Sydney Smith

The Wit and Wisdom of Sydney Smith

A selection of the most memorable passages in his writings and conversations

Sydney Smith

The Wit and Wisdom of Sydney Smith
A selection of the most memorable passages in his writings and conversations

ISBN/EAN: 9783337093655

Printed in Europe, USA, Canada, Australia, Japan

Cover: Foto ©Raphael Reischuk / pixelio.de

More available books at **www.hansebooks.com**

THE

WIT AND WISDOM

OF

THE REV. SYDNEY SMITH

THE

WIT AND WISDOM

OF

THE REV. SYDNEY SMITH

A SELECTION OF

THE MOST MEMORABLE PASSAGES IN HIS WRITINGS

AND CONVERSATION

New Edition

LONDON
LONGMANS, GREEN, AND CO.
1869

BALLANTYNE AND COMPANY, PRINTERS, EDINBURGH.

ADVERTISEMENT.

THE intention of the Editor of this volume has been to unite in a compendious form the most brilliant and instructive sentences in the writings of Sydney Smith. These extracts are purposely separated as much as possible from the context and connection in which they originally stood; and each passage is limited to the smallest compass which could convey with accuracy the detached thoughts of the writer. In this volume the gems are displayed without their setting—the pearls are unstrung. It has frequently been remarked that wit and knowledge strike more forcibly upon the mind, and cling more faithfully to the memory, when they are reduced to the form of maxims or aphorisms; and if this be true in general it is true more especially of writings like those of Sydney Smith, which were for the most part devoted to critical and polemical objects that have already lost much of their interest, by the very success of the warfare he waged against

them.   Posterity will find it hard to comprehend
or to believe the amount of ignorance, prejudice,
intolerance, and cant against which he contended,
and over which he triumphed.

But even when the questions which were fought
out in the earlier portion of this century, with all
the fury of party strife, are forgotten, the writings
of Sydney Smith will be read and cherished
wherever the English tongue is spoken, for their
broad and benevolent wisdom — for their exquisite
flavour of expression — for their gladsome humour
— for that wit which glittered like the good sword
" Joyeuse," but never turned its edge, except on
the false or the vile — for admirable sense applied
to the business of life — and for that enlightened
Christian spirit which rose without affectation to
the loftiest piety, and to the noblest lessons of duty.
The most salient of these passages (though by no
means all which might be selected from his works)
will be found in the present volume.

In the arrangement of them under separate
headings, for which the Editor is responsible, the
chronological order of the series has not been
strictly observed, though the first portion of the
collection is chiefly selected from articles contributed to the *Edinburgh Review,* the second from
pamphlets, sermons, and the Lectures on Moral

Philosophy, the third from the Memoirs and Correspondence. The short reference at the end of each extract denotes the source from which it is taken. But the design of the Editor has rather been to follow the course of subjects, as they arose, and to class together passages relating to the same topic, without reference to the period at which they were written. With very slight exceptions, it will be found that an entire consistency pervades the whole series, though it extends over a period of more than thirty years; and where those exceptions do occur they are attributable to changes in the state of things or in the conduct of other men, not to any modification of the fixed and steadfast principles which governed the mind and the life of Sydney Smith. Not unfrequently it will be observed, that his remarks on the tendency of events have been verified in a very remarkable manner, long after he himself had ceased to watch the courses of the world—thus his prognostications of the results of the French Revolution (p. 7), published in 1802, and of the danger of religious fears as a source of disaffection in British India (p. 70), published in 1808, have been respectively verified by the second Empire and the Indian Mutiny, just fifty years after those passages were composed.

It may be proper to remark, in conclusion, that a volume under a title similar to that which is here adopted, was published in 1856, in the United States, by Mr. Duyckink, and has had, as might be anticipated, a wide circulation in America. The proprietors of the copyrights in this country were desirous that the same facility for procuring the " Wit and Wisdom of Sydney Smith," in a compendious form, should be offered to the British public in addition to the cheap editions of the entire collection of his writings which have already issued from the press. With this view the present selection has been made, but upon a principle differing altogether from the plan adopted by the American Editor. The volume prepared by Mr. Duyckink is in fact an abridgment of the life and of the principal works of Sydney Smith, and an attempt has been made by long extracts to preserve their sequence and connection; in the collection here presented to the reader, on the contrary, each passage is separate, detached, and in itself complete. In this form it is believed that the fragments of Sydney Smith may rank beside the thoughts of Pascal without his mysticism, and eclipse the wit of La Rochefoucauld without his misanthropy.

WIT AND WISDOM OF SYDNEY SMITH.

ORIGIN OF THE EDINBURGH REVIEW (1802).

Towards the end of my residence in Edinburgh, Brougham, Jeffrey, and myself happened to meet in the eighth or ninth story or flat in Buccleugh Place, the then elevated residence of Mr. Jeffrey. I proposed that we should set up a Review. This was acceded to with acclamation. I was appointed editor, and remained long enough in Edinburgh to edit the first number of the Review. The motto I proposed for the Review was, "Tenui Musam meditamur avenâ"—"We cultivate literature on a little oatmeal." But this was too near the truth to be admitted; so we took our present grave motto from Publius Syrus, of whom none of us had, I am sure, read a single line; and so began what has since turned out to be a very important and able journal.

PUBLIC OPINION IN ENGLAND IN 1802.

From the beginning of the century (about which time the Review began), to the death of Lord Liverpool, was an awful period for those who ventured to maintain liberal opinions; and who were too honest to sell them for the ermine of the judge, or the lawn of the prelate. A long and hopeless career in your profession, the chuckling grin of noodles, the sarcastic leer of the genuine political rogue; prebendaries, deans, bishops made over your head; reverend renegades advanced to the highest dignities of the Church, for helping to rivet the fetters of Catholic and Protestant Dissenters; and no more chance of a Whig administration than of a thaw in Zembla. These were the penalties exacted for liberality of opinion at that period; and not only was there no pay, but there were many stripes.

It is always considered a piece of impertinence in England if a man of less than two or three thousand a year has any opinions at all on important subjects; and in addition he was sure to be assailed with all the Billingsgate of the French Revolution. Jacobin, leveller, atheist, Socinian, incendiary, regicide, were the gentlest appellations used; and any man who breathed a syllable against the senseless bigotry of the two Georges, or hinted at the abominable tyranny and persecution exercised against Catholic Ireland, was shunned as unfit for the relations of social life. Not a murmur against any abuse was permitted. To say a word against the suitor-cide delays of the Court of Chancery, or the cruel punishments of the Game-laws, or against any abuse which a rich man inflicted and a poor man suffered, was treason against the plousiocracy, and was bitterly and steadily resented. Lord Grey had not then taken off the bearing-rein from the English people, as Sir Francis Head has now done from horses.

LABOURS OF THE LIBERAL PARTY.

To appreciate the value of the Edinburgh Review, the state of England at the period when that journal began should be had in remembrance. The Catholics were not emancipated—the Corporation and Test Acts were un-repealed—the Game Laws were horribly oppressive—Steel Traps and Spring Guns were set all over the country—Prisoners tried for their Lives could have no Counsel—Lord Eldon and the Court of Chancery pressed heavily upon mankind—Libel was punished by the most cruel and vindictive imprisonments—the principles of Political Economy were little understood—the Law of Debt and of Conspiracy were upon the worst possible footing—the enormous wickedness of the Slave Trade was tolerated—a thousand evils were in existence, which the talents of good and able men have since lessened or removed; and these effects have been not a little assisted by the honest boldness of the Edinburgh Review.

MODERN IMPROVEMENTS.

"The good of ancient times let others state,
I think it lucky I was born so late."

Mr. Editor,—It is of some importance at what period a man is born. A young man, alive at this period, hardly knows to what improvements of human life he has been introduced; and I would bring before his notice the fol-lowing eighteen changes which have taken place in England since I first began to breathe in it the breath of life—a period amounting now to nearly seventy-three years.

Gas was unknown: I groped about the streets of London in all but the utter darkness of a twinkling oil lamp, under the protection of watchmen in their grand climacteric, and exposed to every species of depredation and insult.

I have been nine hours in sailing from Dover to

Calais before the invention of steam. It took me nine hours to go from Taunton to Bath, before the invention of railroads, and I now go in six hours from Taunton to London! In going from Taunton to Bath, I suffered between 10,000 and 12,000 severe contusions, before stone-breaking Macadam was born.

I paid 15*l.* in a single year for repairs of carriage-springs on the pavement of London; and I now glide without noise or fracture, on wooden pavements.

I can walk, by the assistance of the police, from one end of London to the other, without molestation; or if tired, get into a cheap and active cab, instead of those cottages on wheels, which the hackney coaches were at the beginning of my life.

I had no umbrella! They were little used, and very dear. There were no waterproof hats, and *my* hat has often been reduced by rains into its primitive pulp.

I could not keep my smallclothes in their proper place, for braces were unknown. If I had the gout, there was no colchicum. If I was bilious, there was no calomel. If I was attacked by ague, there was no quinine. There were filthy coffee-houses instead of elegant clubs. Game could not be bought. Quarrels about uncommuted tithes were endless. The corruption of Parliament, before Reform, infamous. There were no banks to receive the savings of the poor. The Poor Laws were gradually sapping the vitals of the country; and whatever miseries I suffered, I had no post to whisk my complaints for a single penny to the remotest corners of the empire; and yet, in spite of all these privations, I lived on quietly, and am now ashamed that I was not more discontented, and utterly surprised that all these changes and inventions did not occur two centuries ago.

Z.

I forgot to add, that as the basket of stage coaches, in which luggage was then carried, had no springs, your clothes were rubbed all to pieces; and that even in the best society one third of the gentlemen at least were always drunk. — [*Memoir.*]

SCOTLAND IN 1798.

IT requires a surgical operation to get a joke well into a Scotch understanding. Their only idea of wit, or rather that inferior variety of this electric talent which prevails occasionally in the North, and which, under the name of WUT, is so infinitely distressing to people of good taste, is laughing immoderately at stated intervals. They are so imbued with metaphysics that they even make love metaphysically. I overheard a young lady of my acquaintance, at a dance in Edinburgh, exclaim, in a sudden pause of the music, "What you say, my Lord, is very true of love in the *aibstract*, but—" here the fiddlers began fiddling furiously, and the rest was lost. No nation has so large a stock of benevolence of heart: if you meet with an accident, half Edinburgh immediately flocks to your door to inquire after your *pure* hand or your *pure* foot, and with a degree of interest that convinces you their whole hearts are in the inquiry. You find they usually arrange their dishes at dinner by the points of the compass; "Sandy, put the gigot of mutton to the south, and move the singet sheep's head a wee bit to the nor-wast." If you knock at the door, you hear a shrill female voice from the fifth flat shriek out, "Wha's chapping at the door?" which is presently opened by a lassie with short petticoats, bare legs, and thick ankles. My Scotch servants bargained they were not to have salmon more than three times a week, and always pulled off their stockings, in spite of my repeated objurgations, the moment my back was turned. Their temper stands anything but an attack on their climate. They would have you even believe they can ripen fruit; and, to be candid, I must own in remarkably warm summers I have tasted peaches that made most excellent pickles; and it is upon record that at the siege of Perth, on one occasion, the ammunition failing, their nectarines made admirable cannon balls. Even the enlightened mind of Jeffrey cannot shake off the illusion that myrtles flourished at Craig Crook. In vain I have represented to him that they are of the genus *Carduus*, and pointed out their prickly peculiarities. In vain I have reminded him that I have seen hackney coaches drawn by four horses in the winter, on account of the snow; that I had rescued a man blown flat against my door by the violence of the winds, and black in the face; that even the experienced Scotch fowls did not venture to cross the streets, but sidled along, tails aloft, without venturing to encounter the gale. Jeffrey sticks to his myrtle illusions, and treats my attacks with as much contempt as if I had been a wild visionary, who had never breathed his caller air, nor lived and suffered under the rigour of his climate, nor spent five years in discussing metaphysics and medicine in that garret of the earth — that knuckle-end of England — that land of Calvin, oat-cakes, and sul-phur. — [*Memoir.*]

ANIMOSITY OF ENGLAND AND FRANCE IN 1798.

I now consider the war between France and England no longer as an occasional quarrel or temporary dispute, but as an antipathy and national horror, after the same kind as subsists between the kite and the crow, or the churchwarden and the pauper, the weasel and the rat, the parson and the Deist, the bailiff and the half-pay captain, etc. etc., who have persecuted each other from the beginning of time, and will peck, swear, fly, preach at, and lie in wait for each other till the end of time.— [*Memoir.*]

REVOLUTIONARY STATE OF FRANCE.

If it be visionary to suppose the grandeur and safety of the two nations as compatible and co-existent, we have the important (though the cruel) consolation of reflecting, that the French have yet to put together the very elements of a civil and political constitution ; that they have to experience all the danger and all the inconvenience which result from the rashness and the imperfect views of legislators, who have everything to conjecture, and everything to create ; that they must submit to the confusion of repeated change, or the greater evil of obstinate perseverance in error ; that they must live for a century in that state of perilous uncertainty in which every revolutionised nation remains, before rational liberty becomes feeling and habit, as well as law, and is written in the hearts of men as plainly as in the letter of the statute ; and that the opportunity of beginning this immense edifice of human happiness is so far from being presented to them at present, that it is extremely problematical whether or not they are to be bandied from one vulgar usurper to another, and remain for a century subjugated to the rigour of a military government, at once the scorn and the scourge of Europe.*— [*E. R.* 1803.]

* All this is, unfortunately, as true now as it was when written thirty years ago.—(S. S.) And not less true after the lapse of another period of nearly thirty years in 1860.

REACTION IN FRANCE.

Is not the tide of opinions, at this moment, in France, setting back with a strength equal to its flow? and is there not reason to presume, that, for some time to come, their ancient institutions may be adored with as much fury as they were destroyed?—[*E. R.* 1803.]

REPUBLICAN GOVERNMENT IN FRANCE.

A LOVE of equality is a very strong principle in a republic: therefore it does not tolerate hereditary honour or wealth; and all the effect produced upon the minds of the people by this factitious power is lost, and the government weakened: but, in proportion as the government is less able to command, the people should be more willing to obey; therefore a republic is better suited to a moral than an immoral people.

Yet, though narrowness of territory, purity of morals, and recent escape from despotism, appear to be the circumstances which most strongly recommend a republic, M. Necker proposes it to the most numerous and the most profligate people in Europe, who are disgusted with the very name of liberty, from the incredible evils they have suffered in pursuit of it.

Whatever be the species of free government adopted by France, she can adopt none without the greatest peril. — [*E. R.* 1803.]

POLITICAL EXPERIENCE.

To call upon a nation, on a sudden, totally destitute of such knowledge and experience, to perform all the manifold functions of a free constitution, is to entrust valuable, delicate, and abstruse mechanism, to the rudest skill and the grossest ignorance.—[*E. R.* 1803.]

OBSTACLES TO FREEDOM IN FRANCE.

THE want of all the true elements of constitutional government must retard, for a very long period, the practical enjoyment of liberty in France, and present very serious obstacles to her prosperity; obstacles little dreamed of by men who seem to measure the happiness and future grandeur of France by degrees of longitude and latitude, and who believe she might acquire liberty with as much facility as she could acquire Switzerland or Naples.—[*E. R.* 1803.]

SUDDEN FREEDOM.

A NATION grown free in a single day is a child born with the limbs and the vigour of a man, who would take a drawn sword for his rattle, and set the house in a blaze, that he might chuckle over the splendour.—[*E. R.* 1803.]

VALUE OF ELECTIONS.

THE only foundation of political liberty is the spirit of the people: and the only circumstance which makes a lively impression upon their senses, and powerfully reminds them of their importance, their power, and their rights, is the periodical choice of their representatives.—[*E. R.* 1803.]

POPULAR ELECTIONS.

THE uproar even, and the confusion and the clamour of a popular election in England, have their use: they give a stamp to the names, *Liberty, Constitution,* and *People.* —[*E. R.* 1803.]

ENGLISH MOBS.

AN English mob, which, to a foreigner, might convey the belief of an impending massacre, is often contented by the demolition of a few windows.—[*E. R.* 1803.]

EXTENSION OF THE FRANCHISE.

No person considers himself as so completely deprived of a share in the government, who is to enjoy it when he becomes older, as he would do, were that privilege deferred till he became richer; — time comes to all, wealth to few. — [*E. R.* 1803.]

REPRESENTATIVE GOVERNMENT.

THE sea-ports, the universities, the great commercial towns, should all have their separate organs in the parliament of a great country. There should be some means of bringing in active, able, young men, who would submit to the labour of business from the stimulus of honour and wealth. Others should be there, expressly to speak the sentiments, and defend the interests, of the executive. Every popular assembly must be grossly imperfect, that is not composed of such heterogeneous materials as these. Our own parliament may perhaps contain within itself *too many* of that species of representatives, who could never have arrived at the dignity under a pure and perfect system of election; but, for all

the practical purposes of government, amidst a great
majority fairly elected by the people, we should always
wish to see a certain number of the legislative body
representing interests very distinct from those of the
people. — [*E. R.* 1803.]

SECOND CHAMBERS.

THE institution of two assemblies constitutes a check
upon the passion and precipitation by which the resolutions of any single popular assembly may occasionally be
governed.—[*E. R.* 1803.]

DIVISION OF POWER.

THE prize of supreme power is too tempting to admit
of fair play in the game of ambition; and it is wise to
lessen· its value by dividing it: at least it is wise to do
so, under a form of government that cannot admit the
better expedient of rendering the executive hereditary;
an expedient (gross and absurd as it *seems* to be) the
best calculated, perhaps, to obviate the effects of ambition
upon the stability of governments, by narrowing the
field on which it acts, and the object for which it contends. — [*E. R.* 1803.]

AMERICAN INSTITUTIONS IN 1803.

AMERICA presents such an immediate, and such a
seducing species of provision to all its inhabitants, that
it has no idle discontented populace; its population
amounts only to six millions, and it is not condensed in
such masses as the population of Europe. After all, an
experiment of twenty years is never to be cited in

politics; nothing can be built upon such a slender inference. Even if America were to remain stationary, she might find that she had presented too fascinating and irresistible an object to human ambition: of course, that peril is increased by every augmentation of a people, who are hastening on, with rapid and irresistible pace, to the highest eminences of human grandeur. Some contest for power there must be in every free state: but the contest for vicarial and deputed power, as it implies the presence of a moderator and a master, is more prudent than the struggle for that which is original and supreme. — [*E. R.* 1803.]

THE SALIC LAW.

A MOST sensible and valuable law, banishing gallantry and chivalry from Cabinets, and preventing the amiable antics of grave statesmen. — [*E. R.* 1803.]

LIFE PEERAGES.

THE partial creation of peers for life only, would appear to remedy a very material defect in the English constitution. An hereditary legislative aristocracy not only adds to the dignity of the throne, and establishes that gradation of ranks which is perhaps absolutely necessary to its security, but it transacts a considerable share of the business of the nation, as well in the framing of laws as in the discharge of its juridical functions. But men of rank and wealth, though they are interested by a splendid debate, will not submit to the drudgery of business, much less can they be supposed conversant in all the niceties of law questions. It is therefore necessary to add to their number a certain portion of *novi homines*, men of established character for talents, and upon whom

the previous tenor of their lives has necessarily impressed
the habits of business. The evil of this is that the title
descends to their posterity, without the talents and the
utility that procured it; and the dignity of the peerage
is impaired by the increase of its numbers: not only so,
but as the peerage is the reward of military, as well as
the earnest of civil services, and as the annuity commonly granted with it is only for one or two lives, we
are in some danger of seeing a race of nobles wholly dependent upon the Crown for their support, and sacrificing
their political freedom to their necessities. These evils
are effectually, as it should seem, obviated by the
creation of a *certain number* of peers for life only.
The most useless and offensive tumour in the body
politic, is the titled son of a great man whose merit has
placed him in the peerage. The name, face, and perhaps the pension, remain. The dæmon is gone: or there
is a slight flavour from the cask, but it is empty.—
[*E. R.* 1803.]

DR. PARR.

WHOEVER has had the good fortune to see Dr. Parr's
wig, must have observed, that while it trespasses a little
on the orthodox magnitude of perukes in the anterior
parts, it scorns even episcopal limits behind, and swells
out into boundless convexity of frizz, the $\mu\acute{\epsilon}\gamma a$ $\vartheta a\tilde{\upsilon}\mu a$ of
barbers, and the terror of the literary world. After the
manner of his wig, the Doctor has constructed his sermon, giving us a discourse of no common length, and
subjoining an immeasurable mass of notes, which appear to concern every learned thing, every learned man,
and almost every unlearned man since the beginning of
the world.—[*E. R.* 1802.]

DR. PARR'S STYLE.

DR. PARR seems to think, that eloquence consists not in an exuberance of beautiful images — not in simple and sublime conceptions — not in the feelings of the passions; but in a studious arrangement of *sonorous, exotic, and sesquipedal* words; a very ancient error, which corrupts the style of young, and wearies the patience of sensible men.

In the university of Benares, in the lettered kingdom of Ava, among the Mandarins at Pekin, there must, doubtless, be many men who have the eloquence of Βάῤῥους, the feeling of Ταίλωρος, and the judgment of Ὥκηρος, of whom Dr. Parr might be happy to say, that they have profundity without obscurity — perspicuity without prolixity — ornament without glare — terseness without barrenness — penetration without subtlety — comprehensiveness without digression — and a great number of other things without a great number of other things.—[*E. R.* 1802.]

A SOMNOLENT WRITER.

AN accident, which happened to the gentleman engaged in reviewing this sermon, proves, in the most striking manner, the importance of the charity for which it was preached in restoring to life persons in whom the vital power is suspended. He was discovered with Dr. Langford's discourse lying open before him, in a state of the most profound sleep; from which he could not, by any means, be awakened for a great length of time. By attending, however, to the rules prescribed by the

Humane Society, flinging in the smoke of tobacco, applying hot flannels, and carefully removing the discourse itself to a great distance, the critic was restored to his disconsolate brothers.—[*E. R.* 1802.]

BOOKSELLERS' HACKS.

WE suppose the booksellers have authors at two different prices. Those who do write grammatically, and those who do not; and that they have not thought fit to put any of their best hands upon this work.—[*E. R.* 1802.]

FORESTALLING AND REGRATING.

THE farmer has it not in his power to raise the price of corn : he never has fixed, and never can fix it. He is unquestionably justified in receiving any price he can obtain : for it happens very beautifully, that the effect of his efforts to better his fortune is as beneficial to the public, as if their motive had not been selfish. To insist that he should take a less price when he can obtain a greater, is to insist upon laying on that order of men the whole burden of supporting the poor ; a convenient system enough in the eyes of a rich ecclesiastic; and objectionable only, because it is impracticable, pernicious, and unjust.* —[*E. R.* 1802.]

* If it is pleasant to notice the intellectual growth of an individual, it is still more pleasant to see the public growing wiser. This absurdity of attributing the high price of corn to the combinations of farmers, was the common nonsense talked in the days of my youth. I remember when ten judges out of twelve laid down this doctrine in their charges to the various grand juries on the circuits. The lowest attorney's clerk is now better instructed.—(S. S.)

NATURAL PRODUCTIONS OF AUSTRALIA.

In this remote part of the earth, Nature (having made horses, oxen, ducks, geese, oaks, elms, and all regular and useful productions for the rest of the world), seems determined to have a bit of play, and to amuse herself as she pleases. Accordingly, she makes cherries with the stone on the outside; and a monstrous animal, as tall as a grenadier, with the head of a rabbit, a tail as big as a bed-post, hopping along at the rate of five hops to a mile, with three or four young kangaroos looking out of its false uterus, to see what is passing. Then comes a quadruped as big as a large cat, with the eyes, colour, and skin of a mole, and the bill and web-feet of a duck —puzzling Dr. Shaw, and rendering the latter half of his life miserable, from his utter inability to determine whether it was a bird or a beast. Add to this a parrot, with the legs of a sea-gull; a skate with the head of a shark; and a bird of such monstrous dimensions, that a side-bone of it will dine three real carnivorous Englishmen; — together with many other productions that agitate Sir Joseph, and fill him with mingled emotions of distress and delight.—[*E. R.* 1819.]

AUSTRALIAN ARISTOCRACY.

The time may come, when some Botany Bay Tacitus shall recall the crimes of an emperor lineally descended from a London pickpocket, or paint the valour with which he has led his New Hollanders into the heart of China. At that period, when the Grand Lama is sending to supplicate alliance; when the spice islands are purchasing peace with nutmegs; when enormous tributes of green tea and nankeen are wafted into Port Jackson, and landed on the quays at Sydney, who will ever remember that the sawing of a few planks, and the knocking together of a few nails, were once a serious trial of the energies and resources of the nation?

When the history of the colony has been attentively perused in the parish of St. Giles, the ancient avocation of picking pockets will certainly not become more discreditable from the knowledge that it may eventually lead to the possession of a farm of a thousand acres on the river Hawkesbury. — [*E. R.* 1803.]

FUTURE INDEPENDENCE OF AUSTRALIA.

It may be a curious consideration, to reflect what we are to do with this colony when it comes to years of discretion. Are we to spend another hundred millions of money in discovering its strength, and to humble ourselves again before a fresh set of Washingtons and Franklins? The moment after we have suffered such serious mischief from the escape of the old tiger, we are breeding up a young cub, whom we cannot render less ferocious, or more secure. Endless blood and treasure will be exhausted to support a tax on kangaroos' skins; faithful Commons will go on voting fresh supplies to support a *just and necessary* war; and Newgate, then become a quarter of the world, will evince a heroism, not unworthy of the great characters by whom she was originally peopled. — [*E. R.* 1803.]

ATTRACTIONS OF AUSTRALIA.

A London thief, clothed in kangaroo's skins, lodged under the bark of the dwarf eucalyptus, and keeping sheep, fourteen thousand miles from Piccadilly, with a crook bent into the shape of a picklock, is not an uninteresting picture; and an engraving of it might have a very salutary effect—provided no engraving were made of his convict master, to whom the sheep belong.— [*E. R.* 1823.]

EMANCIPATED CONVICTS.

THE history of emancipated convicts, who have made a great deal of money by their industry and their speculations, necessarily reaches this country, and prevents men who are goaded by want, and hovering between vice and virtue, from looking upon it as a place of suffering—perhaps leads them to consider it as the land of hope and refuge, to them unattainable, except by the commission of crime. And so they lift up their heads at the Bar, hoping to be transported,—

> "Stabant orantes primi transmittere cursum,
> Tendebantque manus, ripæ ulterioris amore."

Another circumstance, which destroys all idea of punishment in transportation to New South Wales, is the enormous expense which that settlement would occasion if it really were made a place of punishment. A little wicked tailor arrives, of no use to the architectural projects of the Governor. He is turned over to a settler, who leases this sartorial Borgia his liberty for five shillings per week, and allows him to steal and snip, what, when, and where he can. The excuse for all this mockery of law and justice is, that the expense of his maintenance is saved to the Government at home. But the expense is not saved to the country at large. The nefarious needleman writes home, that he is as comfortable as a finger in a thimble! that though a fraction only of humanity, he has several wives, and is filled every day with rum and kangaroo. This, of course, is not lost upon the shopboard; and, for the saving of fifteen pence per day, the foundation of many criminal tailors is laid.—[*E. R.* 1803.]

MORAL EQUALITY OF MAN.

ALL honest men, whether counts or cobblers, are of the same rank, if classed by moral distinctions.—[*E. R.* 1823.]

SOCIETY AT BOTANY BAY.

IT is seldom, we suspect, that absolute dunces go to the Bay, but commonly men of active minds, and considerable talents in their various lines — who have not learnt, indeed, the art of self-discipline and control, but who are sent to learn it in the bitter school of adversity. And when this medicine produces its proper effect — when sufficient time has been given to show a thorough change in character and disposition — a young colony really cannot afford to dispense with the services of any person of superior talents. Activity, resolution, and acuteness, are of such immense importance in the hard circumstances of a new State, that they must be eagerly caught at, and employed as soon as they are discovered. Though all may not be quite so unobjectionable as could be wished —

> "Res dura, et regni novitas me talia cogunt
> Moliri" —

To sit down to dinner with men who have not been tried for their lives is a luxury which cannot be enjoyed in such a country. It is entirely out of the question and persons so dainty, and so truly admirable, had better settle at Clapham Common than at Botany Bay.

Mr. Marsden, who has no happiness from six o'clock Monday morning, till the same hour the week following, will not meet pardoned convicts in society. We have no doubt Mr. Marsden is a very respectable clergyman; but is there not something very different from this in the Gospel? The most resolute and inflexible persons in the rejection of pardoned convicts were some of the marching regiments stationed at Botany Bay — men, of course, who had uniformly shunned, in the Old World, the society of· gamesters, prostitutes, drunkards, and blasphemers — who had ruined no tailors, corrupted no wives, and had entitled themselves by a long course of solemnity and decorum, to indulge in all the insolence of purity and virtue. — [*E. R.* 1823.]

DINNERS AT SYDNEY.

An officer, invited to dinner by the Governor, cannot refuse, unless in case of sickness. This is the most complete tyranny we ever heard of. If the officer comes out to his duty at the proper minute, with his proper number of buttons and epaulettes, what matters it to the Governor or any body else, where he dines? He may as well be ordered what to eat, as where to dine — be confined to the upper or under side of the meat — be denied gravy, or refused melted butter. But there is no end to the small tyranny and puerile vexations of a military life. — [*E. R.* 1803.]

TRANSPORTATION.

Men are governed by words; and under the infamous term *convict,* are comprehended crimes of the most dif.

ferent degrees and species of guilt. One man is transported for stealing three hams and a pot of sausages; and in the next berth to him on board the transport is a young surgeon, who has been engaged in the mutiny at the Nore; the third man is for extorting money; the fourth was in a respectable situation of life at the time of the Irish Rebellion, and was so ill read in history as to imagine that Ireland had been ill-treated by England, and so bad a reasoner as to suppose, that nine Catholics ought not to pay tithes to one Protestant. Then comes a man who set his house on fire, to cheat the Phœnix Office; and, lastly, that most glaring of all human villains, a poacher, driven from Europe, wife and child, by thirty lords of manors, at the Quarter Sessions, for killing a partridge. Now, all these are crimes no doubt —particularly the last; but they are surely crimes of very different degrees of intensity, to which different degrees of contempt and horror are attached — and from which those who have committed them may, by subsequent morality, emancipate themselves, with different degrees of difficulty, and with more or less of success. A warrant granted by a reformed bacon-stealer would be absurd; but there is hardly any reason why a foolish hot-brained young blockhead, who chose to favour the mutineers at the Nore when he was sixteen years of age, may not make a very loyal subject, and a very respectable and respected magistrate, when he is forty years of age, and has cast his Jacobine teeth, and fallen into the practical jobbing and loyal baseness which so commonly developes itself about that period of life.

Is it to be believed that a governor, placed over a land of convicts, and capable of guarding his limbs from any sudden collision with odometrous stones, or vertical posts of direction, should make no distinction between

the simple convict and the double and treble convict—
the man of three juries, who has three times appeared
at the Bailey, trilarcenous—three times driven over the
seas?—[*E. R.* 1823.]

TRANSPORT SHIPS.

WE were a little surprised at the scanty limits allowed
to convicts for sleeping on board the transports. Mr.
Bigge (of whose sense and humanity we really have not
the slightest doubt) states eighteen inches to be quite
sufficient—twice the length of a small sheet of letter
paper. The printer's devil, who carries our works to the
press, informs us, that the allowance to the demons of the
type is double foolscap length, or twenty-four inches.
The great city upholsterers generally consider six feet as
barely sufficient for a person rising in business, and assisting occasionally at official banquets.—[*E. R.* 1823.]

A VOYAGE TO BOTANY BAY.

WHILE a convict vessel lay at anchor, about to sail, a
boat from shore reached the ship, and from it stepped a
clerk from the Bank of England. The convicts felici-
tated themselves upon the acquisition of so gentlemanlike
a companion ; but it soon turned out that the visitant had
no intention of making so long a voyage. Finding that
they were not to have the pleasure of his company, the
convicts very naturally thought of picking his pockets;
the necessity of which professional measure was prevented
by a speedy distribution of their contents. Forth from
his bill-case this votary of Plutus drew his nitid Newlands ;
all the forgers and utterers were mustered on deck ; and
to each of them was well and truly paid into his hand a

five pound note : less acceptable, perhaps, than if privately removed from the person, but still joyfully received. This was well intended on the part of the directors : but the consequences it is scarcely necessary to enumerate; a large stock of rum was immediately laid in from the circumambient slop boats ; and the materials of constant intoxication secured for the rest of the voyage. — [*E. R.* 1823.]

ARCHITECTURE AT BOTANY BAY.

ORNAMENTAL architecture in Botany Bay ! How it could enter into the head of any human being to adorn public buildings at the Bay, or to aim at any other architectural purpose but the exclusion of wind and rain, we are utterly at a loss to conceive. Such an expense is not only lamentable for the waste of property it makes in the particular instance, but because it destroys that guarantee of sound sense which the Government at home must require in those who preside over distant colonies. A man who thinks of pillars and pilasters, when half the colony are wet through for want of any covering at all, cannot be a wise or prudent person. He seems to be ignorant, that the prevention of rheumatism in all young colonies is a much more important object than the gratification of taste, or the display of skill.— [*E. R.* 1823.]

COLONIAL BREWERIES.

WHAT two ideas are more inseparable than Beer and Britannia ?—what event more awfully important to an English colony, than the erection of its first brewhouse ?— [*E. R.* 1823.]

SELF-GOVERNMENT IN AUSTRALIA.

THE time of course will come when it would be in the highest degree unjust and absurd, to refuse to that settlement the benefit of popular institutions. But they are too young, too few, and too deficient for such civilised machinery at present. "I cannot come to serve upon the jury—the waters of the Hawkesbury are out, and I have a mile to swim—the kangaroos will break into my corn—the convicts have robbed me—my little boy has been bitten by an ornithorynchus paradoxus—I have sent a man fifty miles with a sack of flour to buy a pair of breeches for the assizes, and he is not returned." These are the excuses which, in new colonies, always prevent Trial by Jury; and make it desirable, for the first half century of their existence, that they should live under the simplicity and convenience of despotism—such modified despotism (we mean) as a British House of Commons will permit, in the governors of their distant colonies.—[*E. R.* 1823.]

CEYLON IN 1803.

THE geographical figure of our possessions in Ceylon is whimsical enough; we possess the whole of the sea-coast, and enclose in a periphery the unfortunate King of Candia, whose rugged and mountainous dominions may be compared to a coarse mass of iron, set in a circle of silver. The Popilian ring, in which this votary of Buddha has been so long held by the Portuguese and Dutch, has infused the most vigilant jealousy into the government, and rendered it as difficult to enter the kingdom of Candia, as if it were Paradise or China; and yet, once there, always there; for the difficulty of departing is just as great as the difficulty of arriving; and his Candian Excellency, who has used every device in his power to keep them out, is seized with such an affection for those who baffle his defensive artifices, that he can on no account suffer them to depart. He has been known to detain a string of four or five Dutch embassies, till various members of the legation died of old age at his court, while they were expecting an answer to their questions, and a return to their presents: and his Majesty once exasperated a little French ambassador to such a degree, by the various pretences under which he kept him at his court, that this lively member of the Corps Diplomatique, one day, in a furious passion, attacked six or seven of his Majesty's largest elephants sword in hand, and would, in all probability, have reduced them to mince-meat, if the poor beasts had not been saved from the unequal combat.— [*E. R.* 1823.]

MALAYS.

THIS is truly a tremendous people! When assassins and blood-hounds will fall into rank and file, and the most furious savages submit (with no diminution of their ferocity) to the science and discipline of war, they only want a Malay Bonaparte to lead them to the conquest of the world. Our curiosity has always been very highly excited by the accounts of this singular people; and we cannot help thinking, that, one day or another, when they are more full of opium than usual, they *will run a muck* from Cape Comorin to the Caspian.—[*E. R.* 1803.]

THE KING OF KANDY.

THE King of Candia is of course despotic; and the history of his life and reign presents the same monotonous ostentation, and baby-like caprice, which characterise Oriental governments. In public audiences he appears like a great fool, squatting on his hams; far surpassing gingerbread in splendour; and, after asking some such idiotical question, as whether Europe is in Asia or Africa, retires with a flourish of trumpets very much out of tune. For his private amusement, he rides on the nose of an elephant, plays with his jewels, sprinkles his courtiers with rose-water, and feeds his gold and silver fish. If his tea is not sweet enough, he impales his footman; and smites off the heads of half a dozen of his noblemen, if he has a pain in his own.—[*E. R.* 1803.]

PEARL FISHERY.

A COMMON mode of theft practised by the common people engaged in the pearl fishery, is by swallowing the pearls. Whenever any one is suspected of having swallowed these precious pills of Cleopatra, the police apothecaries are instantly sent for; a *brisk* cathartic is immediately despatched after the truant pearl, with the strictest orders to apprehend it, in whatever corner of the *viscera* it may be found lurking.—[*E. R.* 1803.]

RELATIONS OF MANKIND.

BY what curious links, and fantastical relations, are mankind connected together! At the distance of half the globe, a Hindoo gains his support by groping at the bottom of the sea for the morbid concretion of a shell-fish, to decorate the throat of a London alderman's wife. —[*E. R.* 1803.]

THE HONEY-BIRD OF CEYLON.

AMONG the great variety of birds in Ceylon, we were struck with Mr. Percival's account of the honey-bird, into whose body the soul of a common informer appears to have migrated. It makes a loud and shrill noise, to attract the notice of anybody whom it may perceive; and thus inducing him to follow the course it points out leads him to the tree where the bees have concealed their treasure; after the apiary has been robbed, this feathered scoundrel gleans his reward from the hive. The list of Ceylonese snakes is hideous; and we become reconciled to the crude and cloudy land in which we live, from reflecting, that the indiscriminate activity of the sun generates what is loathsome, as well as what is lovely; that the asp reposes under the rose; and the scorpion crawls under the fragrant flower, and the luscious fruit.—[*E. R.* 1803.]

AN EAST INDIAN CHAPLAINCY.

THE best history of a serpent we ever remember to have read, was of one killed near one of our settlements in the East Indies; in whose body they found the chaplain of the garrison, all in black, the Rev. Mr. ——, (somebody or other, whose name we have forgotten) and who, after having been missing for above a week, was discovered in this very inconvenient situation.—[*E. R.* 1803.]

THE TALIPOT TREE.

A LEAF of the talipot tree is a tent to the soldier, a parasol to the traveller, and a book to the scholar. It is a natural umbrella, and is of as eminent service in that country as a great-coat tree would be in this. — [*E. R.* 1803.]

COUNTRY GENTLEMEN AS NATURALISTS.

THERE is something, too, to be highly respected and praised in the conduct of a country gentleman who, instead of exhausting life in the chase, has dedicated a considerable portion of it to the pursuit of knowledge. There are so many temptations to complete idleness in the life of a country gentleman, so many examples of it, and so much loss to the community from it, that every exception from the practice is deserving of great praise. Some country gentlemen must remain to do the business of their counties; but, in general, there are many more than are wanted; and, generally speaking also, they are a class who should be stimulated to greater exertions. Sir Joseph Banks, a squire of large fortune in Lincolnshire, might have given up his existence to double-barrelled guns and persecutions of poachers — and all the benefits derived from his wealth, industry, and personal exertion in the cause of science, would have been lost to the community. — [*E. R.* 1826.]

MR. WATERTON'S WANDERINGS.

MR. WATERTON complains, that the trees of Guiana are not more than six yards in circumference — a magnitude in trees which it is not easy for a Scotch imagination to reach. — [*E. R.* 1826.]

THE FORESTS OF GUIANA.

How far does the gentle reader imagine the campanero may be heard, whose size is that of a jay? Perhaps 300 yards. Poor innocent, ignorant reader! unconscious of what Nature has done in the forests of Cayenne, and measuring the force of tropical intonation by the sounds of a Scotch duck! The campanero may be heard three miles!—this single little bird being more powerful than the belfry of a cathedral, ringing for a new dean—just appointed on account of shabby politics, small understanding, and good family!

It is impossible to contradict a gentleman who has been in the forests of Cayenne; but we are determined, as soon as a campanero is brought to England, to make him toll in a public place, and have the distance measured.—[*E. R.* 1826.]

CUI BONO.

THE toucan has an enormous bill, makes a noise like a puppy dog, and lays his eggs in hollow trees. How astonishing are the freaks and fancies of nature! To what purpose, we say, is a bird placed in the woods of Cayenne with a bill a yard long, making a noise like a puppy dog, and laying eggs in hollow trees? The toucans, to be sure, might retort, to what purpose were gentlemen in Bond Street created? To what purpose were certain foolish prating Members of Parliament created?—pestering the House of Commons with their ignorance and folly, and impeding the business of the country? There is no end of such questions. So we will not enter into the metaphysics of the toucan. — [*E. R.* 1826.]

IN SUSPENSE.

THE sloth, in its wild state, spends its life in trees, and never leaves them but from force or accident. The eagle to the sky, the mole to the ground, the sloth to the tree; but what is most extraordinary, he lives not *upon* the branches, but *under* them. He moves suspended, rests suspended, sleeps suspended, and passes his life in suspense—like a young clergyman distantly related to a bishop. — [*E. R.* 1826.]

INSECTS IN THE TROPICS.

INSECTS are the curse of tropical climates. The Bête rouge lays the foundation of a tremendous ulcer. In a moment you are covered with ticks. Chigoes bury themselves in your flesh, and hatch a large colony of young chigoes in a few hours. They will not live together, but every chigoe sets up a separate ulcer, and has his own private portion of pus. Flies get entry into your mouth, into your eyes, into your nose; you eat flies, drink flies, and breathe flies. Lizards, cockroaches, and snakes, get into the bed; ants eat up the books; scorpions sting you on the foot. Every thing bites, stings, or bruises; every second of your existence you are wounded by some piece of animal life that nobody has ever seen before, except Swammerdam and Meriam. An insect with eleven legs is swimming in your teacup, a nondescript with nine wings is struggling in the small beer, or a caterpillar with several dozen eyes in his belly is hastening over the bread and butter! All nature is alive, and seems to be gathering all her entomological hosts to eat you up, as you are standing, out of your coat, waistcoat, and breeches. Such are the tropics. All this reconciles us to our dews, fogs, vapours, and drizzle —to our apothecaries rushing about with gargles and tinctures—to our old, British, constitutional coughs, sore throats, and swelled faces. — [*E. R.* 1826.]

THE DANES.

THE Danish character is not agreeable. It is marked by silence, phlegm, and reserve. A Dane is the excess and extravagance of a Dutchman ; more breeched, more ponderous, and more saturnine. He is not often a bad member of society in the great points of morals, and seldom a good one in the lighter requisites of manners. His understanding is alive only to the useful and the profitable : he never lives for what is merely gracious, courteous, and ornamental. His faculties seem to be drenched and slackened by the eternal fogs in which he resides ; he is never alert, elastic, nor serene. His state of animal spirits is so low, that what in other countries would be deemed dejection, proceeding from casual misfortune, is the habitual tenour and complexion of his mind. In all the operations of his understanding he must have time. He is capable of undertaking great journeys; but he travels only a foot pace, and never leaps nor runs. He loves arithmetic better than lyric poetry, and affects Cocker rather than Pindar. He is slow to speak of fountains and amorous maidens : but can take a spell at porisms as well as another; and will make profound and extensive combinations of thought, if you pay him for it, and do not insist that he shall either be brisk or brief.—[*E. R.* 1803.]

LAPLANDERS.

IN reading Mr. Catteau's account of the congealed and blighted Laplanders, we were struck with the infinite delight they must have in dying; the only circumstance in which they can enjoy any superiority over the rest of mankind; or which tends, in their instance, to verify the theory of the equality of human condition.—[*E. R.* 1803.]

MEDICAL COURAGE.

THE boldness and enterprise of medical men is quite as striking as the courage displayed in battle, and evinces how much the power of encountering danger depends upon habit.   Many a military veteran would tremble to feed upon *pus;* to sleep in sheets running with water; or to draw up the breath of feverish patients.   Dr. White might not, perhaps, have marched up to a battery with great alacrity; but Dr. White, in the year 1801, inoculated himself in the arms with recent matter taken from the bubo of a pestiferous patient, and rubbed the same matter upon different parts of his body.   With somewhat less of courage, and more of injustice, he wrapt his Arab servant in the bed of a person just dead of the plague. The Doctor died; and the Doctor's man (perhaps to prove his master's theory, that the plague was not contagious) ran away.—The bravery of our naval officers never produced any thing superior to this therapeutic heroism of the Doctor's. — [*E. R.* 1803.]

TURKISH DISCIPLINE.

THERE is at present, in the Turkish army, a curious mixture of the severest despotism in the commander, and the most rebellious insolence in the soldier.   When the soldier misbehaves, the Vizier cuts his head off, and places it under his arm.   When the soldier is dissatisfied with the Vizier, he fires his ball through his tent, and admonishes him, by these messengers, to a more pleasant exercise of his authority.—[*E. R.* 1803.]

ENERGY AND EXCESS.

THE governed soon learn to distinguish between systematic energy and the excesses of casual and capricious cruelty; the one awes them into submission, the other rouses them to revenge. — [*E. R.* 1803.]

TURKISH REFORMS.

WHAT is become of all the reforms of the famous Gazi Hassan? The blaze of partial talents is soon extinguished. Never was there so great a prospect of improvement as that afforded by the exertions of this celebrated man, who, in spite of the ridicule thrown upon him by Baron de Tott, was such a man as the Turks cannot expect to see again once in a century. He had the whole power of the Turkish empire at his disposal for fifteen years; and, after repeated efforts to improve the army, abandoned the scheme as totally impracticable. The celebrated Bonneval, in his time, and De Tott since, made the same attempt with the same success. They are not to be taught; and six months after his death, everything the present Capitan Pacha has done will be immediately pulled to pieces.—[*E. R.* 1803.]

NATIONAL CHARACTERISTICS.

THERE are goîtres out of the Valais, extortioners who do not worship Moses, oat cakes south of the Tweed, and balm beyond the precincts of Gilead. If nothing can be said to exist pre-eminently and emphatically in one country, which exists at all in another, then Frenchmen are not gay, nor Spaniards grave, nor are gentlemen of the Milesian race remarkable for their disinterested contempt of wealth in their connubial relations. —[*E. R.* 1803.]

TENACITY OF IGNORANCE.

It must be a general fact, at all times, that gross ignorance more tenaciously adheres to a custom once adopted, because it respects that custom as an ultimate rule, and does not discern cases of exception by appealing to any higher rule upon which the first is found.— [*E. R.* 1803.]

PROVIDENTIAL INTERFERENCE.

There is something so natural, and so closely derived from human governments, in the notion of the immediate interference of Providence, that mankind are only weaned from it by centuries of contradiction and discussion.— [*E. R.* 1803.]

AFRICAN SUPERSTITIONS.

The desire of penetrating into futurity, and the belief that some persons are capable of doing it, is as difficult to eradicate from the human mind, as is the belief in an *immediate* Providence; and consequently, the Africans not only have their ordeal, but their conjurors and magicians, who are appealed to in all the difficulties and uncertainties of life, and who always, of course, preserve their authority, though they are perpetually showing, by the clearest evidence of facts, upon what sort of foundation. — [*E. R.* 1803.]

AFRICAN LITIGATION.

The Africans are very litigious; and display, in their lawsuits or palavers, a most forensic exuberance of images, and loquacity of speech. Their criminal causes are frequently terminated by selling one of the parties into slavery; and the Christians are always ready to purchase either the plaintiff or defendant, or both; together with all the witnesses, and any other human creature who is of a dusky colour, and worships the great idol Boo-Boo-Boo, with eleven heads.—[*E. R.* 1803.]

AFRICAN MERRIMENT.

THE Pagan African is commonly a merry, dancing animal, given to every species of antic and apish amusement; and as he is unacquainted with the future and promised delights of the Arabian prophet, he enjoys the bad music, and imperfect beauty of this world, with a most eager and undisturbed relish.—[*E. R.* 1803.]

BLACKS AND WHITES.

THE Ashantees believe that a higher sort of God takes care of the whites, and that they are left to the care of an inferior species of deities. Still the black kings and black nobility are to go to the upper gods after death, where they are to enjoy eternally the state and luxury which was their portion on earth. For this reason a certain number of cooks, butlers, and domestics of every description, are sacrificed on their tombs.—[*E. R.* 1803.]

FORBIDDEN MEATS.

THE Ashantees please their gods by avoiding particular sorts of meat; but the prohibited viand is not always the same. Some curry favour by eating no veal; some seek protection by avoiding pork; others say, that the real monopoly which the celestials wish to establish is that of beef—and so they piously and prudently rush into a course of mutton.—[*E. R.* 1803.]

USES OF CONQUEST.

NOTHING in this world is created in vain: lions, tigers, conquerors, have their use. Ambitious monarchs, who are the curse of civilised nations, are the civilisers of savage people. With a number of little independent hordes, civilisation is impossible. They must have a common interest before there can be peace; and be directed by one will before there can be order. When mankind are prevented from daily quarrelling and fighting, they first begin to improve; and all this, we are afraid, is only to be accomplished, in the first instance, by some great conqueror. We sympathise, therefore, with the victories of the King of Ashantee—and feel ourselves, for the first time, in love with military glory. The ex-Emperor of the French would, at Coomassie, Dagwumba, or Inta, be an eminent benefactor to the human race. —[*E. R.* 1823.]

THE AMERICAN CHARACTER NOT HEROIC.

THE Americans are a brave, industrious, and acute people; but they have hitherto given no indications of genius; and made no approaches to the heroic, either in their morality or character.

Their Franklins and Washingtons, and all other sages and heroes of their revolution, were born and bred subjects of the King of England—and not among the freest or most valued of his subjects. And, since the period of their separation, a far greater proportion of their statesmen and artists and political writers have been foreigners, than ever occurred before in the history of any civilised and educated people. During the thirty or forty years of their independence, they have done absolutely nothing for the Sciences, for the Arts, for Literature, or even for the statesman-like studies of Politics or Political Economy.— [*E. R.* 1820.]

WHAT HAS AMERICA DONE?

In the four quarters of the globe, who reads an American book? or goes to an American play? or looks at an American picture or statue? What does the world yet owe to American physicians or surgeons? What new substances have their chemists discovered? or what old ones have they analysed? What new constellations have been discovered by the telescopes of Americans? What have they done in the mathematics? Who drinks out of American glasses? or eats from American plates? or wears American coats or gowns? or sleeps in American blankets? Finally, under which of the old tyrannical governments of Europe is every sixth man a slave, whom his fellow-creatures may buy and sell and torture?— [*E. R.* 1820.]

SLAVERY IN THE UNITED STATES.

The great curse of America is the institution of Slavery —of itself far more than the foulest blot upon their national character, and an evil which counterbalances all the excisemen, licensers, and tax-gatherers of England. No virtuous man ought to trust his own character, or the character of his children, to the demoralising effects produced by commanding slaves. Justice, gentleness, pity, and humility, soon give way before them. Conscience suspends its functions. The love of command—the impatience of restraint, get the better of every other feeling; and cruelty has no other limit than fear.—[*E. R.* 1818.]

THE BLOT OF AMERICA.

EVERY American who loves his country should dedicate his whole life, and every faculty of his soul, to efface this foul stain from its character. If nations rank according to their wisdom and their virtue, what right has the American, a scourger and murderer of slaves, to compare himself with the least and lowest of the European nations?—much more with this great and humane country, where the greatest lord dare not lay a finger upon the meanest peasant? What is freedom, where all are not free? where the greatest of God's blessings is limited, with impious caprice, to the colour of the body?—[*E. R.* 1818.]

INCONSISTENCY OF SLAVERY AND FREE INSTITUTIONS.

LET the world judge which is the most liable to censure—we who, in the midst of our rottenness, have torn off the manacles of slaves all over the world;—or they who, with their idle purity, and useless perfection, have remained mute and careless, while groans echoed and whips clanked round the very walls of their spotless Congress. We wish well to America—we rejoice in her prosperity—and are delighted to resist the absurd impertinence with which the character of her people is often treated in this country: but the existence of slavery in America is an atrocious crime, with which no measure can be kept—for which her situation affords no sort of apology—which makes liberty itself distrusted, and the boast of it disgusting.—[*E. R.* 1818.]

RUPTURE OF THE UNION.

THE Americans are a very sensible, reflecting people, and have conducted their affairs extremely well; but it is scarcely possible to conceive that such an empire should very long remain undivided, or that the dwellers on the Columbia should have common interest with the navigators of the Hudson and the Delaware. — [*E. R.* 1818.]

OLD COUNTRIES LEAST EXPENSIVE.

ENGLAND is, to be sure, a very expensive country; but a million of millions has been expended in making it habitable and comfortable; and this is a constant source of revenue, or, what is the same thing, a constant diminution of expense to every man living in it. No country, in fact, is so expensive as one which human beings are just beginning to inhabit;— where there are no roads, no bridges, no skill, no help, no combination of powers, and no force of capital.— [*E. R.* 1818.]

NAVAL POWER OF ENGLAND AND THE UNITED STATES.

IT would be the height of madness in America to run into another naval war with this country if it could be averted by any other means than a sacrifice of proper dignity and character. They have, comparatively, no land revenue; and, in spite of the *Franklin* and *Guerrière*, though lined with cedar and mounted with brass cannon, they must soon be reduced to the same state which has been described by Dr. Seybert, and from which they were so opportunely extricated by the treaty of Ghent.—[*E. R.* 1820.]

BRITISH TAXATION.

WE can inform Jonathan what are the inevitable consequences of being too fond of glory;—TAXES upon every article which enters into the mouth, or covers the back, or is placed under the foot—taxes upon every thing which it is pleasant to see, hear, feel, smell, or taste—taxes upon warmth, light, and locomotion—taxes on every thing on earth, and the waters under the earth—on every thing that comes from abroad, or is grown at home—taxes on the raw material—taxes on every fresh value that is added to it by the industry of man—taxes on the sauce which pampers man's appetite, and the drug that restores him to health—on the ermine which decorates the judge, and the rope which hangs the criminal—on the poor man's salt, and the rich man's spice—on the brass nails of the coffin, and the ribands of the bride—at bed or board, couchant or levant, we must pay.—The schoolboy whips his taxed top—the beardless youth manages his taxed horse, with a taxed bridle, on a taxed road:—and the dying Englishman, pouring his medicine, which has paid 7 per cent. into a spoon that has paid 15 per cent.—flings himself back upon his chintz bed, which has paid 22 per cent.—and expires in the arms of an apothecary who has paid a licence of a hundred pounds for the privilege of putting him to death. His whole property is then immediately taxed from 2 to 10 per cent. Besides the probate, large fees are demanded for burying him in the chancel; his virtues are handed down to posterity on taxed marble; and he is then gathered to his fathers—to be taxed no more.—[*E. R.* 1820.]

AMERICAN PRIVILEGES.

AMERICA is exempted, by its very newness as a nation, from many of the evils of the old governments of Europe. It has no mischievous remains of feudal institutions, and no violations of political economy sanctioned by time, and older than the age of reason. If a man find a partridge upon his ground eating his corn, in any part of Kentucky or Indiana, he may kill it even if his father be not a Doctor of Divinity.—[*E. R.* 1824.]

LIBERTY OF TRADES.

THOUGH America is a confederation of republics, they are in many cases much more amalgamated than the various parts of Great Britain. If a citizen of the United States can make a shoe, he is at liberty to make a shoe any where between Lake Ontario and New Orleans,—he may sole on the Mississippi,— heel on the Missouri,— measure Mr. Birkbeck on the little Wabash, or take (which our best politicians do not find an easy matter) the length of Mr. Munro's foot on the banks of the Potowmac. But woe to the cobbler, who, having made Hessian boots for the alderman of Newcastle, should venture to invest with these coriaceous integuments the leg of a liege subject at York. A yellow ant in a nest of red ants — a butcher's dog in a fox-kennel —a mouse in a bee-hive,—all feel the effects of untimely intrusion; — but far preferable their fate to that of the misguided artisan, who, misled by sixpenny histories of England, and conceiving his country to have been united at the Heptarchy, goes forth from his native town to stitch freely within the sea-girt limits of Albion. Him the mayor, him the alderman, him the recorder, him the quarter sessions would worry. Him the justices before trial would long to get into the treadmill; but the moment he was tried, they would push him in with redoubled energy, and leave him to tread himself into a conviction of the barbarous institutions of his corporation-divided country. — [*E. R.* 1824.]

WIGS AND GOWNS.

THE Americans, we believe, are the first persons who have discarded the tailor in the administration of justice, and his auxiliary the barber — two persons of endless importance in the codes and pandects of Europe. A judge administers justice, without a calorific wig and parti-coloured gown, in a coat and pantaloons. He is obeyed, however; and life and property are not badly protected in the United States. — [*E. R.* 1824.]

EQUALITY OF DRESS.

THE true progress of refinement, we conceive, is to discard all the mountebank drapery of barbarous ages. One row of gold and fur falls off after another from the robe of power, and is picked up and worn by the parish beadle and the exhibitor of wild beasts. Meantime, the afflicted wiseacre mourns over equality of garment; and wotteth not of two men, whose doublets have cost alike, how one shall command and the other obey. — [*E. R.* 1824.]

AMERICAN LITERATURE IN 1818.

LITERATURE the Americans have none — no native literature, we mean. It is all imported. They had a

Franklin, indeed; and may afford to live for half a century on his fame. There is, or was, a Mr. Dwight, who wrote some poems, and his baptismal name was Timothy. There is also a small account of Virginia by Jefferson, and an epic by Joel Barlow: and some pieces of pleasantry by Mr. Irving. But why should the Americans write books, when a six weeks' passage brings them, in their own tongue, our sense, science, and genius, in bales and hogsheads? Prairies, steam-boats, grist-mills, are their natural objects for centuries to come. Then, when they have got to the Pacific Ocean — epic poems, plays, pleasures of memory, and all the elegant grâtifications of an ancient people who have tamed the wild earth, and set down to amuse themselves. — This is the natural march of human affairs. — [*E. R.* 1818.]

AMERICAN SENSITIVENESS.

It is rather surprising that such a people, spreading rapidly over so vast a portion of the earth, and cultivating all the liberal and useful arts so successfully, should be so extremely sensitive and touchy as the Americans are said to be.

It is very natural that we Scotch, who live in a little shabby scraggy corner of a remote island, with a climate which cannot ripen an apple, should be jealous of the aggressive pleasantry of more favoured people; but that Americans, who have done so much for themselves, and received so much from nature, should be flung into such convulsions by English Reviewers and Magazines, is really a sad specimen of Columbian juvenility.—[*E. R.* 1824.]

MR. BULL'S SULKINESS.

THERE is nothing which an Englishman enjoys more than the pleasure of sulkiness,—of not being forced to hear a word from anybody which may occasion to him the necessity of replying. It is not so much that Mr. Bull disdains to talk, as that Mr. Bull has nothing to say. His forefathers have been out of spirits for six or seven hundred years, and seeing nothing but fog and vapour, he is out of spirits too; and when there is no selling or buying; or no business to settle, he prefers being alone and looking at the fire. If any gentleman were in distress, he would willingly lend a helping hand; but he thinks it no part of neighbourhood to talk to a person because he happens to be near him. In short, with many excellent qualities, it must be acknowledged that the English are the most disagreeable of all the nations of Europe,—more surly and morose, with less disposition to please, to exert themselves for the good of society, to make small sacrifices, and to put themselves out of their way. They are content with Magna Charta and Trial by Jury; and think they are not bound to excel the rest of the world in small behaviour, if they are superior to them in great institutions.—[*E. R.* 1818.]

EXPECTORATION.

WE are terribly afraid that some Americans spit upon the floor, even when that floor is covered by good carpets. Now all claims to civilisation are suspended till this secretion is otherwise disposed of. No English gentleman has spit upon the floor since the Heptarchy.—[*E. R.* 1824.]

CAPTAIN ROCK IN AMERICA.

CAPTAIN ROCK has his descendants in America. Mankind cannot live together without some approximation to justice; and if the actual government will not govern well, or cannot govern well, is too wicked or too weak to do so — then men prefer Rock to anarchy. — [*E. R.* 1824.]

AMERICAN FREEDOM AND AMERICAN SLAVERY.

AMERICA seems, on the whole, to be a country possessing vast advantages, and little inconveniences; they have a cheap government, and bad roads; they pay no tithes, and have stage coaches without springs. They have no poor laws and no monopolies — but their inns are inconvenient, and travellers are teased with questions. They have no collections in the fine arts; but they have no Lord Chancellor, and they can go to law without absolute ruin. They cannot make Latin verses, but they expend immense sums in the education of the poor. In all this the balance is prodigiously in their favour: but then comes the great disgrace and danger of America — the existence of slavery, which, if not timeously corrected, will one day entail (and ought to entail) a bloody servile war upon the Americans — which will separate America into slave states and states disclaiming slavery, and which remains at present as the foulest blot in the moral character of that people. A high-spirited nation, who cannot endure the slightest act of foreign aggression, and who revolt at the very shadow of domestic tyranny, beat with cart-whips, and bind with chains, and murder for the merest trifles, wretched human beings

who are of a more dusky colour than themselves; and
have recently admitted into their Union a new State,
with the express permission of ingrafting this atrocious
wickedness into their constitution ! No one can admire
the simple wisdom and manly firmness of the Americans
more than we do, or more despise the pitiful propensity
which exists among Government runners to vent their
small spite at their character; but on the subject of
slavery, the conduct of America is, and has been, most
reprehensible. It is impossible to speak of it with too
much indignation and contempt; but for it we should
look forward with unqualified pleasure to such a land of
freedom and such a magnificent spectacle of human
happiness. — [*E. R.* 1824.]

AMERICAN REPUDIATION.

THE Americans, who boast to have improved the institutions of the old world, have at least equalled its
crimes. A great nation, after trampling under foot all
earthly tyranny, has been guilty of a fraud as enormous
as ever disgraced the worst king of the most degraded
nation of Europe.—[*Letters on American Debts.*]

AMERICAN BAD FAITH.

LITTLE did the friends of America expect it, and sad
is the spectacle to see you rejected by every State in
Europe, as a nation with whom no contract can be made,
because none will be kept; unstable in the very foundations of social life, deficient in the elements of good faith,
men who prefer any load of infamy however great, to
any pressure of taxation however light.—[*Letters on
American Debts.*]

REVULSION CAUSED BY AMERICAN REPUDIATION.

I AM no enemy to America. I loved and admired honest America when she respected the laws of pounds, shillings, and pence; and I thought the United States the most magnificent picture of human happiness: I meddle now in these matters because I hate fraud — because I pity the misery it has occasioned — because I mourn over the hatred it has excited against free institutions. — [*Letters on American Debts.*]

PENNSYLVANIA PLUNDERERS.

I NEVER meet a Pennsylvanian at a London dinner without feeling a disposition to seize and divide him;— to allot his beaver to one sufferer and his coat to another —to appropriate his pocket-handkerchief to the orphan, and to comfort the widow with his silver watch, Broadway rings, and the London Guide, which he always carries in his pockets. How such a man can set himself down at an English table without feeling that he owes two or three pounds to every man in company I am at a loss to conceive: he has no more right to eat with honest men than a leper has to eat with clean men. If he have a particle of honour in his composition he should shut himself up, and say, " I cannot mingle with you, I belong to a degraded people—I must hide myself—I am a plunderer from Pennsylvania."

Figure to yourself a Pennsylvanian receiving foreigners in his own country, walking over the public works with them, and showing them Larcenous Lake, Swindling Swamp, Crafty Canal, and Rogues' Railway, and other dishonest works. "This swamp we gained, (says the patriotic borrower) by the repudiated loan of 1828. Our canal robbery was in 1830; we pocketed your good people's money for the railroad only last year." All this may seem very smart to the Americans; but if I had the misfortune to be born among such a people, the land of my fathers should not retain me a single moment after the act of repudiation. I would appeal from my fathers to my forefathers. I would fly to Newgate for greater purity of thought, and seek in the prisons of England for better rules of life.—[*Letters on American Debts.*]

AMERICAN CREDIT.

This new and vain people can never forgive us for having preceded them 300 years in civilisation. They are prepared to enter into the most bloody wars in England, not on account of Oregon, or boundaries, or right of search, but because our clothes and carriages are better made, and because Bond Street beats Broadway. Wise Webster does all he can to convince the people that these are not lawful causes of war; but wars and long wars, they will one day or another produce; and this, perhaps, is the only advantage of repudiation. The Americans cannot gratify their avarice and ambition at once; they cannot cheat and conquer at the same time. The warlike power of every country depends on their Three per Cents. If Cæsar were to reappear upon earth, Wettenhall's list would be more important than his Commentaries; Rothschild would open and shut the temple of Janus; Thomas Baring, or Bates, would probably command the Tenth Legion, and the soldiers would march to battle with loud cries of Scrip and Omnium reduced, Consols, and Cæsar! Now, the Americans have cut themselves off from all resources of credit. Having been as dishonest as they can be, they are prevented from being as foolish as they wish to be.

In the whole habitable globe they cannot borrow a guinea, and they cannot draw the sword because they have not money to buy it.

If I were an American of any of the honest States, I would never rest till I had compelled Pennsylvania to be as honest as myself. The bad faith of that State brings disgrace on all; just as common snakes are killed because vipers are dangerous.

THE FOLLY OF REPUDIATION.

WE all know that the Americans can fight. Nobody doubts their courage. I see now in my mind's eye a whole army on the plains of Pennsylvania in battle array, immense corps of insolvent light infantry, regiments of heavy horse debtors, battalions of repudiators, brigades of bankrupts, with *Vivre sans payer, ou mourir,* on their banners, and *œre alieno* on their trumpets: all these desperate debtors would fight to the death for their country, and probably drive into the sea their invading creditors. Of their courage, I repeat again, I have no doubt. I wish I had the same confidence in their wisdom. But I believe they will become intoxicated by the flattery of unprincipled orators; and, instead of entering with us into a noble competition in making calico (the great object for which the Anglo-Saxon race appears to have been created), they will waste their happiness and their money (if they can get any) in years of silly, bloody, foolish, and accursed war, to prove to the world that Perkins is a real fine gentleman, and that the carronades of the Washington steamer will carry further than those of the Britisher Victoria, or the Robert Peel vessel of war.

E

AMERICAN PENANCE.

As for me, as soon as I hear that the last farthing is paid to the last creditor, I will appear on my knees at the bar of the Pennsylvanian Senate in the plumeopicean robe of American controversy. Each Conscript Jonathan shall trickle over me a few drops of tar, and help to decorate me with those penal plumes in which the vanquished reasoner of the transatlantic world does homage to the physical superiority of his opponents.

VALUE OF PRINCIPLE.

And now, drab-coloured men of Pennsylvania, there is yet a moment left: the eyes of all Europe are an- chored upon you —

" Surrexit mundus justis furiis:"

start up from that trance of dishonesty into which you are plunged; don't think of the flesh which walls about your life, but of that sin which has hurled you from the heaven of character, which hangs over you like a devouring pestilence, and makes good men sad, and ruffians dance and sing. It is not for Gin Sling and Sherry Cobler alone that man is to live, but for those great principles against which no argument can be listened to — principles which give to every power a double power above their functions and their offices, which are the books, the arts, the academies that teach, lift up, and nourish the world — principles (I am quite serious in what I say) above cash, superior to cotton, higher than currency — principles, without which it is better to die than to live, which every servant of God, over every sea and in all lands, should cherish — *usque ad abdita spiramenta animœ.*

SCIENTIFIC FRUITS OF CONQUEST.

To military men we have been, and must be, indebted for our first acquaintance with the interior of many countries. Conquest has explored more than ever curiosity has done; and the path for science has been commonly opened by the sword.— [*E. R.* 1803.]

ENGLISH RESERVE.

THE society into which a transient stranger gains the most easy access in any country, is not often that which ought to stamp the national character; and no criterion can be more fallible, in a people so reserved and inaccessible as the British, who (even when they open their doors to letters of introduction) cannot for years overcome the awkward timidity of their nature.—[*E. R.* 1803.]

FRENCH PRECIPITATION.

THE late Mr. Pétion, who was sent over into this country to acquire a knowledge of our criminal law, is said to have declared himself thoroughly informed upon the subject, after remaining precisely *two and thirty minutes* in the Old Bailey. — [*E. R.* 1803.]

BENEFITS OF AVARICE.

THE avaricious love of gain, which is so feelingly deplored, appears to us a principle which, in able hands, might be guided to the most salutary purposes. The object is to encourage the love of labour, which is best encouraged by the love of money.—[*E. R.*]

PLAIN WRITING.

Such men, to be sure, have existed as Julius Cæsar; but, in general, a correct and elegant style is hardly attainable by those who have passed their lives in action: and no one has such a pedantic love of good writing, as to prefer mendacious finery to rough and ungrammatical truth. — [*E. R.*]

THE INDICATIVE MOOD.

The whole merit of violent deviations from common style depends upon their rarity, and nothing does, for ten pages together, but the indicative mood. — [*E. R.*]

ACQUISITION OF GOOD FORGOTTEN.

The laborious acquisition of any good we have long enjoyed is apt to be forgotten.—[*E. R.*]

FALSE QUANTITIES.

A young man, who, on a public occasion, makes a false quantity at the outset of life, can seldom or never get over it. — [*E. R.*]

BAD BOOKS.

The immorality of any book (in our estimation) is to be determined by the general impressions it leaves on those minds whose principles, not yet *ossified,* are capable of affording a less powerful defence to its influence.—[*E. R.* 1803.]

GILDING THE GALLOWS.

It is in vain to say the fable evinces, in the last act, that vice is productive of misery. We may decorate a villain with graces and felicities for nine volumes, and hang him in the last page. This is not teaching virtue, but gilding the gallows, and raising up splendid associations in favour of being hanged.—[*E. R.* 1803.]

PUBLIC OPINION AND DESPOTIC POWER.

MANY governments are despotic in law, which are not despotic in fact; not because they are restrained by their own moderation, but because, in spite of their theoretical omnipotence, they are compelled, in many important points, to respect either public opinion or the opinion of other balancing powers, which without the express recognition of law, have gradually sprung up in the state. Russia, and Imperial Rome, had its prætorian guards. Turkey has its uhlema. Public opinion almost always makes some exceptions to its blind and slavish submission ; and in bowing its neck to the foot of a sultan, stipulates how hard he shall tread.—[*E. R.* 1803.]

NUNNERIES.

SOCIETIES of this sort might perhaps be extended to other classes, and to other countries, with some utility. The only objection to a nunnery is, that those who change their minds cannot change their situation. That a number of unmarried females should collect together into one mass, and subject themselves to some few rules of convenience, is a system which might afford great resources and accommodation to a number of helpless individuals, without proving injurious to the community ; unless, indeed, any very timid statesman shall be alarmed at the progress of celibacy, and imagine that the increase and multiplication of the human race may become a mere antiquated habit.—[*E. R.* 1803.]

PROTECTION OF THE ACCUSED.

IT is a principle that should never be lost sight of, that an accused person is presumed to be innocent; and that no other vexation should be imposed upon him than what is absolutely necessary for the purposes of future investigation. The imprisonment of a poor man, because he cannot find bail, is not a gratuitous vexation, but a necessary severity; justified only, because no other, nor milder mode of security can, in that particular instance, be produced.—[*E. R.* 1803.]

ATTRACTION OF HANGING.

A VERY curious circumstance took place in the kingdom of Denmark, in the middle of the last century, relative to the infliction of capital punishments upon malefactors. They were attended from the prison to the place of execution by priests, accompanied by a very numerous procession, singing psalms, &c. &c.: which ended, a long discourse was addressed by the priest to the culprit, who was hung as soon as he had heard it. This spectacle, and all the pious cares bestowed upon the criminals, so far seduced the imaginations of the common people, that many of them committed murder purposely to enjoy such inestimable advantages, and the government was positively obliged to make hanging dull as well as deadly, before it ceased to be an object of popular ambition.—[*E. R.* 1802.]

HOMERIC MORALITY.

THERE is, every now and then, some plain coarse morality in Homer; but the most bloody revenge, and the most savage cruelty in warfare, the ravishing of women, and the sale of men, &c. &c. &c., are circumstances which the old bard seems to relate as the ordinary events of his times, without ever dreaming that there could be much harm in them; and if it be urged that Homer took his ideas of right and wrong from a barbarous age, that is just saying, in other words, that Homer had very imperfect ideas of natural law. — [*E. R.* 1802.]

BLACK FOPS.

THERE is a class of fops not usually designated by that epithet—men clothed in profound black, with large canes, and strange amorphous hats — of big speech, and imperative presence — talkers about Plato — great affecters of senility — despisers of women, and all the graces of life — fierce foes to common sense — abusive of the living, and approving no one who has not been dead for at least a century. Such fops, as vain, and as shallow as their fraternity in Bond Street, differ from these only as Gorgonius differed from Rufillus.—[*E. R.* 1803.]

MEN OF PARADOX.

THERE are some men who continue to astonish and please the world, even in the support of a bad cause. They are mighty in their fallacies, and beautiful in their errors. — [*E. R.*]

SUPERFLUITY OF POETS.

THOUGH we praise Mr. Broughton for his book, and praise him very sincerely, we must warn him against that dreadful propensity which young men have for writing verses.   There is nothing of which Nature has been more bountiful than poets.   They swarm like the spawn of cod-fish, with a vicious fecundity, that invites and requires destruction.   To publish verses is become a sort of evidence that a man wants sense; which is repelled not by writing good verses, but by writing excellent verses. — [*E. R.*]

COLONIAL GOVERNORS.

IT is common, we know, to send a person who is somebody's cousin: but, when a new empire is to be founded, the Treasury *should* send out, into some other part of the town, for a man of sense and character. — [*E. R.*]

QUALIFICATION OF GOVERNORS.

YOUNG surgeons are examined in Surgeons' Hall on the methods of cutting off legs and arms before they are allowed to practise surgery.   An examination on the principles of Adam Smith, and a license from Mr. Ricardo, seem to be almost a necessary preliminary for the appointment of governors. — [*E. R.*]

NOVELS.

THE main question as to a novel is — did it amuse? were you surprised at dinner coming so soon? did you mistake eleven for ten, and twelve for eleven? were you too late to dress? and did you sit up beyond the usual hour?   If a novel produces these effects, it is good; if it does not — story, language, love, scandal itself cannot save it. It is only meant to please; and it must do that, or it does nothing. The objection, indeed, to these compositions, when they are well done, is, that it is impossible to do anything, or perform any human duty, while we are engaged in them. Who can read Mr. Hallam's Middle Ages, or extract the root of an impossible quantity, or draw up a bond, when he is in the middle of Mr. Trebeck and Lady Charlotte Duncan? How can the boy's lesson be heard, about the Jove-nourished Achilles, or his six miserable verses upon Dido be corrected, when Henry Granby and Mr. Courtenay are both making love to Miss Jermyn? Common life palls in the middle of these artificial scenes. All is emotion when the book is open — all dull, flat, and feeble when it is shut. — [*E. R.* 1826.]

CONGRUITY IN FICTION.

NOBODY should suffer his hero to have a black eye, or to be pulled by the nose. The Iliad would never have come down to these times if Agamemnon had given Achilles a box on the ear. We should have trembled for the Æneid, if any Tyrian nobleman had kicked the pious Æneas in the 4th book. Æneas may have deserved it; but he could not have founded the Roman Empire after so distressing an accident. — [*E. R.* 1826.]

A BORE.

LORD CHESTERTON we have often met with; and suffered a good deal from his Lordship: a heavy, pompous, meddling peer, occupying a great share of the conversation—saying things in ten words which required only two, and evidently convinced that he is making a great impression; a large man with a large head, and very landed manner; knowing enough to torment his fellow creatures, not to instruct them—the ridicule of young ladies, and the natural butt and target of wit. It is easy to talk of carnivorous animals and beasts of prey; but does such a man, who lays waste a whole party of civilised beings by prosing, reflect upon the joys he spoils, and the misery he creates, in the course of his life? and that any one who listens to him through politeness, would prefer toothache or ear-ache to his conversation? Does he consider the extreme uneasiness which ensues, when the company have discovered a man to be an extremely absurd person, at the same time that it is absolutely impossible to convey, by words or manner, the most distant suspicion of the discovery? And then, who punishes this bore? What sessions and what assizes for him? What bill is found against him? Who indicts him? When the judges have gone their vernal and autumnal rounds—the sheep-stealer disappears—the swindler gets ready for the Bay — the solid parts of the murderer are preserved in anatomical collections. But, after twenty years of crime, the bore is discovered in the same house, in the same attitude, eating the same soup, —unpunished, untried, undissected—no scaffold, no skeleton—no mob of gentlemen and ladies to gape over his last dying speech and confession.—[*E. R.* 1826.]

DELPHINE.

This dismal trash, which has nearly dislocated the jaws of every critic among us with gaping, so alarmed Buonaparte, that he seized the whole impression, sent Madame de Staël out of Paris, and, for aught we know, sleeps in a nightcap of steel, and dagger-proof blankets.

To us it appears rather an attack upon the Ten Commandments than the government of Buonaparte, and calculated not so much to enforce the rights of the Bourbons, as the benefits of adultery, murder, and a great number of other vices, which have been somehow or other strangely neglected in this country, and too much so (according to the apparent opinion of Madame de Staël) even in France.

Our general opinion of Delphine is, that it is calculated to shed a mild lustre over adultery; by gentle and convenient gradation, to destroy the modesty and the caution of women; to facilitate the acquisition of easy vices, and encumber the difficulty of virtue. What a wretched qualification of this censure to add, that the badness of the principles is alone corrected by the badness of the style, and that this celebrated lady would have been very guilty, if she had not been very dull!—[*E. R.* 1803.]

SUBJECTION OF CLERGY.

THE parochial clergy are as much unrepresented in the English Parliament as they are in the parliament of Brobdignag. The bishops make just what laws they please, and the bearing they may have on the happiness of the clergy at large never for one moment comes into the serious consideration of Parliament.— [*E. R.* 1802.]

UTILITY AND WIT.

THE idea of utility is always inimical to the idea of wit.—[*E. R.*]

A GRACEFUL ILLUSTRATION.

THE resemblance between the sandal tree imparting (while it falls) its aromatic flavour to the edge of the axe, and the benevolent man rewarding evil with good, would be witty, did it not excite virtuous emotions. — [*E. R.*]

IRISH BULLS.

THOUGH the question is not a very easy one, we shall venture to say, that a "*bull*" is an apparent congruity and real incongruity of ideas suddenly discovered. And if this account of bulls be just, they are (as might have been supposed) the very reverse of wit; for as wit discovers real relations that are not apparent, bulls admit apparent relations that are not real. The pleasure arising from wit proceeds from our surprise at suddenly discovering two things to be similar in which we suspected no similarity. The pleasure arising from bulls proceeds from our discovering two things to be dissimilar in which a resemblance might have been suspected.

It is clear that a bull cannot depend upon mere incongruity alone; for if a man were to say that he would ride to London upon a cocked hat, or that he would cut his throat with a pound of pickled salmon, this, though completely incongruous, would not be to make bulls, but to talk nonsense. The stronger the apparent connection, and the more complete the real disconnection of the ideas, the greater the surprise and the better the bull. The less apparent, and the more complete the relations established by wit, the higher gratification does it afford. A great deal of the pleasure experienced from bulls proceeds from the sense of superiority in ourselves. Bulls which we invented, or knew to be invented, might please, but in a less degree, for want of this additional zest. — [*E. R.* 1803.]

TRAINING OF BOYS.

PUT a hundred boys together, and the fear of being laughed at will always be a strong influencing motive with every individual among them. If a master can turn this principle to his own use, and get boys to laugh at vice, instead of the old plan of laughing at virtue, is he not doing a very new, a very difficult, and a very laudable thing? — [*E. R.* 1806.]

EMULATION OF RANK IN SCHOOLS.

IT is, above all things, perilous to create an order of merit in a primary school, because it gives the boys an idea of the origin of nobility. For our part, when we saw these ragged and interesting little nobles, shining in their tin stars, we only thought it probable that the spirit of emulation would make them better ushers, tradesmen, and mechanics. We did, in truth, imagine we had observed, in some of their faces, a bold project for procuring better breeches for keeping out the blasts of heaven, which howled through those garments in every direction, and of aspiring hereafter to greater strength of seam, and more perfect continuity of cloth. But for the safety of the titled orders we had no fear; nor did we once dream that the black rod which whipt these dirty little dukes would one day be borne before them as the emblem of legislative dignity, and the sign of noble blood.

SPECIAL INTERVENTIONS OF PROVIDENCE.

A BELIEF that Providence interferes in all the little actions of our lives, refers all merit and demerit to bad and good fortune; and causes the successful man to be always considered as a good man, and the unhappy man as the object of divine vengeance. It furnishes ignorant and designing men with a power which is sure to be abused: — the cry of, a *judgment*, a *judgment*, it is always easy to make, but not easy to resist. It encourages the grossest superstitions; for if the Deity rewards and punishes on every slight occasion, it is quite impossible, but that such a helpless being as man will set himself at work to discover the will of Heaven in the appearances of outward nature, and to apply all the phenomena of thunder, lightning, wind, and every striking appearance to the regulation of his conduct; as the poor Methodist, when he rode into Piccadilly in a thunder-storm, and imagined that all the uproar of the elements was a mere hint to him not to preach at Mr. Romaine's chapel. Hence a great deal of error, and a great deal of secret misery. — [*E. R.* 1808.]

METHODISTS EXAGGERATE THE DOCTRINE.

THERE is nothing heretical in saying, that God *sometimes* intervenes with his special providence; but these people differ from the Established Church, in the degree in which they insist upon this doctrine. In the hands of a man of sense and education, it is a safe doctrine; — in the management of the Methodists it becomes ridiculous and degrading.

TRUE BASIS OF RELIGION.

THE man who places religion upon a false basis is the greatest enemy to religion. — [*E. R.* 1808.]

PRACTICAL PIETY.

THE honest and the orthodox method is to prepare young people for the world, as it actually exists ; to tell them that they will often find vice perfectly successful, virtue exposed to a long train of afflictions; that they must bear this patiently, and look to another world for its rectification. — [*E. R.* 1808.]

METHODISM.

THE Methodists hate pleasure and amusements; no theatre, no cards, no dancing, no punchinello, no dancing dogs, no blind fiddlers; — all the amusements of the rich and of the poor must disappear, wherever these gloomy people get a footing. It is not the abuse of pleasure which they attack, but the interspersion of pleasure, however much it is guarded by good sense and moderation; — it is not only wicked to hear the licentious plays of Congreve, but wicked to hear Henry the Fifth, or the School for Scandal; — it is not only dissipated to run about to all the parties in London and Edinburgh, — but dancing is not *fit for a being who is preparing himself for Eternity. Ennui,* wretchedness, melancholy, groans and sighs, are the offerings which these unhappy men make to a Deity, who has covered the earth with gay colours, and scented it with rich perfumes; and shown us, by the plan and order of his works, that he has given to man something better than a bare existence, and scattered over his creation a thousand superfluous joys, which are totally unnecessary to the mere support of life. — [*E. R.* 1808.]

OVERWROUGHT PIETY.

MEN must eat, and drink, and work; and if you wish to fix upon them high and elevated notions, as the *ordinary* furniture of their minds, you do these two things; — you drive men of warm temperaments mad, — and you introduce, in the rest of the world, a low and shocking familiarity with words and images, which every real friend to religion would wish to keep sacred. — [*E. R.* 1808.]

MODERN FANATICISM.

THE fanaticism so prevalent in the present day, is one of those evils from which society is never wholly exempt: but which bursts out at different periods, with peculiar violence, and sometimes overwhelms everything in its course. The last eruption took place about a century and a half ago, and destroyed both Church and Throne with its tremendous force. Though irresistible, it was short; enthusiasm spent its force — the usual reaction took place; and England was deluged with ribaldry and indecency, because it had been worried with fanatical restrictions. — [*E. R.* 1808.]

BUOYANCY OF RELIGION.

RELIGION is so noble and powerful a consideration — it is so buoyant and so insubmergible — that it may be made, by fanatics, to carry with it any degree of error and of perilous absurdity. — [*E. R.* 1808.]

CAUSE OF FANATICISM.

THE great and permanent cause of the increase of Methodism, is the cause which has given birth to fanaticism in all ages, — the facility of mingling human errors with the fundamental truths of religion. — [*E. R.* 1808.]

LOW ARTS OF FANATICS.

THE Tabernacle really is to the church what Sadler's Wells is to the Drama. There, popularity is gained by vaulting and tumbling, — by low arts, which the regular clergy are not too idle to have recourse to, but too dignified:—their institutions are chaste and severe — they endeavour to do that which, upon the whole, and for a great number of years, will be found to be the most admirable and the most useful: it is no part of their plan to descend to small artifices, for the sake of present popularity and effect. The religion of the common people under the government of the Church may remain as it is for ever;—the enthusiasm must be progressive, or it will expire.—[*E. R.* 1808.]

INROADS OF METHODISM.

THE Methodists have made an alarming inroad into the Church, and they are attacking the army and navy. The principality of Wales, and the East-India Company, they have already acquired. All mines and subterraneous places belong to them; they creep into hospitals and small schools, and so work their way upwards.—[*E. R.* 1808.]

F

STATUTORY FAITH.

If experience has taught us anything, it is the absurdity of controlling men's notions of eternity by acts of Parliament. — [*E. R.* 1808.]

METHODISM.

In routing out a nest of consecrated cobblers, and in bringing to light such a perilous heap of trash as we were obliged to work through, speaking of the Methodists and Missionaries, we are generally conceived to have rendered an useful service to the cause of rational religion.   In spite of all misrepresentation, we have ever been, and ever shall be, the sincere friends of sober and rational Christianity.   We are quite ready, if any fair opportunity occur, to defend it, to the best of our ability, from the tiger-spring of infidelity; and we are quite determined, if we can prevent such an evil, that it shall not be eaten up by the nasty and numerous vermin of Methodism.—[*E. R.* 1808.]

DESTRUCTION OF VERMIN.

Mr. John Styles should remember that it is not the practice with destroyers of vermin to allow the little victims a *veto* upon the weapons used against them.   If this were otherwise, we should have one set of vermin banishing small tooth-combs; another protesting against mouse-traps; a third prohibiting the finger and thumb; a fourth exclaiming against the intolerable infamy of using soap and water. It is impossible, however, to listen to such pleas. They must all be caught, killed, and cracked, in the manner, and by the instruments which are found most efficacious to their destruction; and the more they cry out, the greater plainly is the skill used against them.—[*E. R.* 1808.]

METHODISTICAL LUBRICITY.

IT is scarcely possible to reduce the drunken declamations of Methodism to a point, to grasp the wriggling lubricity of these cunning animals, and to fix them in one position. —[*E. R.* 1808.]

METHODIST GARMENTS.

THERE is, at this moment, a man in London who prays for what garments he wants, and finds them next morning in his room, tight and fitting. This man, as might be expected, gains between two and three thousand a year from the common people, by preaching. Anna, the prophetess, encamps in the woods of America, with thirteen or fourteen thousand followers, and has visits every night from the prophet *Elijah*. Joanna Southcote raises the dead, &c. &c. Mr. Styles will call us atheists, and disciples of the French school, for what we are about to say; but it is our decided opinion, that there is some fraud in the prophetic visit; and it is but too probable, that the clothes are merely human, and the man measured for them in the common way.—[*E. R.* 1808.]

CANT.

IF the choice rested with us, we should say,— Give us back our wolves again — restore our Danish invaders — curse us with any evil but the evil of a canting, deluded, and Methodistical populace.— [*E. R.* 1809.]

MISSIONARIES IN INDIA.

THE plan, it seems, is this:—We are to educate India in Christianity, as a parent does his child; and, when it is perfect in its catechism, then to pack up, quit it entirely, and leave it to its own management. This is the evangelical project for separating a colony from the parent country. They see nothing of the bloodshed, and massacres, and devastations, nor of the speeches in Parliament, squandered millions, fruitless expeditions, jobs and pensions, with which the loss of our Indian possessions would necessarily be accompanied; nor will they see that these consequences could arise from the *attempt*, and not from the completion, of their scheme of conversion. We should be swept from the peninsula by Pagan zealots; and should lose, among other things, all chance of ever really converting them.—[*E. R.* 1809.]

MISSIONARY LABOURS.

PROVE to us that they are fit men, doing a fit thing, and we are ready to praise the missionaries; but it gives us no pleasure to hear that a man has walked a thousand miles with peas in his shoes, unless we know why and wherefore, and to what good purpose he has done it.— [*E. R.* 1809.]

MISSIONARY PRETENSIONS.

THE missionaries complain of intolerance. A weasel might as well complain of intolerance when he is throttled for sucking eggs.—[*E. R.* 1809.]

EFFECT OF MISSIONS IN INDIA.

THESE men talk of the loss of our possessions in India, as if it made the argument against them only more or less strong; whereas, in our estimation, it makes the argument against them conclusive, and shuts up the case. Two men possess a cow, and they quarrel violently how they shall manage this cow. They will surely both of them (if they have a particle of common sense) agree, that there is an absolute necessity for preventing the cow from running away. It is not only the loss of India that is in question — but how will it be lost? By the massacre of ten or twenty thousand English, by the blood of our sons and brothers, who have been toiling so many years to return to their native country.—[*E. R.* 1809.]

CIVILISATION OF INDIA.

IT may be our duty to make the Hindoos Christians — that is another argument: but, that we shall by so doing strengthen our empire, we utterly deny. What signifies identity of religion to a question of this kind? Diversity of bodily colour and of language would soon overpower this consideration. Make the Hindoos enterprising, active, and reasonable as yourselves—destroy the eternal track in which they have moved for ages — and, in a moment, they would sweep you off the face of the earth.—[*E. R.* 1809.]

CONVERSION OF HINDOOS.

WHEN the tenacity of the Hindoos on the subject of their religion is adduced as a reason against the success of the missions, the friends of this undertaking are always fond of reminding us how patiently the Hindoos submitted to the religious persecution and butchery of Tippo. The inference from such citations is truly alarming. It is the imperious duty of Government to watch some of these men most narrowly. There is nothing of which they are not capable. And what, after all, did Tippo effect in the way of conversion? How many Mahometans did he make? There was all the carnage of Medea's Kettle, and none of the transformation.— [*E. R.* 1809.]

PROBABLE LOSS OF INDIA.

Upon the whole, it appears to us hardly possible to push the business of proselytism in India to any length, without incurring the utmost risk of losing our empire. The danger is more tremendous, because it may be so sudden; religious fears are a very probable cause of disaffection in the troops; if the troops are generally disaffected, our Indian empire may be lost to us as suddenly as a frigate or a fort. — [*E. R.* 1808.]

DANGER OF INDIA.

Nothing is more precarious than our empire in India. Suppose we were to be driven out of it to-morrow, and to leave behind us twenty thousand converted Hindoos; it is most probable they would relapse into heathenism; but their original station in society could not be regained. — [*E. R.* 1808.]

CASTES IN INDIA.

The institution of castes has preserved India in the same state in which it existed in the days of Alexander;

and which would leave it without the slightest change in habits and manners, if we were to abandon the country to-morrow. — [*E. R.* 1808.]

HINDOO PROSELYTES.

THE duty of conversion is less plain, and less imperious, when conversion exposes the convert to great present misery. An African, or an Otaheite proselyte, might not perhaps be less honoured by his countrymen if he became a Christian; a Hindoo is instantly subjected to the most perfect degradation. — [*E. R.* 1808.]

SUPERSTITION BETTER THAN ATHEISM.

CONVERSION is no duty at all, if it merely destroys the old religion, without really and effectually teaching the new one. Brother Ringletaube may write home that he makes a Christian, when, in reality, he ought only to state that he has destroyed a Hindoo. Foolish and imperfect as the religion of a Hindoo is, it is at least some restraint upon the intemperance of human passions. It is better a Brahmin should be respected, than that nobody should be respected. A Hindoo had better believe that a deity, with an hundred legs and arms, will reward and punish him hereafter, than that he is not to be punished at all. — [*E. R.* 1808.]

RELIGIOUS EXCITABILITY OF INDIA.

No man (not an Anabaptist) will, we presume, contend that it is our duty to preach the natives into an insurrection, or to lay before them, so fully and emphatically, the scheme of the Gospel, as to make them rise up in the dead of the night and shoot their instructors through the head. Even for missionary purposes, therefore, the utmost discretion is necessary; and if we wish to teach the natives a better religion, we must take care to do it in a manner which will not inspire them with a passion for political change, or we shall inevitably lose our disciples altogether. To us it appears quite clear, that neither Hindoos nor Mahometans are at all indifferent to the attacks made upon their religion; the arrogance and irritability of the Mahometan are universally acknowledged; nor do the Brahmans show the smallest disposition to behold the encroachments upon their religion with passiveness and unconcern. — [*E. R.* 1808.]

RESPECT FOR OPINION IN INDIA.

How is it in human nature that a Brahman should be indifferent to encroachments upon his religion? His reputation, his dignity, and in great measure his wealth, depend upon the preservation of the present supersttions; and why is it to be supposed that motives which are so powerful with all other human beings, are inoperative with him alone? If the Brahmans, however, are disposed to excite a rebellion in support of their own influence, no man, who knows anything of India, can doubt that they have it in their power to effect it.

Our object, therefore, is not only not to do anything violent and unjust upon subjects of religion, but not to give any strong colour to jealous and disaffected natives for misrepresenting your intentions.

All these observations have tenfold force, when applied to an empire which rests so entirely upon opinion. If physical force could be called in to stop the progress of error, we could afford to be misrepresented for a season; but 30,000 white men living in the midst of 70 millions of sable subjects, must be always in the right, or at least never represented as grossly in the wrong. Attention to the prejudices of the subject is wise in all governments, but quite indispensable in a government constituted as our empire in India is constituted; where an uninterrupted series of dexterous conduct is not only necessary to our prosperity, but to our existence.— [*E. R.* 1808.]

DIFFICULTIES OF CONVERSION OF INDIA.

You have 30,000 Europeans in India, and 60 millions of other subjects. If proselytism were to go on as rapidly as the most visionary Anabaptist could dream or desire, in what manner are these people to be taught the genuine truths and practices of Christianity? Where are the clergy to come from? Who is to defray the expense of the establishment? and who can foresee the immense and perilous difficulties of bending the laws, manners, and institutions of a country, to the dictates of a new religion? If it were easy to persuade the Hindoos that their own religion was folly, it would be infinitely difficult effectually to teach them any other. They would tumble their own idols into the river and you would build them no churches: you would destroy all their present motives for doing right and avoiding wrong, without being able to fix upon their minds the more sublime motives by which you profess to be actuated.

If there were a fair prospect of carrying the Gospel into regions where it was before unknown,—if such a project did not expose the best possessions of the country to extreme danger, and if it was in the hands of men who

were discreet as well as devout, we should consider it to
be a scheme of true piety, benevolence, and wisdom : but
the baseness and malignity of fanaticism shall never
prevent us from attacking its arrogance, its ignorance,
and its activity.   For what vice can be more tremendous than that which, while it wears the outward appearance of religion, destroys the happiness of man, and
dishonours the name of God ? — [*E. R.* 1808.]

TYRANNY OF BISHOPS.

BISHOPS are men; not always the wisest of men;
not always preferred for eminent virtues and talents, or
for any good reason whatever known to the public.   They
are almost always devoid of striking and indecorous vices;
but a man may be very shallow, very arrogant, and very
vindictive, though a bishop ; and pursue with unrelenting
hatred a subordinate clergyman, whose principles he dis-
likes and whose genius he fears. — [*E. R.* 1809.]

PETTICOAT BISHOPS.

I HAVE seen in the course of my life, as the mind of
the prelate decayed, wife bishops, daughter bishops,
butler bishops, and even cook and housekeeper bishops.
— [*E. R.* 1809.]

NON-RESIDENCE.

WE remember Horace's description of the misery of a
parish where there is no resident clergyman.

> ———— ' Illacrymabiles
> Urgentur, ignotique longâ
> Nocte, *carent quia vate sacro.*'

[*E. R.* 1809.]

PENALTIES OF NON-RESIDENCE.

EVERY lay plunderer, and every fanatical coxcomb, is forging fresh chains for the English clergy; and we should not be surprised, in a very little time, to see them absenting themselves from their benefices by a kind of day-rule, like prisoners in the King's Bench. — [*E. R.* 1809.]

FORCED RELIGION.

YOU may drag men into church by main force, and prosecute them for buying a pot of beer, — and cut them off from the enjoyment of a leg of mutton;—and you may do all this, till you make the common people hate Sunday, and the clergy, and religion, and everything which relates to such subjects.—[*E. R.* 1810.]

RELIGION BY INDICTMENT.

A ROBBER and a murderer must be knocked on the head like mad dogs; but we have no great opinion of the possibility of indicting men into piety, or of calling in the Quarter Sessions to the aid of religion. — [*E. R.* 1810.]

OUTWARD CONFORMITY.

To compel men to go to church under a penalty appears to us to be absolutely absurd. The bitterest enemy of religion will necessarily be that person who is driven to a compliance with its outward ceremonies, by informers and justices of the peace.—[*E. R.* 1810.]

RELIGIOUS DUTIES INDEPENDENT OF LAW.

To go to church is a duty of the greatest possible importance; and on the blasphemy and vulgarity of swearing, there can be but one opinion. But such duties are not the objects of legislation; they must be left to the general state of public sentiment; which sentiment must be influenced by example, by the exertions of the pulpit and the press, and, above all, by education. The fear of God can never be taught by constables, nor the pleasures of religion be learnt from a common informer.—[*E. R.* 1810.]

OFFICIAL SUPPRESSION OF VICE.

MEN, whose trade is rat-catching, love to catch rats; the bug-destroyer seizes on his bug with delight; and the suppressor is gratified by finding his vice. The last soon becomes a mere tradesman like the others; none of them moralise, or lament that their respective evils should exist in the world.—[*E. R.* 1810.]

LOVE OF OFFICE.

PROFLIGACY in taking office is so extreme, that we have no doubt public men may be found, who, for half a century, would postpone all remedies for a pestilence, if the preservation of their places depended upon the propagation of the virus.—[*E. R.* 1808.]

PLURALITY OF INFORMERS.

THIRTY or forty informers roaming about the metropolis, may frighten the mass of offenders a little, and do some good; ten thousand informers would either create an insurrection, or totally destroy the confidence and cheerfulness of private life.— [*E. R.* 1809.]

EXTORTION BY INFORMERS.

IF it be lawful for respectable men to combine for the purpose of turning informers, it is lawful for the lowest and most despicable race of informers to do the same thing; and then it is quite clear that every species of wickedness and extortion would be the consequence.— [*E. R.* 1809.]

AUTHORITY OF VIRTUE.

IT is of great importance to keep public opinion on the side of virtue. To their authorised and legal correctors, mankind are, on common occasions, ready enough to submit: but there is something in the self-erection of a voluntary magistracy which creates so much disgust, that it almost renders vice popular, and puts the offence at a premium.—[*E. R.* 1809.]

THE DRAMA.

THERE is something in the word *Playhouse* which seems so closely connected, in the minds of some people, with sin and Satan, that it stands in their vocabulary for every species of abomination. And yet why? Where is every feeling more roused in favour of virtue than at a good play? Where is goodness so feelingly, so enthusiastically learnt? What so solemn as to see the excellent passions of the human heart called forth by a great actor, animated by a great poet? To hear Siddons repeat what Shakspeare wrote! To behold the child and his mother — the noble and the poor artisan — the monarch and his subjects — all ages and all ranks convulsed with one common passion — wrung with one common anguish, and, with loud sobs and cries, doing involuntary homage to the God that made their hearts! What wretched infatuation to interdict such amusements as these! What a blessing that mankind can be allured from sensual gratification, and find relaxation and pleasure in such pursuits! — [*E. R.* 1809.]

POLITICAL OPPOSITION.

IT is the easiest of all things, too, in this country, to make Englishmen believe that those who oppose the Government wish to ruin the country. — [*E. R.* 1809.]

POLITICIANS JUDGED BY RESULTS.

THE visible and immediate stake for which English politicians play, is not large enough to attract the notice of the people, and to call them off from their daily occupations, to investigate thoroughly the characters and motives of men engaged in the business of legislation. The people can only understand, and attend to, the last results of a long series of measures. They are impatient of the details which lead to these results; and it is the easiest of all things to make them believe that those who insist upon such details are actuated only by factious motives. — [*E. R.* 1809.]

JEALOUSY OF FREEDOM.

WHEN a nation has become free, it is extremely difficult to persuade them that their freedom is only to be preserved by perpetual and minute jealousy. — [*E. R.* 1809.]

POLITICAL INDEPENDENCE IN THE CHURCH.

POLITICAL independence—discouraged enough in these times among all classes of men — is sure, in the timid profession of the church, to doom a man to eternal poverty and obscurity.— [*E. R.* 1809.]

LITERARY PROLIXITY.

THERE is an event recorded in the Bible, which men who write books should keep constantly in their remembrance. It is there set forth, that many centuries ago the earth was covered with a great flood, by which the whole of the human race, with the exception of one family, were destroyed. It appears, also, that from thence, a great alteration was made in the longevity of mankind, who, from a range of seven or eight hundred years, which they enjoyed before the flood, were confined to their present period of seventy or eighty years. This epoch in the history of man gave birth to the twofold division of the antediluvian and the postdiluvian style of writing, the latter of which naturally contracted itself into those inferior limits which were better accommodated to the abridged duration of human life and literary labour. Now, to forget this event,— to write without the fear of the deluge before his eyes, and to handle a subject as if mankind could lounge over a pamphlet for ten years, as before their submersion,— is to be guilty of the most grievous error into which a writer can possibly fall. The author of this book should call in the aid of some brilliant pencil, and cause the distressing scenes of the deluge to be portrayed in the most lively colours for his use. He should gaze at Noah, and be brief. The ark should constantly remind him of the little time there is left for reading; and he should learn, as they did in the ark, to crowd a great deal of matter into a very little compass.—[*E. R.* 1809.]

BREVITY OF CHARITY.

BREVITY is in writing what charity is to all other virtues. Righteousness is worth nothing without the one, nor authorship without the other.—[*E. R.* 1809.]

SELF-APPLAUSE.

SOME persons can neither stir hand nor foot without making it clear they are thinking of themselves, and laying little traps for approbation.—[*E. R.* 1809.]

THE BROAD A.

WHO, oh gracious Heaven! who are *a* Burgess,— *a* Tomlin,— *a* Bennet,— *a* Cyril Jackson,— *a* Martin Routh?—A Tom,— a Jack,— a Harry,— a Peter?— All good men enough in their generation doubtless they are. But what have they done for the broad *a?*

Surely, scholars and gentlemen can drink tea with each other, and eat bread and butter, without all this laudatory cackling.—[*E. R.* 1809.]

CAPITAL PUNISHMENT.

WE are scarcely, however, converts to that system which would totally abolish the punishment of death. That it is much too frequently inflicted in this country, we readily admit; but we suspect it will be always necessary to reserve it for the most pernicious crimes. Death is the most terrible punishment to the common people, and therefore the most preventive. It does not perpetually outrage the feelings of those who are innocent, and likely to remain innocent, as would be the case from the spectacle of convicts working in the high roads and public places. Death is the most irrevocable punishment, which is in some sense a good; for, however necessary it might be to inflict labour and imprisonment for life, it would never be done. Kings and Legislatures would take pity after a great lapse of years; the punishment would be remitted, and its preventive efficacy, therefore, destroyed. —[*E. R.* 1809.]

PROMULGATION OF LAWS.

PHILOPATRIS, and Mr. Jeremy Bentham before him, lay a vast stress upon the promulgation of laws, and treat the inattention of the English Government to this point as a serious evil. It may be so — but we do not happen to remember any man punished for an offence which he did not know to be an offence; though he might not know exactly the degree in which it was punishable. Who are to read the laws to the people? who would listen to them if they were read? who would comprehend them if they listened? In a science like law there must be technical phrases, known only to professional men: business could not be carried on without them: and of what avail would it be to repeat such phrases to the people? Again, what laws are to be repeated, and in what places? Is a law respecting the number of threads on the shuttle of a Spitalfields weaver to be read to the corn-growers of the Isle of Thanet? If not, who is to make the selection? If the law cannot be comprehended by listening to the *vivâ voce* repetition, is the reader to explain it, and are there to be law lectures all over the kingdom? The fact is that the evil does not exist.—[*E. R.* 1809.]

POPULAR KNOWLEDGE OF LAWS.

THE people, it is true, are ignorant of the laws; but they are ignorant only of the laws which do not concern them. A poacher knows nothing of the penalties to which he exposes himself by stealing ten thousand pounds from the public. Commissioners of public boards are unacquainted with all the decretals of our ancestors respecting the wiring of hares; but the one pockets his extra per-centage, and the other his leveret, with a perfect knowledge of the laws — the particular laws which it is his business to elude.—[*E. R.* 1809.]

1648 AND 1793.

OUR regicides were serious and original at least, in the bold, bad deeds which they committed. The regicides of France were poor theatrical imitators,—intoxicated with blood and with power, and incapable even of forming a sober estimate of the guilt or the consequences of their actions.—[*E. R.* 1809.]

CAREER OF MR. FOX.

THE whole of Mr. Fox's life was spent in opposing the profligacy and exposing the ignorance of his own court. In the first half of his political career, while Lord North was losing America, and in the latter half, while Mr. Pitt was ruining Europe, the creatures of the Government were eternally exposed to the attacks of this discerning, dauntless, and most powerful speaker. Folly and corruption never had a more terrible enemy in the English House of Commons — one whom it was so impossible to bribe, so hopeless to elude, and so difficult to answer. — [*E. R.* 1811.]

OFFICIAL ACCURACY.

THE term *official accuracy* has of late days become one of very ambiguous import. Mr. Rose, we can see, would imply by it the highest possible accuracy — as we see *office pens* advertised in the window of a shop, by way of excellence. The public reports of those, however, who have been appointed to look into the manner in which public offices are conducted, by no means justify this usage of the term ;— and we are not without apprehensions, that Dutch politeness, Carthaginian faith, Bœotian genius, and official accuracy, may be terms equally current in the world; and that Mr. Rose may, without intending it, have contributed to make this valuable addition to the mass of our ironical phraseology. —[*E. R.* 1811.]

DURATION OF ERROR.

A HUNDRED years, to be sure, is a very little time for the duration of a national error; and it is so far from being reasonable to look for its decay at so short a date, that it can hardly be expected, within such limits, to have displayed the full bloom of its imbecility. — [*E. R.* 1809.]

PURSUIT OF KNOWLEDGE.

NOTHING will do in the pursuit of knowledge but the blackest ingratitude ;— the moment we have got up the ladder, we must kick it down;—as soon as we have passed over the bridge, we must let it rot;—when we have got upon the shoulders of the ancients, we must look over their heads.   The man who forgets the friends of his childhood in real life is base; but he who clings to the props of his childhood in literature, must be content to remain ignorant as he was when a child.—[*E. R.* 1809.]

VALUE OF CLASSICAL LEARNING.

To almost every Englishman up to the age of three or four and twenty, classical learning has been the great object of existence; and no man is very apt to suspect, or very much pleased to hear, that what he has done for so long a time was not worth doing.—[*E. R.* 1809.]

BEAUTY OF CLASSICAL LANGUAGE.

The two ancient languages are as mere inventions — as pieces of mechanism incomparably more beautiful than any of the modern languages of Europe : their mode of signifying time and case, by terminations, instead of auxiliary verbs and particles, would of itself stamp their superiority.   Add to this, the copiousness of the Greek language, with the fancy, majesty, and harmony of its compounds; and there are quite sufficient reasons why the classics should be studied for the beauties of language.   Compared to them, merely as vehicles of thought and passion, all modern languages are dull, ill contrived, and barbarous.—[*E. R.* 1809.]

THE CLASSICAL AUTHORS.

Whatever our conjectures may be, we cannot be sure that the best modern writers can afford us as good models as the ancients;—we cannot be certain that they will live through the revolutions of the world, and continue to please in every climate—under every species of government—through every stage of civilisation. We may still borrow descriptive power from Tacitus; dignified perspicuity from Livy; simplicity from Cæsar; and from Homer some portion of that light and heat which, dispersed into ten thousand channels, has filled the world with bright images and illustrious thoughts. Let the cultivator of modern literature addict himself to the purest models of taste which France, Italy, and England could supply, he might still learn from Virgil to be majestic, and from Tibullus to be tender; he might not yet look upon the face of nature as Theocritus saw it; nor might he reach those springs of pathos with which Euripides softened the hearts of his audience.—[*E. R.* 1809.]

CLASSICAL PEDANTRY.

A LEARNED man!—a scholar!—a man of erudition! Upon whom are these epithets of approbation bestowed? Are they given to men acquainted with the science of government? thoroughly masters of the geographical and commercial relations of Europe? to men who know the properties of bodies, and their action upon each other? No: this is not learning; it is chemistry, or political economy—not learning. The distinguishing abstract term, the epithet of Scholar, is reserved for him who writes on the Æolic reduplication, and is familiar with the Sylburgian method of arranging defectives in ω and $\mu\iota$. The picture which a young Englishman, addicted to the pursuit of knowledge, draws—his *beau idéal,* of human nature—his top and consummation of man's powers — is a knowledge of the Greek language. His object is not to reason, to imagine, or to invent; but to conjugate, decline, and derive. The situations of imaginary glory which he draws for himself, are the detection of an anapæst in the wrong place, or the restoration of a dative case which Cranzius had passed over, and the never-dying Ernesti failed to observe.—[*E. R.* 1809.]

LATIN VERSES.

THERE are few boys who remain to the age of eighteen or nineteen at a public school, without making above ten thousand Latin verses; — a greater number than is contained in the *Æneid:* and after he has made this quantity of verses in a dead language, unless the poet should happen to be a very weak man indeed, he never makes another as long as he lives.—[*E. R.* 1809.]

VERSIFICATION NO TEST OF CAPACITY.

THE prodigious honour in which Latin verses are held at public schools is surely the most absurd of all absurd distinctions. You rest all reputation upon doing that which is a natural gift, and which no labour can attain. If a lad won't learn the words of a language, his degradation in the school is a very natural punishment for his disobedience, or his indolence; but it would be as reasonable to expect that all boys should be witty, or beautiful, as that they should be poets. In either case, it would be to make an accidental, unattainable, and not a very important gift of nature, the only, or the principal, test of merit. This is the reason why boys, who make a considerable figure at school, so very often make no figure in the world;—and why other lads, who are passed over without notice, turn out to be valuable, important men. The test established in the world is widely dif-

ferent from that established in a place which is presumed
to be a preparation for the world; and the head of a
public school, who is a perfect miracle to his contemporaries, finds himself shrink into absolute insignificance,
because he has nothing else to command respect or regard,
but a talent for fugitive poetry in a dead language.—
[*E. R.* 1809.]

EXCLUSIVE CULTURE OF LANGUAGES.

THE passion for languages is just as strong as any
other literary passion.　There are very good Persian and
Arabic scholars in this country.　Large heaps of trash
have been dug up from Sanscrit ruins.　We have seen,
in our own times, a clergyman of the University of Oxford complimenting their Majesties in Coptic and Syro-
phœnician verses; and yet we doubt whether there will
be a sufficient avidity in literary men to get at the
beauties of the finest writers which the world has yet
seen; and though the *Bagvat Gheeta* has (as can be
proved) met with human beings to translate, and other
human beings to read it, we think that, in order to secure
an attention to Homer and Virgil, we must catch up
every man—whether he is to be a clergyman or a duke,
— begin with him at six years of age, and never quit
him till he is twenty; making him conjugate and decline
for life and death; and so teaching him to estimate his
progress in real wisdom as he can scan the verses of the
Greek tragedians. — [*E. R.* 1809.]

NARROWNESS OF ENGLISH EDUCATION.

THE English clergy, in whose hands education entirely
rests, bring up the first young men of the country as if
they were all to keep grammar schools in little country
towns.— [*E. R.* 1809.]

WASTE OF TALENT.

AT present, we act with the minds of our young men, as the Dutch did with their exuberant spices. An infinite quantity of talent is annually destroyed in the Universities of England by the miserable jealousy and littleness of ecclesiastical instructors. — [*E. R.* 1809.]

MISTAKEN OBJECTS OF PURSUIT.

THERE is a delusive sort of splendour in a vast body of men pursuing one object, and thoroughly obtaining it; and yet, though it be very splendid, it is far from being useful. — [*E. R.* 1809.]

TRUE EDUCATION FOR CIVIL LIFE.

WHEN an University has been doing useless things for a long time, it appears at first degrading to them to be useful. If we had to do with a young man going out into public life, we would exhort him to contemn, or at least not to affect the reputation of a great scholar, but to educate himself for the offices of civil life. He should learn what the constitution of his country really was,— how it had grown into its present state,— the perils that had threatened it,— the malignity that had attacked it — the courage that had fought for it, and the wisdom that had made it great. We would bring strongly before his mind the characters of those Englishmen who have been the steady friends of the public happiness; and, by their examples, would breathe into him a pure public taste, which should keep him untainted in all the vicissitudes of political fortune.—[*E. R.* 1809.]

DISCOVERY.

THAT man is not the discoverer of any art who first says the thing; but he who says it so long, and so loud, and so clearly, that he compels mankind to hear him — the man who is so deeply impressed with the importance of the discovery that he will take no denial, but, at the risk of fortune, and fame, pushes through all opposition, and is determined that what he thinks he has discovered shall not perish for want of a fair trial. Other persons had noticed the effect of coal gas in producing light; but Winsor worried the town with bad English for three winters before he could attract any serious attention to his views. Many persons broke stone before Macadam, but Macadam felt the discovery more strongly, stated it more clearly, persevered in it with greater tenacity, wielded his hammer, in short, with greater force than other men, and finally succeeded in bringing his plan into general use.—[*E. R.* 1826.]

ENGLISH PERSEVERANCE.

IF the English were in a paradise of spontaneous productions, they would continue to dig and plough, though they were never a peach nor a pine-apple the better for it.—[*E. R.* 1826.]

THE ELDER GENERATION.

IT is by no means an uncommon wish of the mouldering and decaying part of mankind, that the next generation should not enjoy any advantages from which they themselves have been precluded. — "*Ay, ay, it's all mighty well — but I went through this myself, and I am determined my children shall do the same.*" We are convinced that a great deal of opposition to improvement proceeds from this principle. Crabbe might make a good picture of an unbenevolent old man, slowly retiring from this sublunary scene, and lamenting that the coming race of men would be less bumped on the roads, better lighted in the streets, and less tormented with grammars and lexicons, than in the preceding age. A greal deal of compliment to the wisdom of ancestors, and a great degree of alarm at the dreadful spirit of innovation, are soluble into mere jealousy and envy.— [*E. R.* 1826.]

DIFFICULTIES TO OVERCOME.

NEVER be afraid of wanting difficulties for your pupil; if means are rendered more easy, more will be expected. —[*E. R.* 1826.]

DEAD AND LIVING LANGUAGES.

THE real way of learning a dead language, is to imitate, as much as possible, the method in which a living language is naturally learnt. —[*E. R.* 1826.]

LATIN AND GREEK.

IF there be any thing which fills reflecting men with melancholy and regret, it is the waste of mortal time, parental money, and puerile happiness, in the present method of pursuing Latin and Greek. —[*E. R.* 1826.]

BOYS AND GIRLS.

As long as boys and girls run about in the dirt, and trundle hoops together, they are both precisely alike. If you catch up one half of these creatures, and train them to a particular set of actions and opinions, and the other half to a perfectly opposite set, of course their understandings will differ, as one or the other sort of occupations has called this or that talent into action. There is surely no occasion to go into any deeper or more abstruse reasoning, in order to explain so very simple a phenomenon. — [*E. R.* 1810.]

EDUCATION OF WOMEN.

As the matter now stands, the time of women is considered as worth nothing at all. Daughters are kept to occupations in sewing, patching, mantua-making, and mending, by which it is impossible they can earn tenpence a day. They are kept with nimble fingers and vacant understandings, till the season for improvement is utterly past away, and all chance of forming more important habits completely lost.— [*E. R.* 1810.]

EDUCATION OF COUNTRY GENTLEMEN.

A CENTURY ago, who would have believed that country gentlemen could be brought to read and spell with the ease and accuracy which we now so frequently remark,— or supposed that they could be carried up even to the elements of ancient and modern history? — [*E. R.* 1810.]

AFFECTATION.

ALL affectation and display proceed from the supposition of possessing something better than the rest of the world possesses. Nobody is vain of possessing two legs and two arms;—because that is the precise quantity of either sort of limb which everybody possesses.—[*E. R.* 1810.]

PEDANTRY.

As pedantry is an ostentatious obtrusion of knowledge, in which those who hear us cannot sympathise, it is a fault of which soldiers, sailors, sportsmen, gamesters, cultivators, and all men engaged in a particular occupation, are quite as guilty as scholars; but they have the good fortune to have the vice only of pedantry,—while scholars have both the vice and the name for it too. — [*E. R.* 1810.]

KNOWLEDGE CURES CONCEIT.

Diffuse knowledge generally among women, and you will at once cure the conceit which knowledge occasions while it is rare. —[*E. R.* 1810.]

ENLARGE WOMAN'S EDUCATION.

Why are we necessarily to doom a girl, whatever be her taste or her capacity, to one unvaried line of petty and frivolous occupation? If she be full of strong sense and elevated curiosity, can there be any reason why she should be diluted and enfeebled down to a mere culler of simples, and fancier of birds?— why books of history and reasoning are to be torn out of her hand, and why she is to be sent, like a butterfly, to hover over the idle flowers of the field?—[*E. R.* 1810.]

FEAR OF EDUCATING WOMEN.

There is a very general notion, that if you once suffer women to eat of the tree of knowledge, the rest of the family will very soon be reduced to the same kind of aërial and unsatisfactory diet.—[*E. R.* 1810.]

SIMPLE PLEASURES, SMALL.

IF by a simple pleasure is meant one, the cause of which can be easily analysed, or which does not last long, or which in itself is very faint; then simple pleasures seem to be very nearly synonymous with small pleasures; and if the simplicity were to be a little increased, the pleasure would vanish altogether.—[*E. R.* 1810.]

RESPECT PAID TO EDUCATED WOMEN.

AMONG men of sense and liberal politeness, a woman who has successfully cultivated her mind, without diminishing the gentleness and propriety of her manners, is always sure to meet with a respect and attention bordering upon enthusiasm.—[*E. R.* 1810.]

SOLITARINESS OF WOMEN.

LET any man reflect upon the solitary situation in which women are placed, — the ill treatment to which they are sometimes exposed, and which they must endure in silence, and without the power of complaining,—and he must feel convinced that the happiness of a woman will be materially increased in proportion as education has given to her the habit and the means of drawing her resources from herself. — [*E. R.* 1810.]

OCCUPATION OF WOMEN.

NOTHING, certainly, is so ornamental and delightful in women as the benevolent affections; but time cannot be filled up, and life employed, with high and impassioned virtues. We know women are to be compassionate; but they cannot be compassionate from eight o'clock in the morning till twelve at night:—and what are they to do in the interval?—[*E. R.* 1810.]

DEGRADATION OF UNEDUCATED WOMEN.

IF you neglect to educate the mind of a woman, by the speculative difficulties which occur in literature, it can never be educated at all: if you do not effectually rouse it by education, it must remain for ever languid. Uneducated men may escape intellectual degradation; uneducated women cannot.—[*E. R.* 1810.]

THE DECAY OF WOMAN'S LIFE.

MEN rise in character often as they increase in years; — they are venerable from what they have acquired, and pleasing from what they can impart; but women (such is their unfortunate style of education) hazard every thing upon one cast of the die;—when youth is gone, all is gone. Every human being must put up with the coldest civility, who has neither the charms of youth nor the wisdom of age. Neither is there the slightest commiseration for decayed accomplishments; — no man mourns over the fragments of a dancer, or drops a tear on the relics of musical skill. They are flowers destined to perish; but the decay of great talents is always the subject of solemn pity; and, even when their last memorial is over, their ruins and vestiges are regarded with pious affection. — [*E. R.* 1810.]

ACCOMPLISHMENTS.

ACCOMPLISHMENTS are merely means for displaying the grace and vivacity of youth, which every woman gives up, as she gives up the dress and the manners of eighteen: she has no wish to retain them; or, if she has, she is driven out of them by diameter and derision. The error is, to make such things the grand and universal object,— to insist upon it that every woman is to sing, and draw, and dance, —with nature or against nature,— to bind her apprentice to some accomplishment, and if she cannot succeed in oil or water colours, to prefer gilding, varnishing, burnishing, box-making, to real and solid improvement in taste, knowledge, and understanding. — [*E. R.* 1810.]

THE RESOURCES OF LIFE.

THE object is, to give to children resources that will endure as long as life endures—habits that time will ameliorate, not destroy,— occupations that will render sickness tolerable, solitude pleasant, age venerable, life more dignified and useful, and therefore death less terrible.— [*E. R.* 1810.]

MENTAL CULTURE.

A WOMAN of accomplishments may entertain those who have the pleasure of knowing her for half an hour with great brilliancy; but a mind full of ideas, and with that elastic spring which the love of knowledge only can convey, is a perpetual source of exhilaration and amusement to all that come within its reach ;— not collecting its force into single and insulated achievements, like the efforts made in the fine arts — but diffusing, equally over the whole of existence, a calm pleasure — better loved as it is longer felt — and suitable to every variety and every period of life.—[*E. R.* 1810.]

CHARM OF EDUCATION.

EDUCATION gives fecundity of thought, copiousness of illustration, quickness, vigour, fancy, words, images, and illustrations;— it decorates every common thing, and gives the power of trifling without being undignified and absurd. —[*E. R.* 1810.]

COUNTER ACTION.

THE true way to attack vice, is by setting up something else against it.—[*E. R.* 1810.]

NATURAL LOVE OF GOOD.

TRUST to the natural love of good where there is no temptation to be bad—it operates nowhere more forcibly than in education. —[*E. R.* 1810.]

A NATION'S BEST GIFT.

THE most beautiful possession which a country can have is a noble and rich man, who loves virtue and knowledge;— who without being feeble or fanatical is pious—and who without being factious is firm and independent;— who, in his political life, is an equitable mediator between king and people; and in his civil life, a firm promoter of all which can shed a lustre upon his country, or promote the peace and order of the world.— [*E. R.* 1810.]

GENTLENESS IN EDUCATION.

THOSE young people will turn out to be the best men, who have been guarded most effectually, in their childhood, from every species of useless vexation : and experienced, in the greatest degree, the blessings of a wise and rational indulgence. — [*E. R.* 1810.]

HEAD BOYS.

THE *head* of a public school is generally a very conceited young man, utterly ignorant of his own dimensions, and losing all that habit of conciliation towards others, and that anxiety for self-improvement, which result from the natural modesty of youth. Nor is this conceit very easily and speedily gotten rid of;—we have seen (if we mistake not) public-school importance lasting through the half of after-life, strutting in lawn, swelling in ermine, and displaying itself, both ridiculously and offensively, in the haunts and business of bearded men.—[*E. R.* 1810.]

NATURAL GROWTH AND DECAY.

IN a forest, or public school for oaks and elms, the trees are left to themselves; the strong plants live, and the weak ones die : the towering oak that remains is admired; the saplings that perish around it are cast into the flames and forgotten. — [*E. R.* 1810.]

SCHOOL AND HOME.

THAT education seems to us to be the best which mingles a domestic with a school life, and which gives to a youth the advantage which is to be derived from the learning of a master, and the emulation which results from the society of other boys, together with the affectionate vigilance which he must experience in the house of his parents.—[*E. R.* 1810.]

WAR.

If three men were to have their legs and arms broken, and were to remain all night exposed to the inclemency of weather, the whole country would be in a state of the most dreadful agitation. Look at the wholesale death of a field of battle, ten acres covered with dead, and half dead, and dying; and the shrieks and agonies of many thousand human beings. There is more of misery inflicted upon mankind by one year of war, than by all the civil peculations and oppressions in a century. Yet it is a state into which the mass of mankind rush with the greatest avidity, hailing official murderers, in scarlet, gold, and cock's feathers, as the greatest and most glorious of human creatures. It is the business of every wise and good man to set himself against this passion for military glory, which really seems to be the most fruitful source of human misery.—[*E. R.* 1813.]

FREQUENCY OF WARS.

Alas! we have been at war thirty-five minutes out of every hour since the peace of Utrecht.—[*E. R.* 1827.]

QUAKERS' CHARITY.

Quakers, it must be allowed, are a very charitable and humane people. They are always ready with their money, and, what is of far more importance, with their time and attention for every variety of human misfortune.—[*E. R.* 1814.]

MAD QUAKERS.

A mad Quaker belongs to a small and rich sect; and is, therefore, of greater importance than any other mad person of the same degree in life.—[*E. R.* 1814.]

FRANCE AND ENGLAND.

THE prejudices of the English nation have proceeded a good deal from their hatred to the French ; and, because that country is the native soil of elegance, animation, and grace, a certain patriotic solidity, and loyal awkward ness, have become the characteristics of this.—[*E. R.* 1802.]

FORBIDDEN FRUIT.

A FRENCHWOMAN seems almost always to have wanted the flavour of prohibition, as a necessary condiment to human life.   The provided husband was rejected, and the forbidden husband introduced in ambiguous light, through posterns and secret partitions.   The thing wanted was the wrong man, the gentleman without the ring — the master unsworn to at the altar — the person unconsecrated by priests—

'Oh ! let mo taste thee unexcis'd by kings.'
—[*E. R.* 1818.]

LOVE OF LONDON.

VERY few men who have gratified, and are gratifying their vanity in a great metropolis, are qualified to quit it. Few have the plain sense to perceive, that they must soon inevitably be forgotten,—or the fortitude to bear it when they are.—[*E. R.* 1818.]

OBLIVION IN LONDON.

IN London, as in Law, *de non apparentibus, et non existentibus, eadem est ratio.*—[*E. R.* 1818.]

JEAN JACQUES ROUSSEAU.

JEAN JACQUES ROUSSEAU seems, as the reward of genius and fine writing, to have claimed an exemption from all moral duties.   He borrowed and begged and never paid: —put his children in a poor house—betrayed his friends —insulted his benefactors — and was guilty of every species of meanness and mischief.   His vanity was so great, that it was almost impossible to keep pace with it by any activity of attention; and his suspicion of all mankind amounted nearly, if not altogether, to insanity. —[*E. R.* 1818.]

FASHIONABLE PHYSICIANS.

THERE is always some man, of whom the human viscera stand in greater dread than of any other person, who is supposed, for the time being, to be the only person who can dart his pill into their inmost recesses; and bind them over, in medical recognisance, to assimilate and digest.   In the Trojan war, Podalirius and Machaon were what Dr. Baillie and Sir Henry Halford now are— they had the fashionable practice of the Greek camp; and, in all probability, received many a guinea from Agamemnon dear to Jove, and Nestor the tamer of horses.—[*E. R.* 1818.]

RAILWAY TRAVELLING.

RAILROAD travelling is a delightful improvement of human life.   Man is become a bird; he can fly longer and quicker than a Solan goose.   The mamma rushes sixty miles in two hours to the aching finger of her conjugating and declining grammar boy.   The early

Scotchman scratches himself in the morning mists of the North, and has his porridge in Piccadilly before the setting sun. The Puseyite priest, after a rush of 100 miles, appears with his little volume of nonsense at the breakfast of his bookseller. Every thing is near, every thing is immediate — time, distance, and delay are abolished. But, though charming and fascinating as all this is, we must not shut our eyes to the price we shall pay for it. There will be every three or four years some dreadful massacre—whole trains will be hurled down a precipice, and 200 or 300 persons will be killed on the spot. There will be every now and then a great combustion of human bodies, as there has been at Paris; then all the newspapers up in arms—a thousand regulations, forgotten as soon as the directors dare—loud screams of the velocity whistle—monopoly locks and bolts, as before.—[*Letter on Railways.*]

RAILWAY ACCIDENTS.

WE have been, up to this point, very careless of our railway regulations. The first person of rank who is killed will put every thing in order, and produce a code of the most careful rules. I hope it will not be one of the bench of bishops; but should it be so destined, let the burnt bishop—the unwilling Latimer—remember that, however painful gradual concoction by fire may be, his death will produce unspeakable benefit to the public. Even Sodor and Man will be better than nothing. From that moment the bad effects of the monopoly are destroyed; no more fatal deference to the directors; no despotic incarceration; no barbarous inattention to the anatomy and physiology of the human body; no commitment to locomotive prisons with warrant. We shall then find it possible

"Voyager libre sans mourir."

— [*Letter on Railways.*]

FRANCIS HORNER.

THERE was something very remarkable in his countenance—the commandments were written on his face, and I have often told him there was not a crime he might not commit with impunity, as no judge or jury who saw him would give the smallest degree of credit to any evidence against him : there was in his look a calm settled love of all that was honourable and good—an air of wisdom and of sweetness; you saw at once that he was a great man, whom nature had intended for a leader of human beings; you ranged yourself willingly under his banners and cheerfully submitted to his sway.

The character of his understanding was the exercise of vigorous reasoning, in pursuit of important and difficult truth. He had no wit; nor did he condescend to that inferior variety of this electric talent which prevails occasionally in the North, and which, under the name of *Wut,* is so infinitely distressing to persons of good taste. —[*Letter to L. Horner.*]

GOOD TASTE OF THE HOUSE OF COMMONS.

THE House of Commons, as a near relation of mine once observed, has more good taste than any man in it. — [*Letter to L. Horner.*]

SIR JAMES MACKINTOSH.

CURRAN, the Master of the Rolls, said to Mr. Grattan, "You would be the greatest man of your age, Grattan, if you would buy a few yards of red tape, and tie up your bills and papers." This was the fault or the misfortune of Sir James Mackintosh; he never knew the use of red tape, and was utterly unfit for the common business of life. That a guinea represented a quantity of shillings, and that it would barter for a quantity of cloth, he was well aware; but the accurate number of the baser coin, or the just measurement of the manufactured article, to which he was entitled for his gold, he could never learn, and it was impossible to teach him. Hence his life was often an example of the ancient and melancholy struggle of genius with the difficulties of existence. — [*Letter to Mr. Mackintosh.*]

DESTRUCTION OF LETTERS.

You ask for some of your late father's letters: I am sorry to say I have none to send you. Upon principle, I keep no letters except those on business. I have not a single letter from him, nor from any human being, in my possession. — [*Letter to R. Mackintosh.*]

MR. CANNING'S PARASITES.

NATURE descends down to infinite smallness. Mr. Canning has his parasites; and if you take a large buzzing blue-bottle fly, and look at it in a microscope, you may see twenty or thirty little ugly insects crawling about it, which doubtless think their fly to be the bluest, grandest, merriest, most important animal in the universe, and are convinced that the world would be at an end if it ceased to buzz. — [*P. P. Letters.*]

LIBERTY TO DRINK.

THERE has been in all governments a great deal of absurd canting about the consumption of spirits. We believe the best plan is to let people drink what they like, and wear what they like; to make no sumptuary laws either for the belly or the back. In the first place, laws against rum, and rum and water, are made by men who can change a wet coat for a dry one whenever they choose, and who do not often work up to their knees in mud and water; and, in the next place, if this stimulus did all the mischief it is thought to do by the wise men of claret, its cheapness and plenty would rather lessen than increase the avidity with which it is at present sought for.— [*E. R.* 1819.]

SEPARATION OF SALARY AND DUTY.

THE customary separation of salary and duty is the grand principle which appears to pervade all human institutions, and to be the most invincible of all human abuses. Not only are Church, King, and State, allured by this principle of vicarious labour, but the pot-boy has a lower pot-boy, who, for a small portion of the small gains of his principal, arranges, with inexhaustible sedulity, the subdivided portions of drink, and, intensely perspiring, disperses, in bright pewter, the frothy elements of joy.— [*E. R.* 1823.]

THE HOUR OF DINNER.

AN excellent and well-arranged dinner is a most pleasing occurrence, and a great triumph of civilised life. It is not only the descending morsel, and the enveloping sauce — but the rank, wealth, wit, and beauty which surround the meats — the learned management of light and heat — the silent and rapid services of the attendants — the smiling and sedulous host, proffering gusts and relishes — the exotic bottles — the embossed plate — the pleasant remarks — the handsome dresses — the cunning artifices in fruit and farina! The hour of dinner, in short, includes everything of sensual and intellectual gratification which a great nation glories in producing.

In the midst of all this, who knows that the kitchen chimney caught fire half an hour before dinner!—and that a poor little wretch, of six or seven years old, was sent up in the midst of the flames to put it out. — [*E. R.* 1819.]

SWEEPS.

WE feel for climbing boys as much as anybody can do; but what is a climbing boy in a chimney to a full-grown suitor in the Master's office! —[*E. R.* 1819.]

FERÆ NATURÆ AND DOMESTIC POULTRY.

IT is impossible to make an uneducated man understand in what manner a bird hatched, nobody knows where—to-day living in my field, to-morrow in yours—should be as strictly property as the goose whose whole history can be traced, in the most authentic and satisfactory manner, from the egg to the spit.—[*E. R.* 1819.]

PUNISHMENT OF POACHERS.

IT is expected by some persons, that the severe operation of spring-guns and man-traps will put an end

to the trade of a poacher. This has always been pre-
dicated of every fresh operation of severity, that it was to
put an end to poaching. But if this argument is good
for one thing, it is good for another. Let the first pickpocket who is taken be hung alive by the ribs, and let him
be a fortnight in wasting to death. Let us seize a little
grammar boy, who is robbing orchards, tie his arms and
legs, throw over him a delicate puff-paste, and bake him
in a bunpan in an oven. If poaching can be extirpated
by intensity of punishment, why not all other crimes?
If racks and gibbets and tenterhooks are the best method
of bringing back the golden age, why do we refrain from
so easy a receipt for abolishing every species of wickedness ? The best way of answering a bad argument is not
to stop it, but to let it go on in its course till it leaps
over the boundaries of common sense.—[*E. R.* 1821.]

SALE OF GAME.

THE plan now proposed is, to undersell the poacher,
which may be successful or unsuccessful; but the threat
is, if you attempt this plan there will be no game—and
if there is no game, there will be no country gentlemen.
We deny every part of this enthymeme—the last proposition as well as the first. We really cannot believe that
all our rural mansions would be deserted, although no
game was to be found in their neighbourhood. Some
come into the country for health, some for quiet, for
agriculture, for economy, from attachment to family
estates, from love of retirement, from the necessity of
keeping up provincial interests, and from a vast variety
of causes. Partridges and pheasants, though they form
nine-tenths of human motives, still leave a small residue,
which may be classed under some other head.—[*E. R.*
1823.]

SHOOTING.

A Colonel of the Guards, the second son just entered at Oxford, three diners out from Piccadilly—Major Rock, Lord John, Lord Charles, the Colonel of the regiment quartered at the neighbouring town, two Irish Peers, and a German Baron;—all of this honourable company proceed with fustian jackets, dog-whistles, and chemical inventions, to a solemn destruction of pheasants, how is the country benefited by their presence? or how would earth, air, or sea, be injured by their annihilation?—[*E. R.* 1823.]

PRIVILEGES OF SQUIRES.

We cannot at all comprehend the policy of alluring the better classes of society into the country, by the temptation of petty tyranny and injustice, or of monopoly in sports. How absurd it would be to offer to the higher orders the exclusive use of peaches, nectarines, and apricots, as the premium of rustication—to put vast quantities of men into prison as apricot eaters, apricot buyers, and apricot sellers—to appoint a regular day for beginning to eat, and another for leaving off—to have a lord of the manor for green gages—and to rage with a penalty of five pounds against the unqualified eater of the gage! And yet the privilege of shooting a set of wild poultry is stated to be the bonus for the residence of country gentlemen.—[*E. R.* 1823.]

JUSTICE AMONG SQUIRES.

If gentlemen cannot breathe fresh air without injustice, let them putrefy in Cranborne Alley. Make just laws, and let squires live and die where they please. —[*E. R.* 1823.]

GAME LAWS.

THE first object of a good government is not that rich men should have their pleasures in perfection, but that all orders of men should be good and happy; and if crowded covies and chuckling cock-pheasants are only to be procured by encouraging the common people in vice, and leading them into cruel and disproportionate punishment, it is the duty of the government to restrain the cruelties which the country members, in reward for their assiduous loyalty, have been allowed to introduce into the game laws. — [*E. R.* 1823.]

MISGOVERNMENT OF IRELAND.

So great, and so long has been the misgovernment of Ireland, that we verily believe the empire would be much stronger, if every thing was open sea between England and the Atlantic, and if *skates and cod-fish* swam over the fair land of Ulster. — [*E. R.* 1820.]

CATHOLIC AND PROTESTANT MARRIAGES.

THE Catholics marry upon means which the Protestant considers as insufficient for marriage. A few potatoes and a shed of turf, are all that Luther has left for the Romanist; and, when the latter gets these, he instantly begins upon the great Irish manufacture of children. But a Protestant belongs to the sect that eats the fine flour, and leaves the bran to others; he must have comforts, and he does not marry till he gets them. —[*E. R.* 1820.]

PIG-STYES TO PALACES.

ALL degrees of all nations begin with living in pig-styes. The king or the priest first gets out of them; then the noble, then the pauper, in proportion as each class becomes more and more opulent. Better tastes arise from better circumstances; and the luxury of one period is the wretchedness and poverty of another.—[*E. R.* 1820.]

AN IRISH PLOUGHMAN.

THE most ludicrous of all human objects is an Irishman ploughing. A gigantic figure — a seven-foot machine for turning potatoes into human nature, wrapt up in an immense great coat, and urging on two starved ponies, with dreadful imprecations, and uplifted shillala. The Irish crow discerns a coming perquisite, and is not inattentive to the proceedings of the steeds. The furrow which is to be the depositary of the future crop, is not unlike, either in depth or regularity, to those domestic furrows which the nails of the meek and much-injured wife plough, in some family quarrel, upon the cheeks of the deservedly punished husband. The weeds seem to fall contentedly, knowing that they have fulfilled their destiny, and left behind them, for the resurrection of the ensuing spring, an abundant and healthy progeny. The whole is a scene of idleness, laziness, and poverty; of which it is impossible, in this active and enterprising country, to form the most distant conception. — [*E. R.* 1820.]

AN ENGLISH PLOUGHMAN.

A PLOUGHMAN marries a ploughwoman because she is plump; generally uses her ill; thinks his children an incumbrance; very often flogs them; and, for sentiment, has nothing more nearly approaching to it than the ideas of broiled bacon and mashed potatoes.—[*E. R.* 1806.]

THE IRISH CHARACTER.

THE Irish character contributes something to retard the improvements of that country. The Irishman has many good qualities: he is brave, witty, generous, eloquent, hospitable, and open-hearted; but he is vain, ostentatious, extravagant, and fond of display — light in counsel — deficient in perseverance — without skill in private or public economy—an enjoyer, not an acquirer — one who despises the slow and patient virtues — who wants the superstructure without the foundation — the result without the previous operation — the oak without the acorn and the three hundred years of expectation. The Irish are irascible, prone to debt, and to fight, and very impatient of the restraints of law. Such a people are not likely to keep their eyes steadily upon the main chance, like the Scotch or the Dutch. England strove very hard, at one period, to compel the Scotch to pay a double Church;— but Sawney took his pen and ink; and finding what a sum it amounted to, became furious, and drew his sword. God forbid the Irishman should do the same! the remedy, now, would be worse than the disease: but if the oppressions of England had been more steadily resisted a century ago, Ireland would not have been the scene of poverty, misery, and distress which it now is. —[*E. R.* 1820.]

GRATTAN.

GREAT men hallow a whole people, and lift up all who live in their time. What Irishman does not feel proud that he has lived in the days of GRATTAN? who has not turned to him for comfort, from the false friends and open enemies of Ireland? who did not remember him in the days of its burnings and wastings and murders? No Government ever dismayed him — the world could not bribe him — he thought only of Ireland — lived for no other object — dedicated to her his beautiful fancy, his elegant wit, his manly courage, and all the splendour of his astonishing eloquence. He was so born, and so gifted, that poetry, forensic skill, elegant literature, and all the highest attainments of human genius, were within his reach; but he thought the noblest occupation of a man was to make other men happy and free; and in that straight line he went on for fifty years, without one side-look, without one yielding thought, without one motive in his heart which he might not have laid open to the view of God and man. He is gone!—but there is not a single day of his honest life of which every good Irishman would not be more proud, than of the whole political existence of his countrymen, — the annual deserters and betrayers of their native land. — [*E. R.* 1810.]

ENGLISH TYRANNY TO IRELAND.

ENGLAND seems to have treated Ireland much in the same way as Mrs. Brownrigg treated her apprentice — for which Mrs. Brownrigg is hanged in the first volume of the Newgate Calendar. Upon the whole, we think

the apprentice is better off than the Irishman : as Mrs.
Brownrigg merely starves and beats her, without any
attempt to prohibit her from going to any shop, or praying at any church, her apprentice might select; and once
or twice, if we remember rightly, Brownrigg appears to
have felt some compassion. Not so Old England, who
indulges rather in a steady baseness, uniform brutality,
and unrelenting oppression. — [*E. R.* 1824.]

IRISH PERSECUTIONS.

FOR some centuries after the reign of Henry II. the
Irish were killed like game, by persons qualified or unqualified. Whether dogs were used does not appear
quite certain, though it is probable they were, spaniels
as well as pointers; and that, after a regular point by
Basto, well backed by Ponto and Cæsar, Mr. O'Donnel
or Mr. O'Leary bolted from the thicket, and were bagged
by the English sportsman. — [*E. R.* 1824.]

RELICS.

ENGLAND is almost the only country in the world
(even at present), where there is not some favourite
religious spot, where absurd lies, little bits of cloth,
feathers, rusty nails, splinters, and other invaluable
relics, are treasured up, and in defence of which the
whole population are willing to turn out and perish as
one man. — [*E. R.* 1824.]

MAC'S AND O'S.

THERE are not a few of the best and most humane
Englishmen of the present day, who, when under the

influence of fear or anger, would think it no great crime to put to death people whose names begin with O or Mac. The violent death of Smith, Green or Thomson, would throw the neighbourhood into convulsions, and the regular forms would be adhered to — but little would be really thought of the death of anybody called O'Dogherty or O'Toole. —[*E. R.* 1824.]

ROMAN CATHOLICISM IN ENGLAND.

THE idea of danger from the extension of the Catholic religion in England I utterly deride. The Catholic faith is a misfortune to the world, but those whose faith it conscientiously is are quite right in professing it boldly, and in promoting it by all means which the law allows. A physician does not say, " You will be well *as soon as* the bile is got rid of;" but he says, "You will not be well *until after* the bile is got rid of." He knows, after the cause of the malady is removed, that morbid habits are to be changed, weakness to be supported, organs to be called back to their proper exercise, subordinate maladies to be watched, secondary and vicarious symptoms to be studied. The physician is a wise man—but the anserous politician insists, after 200 years of persecution, and ten of emancipation, that Catholic Ireland should be as quiet as Edmonton or Tooting.—[*Preface to Works.*]

CATHOLIC EMANCIPATION.

IF ever a nation exhibited symptoms of downright madness, or utter stupidity, we conceive these symptoms may be easily recognised in the conduct of this country upon the Catholic question. A man has a wound in his great toe, and a violent and perilous fever at the same time; and he refuses to take the medicines for the fever, because it will disconcert his toe! The mournful and folly-stricken blockhead forgets that his toe cannot survive him; — that if he dies, there can be no digital life apart from him: yet he lingers and fondles over this last part of his body, soothing it madly with little plasters, and anile fomentations, while the neglected fever rages in his entrails, and burns away his whole life. — [*E. R.* 1807.]

SECTARIAN IRRITATION.

GIVE a government only time, and, provided it has the good sense to treat folly with forbearance, it must ultimately prevail. When, therefore, a sect is found, after a lapse of years, to be ill-disposed to the Government, we may be certain that Government has widened its separation by marked distinctions, roused its resentment by contumely, or supported its enthusiasm by persecution. — [*E. R.* 1807.]

TOLERATION.

TOLERATION never had a present tense, nor taxation a future one. The answer which Paul received from Felix, he owed to the subject on which he spoke. When justice and righteousness were his theme, Felix told him to go away, and he would hear him some other time. All men who have spoken to courts upon such disagreeable topics, have received the same answer. Felix, however, trembled when he gave it; but his fear was ill-directed. He trembled at the subject—he ought to have trembled at the delay. — [*E. R.* 1808.]

POLITICAL INACTION.

To lie by in timid and indolent silence,—to *suppose* an inflexibility, in which no court ever could, under pressing circumstances, persevere,—and to neglect a regular and vigorous appeal to public opinion, is to give up all chance of doing good, and to abandon the only instrument by which the few are ever prevented from ruining the many.—[*E. R.* 1808.]

HERESY.

WHAT right has any Government to dictate to any man who shall guide him to heaven, any more than it has to persecute the religious tenets by which he hopes to arrive there? You believe that the heretic professes doctrines utterly incompatible with the true spirit of the Gospel ;—first you burnt him for this,—then you whipt him,—then you fined him,—then you put him in prison. All this did no good ;—and, for these hundred years last past, you have left him alone.— [*E. R.* 1811.]

TENACITY OF INTOLERANCE.

NOTHING dies so hard and rallies so often as intolerance. The fires are put out, and no living nostril has scented the nidor of a human creature roasted for faith ; —then, after this, the prison-doors were got open, and the chains knocked off :—and now Lord Sidmouth only begs that men who disagree with him in religious opinions may be deprived of all civil offices, and not be allowed to hear the preachers they like best. Chains and whips he would not hear of; but these mild gratifications of his bill every orthodox mind is surely entitled to.— [*E. R.* 1811.]

ESTABLISHMENTS.

ALL establishments die of dignity. They are too proud to think themselves ill, and to take a little physic. — [*E. R.* 1811.]

STRENGTH OF THE CHURCH ESTABLISHMENT.

I AM heartily glad that all our disqualifying laws for religious opinions are abolished, and I see nothing in such measures but unmixed good and real increase of strength to our Establishment. — [*Preface to Works.*]

ECCLESIASTICAL BIGOTRY.

IT is a melancholy thing to see a man, clothed in soft raiment, lodged in a public palace, endowed with a rich portion of the product of other men's industry, using all the influence of his splendid situation, however conscientiously, to deepen the ignorance, and inflame the fury, of his fellow creatures. These are the miserable results of that policy which has been so frequently pursued for these fifty years past, of placing men of mean, or middling abilities, in high ecclesiastical stations. In ordinary times, it is of less importance who fills them; but when the bitter period arrives, in which the people must give up some of their darling absurdities;—when the senseless clamour, which has been carefully handed down from father fool to son fool, can be no longer indulged;—when it is of incalculable importance to turn the people to a better way of thinking; the greatest impediments to all amelioration are too often found among those to whose councils, at such periods, the country ought to look for wisdom and peace.—[*E. R.* 1813.]

COUNT YOUR ENEMIES.

KIND providence never sends an evil without a remedy:—and arithmetic is the natural cure for the passion of fear. If a coward can be made to count his enemies, his terrors may be reasoned with, and he may think of ways and means of counteraction.—[*E. R.* 1813.]

EPISCOPAL VIOLENCE.

THE Bishop appears to be in a fog; and as daylight breaks in upon him he will be rather disposed to disown his panic. The noise he hears is not roaring—but braying; the teeth and the mane are all imaginary; there is nothing but ears. It is not a lion that stops the way, but an ass. —[*E. R.* 1813.]

CATHOLIC CONSPIRACIES.

THE Catholics, says his Lordship, will enter into a conspiracy against the English Church. But, is it not also the decided interest of his Lordship's butler that he should be Bishop, and the Bishop his butler? That the crosier and the corkscrew should change hands,—and the washer of the bottles which they had emptied become the diocesan of learned divines? What has prevented this change, so beneficial to the upper domestic, but the extreme improbability of success, if the attempt were made; an improbability so great, that we will venture to say, the very notion of it has scarcely once entered into the understanding of the good man. Why then is the Reverend Prelate, who lives on so safely and contentedly with *John*, so dreadfully alarmed at the Catholics?

And why does he so completely forget, in their instance
alone, that men do not merely strive to obtain a thing
because it is good, but always mingle with the excellence
of the object a consideration of the chance of gaining
it?—[*E. R.* 1813.]

BRITISH EXTRAVAGANCE.

THE world never yet saw so extravagant a government
as the Government of England. Not only is economy
not practised—but it is despised; and the idea of it connected with disaffection, Jacobinism, and Joseph Hume.
Every rock in the ocean where a cormorant can perch is
occupied by our troops—has a governor, deputy-governor,
storekeeper, and deputy storekeeper,—and will soon have
an archdeacon and a bishop. Military colleges, with
thirty-four professors, educating seventeen ensigns per
annum, being half an ensign for each professor, with
every species of nonsense, athletic, sartorial, and plumi-
gerous. A just and necessary war costs this country
about one hundred pounds a minute; whipcord fifteen
thousand pounds; red tape seven thousand pounds; lace
for drummers and fifers, nineteen thousand pounds; a
pension to one man who has broken his head at the Pole;
to another who has shattered his leg at the Equator;
subsidies to Persia; secret service-money to Thibet; an
annuity to Lady Henry Somebody and her seven
daughters—the husband being shot at some place where
we never ought to have had any soldiers at all: and the
elder brother returning four members to Parliament.
Such a scene of extravagance, corruption, and expense as
must paralyse the industry, and mar the fortunes, of the
most industrious, spirited people that ever existed.—[*E.
R.* 1827.]

PROGRESS.

THE follies of one century are scarcely credible in that which succeeds it. A grandmamma of 1827 is as wise as a very wise man of 1727. If the world lasts till 1927, the grandmammas of that period will be far wiser than the tiptop No Popery men of this day. That this childish nonsense will have got out of the drawing-room, there can be no doubt. 'It will most probably have passed through the steward's room, and butler's pantry, into the kitchen. This is the case with ghosts. They no longer loll on couches and sip tea; but are down on their knees scrubbing with the scullion — or stand sweating, and basting with the cook. Mrs. Abigail turns up her nose at them, and the housekeeper declares for flesh and blood, and will have none of their company.—[*E. R.* 1827.]

DISSENTING PREACHERS.

ANY man may dissent from the Church of England, and preach against it, by paying sixpence. Almost every tradesman in a market town is a preacher. It must absolutely be ride-and-tie with them; the butcher must hear the baker in the morning, and the baker listen to the butcher in the afternoon, or there would be no congregation. We have often speculated upon the peculiar trade of the preacher from his style of action. Some have a tying-up or parcel-packing action; some strike strongly against the anvil of the pulpit; some screw, some bore, some act as if they were managing a needle. The occupation of the preceding week can seldom be mistaken. — [*E. R.* 1827.]

LIVE WITH THE TIMES.

WHAT human plan, device, or invention, 270 years old, does not require reconsideration? If a man dressed as he dressed 270 years ago, the pug-dogs in the streets would tear him to pieces. If he lived in the houses of 270 years ago, unrevised and uncorrected, he would die of rheumatism in a week. If he listened to the sermons of 270 years ago, he would perish with sadness and fatigue; and when a man cannot make a coat or a cheese, for 50 years together, without making them better, can it be said that laws made in those days of ignorance, and framed in the fury of religious hatred, need no revision, and are capable of no amendment?—[*E. R.* 1827.]

CORRESPONDENCE WITH ROME.

CAN my Lord Bathurst be ignorant? — can any man, who has the slightest knowledge of Ireland, be ignorant, that the portmanteau which sets out every quarter for Rome, and returns from it, is a heap of ecclesiastical matters, which have no more to do with the safety of the country, than they have to do with the safety of the moon — and which, but for the respect to individual feelings, might all be published at Charing Cross? Mrs. *Flanagan,* intimidated by stomach complaints, wants a dispensation for eating flesh. *Cornelius Oh Bowel* has intermarried by accident with his grandmother; and, finding that she is really his grandmother, his conscience is uneasy. *Mr. Mac Tooley,* the priest, is discovered to be married, and to have two sons, *Castor* and *Pollux Mac Tooley.* Three or four schools-full of little boys have been cursed for going to hear a methodist preacher.

Bargains for shirts and toe-nails of deceased saints — surplices and trencher-caps blessed by the Pope. These are the fruits of double allegiance — the objects of our incredible fear, and the cause of our incredible folly.— [*E. R.* 1827.]

NO MONOPOLY OF FREEDOM.

A GOOD-NATURED and well-conditioned person has pleasure in keeping and distributing anything that is good. If he detects anything with superior flavour, he presses and invites, and is not easy till others participate; — and so it is with political and religious freedom. It is a pleasure to possess it, and a pleasure to communicate it to others. There is something shocking in the greedy, growling, guzzling monopoly of such a bless- ing.— [*E. R.* 1827.]

MARTYRDOM OF BIGOTS.

A BIGOT delights in public ridicule; for he begins to think he is a martyr.— [*P. P. Letters.*]

IMPUNITY OF THEOLOGICAL ERROR.

THE state has nothing whatever to do with theological errors which do not violate the common rules of morality, and militate against the fair power of the ruler. — [*P. P. Letters.*]

PROGRESS OF TOLERATION.

THREE hundred years ago, men burnt and hanged each other for these opinions. Time has softened Catholic as well as Protestant: they both required it; though each perceives only his own improvement, and is blind to that of the other.— [*P. P. Letters.*]

A NAVAL ACTION.

HERE is a frigate attacked by a corsair of immense strength and size, rigging cut, masts in danger of coming by the board, four foot water in the hold, men dropping off very fast; in this dreadful situation how do you think the Captain acts (whose name shall be Perceval)? He calls all hands upon deck; talks to them of King, country, glory, sweethearts, gin, French prison, wooden shoes, Old England, and hearts of oak : they give three cheers, rush to their 'guns, and, after a tremendous conflict, succeed in beating off the enemy. Not a syllable of all this; this is not the manner in which the honourable Commander goes to work; the first thing he does is to secure twenty or thirty of his prime sailors who happen to be Catholics, to clap them in irons, and set over them a guard of as many Protestants; having taking this admirable method of defending himself against his infidel opponents, he goes upon deck, reminds the sailors, in a very bitter harangue, that they are of different religions; exhorts the Episcopal gunner not to trust to the Presbyterian quarter-master; issues positive orders that the Catholics should be fired at upon the first appearance of discontent; rushes through blood and brains, examining his men in the Catechism and Thirty-nine Articles, and positively forbids every one to sponge or ram who has not taken the Sacrament according to the Church of England. Was it right to take out a captain made of excellent British stuff, and to put in such a man as this? Is not he more like a parson, or a talking-lawyer, than a thorough-bred seaman? And built as she is of heart of oak, and admirably manned, is it possible, with such a captain, to save this ship from going to the bottom ?—[*P. P. Letters.*]

HAWKINS BROWN AT THE COURT OF NAPLES.

In the third year of his present Majesty, and in the thirtieth of his own age, Mr. Isaac Hawkins Brown, then upon his travels, danced one evening at the Court of Naples. His dress was a volcano silk with lava buttons. Whether (as the Neapolitan wits said) he had studied dancing under St. Vitus, or whether David, dancing in a linen vest, was his model, is not known; but Mr. Brown danced with such inconceivable alacrity and vigour, that he threw the Queen of Naples into convulsions of laughter, which terminated in a miscarriage, and changed the dynasty of the Neapolitan throne.—[*P. P. Letters.*]

FINALITY.

I hear from some persons in Parliament, and from others in the sixpenny societies for debate, a great deal about unalterable laws passed at the Revolution. When I hear any man talk of an unalterable law, the only effect it produces upon me is to convince me that he is an unalterable fool.—[*P. P. Letters.*]

EPISCOPALIANISM IN SCOTLAND.

For what a length of years was it attempted to compel the Scotch to change their religion : horse, foot, artillery, and armed Prebendaries, were sent out after the Presbyterian parsons and their congregations. The Percevals of those days called for blood: this call is never made in vain, and blood was shed : but to the astonishment and horror of the Percevals of those days, they could not introduce the Book of Common Prayer, nor prevent that metaphysical people from going to heaven their true way, instead of our true way. With a little oatmeal for food, and a little sulphur for friction, allaying cutaneous irritation with the one hand, and holding his Calvinistical creed in the other, Sawney ran away to his flinty hills, sung his psalm out of tune his own way, and listened to his sermon of two hours long, amid the rough and imposing melancholy of the tallest thistles. But Sawney brought up his unbreeched offspring in a cordial hatred of his oppressors; and Scotland was as much a part of the weakness of England then, as Ireland is at this moment. The true and the only remedy was applied; the Scotch were suffered to worship God after their own tiresome manner, without pain, penalty, and privation. No lightning descended from heaven; the country was not ruined; the world is not yet come to an end; the dignitaries, who foretold all these consequences, are utterly forgotten, and Scotland has ever since been an increasing source of strength to Great Britain.—[*P. P. Letters.*]

INVASION.

You cannot imagine, you say, that England will ever be ruined and conquered; and for no other reason that I can find, but because it seems so very odd it should be ruined and conquered. Alas! so reasoned, in their time, the Austrian, Russian, and Prussian Plymleys. But the English are brave: so were all these nations. You might get together a hundred thousand men individually brave; but without generals capable of commanding such a machine, it would be as useless as a first-rate man of war manned by Oxford clergymen, or Parisian shopkeepers. —[*P. P. Letters.*]

EFFECTS OF INVASION.

As for the spirit of peasantry in making a gallant defence behind hedge-rows, and through plate-racks and hen-coops, highly as I think of their bravery, I do not know any nation in Europe so likely to be struck with the panic as the English; and this from their total un-acquaintance with the science of war. Old wheat and beans blazing for twenty miles round; cart mares shot; sows of Lord Somerville's breed running wild over the country; the minister of the parish wounded sorely in his hinder parts; Mrs. Plymley in fits; all these scenes of war an Austrian or a Russian has seen three or four times over; but it is now three centuries since an English pig has fallen in a fair battle upon English ground, or a farm-house been rifled, or a clergyman's wife been subjected to any other proposals of love than the connubial endearments of her sleek and orthodox mate. — [*P. P. Letters.*]

BLOCKADES.

If experience has taught us anything, it is the impossibility of perpetual blockades. The instances are innumerable, during the course of this war, where whole fleets have sailed in and out of harbour, in spite of every vigilance used to prevent it. I shall only mention those cases where Ireland is concerned. In December, 1796, seven ships of the line, and ten transports, reached Bantry Bay from Brest, without having seen an English ship in their passage. It blew a storm when they were off shore, and therefore England still continues to be an independent kingdom. You will observe that at the very time the French fleet sailed out of Brest Harbour,

Admiral Colpoys was cruising off there with a powerful squadron, and still, from the particular circumstances of the weather, found it impossible to prevent the French from coming out.   During the time that Admiral Colpoys was cruising off Brest, Admiral Richery, with six ships of the line, passed him, and got safe into the harbour.   At the very moment when the French squadron was lying in Bantry Bay, Lord Bridport with his fleet was locked up by a foul wind in the Channel, and for several days could not stir to the assistance of Ireland.   Admiral Colpoys, totally unable to find the French fleet, came home.   Lord Bridport, at the change of the wind, cruised for them in vain, and they got safe back to Brest, without having seen a single one of those floating bulwarks, the possession of which we believe will enable us with impunity to set justice and common sense at defiance.   Such is the miserable and precarious state of an anemocracy, of a people who put their trust in hurricanes and are governed by wind. — [*P. P. Letters.*]

FREEDOM OF NEUTRAL TRADE.

It is of the utmost consequence to a commercial people at war with the greatest part of Europe, that there should be a free entry of neutrals into the enemy's ports.—[*P. P. Letters.*]

THE TRUE DEFENCE.

At such a crisis you want the affections of all your subjects, in both islands: there is no spirit which you must alienate, no art you must avert, every man must feel he has a country, and that there is an urgent and pressing cause why he should expose himself to death.—[*P. P. Letters.*]

TREATMENT OF DISSENTERS.

WHEN a country squire hears of an ape, his first feeling is to give it nuts and apples; when he hears of a Dissenter, his immediate impulse is to commit it to the county jail, to shave its head, to alter its customary food, and to have it privately whipped.—[*P. P. Letters.*]

FAITH OF THE CHURCH OF ENGLAND.

THE purest religion in the world, in my humble opinion, is the religion of the Church of England: for its preservation (so far as it is exercised without intruding upon the liberties of others) I am ready at this moment to venture my present life, and but through that religion I have no hopes of any other; yet I am not forced to be silly because I am pious: nor will I ever join in eulogiums on my faith, which every man of common reading and common sense can so easily refute. —[*P. P. Letters.*]

GROWTH OF CATHOLICISM.

As for the enormous wax candles, and superstitious mummeries, and painted jackets of the Catholic priests, I fear them not. Tell me that the world will return again under the influence of the smallpox; that Lord Castlereagh will hereafter oppose the power of the Court; that Lord Howick and Mr. Grattan will do each of them a mean and dishonourable action; that anybody who has heard Lord Redesdale speak once, will knowingly and willingly hear him again; that Lord Eldon has assented to the fact of two and two making four, without shedding tears, or expressing the smallest doubt or scruple; tell me any other thing absurd or incredible, but for the love of common sense, let me hear no more of the danger to be apprehended from the general diffusion of Popery.   It is too absurd to be reasoned upon; every man feels it is nonsense when he hears it stated, and so does every man while he is stating it.—[*P. P. Letters.*]

RED-HAIRED MEN.

I HAVE often thought, if the wisdom of our ancestors had excluded all persons with red hair from the House of Commons, of the throes and convulsions it would occasion to restore them to their natural rights.   What mobs and riots would it produce !   To what infinite abuse and obloquy would the capillary patriot be exposed; what wormwood would distil from Mr. Perceval, what froth would drop from Mr. Canning; how (I will not say *my,* but *our* Lord Hawkesbury, for he belongs to us all)—how our Lord Hawkesbury would work away about the hair of King William and Lord Somers, and the authors of the great and glorious Revolution; how Lord Eldon would appeal to the Deity and his own virtues, and to the hair of his children; some would say that red-haired men were superstitious; some would prove they were atheists ; they would be petitioned against as the friends of slavery, and the advocates for revolt; in short, such a corruptor of the heart and understanding is the spirit of persecution, that these unfortunate people (conspired against by their fellow-subjects of every complexion), if they did not emigrate to countries where hair of another colour was persecuted, would be driven to the falsehood of perukes, or the hypocrisy of the Tricosian fluid.—[*P. P. Letters.*]

GRADUAL EMANCIPATION.

(AN APOLOGUE.)

THERE is a village (no matter where) in which the inhabitants, on one day in the year, sit down to a dinner prepared at the common expense: by an extraordinary piece of tyranny (which Lord Hawkesbury would call the wisdom of the village ancestors), the inhabitants of three of the streets, about a hundred years ago, seized upon the inhabitants of the fourth street, bound them hand and foot, laid them upon their backs, and compelled them to look on while the rest were stuffing themselves with beef and beer; the next year the inhabitants of the persecuted street (though they contributed an equal quota of the expense) were treated precisely in the same manner. The tyranny grew into a custom; and (as the manner of our nature is) it was considered as the most sacred of all duties to keep these poor fellows without their annual dinner: the village was so tenacious of this practice, that nothing could induce them to resign it; every enemy to it was looked upon as a disbeliever in Divine Providence, and any nefarious churchwarden who wished to succeed in his election had nothing to do but to represent his antagonist as an abolitionist, in order to frustrate his ambition, endanger his life, and throw the village into a state of the most dreadful commotion. By degrees, however, the obnoxious street grew to be so well peopled, and its inhabitants so firmly united, that their oppressors, more afraid of injustice, were more disposed to be just. At the next dinner they are unbound, the year after allowed to sit upright, then a bit of bread and a glass of water; till at last, after a long series of concessions, they are emboldened to ask, in pretty plain terms,

that they may be allowed to sit down at the bottom of
the table and to fill their bellies as well as the rest.
Forthwith a general cry of shame and scandal: " Ten
years ago, were you not laid upon your backs? Don't
you remember what a great thing you thought it to get
a piece of bread? How thankful you were for cheese-
parings? Have you forgotten that memorable æra,
when the lord of the manor interfered to obtain for you a
slice of the public pudding? And now, with an audacity
only equalled by your ingratitude, you have the impudence to ask for knives and forks, and to request, in
terms too plain to be mistaken, that you may sit down to
table with the rest, and be indulged even with beef and
beer: there are not more than half-a-dozen dishes which
we have reserved for ourselves; the rest has been thrown
open to you in the utmost profusion; you have potatoes,
and carrots, suet dumplings, sops in the pan, and deli
cious toast and water, in incredible quantities. Beef,
mutton, lamb, pork, and veal are ours; and if you were
not the most restless and dissatisfied of human beings,
you would never think of aspiring to enjoy them.—
[*P. P. Letters.*]

INTOLERANCE AND EMANCIPATION.

IRELAND a millstone about your neck! Why is it not
a stone of Ajax in your hand?—[*P. P. Letters.*]

JUSTICE AND INJUSTICE.

THE only true way to make the mass of mankind see
the beauty of justice, is by showing to them in pretty
plain terms the consequences of injustice.—[*P. P.
Letters.*]

HISTORY OF CHANGE.

Lord Sidmouth, and all the anti-Catholic people, little foresee that they will hereafter be the sport of the antiquary; that their prophecies of ruin and destruction from Catholic emancipation will be clapped into the notes of some quaint history, and be matter of pleasantry even to the sedulous housewife and the rural dean. There is always a copious supply of Lord Sidmouths in the world; nor is there one single source of human happiness, against which they have not uttered the most lugubrious predictions. Turnpike roads, navigable canals, inoculation, hops, tobacco, the Reformation, the Revolution—there are always a set of worthy and moderately-gifted men, who bawl out death and ruin upon every valuable change which the varying aspect of human affairs absolutely and imperiously requires. I have often thought that it would be extremely useful to make a collection of the hatred and abuse that all those changes have experienced, which are now admitted to be marked improvements in our condition. Such a history might make folly a little more modest, and suspicious of its own decisions. — [*P. P. Letters.*]

PARENTAL AMBITION.

Look at human nature:—what is the history of all professions? Joel is to be brought up to the bar: has Mrs. Plymley the slightest doubt of his being Chancellor? Do not his two shrivelled aunts live in the certainty of seeing him in that situation, and of cutting out with their own hands his equity habiliments? And I could name a certain minister of the Gospel who does not, in the bottom of his heart, much differ from these opinions. Do you not think that the fathers and mothers of the holy Catholic Church are not as absurd as Protestant papas and mammas? The probability I admit to be, in each particular case, that the sweet little blockhead will in fact never get a brief; — but I will venture to say, there is not a parent from the Giant's Causeway to Bantry Bay who does not conceive that his child is the unfortunate victim of the exclusion, and that nothing short of positive law could prevent his own dear pre-eminent Paddy from rising to the highest honours of the State. — [*P. P. Letters.*]

WAR AND REFORMS.

How easy it is to shed human blood — how easy it is to persuade ourselves that it is our duty to do so — and that the decision has cost us a severe struggle — how much in all ages have wounds and shrieks and tears been the cheap and vulgar resources of the rulers of mankind — how difficult and how noble it is to govern in kindness and to found an empire upon the everlasting basis of justice and affection! — But what do men call vigour? To let loose hussars and to bring up artillery, to govern with lighted matches, and to cut, and push, and prime — I call this, not vigour, but the *sloth of cruelty and ignorance.* The vigour I love consists in finding out wherein subjects are aggrieved, in relieving them, in studying the temper and genius of a people, in consulting their prejudices, in selecting proper persons to lead and manage them, in the laborious, watchful, and difficult task of increasing public happiness by allaying each particular discontent. — [*P. P. Letters.*]

PROHIBITION OF DRUGS.

CONCEIVE a statesman who would bring the French to reason by keeping them without rhubarb, and exhibit to mankind the awful spectacle of a nation deprived of neutral salts. This is not the dream of a wild apothecary indulging in his own opium; this is not the distempered fancy of a pounder of drugs, delirious from smallness of profits: but it is the sober, deliberate, and systematic scheme of a man to whom the public safety is entrusted, and whose appointment is considered by many as a masterpiece of political sagacity. What a sublime thought, that no purge can now be taken between the Weser and the Garonne; that the bustling pestle is still, the canorous mortar mute, and the bowels of mankind locked up for fourteen degrees of latitude! When, I should be curious to know, were all the powers of crudity and flatulence fully explained to his Majesty's ministers? At what period was this great plan of conquest and constipation fully developed? In whose mind was the idea of destroying the pride and the plasters of France first engendered? Without castor oil they might for some months, to be sure, have carried on a lingering war; but can they do without bark? Will the people live under a government where antimonial powders cannot be procured? Will they bear the loss of mercury? " There's the rub." Depend upon it, the absence of the materia medica will soon bring them to their senses, and the cry of *Bourbon and bolus* burst forth from the Baltic to the Mediterranean.—[*P. P. Letters.*]

TOLERATION IN HUNGARY.

IT is impossible to think of the affairs of Ireland without being forcibly struck with the parallel of Hungary.

Of her seven millions of inhabitants, one half were Protestants, Calvinists, and Lutherans, many of the Greek Church, and many Jews: such was the state of their religious dissensions, that Mahomet had often been called in to the aid of Calvin, and the crescent often glittered on the walls of Buda and of Presburg. At last, in 1791, during the most violent crisis of disturbance, a diet was called, and by a great majority of voices a decree was passed, which secured to all the contending sects the fullest and freest exercise of religious worship and education; ordained (let it be heard in Hampstead) that churches and chapels should be erected for all on the most perfectly equal terms; that the Protestants of both confessions should depend upon their spiritual superiors alone; liberated them from swearing by the usual oath, " the holy Virgin Mary, the saints, and chosen of God ; " and then the decree adds, "that *public offices and honours, high or low, great or small, shall be given to natural-born Hungarians who deserve well of their country, and possess the other qualifications, let their religion be what it may.*" Such was the line of policy pursued in a diet consisting of four hundred members, in a state whose form of government approaches nearer to our own than any other, having a Roman Catholic establishment of great wealth and power, and under the influence of one of the most bigoted Catholic Courts in Europe. This measure has now the experience of eighteen years in its favour; it has undergone a trial of fourteen years of revolution such as the world never witnessed, and more than equal to a century less convulsed: What have been its effects ? When the French advanced like a torrent within a few days' march of Vienna, the Hungarians rose in a mass; they formed what they called the sacred insurrection, to defend their sovereign, their rights and liberties, now common to all: and the apprehension of their approach dictated to the reluctant Bonaparte the immediate signature of the treaty of *Leoben.* The Romish hierarchy of Hungary exists in all its former splendour and opulence; never has the slightest attempt been made to diminish it; and those revolutionary principles, to which so large a portion of civilised Europe has been sacrificed, have here failed in making the smallest successful inroad.—[*P. P. Letters.*]

PREJUDICES REMOVED.

THERE may have been times in England when the quarter sessions would have been disturbed by theological polemics; but now, after a Catholic justice had once been seen on the bench, and it had been clearly ascertained that he spoke English, had no tail, only a single row of teeth, and that he loved port wine,—after all the scandalous and infamous reports of his physical conformation had been clearly proved to be false,—he would be reckoned a jolly fellow, and very superior in flavour to a sly Presbyterian. Nothing, in fact, can be more uncandid and unphilosophical than to say that a man has a tail, because you cannot agree with him upon religious subjects; it appears to be ludicrous: but I am convinced it has done infinite mischief to the Catholics, and made a very serious impression upon the minds of many gentlemen of large landed property.—[*P. P. Letters.*]

IRISH PRIESTS' INCOME.

THE revenue of the Irish Roman Catholic Church is made of half-pence, potatoes, rags, bones, and fragments of old clothes; and those, Irish old clothes. They worship often in hovels, or in the open air, from the *want* of any place of worship. Their religion is the religion of three-fourths of the population! Not far off, in a well-windowed and well-roofed house, is a well-paid Protestant clergyman, preaching to stools and hassocks, and crying in the wilderness; near him the clerk, near him the sexton, near him the sexton's wife—furious against the errors of Popery, and willing to lay down their lives for the great truths established at the Diet of Augsburg.—[*Letter on Irish Clergy.*]

CIVIL WAR AND REPEAL.

CIVIL war is preferable to Repeal. Much as I hate wounds, dangers, privations, and explosions—much as I love regular hours of dinner—foolish as I think men covered with the feathers of the male *Pullus domesticus,* and covered with lace in the course of the ischiatic nerve—much as I detest all these follies and ferocities, I would rather turn soldier myself than acquiesce quietly in such a separation of the Empire.

It is *such* a piece of nonsense, that no man can have any reverence for himself who would stop to discuss such a question. It is such a piece of anti-British villany, that none but the bitterest enemy of our blood and people could entertain such a project! It is to be met only with round and grape—to be answered by Shrapnel and Congreve; to be discussed in hollow squares, and refuted by battalions four deep; to be put down by the *ultima ratio* of that armed Aristotle the Duke of Wellington.—[*Letter on Irish Clergy.*]

OBJECTS OF GOVERNMENT.

WHAT is the object of all government? The object of all government is roast mutton, potatoes, claret, a stout constable, an honest justice, a clear highway, a free chapel. What trash to be bawling in the streets about the Green Isle, the Isle of the Ocean; the bold anthem of *Erin go bragh !* A far better anthem would be Erin go bread and cheese, Erin go cabins that will keep out the rain, Erin go pantaloons without holes in them !—[*Letter on Irish Clergy.*]

PAYMENT OF IRISH CATHOLIC CLERGY.

THE first thing to be done is to pay the priests, and after a little time they will take the money. One man wants to repair his cottage; another wants a buggy; a third cannot shut his eyes to the dilapidations of a cassock. The draft is payable at sight in Dublin, or by agents in the next market town dependent upon the Commission in Dublin. The housekeeper of the holy man is importunate for money, and if it be not procured. by drawing for the salary, it must be extorted by curses and comminations from the ragged worshippers, slowly, sorrowfully, and sadly.—[*Letter on Irish Clergy.*]

DIPLOMATIC RELATIONS WITH ROME.

IT turns out that there is no law to prevent entering into diplomatic engagements with the Pope. The sooner we become acquainted with a gentleman who has so much to say to eight millions of our subjects the better! Can anything be so childish and absurd as a horror of communicating with the Pope, and all the hobgoblins we have imagined of premunires and outlawries for this contraband trade in piety? Our ancestors (strange to say wiser than ourselves) have left us to do as we please, and the sooner Government do, what they *can* do legally, the better.   A thousand opportunities of doing good in Irish affairs have been lost, from our having no avowed and dignified agent at the Court of Rome. If it depended upon me, I would send the Duke of Devonshire there to-morrow, with nine chaplains and several tons of Protestant theology.   I have no love of popery, but the Pope is at all events better than the idol of Juggernaut, whose chaplains I believe we pay, and whose chariot I dare say is made in Long Acre.   We pay 10,000*l.* a year to our ambassador at Constantinople, and are startled with the idea of communicating diplomatically with Rome, deeming the Sultan a better Christian than the Pope ! — [*Letter on Irish Clergy.*]

CABINET DINNERS.

If I were a member of the Cabinet, and met my colleagues once a week to eat birds and beasts, and to talk over the state of the world, I should begin upon Ireland before the soup was finished, go on through fish, turkey, and saddle of mutton, and never end till the last thimbleful of claret had passed down the throat of the incredulous Haddington : but there they sit, week after week ; there they come, week after week ; the Piccadilly Mars, the Scotch Neptune, Themis Lyndhurst, the Tamworth Baronet, dear Goody, and dearer Gladdy, and think no more of paying the Catholic clergy, than a man of real fashion does of paying his tailor ! — [*Letters on Irish Clergy.*]

EPISCOPAL CONTRASTS.

If I were a Bishop, living beautifully in a state of serene plenitude, I don't think I could endure the thought of so many honest, pious, and laborious clergymen of another faith, placed in such disgraceful circumstances! I could not get into my carriage with jelly-springs, or see my two courses every day, without remembering the buggy and the bacon of some poor old Catholic Bishop, ten times as laborious, and with much more, perhaps, of theological learning than myself, often distressed for a few pounds! and burthened with duties utterly disproportioned to his age and strength. — [*Letters on Irish Clergy.*]

LOVE OF TYRANNY.

HUMAN beings cling to their delicious tyrannies, and to their exquisite nonsense, like a drunkard to his bottle, and go on till death stares them in the face. — [*Letters on Irish Clergy.*]

BEEF FOR HINDOOS.

I HAVE always compared the Protestant church in Ireland (and I believe my friend Thomas Moore stole the simile from me) to the institution of butchers' shops in all the villages of our Indian empire. "We *will* have a butcher's shop in every village, and you, Hindoos, shall pay for it. We know that many of you do not eat meat at all, and that the sight of beefsteaks is particularly offensive to you; but still, a stray European may pass through your village, and want a steak or a chop: the shop *shall* be established; and you shall pay for it." This is English Legislation for Ireland!! — [*Letters on Irish Clergy.*]

EFFECTS OF PAYMENT OF CATHOLIC CLERGY.

I AM thoroughly convinced that State payments to the Catholic clergy would remove a thousand causes of hatred between the priest and his flock, and would be as favourable to the increase of his useful authority, as it would be fatal to his factious influence over the people. — [*Letters on Irish Clergy.*]

GORED TO DEATH.

IF a lawyer is wounded, the rest of the profession pursue him, and put him to death. If a churchman is hurt, the others gather round for his protection, stamp with their feet, push with their horns, and demolish the dissenter who did the mischief.—[*E. R.* 1822.]

INTERROGATION OF CURATES.

IF a man is a captain in the army in one part of England, he is a captain in all. The general who commands north of the Tweed does not say, You shall never appear in my district, or exercise the functions of an officer, if you do not answer eighty-seven questions on the art of war, according to my notions. The same officer who commands a ship of the line in the Mediterranean, is considered as equal to the same office in the North Seas. The sixth commandment is suspended, by one medical diploma, from the north of England to the south. But, by this new system of interrogation, a man may be admitted into orders at Barnet, rejected at Stevenage, readmitted at Brogden, kicked out as a Calvinist at Witham Common, and hailed as an ardent Arminian on his arrival at York.—[*E. R.* 1822.]

VARIETIES OF BELIEF.

MR. GREENOUGH has made a map of England, according to its geological varieties;—blue for the chalk, green for the clay, red for the sand, and so forth. Under the system of Bishop Marsh, we must petition for the assistance of the geologist in the fabrication of an ecclesiastical map. All the Arminian districts must be purple. Green for one theological extremity—sky-blue for another—as many colours as there are bishops—as many shades of these colours as there are Archdeacons—a tailor's pattern card—the picture of vanity, fashion, and caprice.—[*E. R.* 1822.]

COMMON SENSE.

THE longer we live, the more we are convinced of the justice of the old saying, that an *ounce of mother wit is worth a pound of clergy*; that discretion, gentle manners, common sense, and good nature, are, in men of high ecclesiastical station, of far greater importance than the greatest skill in discriminating between sublapsarian and supralapsarian doctrines.—[*E. R.* 1822.]

BITTER BISHOPS.

WHAT would the worst enemy of the English Church require?—a bitter, bustling, theological Bishop, accused by his clergy of tyranny and oppression—the cause of daily petitions and daily debates in the House of Commons — the idoneous vehicle of abuse against the Establishment—a stalking-horse to bad men for the introduction of revolutionary opinions, mischievous ridicule, and irreligious feelings.

It is inconceivable how such a prelate shakes all the upper works of the Church, and ripens it for dissolution and decay. Six such Bishops, multiplied by eighty-seven, and working with five hundred and twenty-two questions, would fetch every thing to the ground in less than six months. But what if it pleased Divine Providence to afflict every prelate with the spirit of putting eighty-seven queries, and the two Archbishops with the spirit of putting twice as many, and the Bishop of Sodor and Man with the spirit of putting only forty-three queries?—there would then be a grand total of two thousand three hundred and thirty-five interrogations flying about the English Church; and sorely vexed would the land be with Question and Answer.—[*E. R.* 1822.]

THE STANDARD OF FAITH.

The Bishop not only puts the questions, but he actually assigns the limits within which they are to be answered. Spaces are left in the paper of interrogations, to which limits the answer is to be confined;—two inches to original sin; an inch and a half to justification; three quarters to predestination; and to free will only a quarter of an inch. But if his Lordship gives them an inch, they will take an ell.—[*E. R.* 1822.]

MODERATE PUNISHMENT.

His Lordship boasts, that he has excluded only two curates. So the Emperor of Hayti boasted that he had only cut off two persons' heads for disagreeable behaviour at his table.—[*E. R.* 1822.]

EPISCOPAL BREVITY.

We never met with any style so entirely clear of all redundant and vicious ornament, as that which the ecclesiastical Lord of Peterborough has adopted towards his clergy. It, in fact, may be all reduced to these few words—" Reverend Sir, I shall do what I please. Peterborough."—[*E. R.* 1822.]

CURATES.

A CURATE—there is something which excites compassion in the very name of a Curate!!! How any man of Purple, Palaces, and Preferment, can let himself loose against this poor working man of God, we are at a loss to conceive,—a learned man in an hovel, with sermons and saucepans, lexicons and bacon, Hebrew books and ragged children—good and patient—a comforter and a preacher—the first and purest pauper in the hamlet, and yet showing, that, in the midst of his worldly misery, he has the heart of a gentleman, and the spirit of a Christian, and the kindness of a pastor; and this man, though he has exercised the duties of a clergyman for twenty years —though he has most ample testimonies of conduct from clergymen as respectable as any Bishop—though an Archbishop add his name to the list of witnesses, is not good enough for Bishop Marsh; but is pushed out in the street, with his wife and children, and his little furniture, to surrender his honour, his faith, his conscience, and his learning—or to starve!—[*E. R.* 1822.]

SENSITIVENESS OF CURATES.

MEN of very small incomes, be it known to his Lordship, have very often very acute feelings; and a Curate trod on feels a pang as great as when a Bishop is refuted. —[*E. R.* 1822.]

PAYMENT BY LOTTERY.

IT seems a paradoxical statement; but the fact is, that the respectability of the Church, as well as of the Bar, is almost entirely preserved by the unequal division of their revenues. A Bar of one hundred lawyers travel the Northern Circuit, enlightening provincial ignorance, curing local partialities, diffusing knowledge, and dispensing justice in their route: it is quite certain that all they gain is not equal to all that they spend; if the profits were equally divided there would not be six and eight-pence for each person, and there would be no Bar at all. At present, the success of the leader animates them all—each man hopes to be a Scarlett or a Brougham —and takes out his ticket in a lottery by which the mass must infallibly lose, trusting (as mankind are so apt to do) to his good fortune, and believing that the prize is reserved for him—disappointment and defeat for others. So it is with the clergy; the whole income of the Church, if equally divided, would be about 250*l.* for each minister. Who would go into the Church and spend 1200*l.* or 1500*l.* upon his education, if such were the highest remuneration he could ever look to? At present, men are tempted into the Church by the prizes of the Church, and bring into that Church a great deal of capital, which enables them to live in decency, supporting themselves, not with the money of the public, but with their own money, which, but for this temptation, would have been carried into some retail trade. The offices of the Church would then fall down to men little less coarse and ignorant than agricultural labourers —the clergyman of the parish would soon be seen in the squire's kitchen; and all this would take place in a country where poverty is infamous. — [*Letter to Archdeacon Singleton.*]

DEMOCRACY IN THE CHURCH.

I AM surprised it does not strike the mountaineers how very much the great emoluments of the Church are flung open to the lowest ranks of the community. Butchers, bakers, publicans, schoolmasters, are perpetually seeing their children elevated to the mitre. Let a respectable baker drive through the city from the west end of the town, and let him cast an eye on the battlements of Northumberland House, has his little muffin-faced son the smallest chance of getting in among the Percies, enjoying a share of their luxury and splendour, and of chasing the deer with hound and horn upon the Cheviot Hills? But let him drive his alum-steeped loaves a little further, till he reaches St. Paul's Churchyard, and all his thoughts are changed when he sees that beautiful fabric; it is not impossible that his little penny roll may be introduced into that splendid oven. Young Crumpet is sent to school — takes to his books — spends the best years of his life, as all eminent Englishmen do, in making Latin verses — knows that the *crum* in crum-pet is long, and the *pet* short — goes to the University — gets a prize for an Essay on the Dispersion of the Jews — takes orders — becomes a Bishop's chaplain — has a young nobleman for his pupil — publishes an useless classic, and a serious call to the unconverted — and then goes through the Elysian transitions of Prebendary, Dean, Prelate, and the long train of purple, profit, and power. — [*Letter to Archdeacon Singleton.*]

PAYMENT OF THE CLERGY.

THIS, it will be said, is a Mammonish view of the subject: it is so, but those who make this objection forget the immense effect which Mammon produces upon religion itself. Shall the Gospel be preached by men paid by the State? shall these men be taken from the lower orders, and be meanly paid? shall they be men of learning and education? and shall there be some magnificent endowments to allure such men into the Church? Which of these methods is the best for diffusing the rational doctrines of Christianity? Not in the age of the apostles, not in the abstract, timeless, nameless, placeless land of the philosophers, but in the year 1837, in the porter-brewing, cotton-spinning, tallow-melting kingdom of Great Britain, bursting with opulence, and flying from poverty as the greatest of human evils. Many different answers may be given to these questions; but they are questions which, not ending in Mammon, have a powerful bearing on real religion, and deserve the deepest consideration from its disciples and friends. Let the comforts of the Clergy go for nothing. Consider their state only as religion is affected by it. If upon this principle I am forced to allot to some an opulence which my clever friend the Examiner would pronounce to be unapostolical, I cannot help it; I must take this people with all their follies, and prejudices, and circumstances, and carve out an establishment best suited for them, however unfit for early Christianity in barren and conquered Judea.—[*Letter to Archdeacon Singleton.*]

BISHOPS NOT TO BE SUSPECTED.

It is a very singular thing that the law always suspects Judges, and never suspects Bishops. If there be any way in which the partialities of the Judge may injure laymen, the subject is fenced round with all sorts of jealousies, and enactments, and prohibitions — all partialities are guarded against, and all propensities watched. Where Bishops are concerned, Acts of Parliament are drawn up for beings who can never possibly be polluted by pride, prejudice, passion, or interest. Not otherwise would be the case with Judges, if they, like the heads of the Church, legislated for themselves. — [*Letter to Archdeacon Singleton.*]

THE PUBLIC EYE.

WITH regard to that common newspaper phrase *the public eye* — there's nothing (as the Bench well know) more wandering and slippery than the *public eye.* In five years hence the public eye will no more see what description of men are promoted by Bishops, than it will see what Doctors of Law are promoted by the Turkish Uhlema; and at the end of this period (such is the example set by the Commission), the *public eye* turned in every direction may not be able to see any Bishops at all.— [*Letter to Archdeacon Singleton.*]

EPISCOPAL CORRESPONDENCE.

THE first of three bishops whom I remember was a man of careless easy temper, and how patronage went in those early days may be conjectured by the following letters—which are not his, but serve to illustrate a system : —

The Bishop to Lord A ——.

My dear Lord,

I have noticed with great pleasure the behaviour of your Lordship's second son, and am most happy to have it in my power to offer to him the living of * * *. He will find it of considerable value; and there is, I understand, a very good house upon it, &c. &c.

This is to confer a living upon a man of real merit out of the family; into which family, apparently sacrificed to the public good, the living is brought back by the second letter:

The same to the same a year after.

My dear Lord,

Will you excuse the liberty I take in soliciting promotion for my grandson?   He is an officer of great skill and gallantry, and can bring the most ample testimonials from some of the best men in the profession: the Arethusa frigate is, I understand, about to be commissioned; and if, &c. &c. — [*Letter to Archdeacon Singleton.*]

EPISCOPAL GRANDEUR.

A GOOD and honest bishop (I thank God there are many who deserve that character!) ought to suspect himself, and carefully to watch his own heart.   He is all of a sudden elevated from being a tutor, dining at an early hour with his pupil, (and occasionally, it is believed, on cold meat,) to be a spiritual Lord; he is dressed in a magnificent dress, decorated with a title, flattered by Chaplains, and surrounded by little people looking up for the things which he has to give away; and this often happens to a man who has had no opportunities of seeing the world, whose parents were in very humble life, and who has given up all his thoughts to the frogs of Aristophanes and the Targum of Onkelos.   How is it possible that such a man should not lose his head? that he should not swell? that he should not be guilty of a thousand follies, and worry and tease to death (before he recovers his common sense) a hundred men as good, and as wise, and as able as himself?—[*Letter to Archdeacon Singleton.*]

DEMOCRATS AND PRELATISTS.

We are told, If you agitate these questions among yourselves, you will have the democratic Philistines come down upon you, and sweep you all away together. Be it so; I am quite ready to be swept away when the time comes. Every body has their favourite death: some delight in apoplexy, and others prefer marasmus. I would infinitely rather be crushed by democrats, than, under the plea of the public good, be mildly and blandly absorbed by bishops.—[*Letter to Archdeacon Singleton.*]

CLERICAL SUBJECTION.

What Bishops like best in their Clergy is a dropping-down-deadness of manner.—[*Letter to Archdeacon Singleton.*]

SYDNEY SMITH'S CAREER IN THE CHURCH.

You tell me I shall be laughed at as a rich and over-grown Churchman. Be it so. I have been laughed at a hundred times in my life, and care little or nothing about it. If I am well provided for now—I have had my full share of the blanks in the lottery as well as the prizes. Till thirty years of age I never received a farthing from the Church; then 50*l.* per annum for two years—then nothing for ten years—then 500*l.* per annum, increased for two or three years to 800*l.*, till in my grand climacteric, I was made Canon of St. Paul's; and before that period, I had built a Parsonage-house with farm offices for a large farm, which cost me 4000*l.*, and had reclaimed another from ruins at the expense of 2000*l.* A lawyer, or a physician in good practice, would smile at this picture of great ecclesiastical wealth; and yet I am considered as a perfect monster of ecclesiastical prosperity.

I should be very sorry to give offence to the dignified ecclesiastics who are in the Commission: I hope they will allow for the provocation, if I have been a little too warm in the defence of St. Paul's, which I have taken a solemn oath to defend.   I was at school and college with the Archbishop of Canterbury: fifty-three years ago he knocked me down with the chess-board for checkmating him—and now he is attempting to take away my patronage.   I believe these are the only two acts of violence he ever committed in his life; the interval has been one of gentleness, kindness, and the most amiable and high-principled courtesy to his Clergy.—[*Letter to Archdeacon Singleton.*]

AN OLD WHIG.

As for my friends the Whigs, I neither wish to offend them nor any body else.   I consider myself to be as good a Whig as any amongst them.   I was a Whig before many of them were born—and while some of them were Tories and Waverers.   I have always turned out to fight their battles, and when I saw no other Clergyman turn out but myself—and this in times before liberality was well recompensed, and therefore in fashion, and when the smallest appearance of it seemed to condemn a Churchman to the grossest obloquy, and the most hopeless poverty.   It may suit the purpose of the Ministers to flatter the Bench; it does not suit mine. I do not choose in my old age to be tossed as a prey to the Bishop; I have not deserved this of my Whig friends.—[*Letter to Archdeacon Singleton.*]

THE WHIG ADMINISTRATION.

NOBODY admires the general conduct of the Whig Administration more than I do. They have conferred, in their domestic policy, the most striking benefits on the country. To say that there is no risk in what they have done is mere nonsense: there is great risk; and all honest men must balance to counteract it—holding back as firmly down hill as they pulled vigorously up hill. Still, great as the risk is, it was worth while to incur it in the Poor Law Bill, in the Tithe' Bill, in the Corporation Bill, and in the circumscription of the Irish Protestant Church. In all these matters, the Whig Ministry, after the heat of party is over, and when Joseph Hume and Wilson Croker are powdered into the dust of death, will gain great and deserved fame. — [*Letter to Archdeacon Singleton, 1835.*]

A WHIG JEHU.

YOU will, of course, consider me as a defender of abuses. I have all my life been just the contrary, and I remember, with pleasure, thirty years ago, old Lord Stowell saying to me, " Mr. Smith, you would have been a much richer man if you had joined us." I like, my dear Lord, the road you are travelling, but I don't like the pace you are driving: too similar to that of the son of Nimshi. I always feel myself inclined to cry out, Gently, John, gently down hill. Put on the drag. We shall be over, if you go so quick — you'll do us a mischief.·—[*Letter to Archdeacon Singleton.*]

DISSENTERS WITHOUT A GRIEVANCE.

REMEMBER, as a philosopher, that the Church of England now is a very different Institution from what it was twenty years ago. It then oppressed every sect, they are now all free — all exempt from the tyranny of an Establishment; and the only real cause of complaint for Dissenters is, that they can no longer find a grievance, and enjoy the distinction of being persecuted. I have always tried to reduce them to this state, and I do not pity them. — [*Letter to Archdeacon Singleton.*]

HIGH-PRESSURE WISDOM.

ALL gradation and caution have been banished since the Reform Bill — rapid high-pressure wisdom is the only agent in public affairs. — [*Letter to Archdeacon Singleton.*]

LORD MELBOURNE.

VISCOUNT MELBOURNE declared himself quite satisfied with the Church as it is; but if the public had any desire to alter it, they might do as they pleased. He might have said the same thing of the Monarchy, or of any other of our institutions; and there is in the declaration a permissiveness and good humour which in public men have seldom been exceeded. Carelessness, however, is but a poor imitation of genius, and the formation of a wise and well-reflected plan of Reform conduces more to the lasting fame of a Minister than that affected contempt of duty which every man sees to be mere vanity, and a vanity of no very high description.

But if the truth must be told, our Viscount is somewhat of an impostor. Everything about him seems to betoken careless desolation: any one would suppose from his manner that he was playing at chuck-farthing with human happiness; that he was always on the heel of pastime; that he would giggle away the Great Charter,

and decide by the method of tee-totum whether my
Lords the Bishops should or should not retain their
seats in the House of Lords. All this is the mere vanity
of surprising and making us believe that he can play
with kingdoms as other men can with nine-pins. Instead of this lofty nebulo, this miracle of moral and
intellectual felicities, he is nothing more than a sensible
honest man, who means to do his duty to the Sovereign
and to the Country: instead of being the ignorant man
he pretends to be, before he meets the deputation of
Tallow-Chandlers in the morning, he sits up half the
night talking with Thomas Young about melting and
skimming, and then, though he has acquired knowledge
enough to work off a whole vat of prime Leicester tallow,
he pretends next morning not to know the difference
between a dip and a mould. In the same way, when he
has been employed in reading Acts of Parliament, he
would persuade you that he has been · reading *Cleghorn
on the Beatitudes,* or *Pickler on the Nine Difficult
Points.* Neither can I allow to this Minister (however
he may be irritated by the denial) the extreme merit of
indifference to the consequences of his measures. I
believe him to be conscientiously alive to the good or
evil that he is doing, and that his caution has more than
once arrested the gigantic projects of the Lycurgus of
the Lower House. I am sorry to hurt any man's feelings, and to brush away the magnificent fabric of levity
and gaiety he has reared; but I accuse our Minister of
honesty and diligence: I deny that he is careless or
rash: he is nothing more than a man of good understanding, and good principle, disguised in the eternal
and somewhat wearisome affectation of a political Roué.
—[*Letter to Archdeacon Singleton.*]

BISHOP BLOMFIELD.

IN not acting so as to be suspected, the Bishop of London should resemble Cæsar's wife. In other respects, this excellent prelate would not have exactly suited for the partner for that great and self-willed man; and an idea strikes me, that it is not impossible he might have been in the Senate-house instead of Cæsar. —[*Letter to Archdeacon Singleton.*]

LORD JOHN RUSSELL.

THERE is not a better man in England than Lord John Russell; but his worst failure is that he is utterly ignorant of all moral fear; there is nothing he would not undertake. I believe he would perform the operation for the stone — build St. Peter's — or assume (with or without ten minutes' notice) the command of the Channel Fleet; and no one would discover by his manner that the patient had died—the Church tumbled down — and the Channel Fleet been knocked to atoms. I believe his motives are always pure, and his measures often able; but they are endless, and never done with that pedetentous pace and pedetentous mind in which it behoves the wise and virtuous improver to walk. He alarms the wise Liberals: and it is impossible to sleep soundly while he has the command of the watch.*

Do not say, my dear Lord John, that I am too severe upon you. A thousand years have scarce sufficed to make our blessed England what it is; an hour may lay it in the dust: and can you with all your talents reno-

---

* Another peculiarity of the Russells is, that they never alter their opinions: they are an excellent race, but they must be trepanned before they can be convinced.— [*Letter to Archdeacon Singleton.*]

vate its shattered splendour — can you recall back its virtues — can you vanquish time and fate ?   But, alas ! you want to shake the world, and be the Thunderer of the scene !—[*Letter to Archdeacon Singleton.*]

BISHOPS' INCOMES.

THE Bishops and Commissioners wanted a fund to endow small Livings ; they did not touch a farthing of their own incomes, only distributed them a little more equally ; and proceeded lustily at once to confiscate Cathedral property.   But why was it necessary, if the fund for small Livings was such a paramount consideration, that the future Archbishops of Canterbury should be left with two palaces, and 15,000*l.* per annum ? Why is every future Bishop of London to have a palace in Fulham, a house in St. James's Square, and 10,000*l.* a year ?   Could not all the Episcopal functions be carried on well and effectually with the half of these incomes ? Is it necessary that the Archbishop of Canterbury should give feasts to Aristocratic London ; and that the domestics of the Prelacy should stand with swords and bag-wigs round pig, and turkey, and venison, to defend, as it were, the Orthodox gastronome from the fierce Unitarian, the fell Baptist, and all the famished children of Dissent ?—[*Letter to Archdeacon Singleton.*]

A MODERN FABLE.

THIS comes of calling a meeting of one species of cattle only.   The horned cattle say,—" If you want any meat, kill the sheep ; don't meddle with us, there is no beef to spare."   They said this, however, to the lion : and the cunning animal, after he had gained all the information necessary for the destruction of the muttons, and learnt how well and widely they pastured, and how they could be most conveniently eaten up, turns round and informs the cattle, who took him for their best and tenderest friend, that he means to eat them up also. Frequently did Lord John meet the destroying Bishops: much did he commend their daily heap of ruins; sweetly did they smile on each other, and much charming talk was there of meteorology and catarrh, and the particular Cathedral they were pulling down at each period; till one fine day the Home Secretary, with a voice more bland, and a look more ardently affectionate, than that which the masculine mouse bestows on his nibbling female, informed them that the Government meant to take all the Church property into their own hands, to pay the rates out of it and deliver the residue to the rightful possessors. Such an effect, they say, was never before produced by a *coup de théâtre*. The Commission was separated in an instant: London clenched his fist; Canterbury was hurried out by his chaplains, and put into a warm bed; a solemn vacancy spread itself over the face of Gloucester; Lincoln was taken out in strong hysterics. What a noble scene Serjeant Talfourd would have made of this! Why are such talents wasted on *Ion* and the *Athenian Captive?* —[*Letter to Archdeacon Singleton.*]

GOVERNMENT MANAGEMENT.

If Government are to take into their own hands all property which is not managed with the greatest sharpness and accuracy, they may squeeze one-eighth per cent out of the Turkey Company; Spring Rice would become Director of the Hydro-impervious Association, and clear a few hundreds for the Treasury. The British

Roasted Apple Society is notoriously mismanaged, and Lord John and Brother Lister, by a careful selection of fruit, and a judicious management of fuel, would soon get it up to par.—[*Letter to Archdeacon Singleton.*]

THE BISHOPS' SATURDAY NIGHT.

A CHURCH is in danger when it is degraded. It costs mankind much less to destroy it when an institution is associated with mean, and not with elevated, ideas. I should like to see the subject in the hands of H. B. I would entitle the print—

"The Bishops' Saturday Night; or, Lord John Russell at the Pay-Table."

The Bishops should be standing before the pay-table, and receiving their weekly allowance; Lord John and Spring Rice counting, ringing, and biting the sovereigns, and the Bishop of Exeter insisting that the Chancellor of the Exchequer has given him one which was not weight. Viscount Melbourne, in high chuckle, should be standing, with his hat on, and his back to the fire, delighted with the contest; and the Deans and Canons should be in the back-ground, waiting till their turn came. and the Bishops were paid; and among them a Canon, of large composition, urging them not to give way too much to the Bench. Perhaps I should add the President of the Board of Trade, recommending the truck principle to the Bishops, and offering to pay them in hassocks, cassocks, aprons, shovel-hats, sermon-cases, and such like ecclesiastical gear.—[*Letter to Archdeacon Singleton.*]

THE FOOLOMETER.

I AM astonished that these Ministers neglect the common precaution of a foolometer *, with which no public man should be unprovided : I mean, the acquaintance and society of three or four regular British fools as a test of public opinion. Every Cabinet Minister should judge of all his measures by his foolometer, as a navigator crowds or shortens sail by the barometer in his cabin. I have a very valuable instrument of that kind myself, which I have used for many years; and I would be bound to predict, with the utmost nicety, by the help of this machine, the precise effect which any measure would produce on public opinion. Certainly, I never saw anything so decided as the effects produced upon my machine by the Rate Bill. No man who had been accustomed in the smallest degree to handle philosophical instruments could have doubted of the storm which was coming on, or of the thoroughly un-English scheme, in which the Ministry had so rashly engaged themselves.

CATHEDRALS AND PARISH CHURCHES.

THE word *parochial* is a fine deceitful word, and eminently calculated to coax the public. If he means simply that Cathedrals do not belong to parishes, that

---

* Mr. Fox very often used to say, "I wonder what Lord B. will think of this!" Lord B. happened to be a very stupid person, and the curiosity of Mr. Fox's friends was naturally excited to know why he attached such importance to the opinion of such an ordinary commonplace person. "His opinion," said Mr. Fox, "is of much more importance than you are aware of. He is an exact representative of all commonplace English prejudices, and what Lord B. thinks of any measure, the great majority of English people will think of it." It would be a good thing if every Cabinet of philosophers had a Lord B, among them.—[*Letter to Archdeacon Singleton.*]

St. Paul's is not the parish church of Upper Puddi-
comb, and that the vicar of St. Fiddlefrid does not
officiate in Westminster Abbey: all this is true enough,
but do they not in the most material points instruct the
people precisely in the same manner as the parochial
Clergy? Are not prayers and sermons the most important means of spiritual instruction? And are there not
eighteen or twenty services in every Cathedral for one
which is heard in parish churches? I have very often
counted in the afternoon of week days in St. Paul's 150
people, and on Sundays it is full to suffocation. Is all
this to go for nothing? and what right has the Bishop
of London to suppose that there is not as much real
piety in Cathedrals, as in the most roadless, postless,
melancholy, sequestered hamlet, preached to by the most
provincial, sequestered, bucolic Clergyman in the Queen's
dominions?—[*E. R.* 1826.]

EPISCOPAL INCENDIARIES.

I AM thinking of something else, and I see all of a
sudden a great blaze of light: I behold a great number of
gentlemen in short aprons, neat purple coats, and gold
buckles, rushing about with torches in their hands, calling each other " My Lord," and setting fire to all the
rooms in the house, and the people below delighted with
the combustion: finding it impossible to turn them from
their purpose, and finding that they are all what they
are, by divine permission; I endeavour to direct their
holy innovations into another channel; and I say to
them, " My Lords, had not you better set fire to the out-
of-door offices, to the barns and stables, and spare this
fine library and this noble drawing-room? Yonder are
several cow-houses of which no use is made; pray direct

your fury against them, and leave this beautiful and venerable mansion as you found it." If I address the divinely permitted in this manner, has the Bishop of London any right to call me a brother incendiary?— [*Letter to Archdeacon Singleton.*]

SHEEP AND SHEPHERDS.

WE want (and he prints it in italics) for these purposes "*all that we can obtain from whatever sources derived.*" I never remember to have been more alarmed in my life than by this passage. I said to myself, the necessities of the Church have got such complete hold of the imagination of this energetic Prelate, who is so captivated by the holiness of his innovations, that all grades and orders of the Church and all present and future interests will be sacrificed to it. I immediately rushed to the Acts of Parliament which I always have under my pillow to see at once the worst of what had happened. I found present revenues of the Bishops all safe; that is some comfort, I said to myself: Canterbury, 24,000*l.* or 25,000*l.* per annum; London, 18,000*l.* or 20,000*l.* I began to feel some comfort: " things are not so bad; the Bishops do not mean to sacrifice to *sheep and shepherd's money* their present revenues; the Bishop of London is less violent and headstrong than I thought he would be." I looked a little further, and found that 15,000*l.* per annum is allotted to the future Archbishop of Canterbury, 10,000*l.* to the Bishop of London, 8000*l.* to Durham, and 8000*l.* each to Winchester and Ely. "Nothing of *sheep and shepherd* in all this," I exclaimed, and felt still more comforted. It was not till after the Bishops were taken care of, and the revenues of the Cathedrals came into full view, that I saw the perfect development of the *sheep and shepherd principle*, the deep and heartfelt compassion for spiritual labourers, and that inward groaning for the destitute state of the Church, and that firm purpose, printed in italics, of taking *for these purposes all that could be obtained from whatever source derived;* and even in this delicious rummage of Cathedral property, where all the fine church feelings of the Bishop's heart could be indulged without costing the poor sufferer a penny, stalls for Archdeacons in Lincoln and St. Paul's are, to the amount of 2000*l.* per annum, taken from the *sheep and shepherd fund,* and the patronage of them divided between two Commissioners, the Bishop of London and the Bishop of Lincoln, instead of being paid to additional *labourers in the Vineyard.*—[*Letter to Archdeacon Singleton.*]

PROSPECTS OF PREFERMENT.

THE truth is, the greater number of the Clergymen go into Church in order that they may derive a comfortable income *from* the Church.   Such men intend to do their duty, and they do it; but the duty is, however, not the motive, but the adjunct.

I have no manner of doubt, that the immediate effect of passing the Dean and Chapter Bill will be, that a great number of fathers and uncles, judging, and properly judging, that the Church is a very altered and deteriorated profession, will turn the industry and capital of their *élèves* into another channel.   My friend, Robert Eden, says, "This is of the earth earthy:" be it so; I cannot help it, I paint mankind as I find them, and am not answerable for their defects.—[*Letter to Archdeacon Singleton.*]

CHEAP PARSONS.

A PICTURE may be drawn of a Clergyman with 130*l.*
per annum, who combines all moral, physical, and intellectual advantages, a learned man, dedicating himself
intensely to the care of his parish—of charming manners
and dignified deportment—six feet two inches high,
beautifully proportioned, with a magnificent countenance, expressive of all the cardinal virtues and the Ten
Commandments,—and it is asked with an air of triumph
if such a man as this will fall into contempt on account
of his poverty? But substitute for him an average,
ordinary, uninteresting Minister; obese, dumpy, neither
ill-natured nor good-natured: neither learned nor
ignorant, striding over the stiles to Church, with a
second-rate wife—dusty and deliquescent—and four
parochial children, full of catechism and bread and
butter; or let him be seen in one of those Shem-Ham-
and-Japhet buggies—made on Mount Ararat soon after
the subsidence of the waters, driving in the High Street
of Edmonton,—among all his pecuniary, saponaceous,
oleaginous parishioners. Can any man of common sense
say that all these outward circumstances of the Ministers
of religion have no bearing on religion itself?—[*Letter
to Archdeacon Singleton.*]

MOCK TURTLE.

I ASK the Bishop of London, a man of honour and
conscience, as he is, if he thinks five years will elapse
before a second attack is made upon Deans and Chapters?
Does he think, after Reformers have tasted the flesh of
the Church, that they will put up with any other diet?
Does he forget that Deans and Chapters are but mock

turtle—that more delicious delicacies remain behind?
Five years hence he will attempt to make a stand, and
he will be laughed at and eaten up.—[*Letter to Archdeacon Singleton.*]

BISHOP MONK.

You must have read an attack upon me by the Bishop
of Gloucester, in the course of which he says that I have
not been appointed to my situation as Canon of St.
Paul's for my piety and learning, but because I am a
scoffer and a jester. Is not this rather strong for a
Bishop, and does it not appear to you, Mr. Archdeacon,
as rather too close an imitation of that language which
is used in the apostolic occupation of trafficking in fish?
Whether I have been appointed for my piety or not,
must depend upon what this poor man means by piety.
He means by that word, of course, a defence of all the
tyrannical and oppressive abuses of the Church which
have been swept away within the last fifteen or twenty
years of my life; the Corporation and Test Acts; the
Penal Laws against the Catholics; the Compulsory Marriages of Dissenters, and all those disabling and disqualifying laws which were the disgrace of our Church,
and which he has always looked up to as the consummation of human wisdom. If piety consisted in the defence
of these—if it was impious to struggle for their abroga-
tion, I have indeed led an ungodly life.

There is nothing pompous gentlemen are so much afraid
of as a little humour. It is like the objection of certain
cephalic animalculæ to the use of small-tooth combs,
" Finger and thumb, precipitate powder, or anything else
you please; but for heaven's sake no small-tooth combs!"
After all, I believe, Bishop Monk has been the cause of
much · more laughter than ever I have been; I cannot

account for it, but I never see him enter a room without exciting a smile on every countenance within it.—[*Letter to Archdeacon Singleton.*]

MEN OF THE WORLD.

MUCH writing and much talking are very tiresome; and, above all, they are so to men who, living in the world, arrive at those rapid and just conclusions which are only to be made by living in the world.—[*Memoir.*]

SERMONS.

PREACHING has become a bye-word for long and dull conversation of any kind; and whoever wishes to imply, in any piece of writing, the absence of every thing agreeable and inviting, calls it a sermon.—[*Memoir.*]

PULPIT ELOCUTION.

To this cause of the unpopularity of sermons may be added the extremely ungraceful manner in which they are delivered. The English, generally remarkable for doing very good things in a very bad manner, seem to have reserved the maturity and plenitude of their awkwardness for the pulpit. A clergyman clings to his velvet cushion with either hand, keeps his eye riveted upon his book, speaks of the ecstasies of joy and fear with a voice and a face which indicate neither, and pinions his body and soul into the same attitude of limb and thought, for fear of being called theatrical and affected. The most intrepid veteran of us all dares no more than wipe his face with his cambric sudarium; if, by mischance, his hand slip from its orthodox gripe of the velvet, he draws it back as from liquid brimstone, or the caustic iron of the law, and atones for this indecorum by fresh inflexibility and more rigorous sameness. Is it wonder, then, that every semi-delirious sectary who pours forth his animated nonsense with the genuine look and voice of passion should gesticulate away the congregation of the most profound and learned divine of the Established Church, and in two Sundays preach him bare to the very sexton? Why are we natural everywhere but in the pulpit? No man expresses warm and animated feelings anywhere else, with his mouth alone, but with his whole body; he articulates with every limb, and talks from head to foot with a thousand voices. Why this holoplexia on sacred occasions alone? Why call in the aid of paralysis to piety? Is it a rule of oratory to balance the style against the subject, and to handle the most sublime truths in the dullest language and the driest manner? Is sin to be taken from man, as Eve was from Adam, by casting them into a deep slumber? Or from what possible perversion of common sense are we all to look like field preachers in Zembla, holy lumps of ice, numbed into quiescence, and stagnation, and mumbling?—[*Memoir.*]

INSIPIDITY OF SERMONS.

THE great object of modern sermons is to hazard nothing: their characteristic is, decent debility; which alike guards their authors from ludicrous errors, and precludes them from striking beauties.—[*E. R.* 1802.]

READING OF SERMONS.

PULPIT discourses have insensibly dwindled from speaking to reading; a practice, of itself, sufficient to stifle every germ of eloquence. It is only by the fresh feelings of the heart, that mankind can be very powerfully affected. What can be more ludicrous, than an orator delivering stale indignation, and fervour of a week old; turning over whole pages of violent passions, written out in German text; reading the tropes and apostrophes into which he is hurried by the ardour of his mind; and so affected at a preconcerted line and page, that he is unable to proceed any further!—[*E. R.* 1802.]

CONFUTATION OF INFIDELITY.

IT is a very easy thing to talk about the shallow impostures, and the silly ignorant sophisms of Voltaire, Rousseau, Condorcet, D'Alembert, and Volney, and to say that Hume is not worth answering. This affectation of contempt will not do. While these pernicious writers have power to allure from the Church great numbers of proselytes, it is better to study them diligently, and to reply to them satisfactorily, than to veil insolence, want of power, or want of industry, by a pretended contempt; which may leave infidels and wavering Christians to suppose that such writers are abused, because they are feared: and not answered, because they are unanswerable. [*E.R.* 1802.]

COLD CHURCHES.

I AM convinced we should do no great injury to the cause of religion if we remembered the old combination of *arœ et foci,* and kept our churches a little warmer. An experienced clergyman can pretty well estimate the number of his audience by the indications of a sensible thermometer. The same blighting wind chills piety which is fatal to vegetable life; yet our power of encountering weather varies with the object of our hardihood; we are very Scythians when pleasure is concerned, and Sybarites when the bell summons us to church.— [*Memoir.*]

CEREMONIES.

IF anything, there is, perhaps, too little pomp and ceremony in our worship, instead of too much. We quarrelled with the Roman Catholic Church, in a great hurry and a great passion, and furious with spleen; clothed ourselves with sackcloth, because she was habited in brocade; rushing, like children, from. one extreme to another, and blind to all medium between complication and barrenness, formality and neglect.—[*Memoir.*]

PRESENT AND FUTURE.

A MAN who was sure to die a death of torture in ten years would think more of the most trifling gratification or calamity of the day than of his torn flesh and twisted nerves years hence.—[*Memoir.*]

LEVITY OF ATTENTION.

THE cry of a child, the fall of a book, the most trifling occurrence, is sufficient to dissipate religious thought, and to introduce a more willing train of ideas; a sparrow fluttering about the church is an antagonist which the most profound theologian in Europe is wholly unable to overcome.—[*Memoir.*]

CHRISTIAN INFLUENCE.

THE beauty of the Christian religion is, that it carries the order and discipline of heaven into our very fancies and conceptions, and, by hallowing the first shadowy notions of our minds from which actions spring, makes our actions themselves good and holy.—[*Memoir.*]

THE MEASURE OF PIETY.

PIETY, stretched beyond a certain point, is the parent of impiety.—[*Memoir.*]

THE BASIS OF FAITH.

THE awe and respect which a child entertains for its parent and instructor, is the first scaffolding upon which the sacred edifice of religion is reared. A child *begins* to pray, to act, and to abstain, not to please God but to please the parent, who tells him that such is the will of God.—[*E. R.* 1806.]

TRUE CHRISTIANITY.

TRUE, modest, unobtrusive religion—charitable, for giving, indulgent Christianity, is the greatest ornament and the greatest blessing that can dwell in the mind of man. But if there be one character more base, more infamous, and more shocking than another, it is *he* who, for the sake of some paltry distinction in the world, is ever ready to accuse conspicuous persons of irreligion— to turn common informer for the Church—and , to convert the most beautiful feelings of the human heart to the destruction of the good and great, by fixing upon talents the indelible stigma of irreligion. It matters not how trifling and how insignificant the accuser; cry out that the *Church is in danger,* and your object is accomplished; lurk in the walk of hypocrisy, to accuse your enemy of the crime of atheism, and his ruin is quite certain; acquitted or condemned, is the same thing ; it is only sufficient that he be accused, in order that his destruction be accomplished. If we could satisfy ourselves that such were the real views of Mrs. Trimmer, and that she were capable of such baseness, we would have drawn blood from her at every line, and left her in a state of martyrdom more piteous than that of St. Uba.—[*E. R.* 1806.]

THE WORDS OF TRUTH.

In the Gospels, and the various parts of the New Testament, the words of our Saviour and of St. Paul, when they contain any opinion, are always to be looked upon as lessons of wisdom to us, however incidentally they may have been delivered, and however shortly they may have been expressed. As their words were to be recorded by inspired writers, and to go down to future ages, nothing can have been said without reflection and design. Nothing is to be lost, everything is to be studied : a great moral lesson is often conveyed in a few words. Read slowly, think deeply, let every word enter into your soul, for it was intended for your soul.—[*Sermons.*]

SIMPLICITY OF GOSPEL TRUTH.

No man preaches novelties and discoveries; the object of preaching is constantly to remind mankind of what mankind are constantly forgetting ; not to supply the defects of human intelligence, but to fortify the feebleness of human resolutions, to recall mankind from the by-paths where they turn, into that broad path of salvation which all know, but few tread. These plain lessons the humblest ministers of the Gospel may teach, if they are honest, and the most powerful Christians will ponder, if they are wise.—[*Sermons.*]

WE pray also for that Infant of the Royal Race whom
in thy good Providence thou hast given us for our future
King.   We beseech Thee so to mould his heart and
fashion his spirit, that he may be a blessing and not an
evil to the land of his birth.   May he grow in favour
with man, by leaving to its own force and direction the
energy of a free People!   May he grow in favour with
God, by holding the Faith in Christ fervently and
feelingly, without feebleness, without fanaticism, without folly!   As he will be the first man in these realms,
so may he be the best;— disdaining to hide bad actions
by high station, and endeavouring always, by the example of a strict and moral life, to repay those gifts
which a loyal people are so willing to spare from their
own necessities to a good King.

THE JUDICIAL OFFICE.

HE who takes the office of a Judge as it now exists in
this country, takes in his hands a splendid gem, good
and glorious, perfect and pure.   Shall he give it up
mutilated, shall he mar it, shall he darken it, shall it
emit no light, shall it be valued at no price, shall it
excite no wonder?   Shall he find it a diamond, shall he
leave it a stone?   What shall we say to the man who
would wilfully destroy with fire the magnificent temple
of God, in which I am now preaching?   Far worse is
he who ruins the moral edifices of the world, which time
and toil, and many prayers to God, and many sufferings
of men, have reared; who puts out the light of the
times in which he lives, and leaves us to wander amid

the darkness ot corruption and the desolation of sin. There may be, there probably is, in this church, some young man who may hereafter fill the office of an English Judge, when the greater part of those who hear me are dead, and mingled with the dust of the grave. Let him remember my words, and let them form and fashion his spirit: he cannot tell in what dangerous and awful times he may be placed; but as a mariner looks to his compass in the calm, and looks to his compass in the storm, and never keeps his eyes off his compass, so in every vicissitude of a judicial life, deciding for the people, deciding against the people, protecting the just rights of kings, or restraining their unlawful ambition, let him ever cling to that pure, exalted, and Christian independence, which towers over the little motives of life; which no hope of favour can influence, which no effort of power can control.—[*Sermons.*]

THE SAFETY OF NATIONS.

THE most obvious and important use of this perfect Justice is, that it makes nations safe: under common circumstances, the institutions of Justice seem to have little or no bearing upon the safety and security of a country, but in periods of real danger, when a nation surrounded by foreign enemies contends not for the boundaries of empire, but for the very being and existence of empire; then it is that the advantage of just institutions are discovered. Every man feels that he has a country, that he has something worth preserving, and worth contending for. Instances are remembered where the weak prevailed over the strong: one man recalls to mind when a just and upright judge protected him from unlawful violence, gave him back his vineyard, rebuked his oppressor, restored him to his rights, published, condemned, and rectified the wrong. This is what is called country. Equal rights to unequal possessions, equal justice to the rich and poor: this is what men come out to fight for, and to defend.— [*Sermons.*]

ENGLAND'S LAW.

I CALL you all to witness if there be any exaggerated picture in this: the sword is just sheathed, the flag is just furled, the last sound of the trumpet has just died away. You all remember what a spectacle this country exhibited: one heart, one voice—one weapon, one purpose. And why? Because this country is a country of the law; because the Judge is a judge for the peasant as well as for the palace; because every man's happiness is guarded by fixed rules from tyranny and caprice. This town, this week, the business of the few next days, would explain to any enlightened European why other nations *did* fall in the storms of the world, and why we did *not* fall. The Christian patience you may witness, the impartiality of the judgment-seat, the disrespect of persons, the disregard of consequences. These attributes of justice do not end with arranging your conflicting rights, and mine; they give strength to the English people, duration to the English name; they turn the animal courage of this people into moral and religious courage, and present to the lowest of mankind plain reasons and strong motives why they should resist aggression from without, and bind themselves a living rampart round the land of their birth.—[*Assize Sermon.*]

THE MARCH OF JUSTICE.

THE whole tone and tenor of public morals is affected by the state of supreme Justice; it extinguishes revenge, it communicates a spirit of purity and uprightness to inferior magistrates; it makes the great good, by taking away impunity; it banishes fraud, obliquity, and solicitation, and teaches men that the law is their right. Truth is its handmaid, freedom is its child, peace is its companion; safety walks in its steps, victory follows in its train: it is the brightest emanation of the Gospel, it is the greatest attribute of God; it is that centre round which human motives and passions turn: and Justice, sitting on high, sees Genius and Power, and Wealth and Birth, revolving round her throne; and teaches their paths and marks out their orbits, and warns with a loud voice, and rules with a strong arm, and carries order and discipline into a world, which but for her would only be a wild waste of passions.—[*Sermons.*]

PRISON LIFE.

THERE are, in every county in England, large public schools maintained at the expense of the county, for the encouragement of profligacy and vice, and for providing a proper succession of housebreakers, profligates, and thieves. They are schools, too, conducted without the smallest degree of partiality or favour; there being no man (however mean his birth, or obscure his situation,) who may not easily procure admission to them. The moment any young person evinces the slightest propensity for these pursuits, he is provided with food, clothing, and lodging, and put to his studies under the most accomplished thieves and cut-throats the county can supply. — [*E. R.* 1821.]

PRISON REFORM.

It is inconceivable to what a spirit of party this has given birth;—all the fat and sleek people—the enjoyers —the mumpsimus, and "well as we are" people, are perfectly outrageous at being compelled to do their duty, and to sacrifice time and money to the lower orders of mankind.—[*E. R.* 1821.]

THE ENEMIES OF IMPROVEMENT.

Dislike of innovation proceeds sometimes from the disgust excited by false humanity, canting hypocrisy, and silly enthusiasm. It proceeds also from a stupid and indiscriminate horror of change, whether of evil for good, or good for evil. There is also much party spirit in these matters. A good deal of these humane projects and · institutions originate from Dissenters. The plunderers of the public, the jobbers, and those who sell themselves to some great man, who sells himself to a greater, all scent, from afar, the danger of political change,—are sensible that the correction of one abuse may lead to that of another—feel uneasy at any visible operation of public spirit and justice—hate and tremble at a man who exposes and rectifies abuses from a sense of duty— and think, if such things are suffered to be, that their candle-ends and cheese-parings are no longer safe : and these sagacious persons, it must be said for them, are not very wrong in this feeling. Providence, which has denied to them all that is great and good, has given them a fine tact for the preservation of their plunder : their real enemy is the spirit of inquiry—the dislike of wrong—the love of right—and the courage and dili- gence which are the concomitants of these virtues.— [*E. R.* 1823.]

EFFECTS OF GAOL DISCIPLINE.

IT is quite obvious that, if men were to appear again, six months after they were hanged, handsomer, richer, and more plump than before execution, the gallows would cease to be an object of terror. But here are men who come out of gaol, and say, " Look at us—we can read and write, we can make baskets and shoes, and we went in ignorant of everything: and we have learnt to do without strong liquors, and have no longer any objection to work; and we did work in the gaol, and have saved money, and here it is." What is there of terror and detriment in all this? and how are crimes to be lessened if they are thus rewarded?—[*E. R.* 1821.]

TRACTS FOR CULPRITS.

IF education is to be continued in gaols, and tracts are to be dispersed, we cannot help lamenting that the tracts, though full of good principles, are so intolerably stupid — and all apparently constructed upon the supposition, that a thief or a peccant ploughman are inferior in common sense to a boy of five years old. The story generally is, that a labourer with six children has nothing to live upon but mouldy bread and dirty water; yet nothing can exceed his cheerfulness and content — no murmurs — no discontent: of mutton he has scarcely heard — of bacon he never dreams: furfurous bread and the water of the pool constitute his food, establish his felicity, and excite his warmest gratitude. The squire or parson of the parish always happens to be walking by, and overhears him praying for the king and the members for the county, and for all in authority; and it generally ends with their offering him a shilling, which this excellent man declares he does not want, and will not accept! These are the pamphlets which Goodies and Noodles are dispersing with unwearied diligence.— [*E. R.* 1821.]

GAOL EDUCATION.

A POOR man, who is lucky enough to have his son committed for a felony, educates him, under such a system, for nothing; while the virtuous simpleton on the other side of the wall is paying by the quarter for these attainments. He sees clergymen and ladies busy with the larcenous pupil; while the poor lad, who respects the eighth commandment, is consigned, in some dark alley, to the frowns and blows of a ragged pedagogue.— [*E. R.* 1821.]

DISCIPLINE.

MRS. FRY is an amiable excellent woman, and ten thousand times better than the infamous neglect that preceded her; but hers is not the method to stop crimes. In prisons which are really meant to keep the multitude in order, and to be a terror to evil doers, there must be no sharing of profits—no visiting of friends — no education but religious education — no freedom of diet — no weavers' looms or carpenters' benches. There must be a great deal of solitude; coarse food; a dress of shame; hard, incessant, irksome, eternal labour; a planned and regulated and unrelenting exclusion of happiness and comfort.—[*E. R.* 1822.]

SCARLETT'S POOR BILL.

MR. SCARLETT is a very strong man; and before he works his battering-ram, he chooses to have the wall made of a thickness worthy of his blow—capable of evincing, by the enormity of its ruins, the superfluity of his vigour, and the certainty of his aim.

If this bill had passed, he could not have passed. His post-chaise on the Northern Circuit would have been impeded by the crowds of houseless villagers, driven from their cottages by landlords rendered merciless by the bill. In the mud—all in the mud (for such cases made and provided) would they have rolled this most excellent counsellor. Instigated by the devil and their own malicious purposes, his wig they would have polluted, and tossed to a thousand winds the parchment bickerings of Doe and Roe.

His bill, we cannot help saying, appears to us to be a receipt for universal and interminable litigation all over England—a perfect law-hurricane—a conversion of all flesh into plaintiffs and defendants. The parish A. has pulled down houses, and burthened the parish B. ; B. has demolished to the misery of C. ; which has again misbehaved itself in the same manner to the oppression of other letters of the alphabet. All run into parchment, and pant for revenge and exoneration.—[*E. R.* 1821.]

. ANTICIPATED REFORM OF THE POOR LAW.

As soon as it becomes *really impossible* to increase the poor fund by law—when there is but little, and there *can* be no more, that little will be administered with the utmost caution ; claims will be minutely inspected ; idle manhood will not receive the scraps and crumbs which belong to failing old age ; distress will make the poor provident and cautious ; and all the good expected from

the abolition of the Poor-Laws will begin to appear.—
[*E. R.* 1821.]

JUSTICE BEFORE DISCIPLINE.

PRISON discipline is an object of considerable importance; but the common rights of mankind, and the common principles of justice, and humanity, and liberty, are of greater consequence even than prison discipline. Right and wrong, innocence and guilt, must not be confounded, that a prison-fancying Justice may bring his friend into the prison and say, "Look what a spectacle of order, silence, and decorum we have established! here no idleness, all grinding!—we produce a penny roll every second,—our prison is supposed to be the best regulated prison in England,—Cubitt is making us a new wheel of forty-felon power,—look how white the flour is, all done by untried prisoners—as innocent as lambs!"—[*E. R.* 1824.]

EFFECTS OF PUNISHMENT.

Because punishment does not annihilate crime, it is folly to say it does not lessen it. It did not stop the murder of Mrs. Donatty; but how many Mrs. Donattys has it kept alive!—[*E. R.* 1824.]

THE TREAD-MILL.

THE labour of the tread-mill is irksome, dull, monotonous, and disgusting to the last degree. A man does not see his work, does not know what he is doing, what progress he is making; there is no room for art, contrivance, ingenuity, and superior skill — all which are the cheering circumstances of human labour. The husbandman sees the field gradually subdued by the plough; the smith beats the rude mass of iron by degrees into its meditated shape, and gives it a meditated utility; the tailor accommodates his parallelogram of cloth to the lumps and bumps of the human body, and, holding it up, exclaims, "This will contain the lower moiety of a human being." But the treader does nothing but tread; he sees no change of objects, admires no new relation of parts, imparts no new qualities to matter, and gives to it no new arrangements and positions; or, if he does, he sees and knows it not, but is turned at once from a rational being, by a justice of peace, into a *primum mobile,* and put upon a level with a rush of water or a puff of steam. It is impossible to get gentlemen to attend to the distinction between raw and roasted prisoners, without which all discussion on prisoners is perfectly ridiculous. — [*E. R.* 1824.]

PRIVILEGE OF PUNISHMENT.

It is said, that labour may be a privilege as well as a punishment. So may taking physic be a privilege, in cases where it is asked for as a charitable relief, but not if it is stuffed down a man's throat whether he say yea or nay. — [*E. R.* 1824.]

UNTRIED PRISONERS.

You take up a poor man upon suspicion, deprive him of all his usual methods of getting his livelihood, and then giving him the first view of the tread-mill, he of the

Quorum thus addresses him : — " My amiable friend, we use no compulsion with untried prisoners.   You are free as air till you are found guilty; only it is my duty to inform you, as you have no money of your own, that the disposition to eat and drink which you have allowed you sometimes feel, and upon which I do not mean to cast any degree of censure, cannot possibly be gratified but by constant grinding in this machine.   It has its inconveniences, I admit; but balance them against the total want of meat and drink, and decide for yourself.   You are perfectly at liberty to make your choice, and I by no means wish to influence your judgment." — [*E. R.* 1824.]

PUNISHMENT ON SUSPICION.

If there are, according to the doctrines of the millers, to be two punishments, the first for being suspected of committing the offence, and the second for committing it, there should be two trials as well as two punishments. Is the man really suspected, or do his accusers only pretend to suspect him?   Are the suspecting of better character than the suspected?   Is it a light suspicion which may be atoned for by grinding a peck a day?   Is it a bushel case? or is it one deeply criminal, which requires the flour to be ground fine enough for French rolls?

Such reasoning is doubly important, when it comes from an author, the leader of the Quorum, who may say with the pious Æneas, —

> —— Quæque ipse miserrima vidi,
> Et *quorum* pars magna fui.

—[*E. R.* 1824.]

THE TREADER.

To compel prisoners before trial to work at the tread-mill, as the condition of their support, must, in a great number of instances, operate as a very severe punishment. Is it no punishment to such a man to walk up hill like a turnspit dog, in an infamous machine, for six months? and yet there are gentlemen who suppose that the common people do not consider this as punishment!—that the gayest and most joyous of human beings is a treader, untried by a jury of his countrymen, in the fifth month of lifting up the leg, and striving against the law of gravity, supported by the glorious information which he receives from the turnkey, that he has all the time been grinding flour on the other side of the wall.—[*E. R.* 1824.]

MENTAL PUNISHMENT.

PUNISHMENTS are not merely to be estimated by pain to the limbs, but by the feelings of the mind.—[*E. R.* 1824.]

COUNSEL FOR PRISONERS.

A MOST absurd argument was advanced in the honourable House, that the practice of employing counsel would be such an expense to the prisoner!—just as if any thing was so expensive as being hanged! What a fine topic for the ordinary! "You are going" (says that exquisite divine) "to be hanged to-morrow, it is true, but consider what a sum you have saved! Mr. Scarlett or Mr. Brougham might certainly have presented arguments to the jury, which would have insured your acquittal; but do you forget that gentlemen of their eminence must be recompensed by large fees, and that if your life had been saved, you would actually have been out of pocket above 20*l.*?   You will now die with the consciousness of having obeyed the dictates of a wise economy; and with a grateful reverence for the laws of your country, which prevents you from running into such unbounded expense—so let us now go to prayers."—[*E. R.* 1826.]

BARBARITY OF THE OLD LAW.

It is a most affecting moment in a court of justice, when the evidence has all been heard, and the Judge asks the prisoner what he has to say in his defence.   The prisoner, who has (by great exertions, perhaps, of his friends) saved up money enough to procure counsel, says to the Judge, "that he leaves his defence to his counsel." We have often blushed for English humanity to hear the reply.   "Your counsel cannot speak for you, you must speak for yourself;" and this is the reply given to a poor girl of eighteen—to a foreigner—to a deaf man—to a stammerer—to the sick—to the feeble—to the old—to the most abject and ignorant of human beings!   It is a reply, we must say, at which common sense and common feeling revolt:—for it is full of brutal cruelty, and of base inattention of those who make laws, to the happiness of those for whom laws were made.   We wonder that any juryman can convict under such a shocking violation of all natural justice.   The iron age of Clovis and Clottaire can produce no more atrocious violation of every good feeling and every good principle.   Can a sick man find strength and nerves to speak before a large assembly?

—can an ignorant man find words?—can a low man find confidence? Is not he afraid of becoming an object of ridicule?— can he believe that his expressions will be understood? How often have we seen a poor wretch, struggling against the agonies of his spirit, and the rudeness of his conceptions, and his awe of better-dressed men and better-taught men, and the shame which the accusation has brought upon his head, and the sight of his parents and children gazing at him in the Court, for the last time, perhaps, and after a long absence! The mariner sinking in the wave does not want a helping hand more than does this poor wretch. But help is denied to all! Age cannot have it, nor ignorance, nor the modesty of women! One hard uncharitable rule silences the defenders of the wretched, in the worst of human evils; and at the bitterest of human moments, mercy is blotted out from the ways of men!*—[*E. R.* 1826.]

FIAT EXPERIMENTUM.

HOWARD devoted himself to his country. It was a noble example. Let two gentlemen on the Ministerial side of the House (we only ask for two) commit some crimes, which will render their execution a painful necessity. Let them feel, and report to the House, all the injustice and inconvenience of having neither a copy of the indictment, nor a list of witnesses, nor counsel to defend them. We will venture to say, that the evidence of two such persons would do more for the

---

* All this nonsense is now put an end to. Counsel is allowed to the prisoner, and they are permitted to speak in his defence.

improvement of the criminal law, than all the orations of Mr. Lamb or the lucubrations of Beccaria. Such evidence would save time, and bring the question to an issue. It is a great duty, and ought to be fulfilled—and in ancient Rome, would have been fulfilled.—[*E. R.* 1826.]

CURRENCY OF FALLACIES.

THERE are a vast number of absurd and mischievous fallacies, which pass readily in the world for sense and virtue, while in truth they tend only to fortify error and encourage crime. — [*E. R.* 1825.]

THE FALLACY OF AGE.

Our Wise Ancestors — the Wisdom of our Ancestors — the Wisdom of Ages—venerable Antiquity—Wisdom of Old Times.—This mischievous and absurd fallacy springs from the grossest perversion of the meaning of words. Experience is certainly the mother of wisdom, and the old have, of course, a greater experience than the young; but the question is, who are the old? and who are the young? Of *individuals* living at the same period, the oldest has, of course, the greatest experience; but among *generations* of men the reverse of this is true. Those who come first (our ancestors), are the young people, and have the least experience. We have added to their experience the experience of many centuries: and, therefore, as far as experience goes, are wiser, and more capable of forming an opinion than they were. The real feeling should be, *not*, can we be so presumptuous as to put our opinions in opposition to those of our ancestors? but can such young, ignorant, inexperienced persons as our ancestors necessarily were, be expected to have understood a subject as well as those who have seen so much more, lived so much longer, and enjoyed the experience of so many centuries ? — [*E. R.* 1825.]

WISDOM OF OUR ANCESTORS.

OUR ancestors, up to the Conquest, were children in arms; chubby boys in the time of Edward the First; striplings under Elizabeth; men in the reign of Queen Anne; and *we* only are the white-bearded, silver-headed ancients, who have treasured up, and are prepared to profit by, all the experience which human life can supply. It is necessary to insist upon this; for upon sacks of wool, and on benches forensic, sit grave men, and agricolous persons in the Commons, crying out "Ancestors, Ancestors ! *hodie non !* Saxons, Danes, save us ! Fiddlefrig, help us ! Howel, Ethelwolf, protect us ! " — Any cover for nonsense — any veil for trash — any pretext for repelling the innovations of conscience and of duty ! — [*E. R.* 1825.]

IRREVOCABLE LAWS.

THE despotism of Nero or Caligula would be more tolerable than an *irrevocable law.* The despot, through fear or favour, or in a lucid interval, might relent; but how are the Parliament, who made the Scotch Union, for example, to be awakened from that dust in which they repose—the jobber and the patriot, the speaker and the doorkeeper, the silent voters and the men of rich allusions—Cannings and cultivators, Barings and beggars—

making irrevocable laws for men who toss their remains about with spades, and use the relics of these legislators, to give breadth to broccoli, and to aid the vernal eruption of asparagus ?

To suppose that there is anything which a whole nation cannot do, which they deem to be essential to their happiness, and that they cannot do it, because *another* generation, long ago dead and gone, said it must not be done, is mere nonsense. While you are captain of the vessel, do what you please; but the moment you quit the ship, I become as omnipotent as you. You may leave me as much *advice* as you please, but you cannot leave me *commands;* though, in fact, this is the only meaning which can be applied to what are called irrevocable laws.

In every year, and every day of that year, living men have a right to make their own laws, and manage their own affairs; to break through the tyranny of the ante-spirants — the people who breathed before them, and to do what they please for themselves.

When a law is considered as immutable, and the immutable law happens at the same time to be too foolish and mischievous to be endured, instead of being repealed, it is clandestinely evaded, or openly violated; and thus the authority of all law is weakened.

An irrevocable law is a piece of absurd tyranny exercised by the rulers of Queen Anne's time upon the government of 1825 — a certain art of potting and preserving a kingdom, in one shape, attitude, and flavour — and in this way it is that an institution appears like old Ladies' Sweetmeats and made Wines — Apricot Jam 1822 — Currant Wine 1819 — Court of Chancery 1427 — Penal Laws against Catholics 1676. The difference is, that the Ancient Woman is a better judge of mouldy commodities than the liberal part of his Majesty's Ministers. The potting lady goes sniffing about and admitting light and air to prevent the progress of decay; while to him of the Woolsack, all seems doubly dear in proportion as it is antiquated, worthless, and unusable. — [*E. R.* 1825.]

SUBMISSION OF JUDGMENT.

CAN there be greater absurdity than to say that a man is acting contrary to his conscience who surrenders his opinion upon any subject to those who must understand the subject better than himself? — [*E. R.* 1825.]

NO INNOVATION.

No Innovation! — To say that all new things are bad, is to say that all old things were bad in their commencement: for of all the old things ever seen or heard of, there is not one that was not once new. Whatever is now establishment was once innovation. The first inventor of pews and parish clerks, was no doubt considered as a Jacobin in his day. Judges, juries, criers of the court, are all the inventions of ardent spirits, who filled the world with alarm, and were considered as the great precursors of ruin and dissolution. No inoculation, no turnpikes, no reading, no writing, no popery! The fool sayeth in his heart, and crieth with his mouth, " I will have nothing new!" — [*E. R.* 1825.]

CONDUCT AND RESPECT.

THE greater the quantity of respect a man receives, independently of good conduct, the less good is his behaviour likely to be. — [*E. R.* 1825.]

WHEN TO DO GOOD.

WHICH is the properest day to do good? which is the properest day to remove a nuisance? we answer, the very first day a man can be found to propose the removal of it; and whoever opposes the removal of it on that day will (if he dare) oppose it on every other. There is in the minds of many feeble friends to virtue and improvement, an imaginary period for the removal of evils, which it would certainly be worth while to wait for, if there was the smallest chance of its ever arriving — a period of unexampled peace and prosperity, when a patriotic king and an enlightened mob united their ardent efforts for the amelioration of human affairs; when the oppressor is as delighted to give up the oppression, as the oppressed is to be liberated from it; when the difficulty and the unpopularity would be to continue the evil, not to abolish it! These are the periods when fair-weather philosophers are willing to venture out, and hazard a little for the general good. But the history of human nature is so contrary to all this, that almost all improvements are . made after the bitterest resistance, and in the midst of tumults and civil violence —-the worst period at which they can be made, compared to which any period is eligible, and should be seized hold of by the friends of salutary reform. — [*E. R.* 1825.]

SOCIAL ORDER.

AMONG the several cloudy appellatives which have been commonly employed as cloaks for misgovernment, there is none more conspicuous in this atmosphere of illusion than the word Order. As often as any measure is brought forward which has for its object to lessen the sacrifice made by the many to the few, *social order* is the phrase commonly opposed to its progress. — [*E. R.* 1825.]

PRAISE OF DELINQUENTS.

IT is the fashion very much among the Tories of the House of Commons, and all those who love the effects of public liberty, without knowing or caring how it is preserved, to attack every person who complains of abuses, and to accuse him of gross exaggeration. No sooner is the name of any public thief, or of any tormentor, or oppressor, mentioned in that Honourable House, than out bursts the spirit of jobbing eulogium, and there is not a virtue under heaven which is not ascribed to the delinquent in question, and vouched for by the most irrefragable testimony. — [*E. R.* 1821.]

NOODLE'S ORATION.

"WHAT would our ancestors say to this, Sir? How does this measure tally with their institutions? How does it agree with their experience? Are we to put the wisdom of yesterday in competition with the wisdom of centuries? (*Hear, hear!*) Is beardless youth to show no respect for the decisions of mature age? (*Loud cries of hear! hear!*) If this measure be right, would it have escaped the wisdom of those Saxon progenitors to whom we are indebted for so many of our best political institutions? Would the Dane have passed it over? Would the Norman have rejected it? Would such a notable discovery have been reserved for these modern and degenerate times? Besides, Sir, if the measure itself is good, I ask the honourable gentleman if this is the time for carrying it into execution — whether, in fact, a more unfortunate period could have been selected than that which he has chosen? If this were an ordinary measure, I should not oppose it with so much vehemence; but, Sir, it calls in question the wisdom of an irrevocable law — of a law passed at the memorable period of the Revolution. What right have we, Sir, to break down this firm column, on which the great men of that age stamped a character of eternity? Are not all authorities against this measure — Pitt, Fox, Cicero, and the Attorney and Solicitor General? The proposition is new, Sir; it is the first time it was ever heard in this House. I am not prepared, Sir—this House is not prepared, to receive it. The measure implies a distrust of his Majesty's government; their disapproval is sufficient to warrant opposition. Precaution only is requisite where danger is apprehended. Here the high character of the individuals in question is a sufficient guarantee against any ground of alarm. Give not, then, your sanction to this measure; for, whatever be its character, if you do give your sanction to it, the same man by whom this is proposed, will propose to you others to which it will be impossible to give your consent. I care very little, Sir, for the ostensible measure; but what is there behind? What are the honourable gentleman's future schemes? If we pass this bill, what fresh concessions may he not require? What further degradation is he planning for his country?

Talk of evil and inconvenience, Sir! look to other countries—study other aggregations and societies of men, and then see whether the laws of this country demand a remedy or deserve a panegyric. Was the honourable gentleman (let me ask him) always of this way of thinking? Do I not remember when he was the advocate in this House of very opposite opinions? I not only quarrel with his present sentiments, Sir, but I declare very frankly I do not like the party with which he acts. If his own motives were as pure as possible, they cannot but suffer contamination from those with whom he is politically associated. This measure may be a boon to the constitution, but I will accept no favour to the constitution from such hands. (*Loud cries of hear! hear!*) I profess myself, Sir, an honest and upright member of the British Parliament, and I am not afraid to profess myself an enemy to all change, and all innovation. I am satisfied with things as they are; and it will be my pride and pleasure to hand down this country to my children as I received it from those who preceded me. The honourable gentleman pretends to justify the severity with which he has attacked the Noble Lord who presides in the Court of Chancery. But I say such attacks are pregnant with mischief to Government itself. Oppose Ministers, you oppose Government; disgrace Ministers, you disgrace Government; bring Ministers into contempt, you bring Government into contempt; and anarchy and civil war are the consequences. Besides, Sir, the measure is unnecessary. Nobody complains of disorder in that shape in which it is the aim of your measure to propose a remedy to it. The business is one of the greatest importance; there is need of the greatest caution and circumspection. Do not let us be precipitate, Sir; it is impossible to foresee all consequences. Every thing should be gradual; the example of a neighbouring nation should fill us with alarm! The honourable gentleman has taxed me with illiberality, Sir. I deny the charge. I hate innovation, but I love improvement. I am an enemy to the corruption of Government, but I defend its influence. I dread reform, but I dread it only when it is intemperate. I consider the liberty of the press as the great Palladium of the Constitution; but at the same time, I hold the licentiousness of the press in the greatest abhorrence. Nobody is more conscious than I am of the splendid abilities of the honourable mover, but I tell him at once, his scheme is too good to be practicable. It savours of Utopia. It looks well in theory, but it won't do in practice. It will not do, I repeat, Sir, in practice; and so the advocates of the measure will find, if, unfortunately, it should find its way through Parliament. (*Cheers.*) The source of that corruption to which the honourable member alludes, is in the minds of the people; so rank and extensive is that corruption, that no political reform can have any effect in removing it. Instead of reforming others — instead of reforming the State, the Constitution, and every thing that is most excellent, let each man reform himself! let him look at home, he will find there enough to do, without looking abroad, and aiming at what is out of his power. (*Loud cheers.*) And now, Sir, as it is frequently the custom in this House to end with a quotation, and as the gentleman who preceded me in the debate has anticipated me in my favourite quotation of the 'Strong pull and the long pull,' I shall end with the memorable words of the assembled Barons — *Nolumus leges Angliæ mutari.*" — [*E. R.* 1825.]

THE RULE OF PUBLIC CONDUCT.

THERE is only one principle of public conduct — *Do what you think right, and take place and power as an accident.* Upon any other plan, office is shabbiness, labour, and sorrow. — [*Taunton Speech*, 1832.]

ROTTEN BOROUGHS.

THERE happens, gentlemen, to live near my parsonage a labouring man, of very superior character and understanding to his fellow-labourers ; and who has made such good use of that superiority, that he has saved what is (for his station in life) a very considerable sum of money, and if his existence be extended to the common period, he will die rich. It happens, however, that he is (and long has been) troubled with violent stomachic pains, for which he has hitherto obtained no relief, and which really are the bane and torment of his life. Now, if my excellent labourer were to send for a physician, and to consult him respecting this malady, would it not be very singular language if our doctor were to say to him, " My good friend, you surely will not be so rash as to attempt to get rid of these pains in your stomach. Have you not grown rich with these pains in your stomach ? have you not risen under them from poverty to prosperity ? has not your situation, since you were first attacked, been improving every year ? You surely will not be so foolish and so indiscreet as to part with the pains in your stomach ? " — Why, what would be the answer of the rustic to this nonsensical monition ? " Monster of Rhubarb ! (he would say) I am not rich in consequence of the pains in my stomach, but in spite of the pains in my stomach ; and I should have been ten times richer, and fifty times happier, if I had never had any pains in my stomach at all." Gentlemen, these rotten boroughs are your pains in the stomach — and you would have been a much richer and greater people if you had never had them at all. Your wealth and your power have been owing, not to the debased and corrupted parts of the House of Commons, but to the many independent and honourable Members, whom it has always contained within its walls. If there had been a few more of these very valuable members for close boroughs, we should, I verily believe, have been by this time about as free as Denmark, Sweden, or the Germanised States of Italy. — [*Taunton Speech*, 1832.]

LET THEM ALONE.

ALL would be well, it is urged, if they would but let the people alone. But what chance is there, I demand of these wise politicians, that the people will ever be let alone; that the orator will lay down his craft, and the demagogue forget his cunning? If many things were let alone, which never will be let alone, the aspect of human affairs would be a little varied. If the winds would let the waves alone there would be no storms. If gentlemen would let ladies alone, there would be no unhappy marriages, and deserted damsels. If persons who can reason no better than this, would leave speaking alone, the school of eloquence might be improved. I have little hopes, however, of witnessing any of these acts of forbearance, particularly the last, and so we must (however foolish it may appear) proceed to make laws for a people who we are sure will not be let alone. — [*Taunton Speech*, 1832.*]

THE NATIVE SOIL OF ELOQUENCE.

I HAVE always found that all things, moral or physical, grow in the soil best suited for them. Show me a deep and tenacious earth — and I am sure the oak will spring up in it. In a low and damp soil I am equally certain of the alder and the willow. Gentlemen, the free Parliament of a free People is the native soil of eloquence — and in that soil will it ever flourish and abound — there it will produce those intellectual effects which drive before them whole tribes and nations of the human race, and settle the destinies of man.—[*Taunton Speech,* 1832.]

POPULAR MISTAKES.

THE people are sometimes, it is urged, grossly mistaken; but are Kings never mistaken? Are the higher orders never mistaken?—never wilfully corrupted by their own interests? The people have at least this superiority, that they always intend to do what is right.—[*Taunton Speech,* 1832.]

PROTECTION TO HIGHWAYMEN.

WHEN I was a young ·man, the place in England I remember as most notorious for highwaymen and their exploits was Finchley Common, near the metropolis; but Finchley Common, gentlemen, in the progress of improvement, came to be enclosed, and the highwaymen lost by these means the opportunity of exercising their gallant vocation. I remember a friend of mine proposed to draw up for them a petition to the House of Commons for compensation, which ran in this manner—" We, your loyal highwaymen of Finchley Common and its neighbourhood, having, at a great expense, laid in a stock of blunderbusses, pistols, and other instruments for plundering the public, and finding ourselves impeded in the exercise of our calling by the said enclosure of the said Common of Finchley, humbly petition your Honourable House will be pleased to assign to us such compensation as your Honourable House in its wisdom and justice may think fit."—Gentlemen, I must leave the application to you.—[*Taunton Speech*, 1832.]

MRS. PARTINGTON.

I DO not mean to be disrespectful, but the attempt of the Lords to stop the progress of reform, reminds me very forcibly of the great storm of Sidmouth, and of the conduct of the excellent Mrs. Partington on that occasion. In the winter of 1824, there set in a great flood upon that town—the tide rose to an incredible height—the waves rushed in upon the houses, and every thing was threatened with destruction! In the midst of this sublime and terrible storm, Dame Partington who lived upon the beach, was seen at the door of her house with mop and pattens, trundling her mop, squeezing out the sea-water, and vigorously pushing away the Atlantic Ocean. The Atlantic was roused. Mrs. Partington's spirit was up; but I need not tell you that the contest was unequal. The Atlantic Ocean beat Mrs. Partington. She was excellent at a slop, or a puddle, but she should not have meddled with a tempest. Gentlemen, be at your ease— be quiet and steady. You will beat Mrs. Partington.— [*Taunton Speech*, 1832.]

BOROUGH-MONGERING.

THE thing I cannot, and will not bear, is this;—what right has *this* Lord, or *that* Marquis, to buy ten seats in Parliament, in the shape of Boroughs, and then to make laws to govern me? And how are these masses of power re-distributed? The eldest son of my Lord is just come from Eton—he knows a good deal about Æneas and Dido, Apollo and Daphne—and that is all; and to this boy his father gives a six-hundredth part of the power of making laws, as he would give him a horse or a double-barrelled gun. Then Vellum, the steward, is put in—an admirable man;—he has raised the estates —watched the progress of the family Road, and Canal Bills—and Vellum shall help to rule over the people of Israel. A neighbouring country gentleman, Mr. Plumpkin, hunts with my Lord—opens him a gate or two, while the hounds are running—dines with my Lord— agrees with my Lord—wishes he could rival the South-Down sheep of my Lord—and upon Plumpkin is conferred a portion of the government. Then there is a distant relation of the same name, in the County Militia, with white teeth, who calls up the carriage at the opera, and is always wishing O'Connell was hanged, drawn, and quartered—then a barrister, who has written an article in the Quarterly, and is very likely to speak, and refute M'Culloch; and these five people, in whose nomination I have no more agency than I have in the nomination of the toll-keepers of the Bosphorus, are to make laws for me and my family—to put their hands in my purse, and to sway the future destinies of this country; and when the neighbours step in, and beg permission to say a few words before these persons are chosen, there is an universal cry of ruin, confusion, and destruction;—we have become a great people under Vellum and Plumpkin —under Vellum and Plumpkin our ships have covered the ocean—under Vellum and Plumpkin our armies have secured the strength of the hills—to turn out Vellum and

Plumpkin is not Reform, but Revolution.—[*Taunton Speech*, 1832.]

LORD BROUGHAM AND LORD GREY.

THEN look at the gigantic Brougham, sworn in at twelve o'clock, and before six, has a bill on the table, abolishing the abuses of a Court which has been the curse of the people of England for centuries. For twenty-five long years did Lord Eldon sit in that Court, surrounded with misery and sorrow, which he never held up a finger to alleviate. The widow and the orphan cried to him, as vainly as the town crier cries when he offers a small reward for a full purse; the bankrupt of the Court became the lunatic of the Court; estates mouldered away, and mansions fell down; but the fees came in, and all was well. But in an instant the iron mace of Brougham shivered to atoms this house of fraud and of delay; and this is the man who will help to govern you; who bottoms his reputation on doing good to you; who knows, that to reform abuses is the safest basis of fame, and the surest instrument of power; who uses the highest gifts of reason, and the most splendid efforts of genius, to rectify those abuses, which all the genius and talent of the profession have hitherto been employed to justify, and to protect. Look to Brougham, and turn you to that side where he waves his long and lean finger; and mark well that face which nature has marked so forcibly — which dissolves pensions — turns jobbers into honest men — scares away the plunderer of the public—and is a terror to him who doeth evil to the people. But, above all, look to the Northern Earl, victim, before this honest and manly reign, of the spite-fulness of the Court. You may now, for the first time, learn to trust in the professions of a Minister; you are directed by a man who prefers character to place, and who has given such unequivocal proofs of honesty and patriotism, that his image ought to be amongst your household gods, and his name to be lisped by your children: two thousand years hence it will be a legend like the fable of Perseus and Andromeda: Britannia chained to a mountain — two hundred rotten animals menacing her destruction, till a tall Earl, armed with Schedule A., and followed by his page Russell, drives them into the deep, and delivers over Britannia in safety to crowds of ten-pound renters, who deafen the air with their acclamations. Forthwith, Latin verses upon this — school exercises — boys whipt, and all the usual absurdities of education. Don't part with the Administration composed of Lord Grey and Lord Brougham; and not only these, but look at them all — the mild wisdom of Lansdowne — the genius and extensive knowledge of Holland, in whose bold and honest life there is no varying nor shadow of change—the unexpected and exemplary activity of Lord Melbourne — and the rising parliamentary talents of Stanley. You are ignorant of your best interests, if every vote you can bestow is not given to such a ministry as this. — [*Taunton Speech*, 1832.]

A DOSE IN TIME.

ALL former political changes, proposed by these very men, it is said, were mild and gentle, compared to this: true, but are you on Saturday night to seize your apothecary by the throat, and to say to him, "Subtle compounder, fraudulent posologist, did not you order me a drachm of this medicine on Monday morning, and now you declare that nothing short of an ounce can do me

any good ?"   "True enough," would he of the phials
reply, "*but you did not take the drachm on Monday
morning* — that makes all the difference, my dear Sir;
if you had done as I advised you at first, the small
quantity of medicine would have sufficed; and, instead
of being in a night-gown and slippers up stairs, you
would have been walking vigorously in Piccadilly. Do
as you please — and die if you please; but don't blame
me because you despised my advice, and by your own
ignorance and obstinacy have entailed upon yourself
tenfold rhubarb and unlimited infusion of senna." —
[*Taunton Speech*, 1832.]

THE REFORMED HOUSE OF COMMONS.

THE majority of the new Members will be landed
gentlemen: their genus is utterly distinct from the
revolutionary tribe; they have Molar teeth; they are
destitute of the carnivorous and incisive jaws of political
adventurers.

There will be mistakes at first, as there are in all
changes. All young ladies will imagine (as soon as this
Bill is carried) that they will be instantly married.
Schoolboys believe that Gerunds and Supines will be
abolished, and that Currant Tarts must ultimately come
down in price; the Corporal and Sergeant are sure of
double pay; bad Poets will expect a demand for their
Epics; Fools will be disappointed, as they always are;
reasonable men, who know what to expect, will find that
a very serious good has been obtained.—[*Taunton
Speech*, 1832.]

RESULTS OF REFORM.

IF peace, economy, and justice, are the results of
Reform, a number of small benefits, or rather of benefits

which appear small to us, but not to them, will accrue to millions of the people; and the connection between the existence of John Russell, and the reduced price of bread and cheese, will be as clear as it has been the object of his honest, wise, and useful life to make it. — [*Taunton Speech*, 1832.]

THIRST FOR REFORM.

OF what use have all the cruel laws been of Perceval, Eldon, and Castlereagh, to extinguish Reform? Lord John Russell, and his abettors, would have been committed to gaol twenty years ago for half only of his present Reform; and now relays of the people would drag them from London to Edinburgh; at which latter city we are told, by Mr. Dundas, that there is no eagerness for Reform. Five minutes before Moses struck the rock, this gentleman would have said that there was no eagerness for water. — [*Taunton Speech*, 1832.]

CATCH A KING.

IT is not enough that a political institution works well practically; it must be defensible; it must be such as will bear discussion, and not excite ridicule and contempt. It might work well for ought I know, if, like the savages of Onelashka, we sent out to catch a king: but who could defend a coronation by chase? — [*Taunton Speech*, 1832.]

THE BALLOT BOX.

IT is possible, and perhaps not very difficult, to invent a machine, by the aid of which electors may vote for a candidate, or for two or three candidates, out of a greater

number, without its being discovered for whom they vote;
it is less easy than the rabid and foaming Radical sup-
poses; but I have no doubt that it may be accomplished.
In Mr. Grote's dagger ballot box, which has been carried
round the country by eminent patriots, you stab the card
of your favourite candidate with a dagger.   I have seen
another, called a mouse-trap ballot box, in which you
poke your finger into the trap of the member you prefer,
and are caught and detained till the trap-clerk below
(who knows by means of a wire when you are caught)
marks your vote, pulls the liberator, and releases you.
Which may be the most eligible of these two methods
I do not pretend to determine, nor do I think my excellent friend Mr. Babbage has as yet made up his
mind on the subject; but, by some means or another, I
have no doubt the thing may be done. — [*Letter on the
Ballot.*]

ODIUM OF UNDUE INFLUENCE.

I DISTINCTLY admit that every man has a right to do
what he pleases with his own.   I cannot, by law, prevent
any one from discharging his tenants, and changing his
tradesmen, for political reasons;   but I may judge
whether that man exercises his right to the public detriment, or for the public advantage.   A man has a right
to refuse dealing with any tradesman who is not five feet
eleven inches high; but if he act upon this rule, he is
either a madman or a fool.   He has a right to lay waste
his own estate, and to make it utterly barren; but I have
also a right to point him out as one who exercises his
right in a manner very injurious to society.   He may set
up a religious or a political test for his tradesmen; but
admitting his right, and deprecating all interference with

law, I must tell him he is making the aristocracy odious to the great mass, and that he is sowing the seeds of revolution. His purse may be full, and his fields may be wide; but the moralist will still hold the rod of public opinion over his head, and tell the money-bloated blockhead that he is shaking those laws of property which it has taken ages to extort from the wretchedness and rapacity of mankind; and that what he calls his own will not long be his own, if he tramples too heavily on human patience. — [*Letter on the Ballot.*]

THE PLOUGH AND THE LOOM.

THE plough is not a political machine : the loom and the steam-engine are furiously political, but the plough is not. — [*Letter on the Ballot.*]

INTIMIDATION BY MOBS.

Is intimidation confined to the aristocracy? Can anything be more scandalous and atrocious than the intimidation of mobs? Did not the mob of Bristol occasion more ruin, wretchedness, death, and alarm than all the ejection of tenants, and combinations against shopkeepers, from the beginning of the century? and did not the Scotch philosophers tear off the clothes of the Tories in Mintoshire? or at least such clothes as the customs of the country admit of being worn? — and did not they, without any reflection at all upon the customs of the country, wash the Tory voters in the river? — [*Letter on the Ballot.*]

RULE OF THE MANY BY THE DEFECTS OF THE FEW.

IT is really a curious condition that all men must imitate the defects of a few, in order that it may not be known who have the natural imperfection, and who put it on from conformity. In this way in former days, to hide the grey hairs of the old, every body was forced to wear powder pomatum. — [*Letter on the Ballot.*]

THE TIMES OF LOG.

THERE is no end to these eternal changes; we have made an enormous revolution within the last ten years — let us stop a little and secure it, and prevent it from being turned into ruin; I do not say the Reform Bill is final, but I want a little time for breathing; and if there are to be any more changes, let them be carried into execution hereafter by those little legislators who are now receiving every day after dinner a cake or a plum, in happy ignorance of Mr. Grote and his ballot. I long for the quiet times of *Log* when all the English common people are making calico, and all the English gentlemen are making long and short verses, with no other interruption of their happiness than when false quantities are discovered in one or the other. — [*Letter on the Ballot.*]

SYSTEMATIC DISSIMULATION.

THE single lie on the hustings would not suffice; the concealed democrat who voted against his landlord must talk with the wrong people, subscribe to the wrong club, huzza at the wrong dinner, break the wrong head, lead (if he wish to escape from the watchful jealousy of his landlord) a long life of lies between every election; and he must do this, not only *eundo* in his calm and prudential state, but *redeundo* from the market, warmed with beer, and expanded by alcohol; and he must not only carry on his seven years of dissimulation before the

world, but in the very bosom of his family, or he must
expose himself to the dangerous garrulity of wife,
children, and servants, from whose indiscretion every kind
of evil report would be carried to the ears of the watchful
steward.— [*Letter on the Ballot.*]

A BALLOT MOB.

THE noise and jollity of a ballot mob must be such as
the very devils would look on with delight. A set of
deceitful wretches wearing the wrong colours, abusing
their friends, pelting the man for whom they voted,
drinking their enemies' punch, knocking down persons
with whom they entirely agreed, and roaring out eternal
duration to principles they abhorred. A scene of wholesale bacchanalian fraud, a *posse comitatus* of liars, which
would disgust any man with a free government, and
make him sigh for the monocracy of Constantinople.—
[*Letter on the Ballot.*]

INTIMIDATION BY THE MULTITUDE.

A STATE of things may (to be sure) occur where the
aristocratic part of the voters may be desirous, by con-
cealing their votes, of protecting themselves from the
fury of the multitude; but precisely the same objection
obtains against ballot, whoever may be the oppressor or
the oppressed. · It is no defence; the single falsehood
at the hustings will not suffice. Hypocrisy for seven
years is impossible: the multitude will be just as jealous
of preserving the power of intimidation, as aristocrats are
of preserving the power of property, and will in the same
way redouble their vicious activity from the attempt at
destroying their empire by ballot. — [*Letter on the
Ballot.*]

EFFECTS OF BALLOT.

OLD John Randolph, the American orator, was asked one day at a dinner party in London, whether the ballot prevailed in his state of Virginia—"I scarcely believe," he said, "we have such a fool in all Virginia, as to mention even the vote by ballot; and I do not hesitate to say that the adoption of the ballot *would make any nation a nation of scoundrels if it did not find them so.*" John Randolph was right; he felt that it was not necessary that a people should be false in order to be free; universal hypocrisy would be the consequence of ballot: we should soon say on deliberation what David only asserted in his haste, *that all men were liars.* — [*Letter on the Ballot.*]

A BALLOTO-GROTICAL FAMILY.

I HAVE often drawn a picture in my own mind of a Balloto-Grotical family voting and promising under the new system. There is one vacancy, and three candidates, Tory, Whig, and Radical. Walter Wiggins, a small artificer of shoes, for the moderate gratuity of five pounds, promises his own vote, and that of the chaste Arabella his wife, to the Tory candidate; he, Walter Wiggins, having also sold, for one sovereign, the vote of the before-named Arabella to the Whigs. Mr. John Wiggins, a tailor, the male progeny of Walter and Arabella, at the solicitation of his master, promises his vote to the Whigs, and persuades his sister Honoria to make a similar promise in the same cause. Arabella, the wife, yields implicitly to the wishes of her husband. In this way, before the election, stand committed the highly moral family of Mr. Wiggins. The period for lying arrives, and the mendacity machine is exhibited to the view of the Wigginses. What happens? Arabella, who has in the interim been chastised by her drunken husband, votes secretly for the Radicals, having been sold both to Whig and Tory. Mr. John Wiggins, pledged beyond redemption to Whigs, votes for the Tory; and Honoria, extrinsically furious in the cause of Whigs, is persuaded by her lover to vote for the Radical member. The following table exhibits the state of this moral family, before and after the election :

Walter Wiggins sells himself once and his wife twice.
Arabella Wiggins, sold to Tory and Whig, votes for Radical.
John Wiggins, promised to Whig, votes for Tory.
Honoria Wiggins, promised to Whig, votes for Radical.

— [*Letter on the Ballot.*]

BALLOT AN ILLUSION.

BALLOT is a mere illusion, but universal suffrage is not an illusion. The common people will get nothing by the one, but they will gain every thing, and *ruin* every thing, by the last.—[*Letter on the Ballot.*]

STRONG BOX *v.* BALLOT BOX.

BUT it is madness to make laws of society which attempt to shake off the great laws of nature. As long as men love bread, and mutton, and broad cloth, wealth, in a long series of years, must have enormous effects upon human affairs, and the strong box will beat the ballot box. — [*Letter on the Ballot.*]

PATH AND NO PATH.*

To say there is no path, because we have often got into the wrong path, puts an end to all other knowledge as well as to this.

ERROR MINGLED WITH TRUTH.

ERRORS, to be dangerous, must have a great deal of truth mingled with them; it is only from this alliance that they can ever obtain an extensive circulation: from pure extravagance, and genuine, unmingled false-hood, the world never has, and never can sustain any mis-chief.

THE GREAT STREAM OF NATURE.

IF you will build an error upon some foundation of truth, you may effect your object; you may divert a little rivulet from the great stream of nature, and train it cau-tiously, and obliquely, away; but if you place yourself in the very depth of her almighty channel, and combat with her eternal streams, you will be swept off without ruffling the smoothness, or impeding the vigour, of her course.

NO REAL RESULTS OF SCEPTICISM.

BISHOP BERKELEY destroyed this world in one volume octavo; and nothing remained after his time, but mind; which experienced a similar fate from the hand of Mr. Hume in 1737: — so that, with all the tendency to de-

---

* This and the following passages are from the Lectures on "Moral Philosophy," delivered by Mr. Sydney Smith at the Royal Institution in 1804, 1805, and 1806.

stroy, there remains nothing left for destruction: but I would fain ask if there be any one human being, from the days of Protagoras the Abdērite to this present hour, who was ever for a single instant a convert to these subtle and ingenious follies? Is there any one out of Bedlam who *doubts* of the existence of matter? who doubts of his own personal identity? or of his consciousness? or of the general credibility of memory? Men *talk* on such subjects from ostentation, or because such wire-drawn speculations are an agreeable exercise to them; but they are perpetually recalled by the necessary business and the inevitable feelings of life to sound and sober opinions on these subjects.

THE MORAL EVIDENCE OF A CREATOR.

THE school of natural religion is the contemplation of nature; the ancient anatomist who was an atheist, was converted by the study of the human body: he thought it impossible that so many admirable contrivances should exist, without an intelligent cause;—and if men can become religious from looking at an entrail, or a nerve, can they be taught atheism from analysing the structure of the human mind? Are not the affections and passions which shake the very entrails of man, and the thoughts and feelings which dart along those nerves, more indicative of a God than the vile perishing instruments themselves? Can you remember the nourishment which springs up in the breast of a mother, and forget the *feelings which spring up in her heart?* If God made the blood of man, did he not make that *feeling,* which summons the blood to his face, and makes it the sign of guilt and of shame? You may show me a human hand, expatiate upon the singular contrivance of its sinews, and bones; how admirable, how useful, for all the purposes of grasp, and flexure: *I* will show you, in return, the mind, receiving her tribute from the senses;—*comparing, reflecting, compounding, dividing, abstracting;*—the passions *soothing, aspiring, exciting,* till the whole *world* falls under the dominion of *man;* evincing that in his mind the Creator has reared up the noblest emblem of his wisdom, and his power. The philosophy of the human mind is *no* school for infidelity, but it excites the warmest feelings of piety, and defends them with the soundest reason.

NO GENERAL DISCOVERIES IN MORAL PHILOSOPHY.

SOME very considerable men are accustomed to hold very strong and sanguine language respecting the important discoveries which are to be made in Moral Philosophy, from a close attention to facts; and by that method of induction which has been so invaluably employed in Natural Philosophy: but then this appears to be the difference;—that Natural Philosophy is directed to subjects with which we are little or imperfectly acquainted; Moral Philosophy investigates faculties we have always exercised, and passions we have always felt. Chemistry, for instance, is perpetually bringing to light fresh existences; four or five new metals have been discovered within as many years, of the existence of which no human being could have had any suspicion, but no man, that I know of, pretends to discover four or five new passions, neither can anything very new be discovered of those passions and faculties with which mankind are already familiar. We are, in natural philosophy, perpetually making discoveries of new properties in bodies, with whose existence we have been acquainted for

centuries: Sir James Hall has just discovered that lime
can be melted by carbonic acid;—but who hopes that he
can discover any new flux for avarice? or any improved
method of judging, and comparing? We have had no
occasion to busy ourselves with the chromian or Titanian
metal; but we have commonly employed our minds for
twenty or thirty years, before we begin to speculate upon
them.

THE TRUE RANGE OF DISCOVERY.

I HAVE said that no practical discoveries can be made
in Moral Philosophy, because I think the word *discovery*
implies so much originality, and novelty, that I can
hardly suppose they will be met with in a subject with
which mankind are so familiar. But then opinions may
be discoveries to the individual, which are not discoveries
to the world at large.

THE SCOPE OF MORAL PHILOSOPHY.

MORAL Philosophy teaches, for the conduct of the
understanding, a variety of delicate rules which can result
only from such sort of meditation; and it gradually
subjects the most impetuous feelings to patient examination and wise control: it inures the youthful mind to
intellectual difficulty, and to enterprise in thinking; and
makes it as keen as an eagle, and as unwearied as the
wing of an angel. In looking round the region of spirit,
from the mind of the brute and the reptile, to the
sublimest exertions of the human understanding, this
philosophy lays deep the foundations of a fervent and
grateful piety, for those intellectual riches which have
been dealt out to us with no scanty measure. With
sensation alone, we might have possessed the earth, as it

is possessed by the lowest order of beings: but we have talents which bend *all* the laws of nature to our service; memory for the past, providence for the future,—senses which mingle pleasure with intelligence, the surprise of novelty, the boundless energy of imagination, accuracy in comparing, and severity in judging; an original affection, which binds us together in society; a swiftness to pity; a fear of shame; a love of esteem; a detestation of all that is cruel, mean, and unjust. All these things Moral Philosophy observes, and, observing, adores the Being from whence they proceed.

PHILOSOPHY OF SOCRATES.

THE morality of Socrates was reared upon the basis of religion. The principles of virtuous conduct which are common to all mankind, are, according to this wise and good man, laws of God; and the argument by which he supports this opinion is, that no man departs from these principles with impunity. "It is frequently possible," says he, "for men to screen themselves from the penalty of human laws, but no man can be unjust or ungrateful without suffering for his crime — hence I conclude that these laws must have proceeded from a more excellent legislator than man." Socrates taught that true felicity is not to be derived from external possessions, but from wisdom; which consists in the knowledge and practice of virtue; — that the cultivation of virtuous manners is necessarily attended with pleasure as well as profit; — that the honest man alone is happy; and that it is absurd to attempt to separate things which are in their nature so united as virtue and interest.

Socrates was, in truth, not very fond of subtle and re-fined speculations; and upon the intellectual part of our

nature, little or nothing of his opinions is recorded. If
we may infer anything from the clearness and simplicity
of his opinions on moral subjects, and from the bent
which his genius had received from the useful and the
practical, he would certainly have laid a strong foundation for rational metaphysics. The slight sketch I have
given of his moral doctrines contains nothing very new
or very brilliant, but comprehends those moral doctrines
which every person of education has been accustomed to
hear from his childhood; — but two thousand years ago
they were great discoveries, — two thousand years since,
common sense was not invented. If Orpheus, or Linus,
or any of those melodious moralists, sung, in bad verses,
such advice as a grandmamma would now give to a child
of six years old, he was thought to be inspired by the gods,
and statues and altars were erected to his memory. In
Hesiod there is a very grave exhortation to mankind to
wash their faces: and I have discovered a very strong
analogy between the precepts of Pythagoras and Mrs.
Trimmer; — both think that a son ought to obey his
father, and both are clear that a good man is better than
a bad one. Therefore, to measure aright this extraordinary man, we must remember the period at which he lived;
that he was the first who called the attention of mankind
from the pernicious subtleties which engaged and per-
plexed their wandering understandings to the practical
rules of life; — he was the great father and inventor of
common sense, as Ceres was of the plough, and Bacchus
of intoxication. First he taught his contemporaries that
they did not know what they pretended to know; then
he showed them that they knew nothing; then he told
them what they ought to know. Lastly, to sum up the
praise of Socrates, remember that two thousand years ago,
while men were worshipping the stones on which they

trod, and the insects which crawled beneath their feet;
— two thousand years ago, with the bowl of poison in his
hand, Socrates said, "I am persuaded that my death,
which is now just coming, will conduct me into the presence of the gods, who are the most righteous governors,
and into the society of just and good men; and I derive
confidence from the hope that something of man remains
after death, and that the condition of good men will then
be much better than that of the bad." Soon after this he
covered himself up with his cloak and expired.

PLATO.

Of all the disciples of Socrates, Plato, though he calls
himself the least, was certainly the most celebrated. As
long as philosophy continued to be studied among the
Greeks and Romans, his doctrines were taught and
his name revered. Even to the present day his writings
give a tinge to the language and speculations of philosophy and theology. Of the majestic beauty of Plato's
style, it is almost impossible to convey an adequate idea.
He keeps the understanding up to a high pitch of enthusiasm longer than any existing writer; and, in reading
Plato, zeal and animation seem rather to be the regular
feelings than the casual effervescence of the mind.
He appears almost disdaining the mutability and imperfection of the earth on which he treads, to be drawing
down fire from heaven, and to be seeking among the
gods above, for the permanent, the beautiful, and the
grand !

ARISTOTLE.

Whoever is fond of the biographical art, as a reposi-
tory of the actions and the fortunes of great men, may

enjoy an agreeable specimen of its certainty in the life of Aristotle. Some writers say he was a Jew, others, that he got all his information from a Jew; that he kept an apothecary's shop, and was an atheist; others say, on the contrary, that he did not keep an apothecary's shop, and that he was a Trinitarian. Some say he respected the religion of his country; others that he offered sacrifices to his wife, and made hymns in favour of his father-in-law. Some are of opinion he was poisoned by the priests; others are clear that he died of vexation, because he could not discover the causes of the ebb and flow in the Euripus. We now care or know so little about Aristotle, that Mr. Fielding, in one of his novels, says, " Aristotle is not such a fool as many people believe, who never read a syllable of his works."

Before the Reformation, his morals used to be read to the people in some of the churches of Germany, instead of the Scriptures; his philosophy had an exclusive monopoly granted to it by the Parliament at Paris, who forbad the use of any other in France; and the President De Thou informs us, that Paul de Foix, one of the most learned and elegant men of his time, in passing through Ferrara, refused to see the famous Patricius, or to meet him at any third house, because he disbelieved in some of the doctrines of Aristotle. Certainly the two human beings who have had the greatest influence upon the understandings of mankind have been Aristotle and Lord Bacon. To Lord Bacon we are indebted for an almost daily extension of our knowledge of the laws of nature in the outward world; and the same modest and cautious spirit of inquiry extended to Moral Philosophy, will probably at last give us clear, intelligible ideas of our spiritual nature. Every succeeding year is an additional confirmation to us that we are travelling in the true path of knowledge; and as it brings in fresh tributes of science for the increase of human happiness, it extorts from us fresh tributes of praise to the guide and father of true philosophy. To the understanding of Aristotle, equally vast, perhaps, and equally original, we are indebted for fifteen hundred years of quibbling and ignorance; in which the earth fell under the tyranny of words, and philosophers quarrelled with one another, like drunken men in dark rooms who hate peace without knowing why they fight, or seeing how to take aim. Professors were multiplied without the world becoming wiser; and volumes of Aristotelian philosophy were written which, if piled one upon another, would have equalled the Tower of Babel in height, and far exceeded it in confusion. Such are the obligations we owe to the mighty Stagirite; for that he *was* of very mighty understanding, the broad circumference and the deep root of his philosophy most lamentably evince.

THE FRIENDSHIP OF PHILOSOPHERS.

THE friendship of the Epicurean sect is described by Cicero, in his treatise "De Finibus," as unexampled in the history of human attachments; and Valerius Maximus relates a memorable example of friendship between Polycrates and Hippoclides, two disciples of this sect. It is impossible, however, to receive these accounts without some sort of mistrust. A set of graminivorous metaphysicians living together in a garden, and employing their whole time in acts of benevolence towards each other, carries with it such an air of romance, that I am afraid it must be considerably lowered, and rendered more tasteless, before it can be brought down to the standard of credibility and the probabilities of real life.

At least we may be tolerably sure, that if half a dozen metaphysicians, such as metaphysicians are in these modern days, were to live in a garden in Battersea or Kew, that their friendship would not be of very long duration; and their learned labours would probably be interrupted by the same reasons which prevented Reaumur's spiders from spinning, — they fabricated a very beautiful and subtle thread, but, unfortunately, they were so extremely fond of fighting, that it was impossible to keep them together in the same place.

THE PRINCIPLE OF PITY.

I LEARN what pain is in *another man* by knowing what it is in *myself;* but I might know this without feeling the pity. I might have been so constituted as to rejoice that another man was in agony; how can you prove that my own aversion to pain must necessarily make me feel for the pain of another? I have a great horror of breaking my own leg, and I will avoid it by all means in my power; but it does not *necessarily* follow from thence that I should be struck with horror because you have broken yours. The reason why we *do* feel horror, is, that nature has superadded to these two principles of Epicurus the principle of pity ; which, unless it can be shown by stronger arguments to be derived from any other feeling, must stand as an ultimate fact in our nature.

PERSONAL IDENTITY.

ALL that sceptics have said of the outer and the inner world may, with equal justice, be applied to every other radical truth. Who can prove his own personal identity? A man may think himself a clergyman, and believe he has preached for these ten years last past; but I defy him to offer any sort of *proof* that he has not been a fish-monger all the time.

RELATION IF NOT REALITY.

The sceptics may call the philosophy of the human mind merely hypothetical; but if it be so, all other knowledge must of course be hypothetical also; and if it be so, and all is erroneous, it will do quite as well as reality, if we keep up a certain proportion in our errors: for there *may* be no such things as lunar tables, no sea, and no ships; but, by falling into one of these errors after the other, we avoid shipwreck, or, what is the same thing, as it gives the same pain, the idea of shipwreck. So with the philosophy of the human mind; I may have no memory, and no imagination,—they may be mistakes; but if I cultivate them both I derive honour and respect from my fellow-creatures, which may be mistakes also; but they harmonise so well together, that they are quite as good as realities. The only evil of error is, that they are never supported by consequences; if they were, they would be as good as realities.

SIR JAMES MACKINTOSH AND DUGALD STEWART.

May I be allowed to introduce the names of two gentlemen now living, — to one of whom the world may fairly look for no common improvement of this science, and from the other of whom it has already received it: I mean Sir James Mackintosh and Mr. Dugald Stewart. In my expectations from the first of these gentlemen, those will not think I am too sanguine who have witnessed the circumference, the order, and the connection of his knowledge, his zeal in prosecuting it,

his perspicuity in detailing it, and that extraordinary mixture of enterprise and judgment which makes him as new
and original as he is judicious and safe. Of the latter gentleman, if I am not misled by the suavity of his manners,
the spotless integrity of his life, and the marvellous effects
of that eloquence to which many others here can bear
witness as well as myself,—if all these circumstances do
not mislead me, I think I may say that never any man
has taken up the science of the human mind with such
striking and comprehensive views of man's nature. You
begin with thinking you are taking up a curious, yet
barren, speculation ; and you find it, under the masterly
hand of this writer, gradually unfolding itself into a wide
survey of passions, motives, and faculties, made in chaste
language, watched over with correct taste, and adorned
with beautiful illustrations. He is ever drawing from
those discussions which, in the hands of common men,
are mere scholastic subtleties, principles useful in the
conduct of life, and valuable for the improvement of the
understanding. He is the *first* writer who ever carried a
feeling heart and a creative fancy into the depth of these
abstract sciences, without rendering them a mass of declamatory confusion. He has not rendered his metaphysics dry and disgusting, like Reid ; he has not involved
them in lofty obscurity, like Plato ; nor has he poisoned
them with impiety, like Hume. Above all, he has
that invaluable talent of inspiring the young with the
love of knowledge, the love of virtue, and that feeling of
modest independence which has ever been the ornament
of his conduct. I have been his pupil, and have received
kindness at his hands. Perhaps I am over-rating his
merit ; but I am truly sincere when I say, that I know
no reason why he is not ranked among the first writers
of the English language, except that he is still alive ;

and my most earnest and hearty wish is, that *that* cause
of his depreciation may operate for many, many years to
come!

ENGLISH PHILOSOPHERS.

I CANNOT conclude this lecture without remarking the
high destiny and splendid fortune of this country, in
giving to the world its great masters of philosophy.   We
will allow to other countries the most splendid efforts of
genius directed to this object; but they have passed
away, and are now no more than beautiful and stupendous errors.   We will give up to them the mastery
in all that class of men who can diffuse over bad and
unsocial principles, the charms of eloquence and wit;
but the great teachers of mankind, big with better hopes
than their own days could supply,—who have looked
backward to the errors, and forward to the progress of
mankind,—who have searched for knowledge only from
experience, and applied it only to the promotion of
human happiness,—who have disdained paradox and
impiety, and coveted no other fame than that which was
founded upon the modest investigation of truth,—such
men have sprung from this country, and have shed upon
it the everlasting lustre of their names.   Descartes has
perished, Leibnitz is fading away; but Bacon, and
Locke, and Newton remain, as the Danube and the Alps
remain:—the learned examine them, and the ignorant,
who forget lesser streams and humbler hills, remember
them as the glories and prominences of the world.   And
let us never, in thinking of perpetuity and duration,
confine that notion to the physical works of nature, and
forget the eternity of fame!   God has shown his power
in the stars and the firmament, in the aged hills and in

the perpetual streams; but he has shown it as much, in the minds of the greatest of human beings! Homer and Virgil and Milton, and Locke and Bacon and Newton, are as great as the hills and the streams; and will endure till heaven and earth shall pass away, and the whole fabric of nature is shaken into dissolution and eternal ashes.

THE ENGLISH CHARACTER.

I HAVE a boundless confidence in the English character; I believe that they have more real religion, more probity, more knowledge, and more genuine worth, than exists in the whole world besides. They are the guardians of pure Christianity; and from this prostituted nation of merchants (as they are in derision called) I believe more heroes will spring up in the hour of danger than all the military nations of ancient and modern Europe have ever produced.

A DEFENCE OF DULLNESS.

I PROMISED, in the beginning of these lectures, to be very dull and unamusing; and I am of opinion that I have hitherto acted up to the spirit of my contract; but if there should perchance exist in any man's mind the slightest suspicion of my good faith, I think this day's lecture will entirely remove that suspicion, and that I shall turn out to be a man of unsullied veracity!

A list of great and splendid names, such as I gave in my last lecture, of itself was *some* obstacle to the completion of my promise. I have no doubt, however, but that I overcame that obstacle with sufficient success; and, of course, that, aided as I am by the subject to-day, it will be still more perfect, and my fortune more complete.

It is some encouragement to me, however, in the execution of my plan, to perceive the extreme patience with
which subjects are listened to, upon other occasions,
which in their nature are not capable of eloquence, and
in which all ornament would be impertinent and misplaced.   I think I have observed, that the ornaments
called for here are established facts and fair reasonings;
and that the object for which both sexes pass an hour in
this place is, to hear the investigation of some important
subject, made with some care, and conducted without
any pretence.   Without offering, therefore, any other
apology in future, for the dryness and barrenness of the
subject, but trusting to the candour and good sense of
those who hear me, I shall at once proceed upon my
subject.

LIFE OF SOCIETY.

NOTHING can be plainer than that a life of society is
unfavourable to all the animal powers of man.

CIVILISED AND SAVAGE MAN.

A CHOCTAW could run from here to Oxford without
stopping: I go in the mail coach; and the time that the
savage has been employed in learning to run so far, I
have employed in something else.   It would not only be
useless in me to run like a Choctaw, but foolish and
disgraceful.

SIGHT.

THE author of the book of Ecclesiastes has told us
" that the light is sweet, that it is a pleasant thing for
the eyes to behold the sun."   The sense of sight is

indeed the highest bodily privilege, the purest physical
pleasure, which man has derived from his Creator. To
see that wandering fire, after he has finished his journey through the nations, coming back to his eastern
heavens, the mountains painted with light, the floating
splendour of the sea, the earth waking from deep slumber, the day flowing down the sides of the hills till it
reaches the secret valleys, the little insect recalled to life,
the bird trying her wings, man going forth to his labour,
—each created being moving, thinking, acting, contriv-
ing, according to the scheme and compass of its nature,
by force, by cunning, by reason, by necessity. Is it
possible to joy in this animated scene, and feel no pity
for the sons of darkness? for the eyes that will never
see light? for the poor clouded in everlasting gloom?
If you ask me why they are miserable and dejected, I
turn you to the plentiful valleys; to the fields now bringing forth their increase ; to the freshness and the flowers
of the earth; to the endless variety of its colours; to the
grace, the symmetry, the shape of all it cherishes and all
it bears ; these you have forgotten, because you have
always enjoyed them : but these are the means by which
God Almighty makes man what he is—cheerful, lively,
erect, full of enterprise, mutable, glancing from heaven
to earth, prone to labour and to act. Why was not the
earth left without form and void ? Why was not darkness suffered to remain on the face of the deep? Why
did God place lights in the firmament, for days, for
seasons, for signs, and for years? That He might make
man the happiest of creative beings; that He might
give to this His favourite creation a wider scope, a more
permanent duration, a richer diversity of joy. This is
the reason why the blind are miserable and dejected—
because their soul is mutilated, and dismembered of its

best sense — because they are a laughter and a ruin, and the boys of the streets mock at their stumbling feet. [*Memoir.*]

READING BY SCENT.

It seems, at first sight, very singular that a blind child should be taught to read; but observe what the common process is with every child; a child sees certain marks upon a plain piece of paper, which he is taught to call A, B, C; but if you were to raise certain marks in relief upon pasteboard, as you may of course do, and teach a blind child to call these marks which he felt A, B, C, a blind child would as easily learn his alphabet by his fingers as another would do by his eyes, and might go on feeling through Homer or Virgil as we do by persevering in looking at the book. Just in the same manner, I should not be surprised if the alphabet could be taught by a series of well-contrived flavours; and we may even live to see the day when men may be taught to smell out their learning, and when a fine scenting day shall be (which it certainly is not at present) considered as a day peculiarly favourable to study.

CONNECTION OF THE SENSES.

A curious question may be agitated as to the resemblance of the senses to each other. All the ideas of seeing bear a resemblance to each other, and all of hearing, and so forth; or do we only conceive them to resemble each other because they enter the mind by the same channel? Is there any more resemblance in the taste of vinegar and the taste of a peach, than there is between the taste of vinegar and the sound of an Æolian harp?

I am very much inclined to think there is not; and that the only reason of supposing a resemblance is, that they affect the same organ.   I believe there is a much greater analogy between those ideas of every sense which produce a similar tone of mind, whether of excitement, or soothing, or dislike, or horror, than there is between ideas of the same sense which stand in very different degrees of favour with the mind.   The resemblance seems to be much more intimate between soft sounds, fragrant smells, smooth surfaces, pleasant tastes, and refreshing colours, than between soft sounds and horrible crashes, smooth surfaces and lacerating inequalities, pleasant tastes and caustic bitterness, refreshing colour and sable gloom.

MADNESS.

A MADMAN has the conception of all the pageantry of a court, and so may any man in his senses; the difference is, the one knows it to be only a creation of his mind, the other really believes he sees dukes, and marquises, and all the splendour of a real court.   If he is not very far gone, he pays some attention to the objects of sense about him, and tells you that he is confined in this sorry situation by the perfidy and rebellion of his subjects.   As the disease further advances, he totally neglects the objects of his senses; — does not see that he sleeps on straw and is chained down, but abandons himself wholly to the creations of his mind, and riots in every extravagance of thought.

TEST OF REASON.

SENSE and nonsense, congruity and incongruity, are only determined by the outer world; and we consider our conceptions to be wild or rational only as they correspond with it.

SENSATIONS AND CONCEPTIONS.

NATURE has *probably* made a strong original difference between our sensations and conceptions; but whatever the *original* difference may be, it is considerably strengthened by habit.

MEMORY AND CONCEPTION.

THERE seems to be a regular process carried on in the mind throughout its whole existence, by which ideas of memory are converted into ideas of conception. If a poet writes two or three hundred verses, very many of the combinations of words, perhaps whole verses, will be faithful copies of what he has once remembered, and which, divested of all the marks of their origin, have reappeared to the writer as productions of his own brain. In the same manner, in a fancy landscape, or in grounds laid out by a man of taste, many of the combinations are in all probability copies of real scenes, which the person who introduced them could once have referred to some particular spot, but have now become his own property, from an inability to discover their former master, —like domestic animals which run away into the woods, and belong to whoever can catch them.

CONCEPTION STRENGTHENED BY HABIT.

MEN differ in their power of lively conception, but more in their habits of attention; but conception is in all men much strengthened by habit.

CONTEMPLATION AND ACTION.

He who can thus manage his mind has two worlds before him instead of one: he can contemplate and act; and, dispelling the vision of a rich and creative mind, can come down into the world of realities to observe with steadfastness and to act with consistency.

VOLUNTARY AGE.

I am convinced, that it is for a long time in every man's power to determine whether he will be old or not. The *outward* marks of age we are all of us very willing to defer; forgetting that we may wear the inward bloom of youth with true dignity and grace, and be ready to learn, and eager to give pleasure to others, to the latest moment of our existence.

PORTABLE KNOWLEDGE.

The desirable and the useful thing is, that we should carry our knowledge about with us, as we carry our health about with us; that the one should be exhibited in the alacrity of our actions, and the other proved by the vigour of our thoughts. I would as soon call a man healthy who had a physician's prescription in his pocket, which he could take and recover from, as I would say that a man had knowledge who had no other proof of it to afford, than a pile of closely-written common-place books.

IMPROVEMENT BY HABIT.

Imagination of all sorts, though originally dealt out with very different degrees of profusion to different men, ıs capable of great improvement from habit.   As great part of imagination depends upon association, and the power of association always increases with practice, men acquire extraordinary command over particular classes of ideas, and are supplied with copiousness of materials for their collection, to which inexperienced and unpractised minds can never attain.   What a prodigious command, for instance, over all those associations which are productive of wit, must the head wit of such a city as this or Paris have acquired in twenty years of facetiousness, — having been accustomed, for that space of time, to view all the characters and events which have fallen under his notice with a reference to these relations!   What an enormous power of versification must Pope have gained, after his translations of the Iliad and the Odyssey! so that no combination of words or inflection of sounds, could possibly have been new to him ; and he must have almost meditated in hexameters, and conversed in rhyme.   What a powerful human being must that man become who, beginning with original talents, has been accustomed, for half his life, to the eloquence of the bar or the senate! No combination of circumstances can come before him for which he is unprepared ; he is always ready for every purpose of defence and attack : and trusts, with the most implicit confidence, to that host of words and images which he knows from long experience will rise up at any moment of exigence for his ornament and support.

THE CONCORD OF TRUTH.

IF a question be discussed coolly, if the parties have no other interest in its termination but that of truth, if they thoroughly understand the *terms* they employ, if they are well informed upon the relative facts, and if they are, both, in the habit of guarding against accidental associations, the conclusions in which they terminate will probably be the same: there is hardly any difference of opinion not resolvable into one or the other of these causes. Here, then, we have an outline of that manly and high-prized reason, which, under the blessing and direction of God, arranges the affairs of this world; which cools passion, unravels sophism, enlightens ignorance, and detects mistake; which wit cannot disconcert, nor eloquence bear down; which appeals always to realities, and ever follows truth without insolence and without fear. For it is disgraceful to the immortal understanding of man to be governed by *sounds*, and to be the slave of that speech which was given to do him service. It is beneath the loftiness of his faculties to take his notions of truth from the little hamlet in which he was bred, or from the fashions of thought which prevailed in his hour of life: for truth dwells not on the Danube, or the Seine, or the Thames; she is not this thing to-day, and to-morrow another; but she is of all places, and all times the same, in every change, and in every chance— as firm as the pillars of the earth, and as beautiful as its fabric.

NOURISHMENT OF THE MIND.

THE first thing to be done in conducting the understanding is precisely the same as in conducting the body, — to give it regular and copious supplies of food, to prevent that atrophy and marasmus of mind, which comes on from giving it no new ideas. It is a mistake equally fatal to the memory, the imagination, the powers of reasoning, and to every faculty of the mind, to think too early that we can live upon our stock of understanding, — that it is time to leave off business, and make use of the acquisitions we have already made, without troubling ourselves any further to add to them. It is no more possible for an idle man to keep together a certain stock of knowledge, than it is possible to keep together a stock of ice exposed to the meridian sun. Every day destroys a fact, a relation, or an inference; and the only method of preserving the bulk and value of the pile is by constantly adding to it.

ONE ROAD TO GREATNESS.

THERE is but one method, and that is hard-labour; and a man who will not pay that price for distinction, had better at once dedicate himself to the pursuit of the fox, — or sport with the tangles of Neæra's hair, — or talk of bullocks, and glory in the goad! There are many modes of being frivolous, and not a few of being useful; there is but one mode of being intellectually great.

GREAT SUCCESS THE FRUIT OF GREAT LABOUR.

GENERALLY speaking, the life of all truly great men has been a life of intense and incessant labour. They have commonly past the first half of life in the gross darkness of indigent humility, — overlooked, mistaken, contemned, by weaker men, — thinking while others slept, reading while others rioted, feeling something within them that told them they should not always be kept down among the dregs of the world; and then, when their time was come, and some little accident has given them their first occasion, they have burst out into the light and glory of public life, rich with the spoils of time, and mighty in all the labours and struggles of the mind. Then do the multitude cry out " a miracle of genius;" Yes, he *is* a miracle of genius, because he is a miracle of labour; because, instead of trusting to the resources of his own single mind, he has ransacked a thousand minds; because he makes use of the accumulated wisdom of ages, and takes as his point of departure the very last line and boundary to which science has advanced; because it has ever been the object of his life to assist every intellectual gift of nature, however munificent, and however splendid, with every resource that art could suggest, and every attention diligence could bestow.

ODD QUOTATIONS.

THERE is a sort of vanity some men have, of talking of, and reading, obscure and half-forgotten authors, because it passes as a matter of course, that he who quotes authors which are so little read, must be completely and thoroughly acquainted with those authors which are in every man's mouth. For instance, it is very common to quote Shakspeare; but it makes a sort of stare to quote Massinger. I have very little credit for being well acquainted with Virgil; but if I quote Silius Italicus, I may stand some chance of being reckoned a great scholar. In short, whoever wishes to strike out the great road, and to make a short cut to fame, let him neglect Homer, Virgil, and Horace, and Ariosto and Milton, and, instead of these, read and talk of Fracastorius, Sannazarius, Lorenzini, Pastorini, and the thirty-six primary sonneteers of Bettinelli;—let him neglect everything which the suffrage of ages has made venerable and grand, and dig out of their graves a set of decayed scribblers, whom the silent verdict of the public has fairly condemned to everlasting oblivion. If he complain of the injustice with which they have been treated, and call for a new trial with loud and importunate clamour, though I am afraid he will not make much progress in the estimation of men of sense, he will be sure to make some noise in the crowd, and to be dubbed a man of very curious and extraordinary erudition.

THE POWER TO SAY " NO."

THE purity of moral habits is, I am afraid, of very little use to a man unless it is accompanied with that degree of firmness which enables him to act up to what he may think right, in spite of solicitation to the contrary. Very few young men have the power of negation in any great degree at first. It increases with the increase of confidence, and with the experience of those inconveniences which result from the absence of this virtue. Every young man must be exposed to temptation : he cannot learn the ways of men without being witness to their vices. If you attempt to preserve him from danger by keeping him out of the way of it, you render him quite unfit for any style of life in which he may be placed. The great point is, not to turn him out too soon, and to give him a pilot at first.

EARLY INDEPENDENCE.

I HAVE always said that the greatest object in education is to accustom a young man gradually to be his own master.

MERE READERS.

WE do not want readers, for the number of readers seems to be very much upon the increase, and mere readers are very often the most idle of human beings.

RESULTS OF READING.

IT is no more necessary that a man should remember the different dinners and suppers which have made him healthy, than the different books which have made him wise. Let us see the result of good food in a strong body, and the result of great reading in a full and powerful mind.

QUICK READING.

THE best way of reading books with rapidity is, to acquire that habit of severe attention to what they contain, that perpetually confines the mind to the single object it has in view. When you have read enough to have acquired the habit of reading without suffering your mind to wander, and when you can bring to bear upon your subject a great share of previous knowledge, you may then read with rapidity; before that, as you have taken the wrong road, the faster you proceed the more you will be sure to err.

LOVE OF TRUTH.

A SINCERE attachment to truth, moral and scientific, is a habit which cures a thousand little infirmities of mind, and is as honourable to a man who possesses it, in point of character, as it is profitable in point of improvement.

ABSTRACT PROPOSITIONS.

HAVE you definite notions of justice? How do you explain the word chance? What is virtue? Men are every day framing the rashest propositions on such sort of subjects, and prepared to kill and to die in their defence.

DISTINCT MEANING OF WORDS.

IF you choose to quarrel with your eldest son, do it; if you are determined to be disgusted with the world, and to go and live in Westmoreland, do so; if you are resolved to quit your country and settle in America, go!—only, when you have settled the reasons upon which you take one or the other of these steps, have the goodness to examine whether the *words* in which those reasons are contained have really any distinct meaning; and if you find they have not, embrace your firstborn, forget America, unloose your packages, and remain where you are.

BARREN GENERALITIES.

THERE are men who suffer certain barren generalities to get the better of their understandings, by which they try all their opinions, and make them their perpetual standards of right and wrong: as thus—Let us beware of *novelty*; The excesses of the people are *always* to be feared: or these contrary maxims—that there is a natural tendency in all governments to encroach upon the liberties of the people; or, that everything modern is probably an improvement of antiquity. Now what can the use be of sawing about a set of maxims to which there are a complete set of antagonist maxims? For of what use is it to tell me that governors have a tendency to encroach upon the liberties of the people? and is that a reason why you should throw yourself systematically in opposition to the government? What you *say* is very true; what you *do* is very foolish. For is there not another maxim quite as true, that the excesses of the people are to be guarded against? and does not one

evil *à priori* require your attention as well as another?
The business is, to determine, at any one particular
period of affairs, which is in danger of being weakened,
and to act accordingly, like an honest and courageous
man; not to lie like a dead weight at one end of the
beam, without the smallest recollection there is any
other, and that the equilibrium will be violated alike
whichever extreme shall preponderate.

COURAGE ESSENTIAL TO TALENT.

A GREAT deal of talent is lost to the world for the
want of a little courage.

ACT.

THE fact is, that in order to do anything in this world
worth doing, we must not stand shivering on the bank,
and thinking of the cold and the danger, but jump in
and scramble through as well as we can. It will not do
to be perpetually calculating risks, and adjusting nice
chances: it did all very well before the Flood, when a
man could consult his friends upon an intended publication for a hundred and fifty years, and then live to see its
success for six or seven centuries afterwards; but at
present a man waits, and doubts, and hesitates, and con-
sults his brother, and his uncle, and his first cousins, and
his particular friends, till one fine day he finds that he
is sixty-five years of age,—that he has lost so much
time in consulting first cousins and particular friends,
that he has no more time left to follow their advice.

ECONOMY OF PRAISE.

AMONG the smaller duties of life, I hardly know any
one more important than that of not praising where

praise is not due.   Reputation is one of the prizes for which men contend: it is, as Mr. Burke calls it, " the cheap defence and ornament of nations, and the nurse of manly exertions; " it produces more labour and more talent than twice the wealth of a country could ever rear up.   It is the coin of genius; and it is the imperious duty of every man to bestow it with the most scrupulous justice and the wisest economy.

ARGUMENTATIVENESS.

IT is as unfair to compel a man to discuss with you, who cannot play the game, or does not like it, as it would be to compel a person to play at chess with you under similar circumstances: neither is such a sort of exercise of the mind suitable to the rapidity and equal division of general conversation.

FAIR DISCUSSION.

WHEN two men meet together who love truth, and discuss any difficult point with good-nature and a respect for each other's understandings, it always imparts a high degree of steadiness and certainty to our knowledge; or, what is nearly of equal value, and certainly of greater difficulty, it convinces us of our ignorance.   It is an exercise grossly abused by those who have recourse to it, and is very apt to degenerate into a habit of perpetual contradiction, which is the most tiresome and most *disgusting* in all the catalogue of imbecilities.   It is an exercise which timid men dread, — from which irritable men ought to abstain; but which, in my humble opinion, advances a man, who is calm enough for it, and strong enough for it, far beyond any other method of employing the mind.

THE MISUSE OF KNOWLEDGE.

THE truth is, that most men want knowledge, not for itself, but for the superiority which knowledge confers; and the means they employ to secure this superiority are as wrong as the ultimate object, for no man can ever end with being superior, who will not begin with being inferior.

MODEST MERIT.

THERE are some sayings in our language about merit being always united with modesty, &c. (I suppose because they both begin with an *m*, for alliteration has a great power over proverbs, and proverbs over public opinion); but I fancy that in the majority of instances, the fact is directly the reverse, — that talents and arrogance are commonly united, and that most clever young men of eighteen or nineteen believe themselves to be about the level of Demosthenes, or Virgil, or the Admirable Crichton, or John Duke of Marlborough.

AXIOMS THE BASE OF BELIEF.

As for general scepticism, the only way to avoid it is, to seize on some first principles arbitrarily, and not to quit them. Take as few as you can help, — about a tenth part of what Dr. Reid has taken will suffice, — but take some and proceed to build upon them. Some of his disciples, however, could never get a single step further; — they admitted their own existence, but could never deduce any one single truth from it. One might almost wish that these gentlemen had disencumbered themselves of this their only idea, by running down steep places, or walking very far into profound ponds, rather than that they should exhibit such a spectacle of stupidity and perversion.

IS KNOWLEDGE HYPOTHETICAL?

IF you choose to call all knowledge hypothetical, because first principles are arbitrarily assumed, you certainly *may* call it so, if you please ; but then I only contend that it does quite as well as if it were not hypothetical, because all the various errors agree perfectly well together, and produce that happiness which is the end of knowledge.

IDIOSYNCRASY.

IT is a very wise rule in the conduct of the understanding, to acquire early a correct notion of your own peculiar [constitution of mind, and to become well acquainted, as a physician would say, with your *idiosyncrasy.*   Are you an acute man, and see sharply for small distances ? or are you a comprehensive man, and able to take in wide and extensive views into your mind ?   Does your mind turn its ideas into wit ? or are you apt to take a common-sense view of the objects presented to you ? Have you an exuberant imagination, or a correct judgment ?   Are you quick, or slow ?   accurate, or hasty ? a great reader, or a great thinker ?   It is a prodigious point gained if any man can find out where his powers lie, and what are his deficiencies,—if he can contrive to ascertain what Nature intended him for.

SQUARE PERSONS AND ROUND HOLES.

IF you choose to represent the various parts in life by holes upon a table, of different shapes, — some circular, some triangular, some square, some oblong,—and the persons acting these parts by bits of wood of similar shapes, we shall generally find that the triangular person has got into the square hole, the oblong into the trian-gular, and a square person has squeezed himself into the round hole. The officer and the office, the doer and the thing done, seldom fit so exactly, that we can say they were almost made for each other.

THE LOVE OF KNOWLEDGE.

I SOLEMNLY declare that, but for the love of knowledge, I should consider the life of the meanest hedger and ditcher, as preferable to that of the greatest and richest man here present: for the fire of our minds is like the fire which the Persians burn in the mountains,—it flames night and day, and is immortal, and not to be quenched! Upon something it *must* act and feed, — upon the pure spirit of knowledge, or upon the foul dregs of polluting passions. Therefore, when I say, in conducting your understanding, love knowledge with a great love, with a vehement love, with a love co-eval with life, what do I say, but love innocence, — love virtue, — love purity of conduct, — love that which, if you are rich and great, will sanctify the blind fortune which has made you so, and make men call it justice, — love that which, if you are poor, will render your poverty respectable, and make the proudest feel it unjust to laugh at the meanness of your fortunes,—love that which will comfort you, adorn you, and never quit you, — which will open to you the kingdom of thought, and all the boundless regions of conception, as an asylum against the cruelty, the in-justice, and the pain that may be your lot in the outer world, — that which will make your motives habitually great and honourable, and light up in an instant a

thousand noble disdains at the very thought of meanness
and of fraud!   Therefore, if any young man here have
embarked his life in pursuit of knowledge, let him go
on without doubting or fearing the event;—let him not
be intimidated by the cheerless beginnings of knowledge,
by the darkness, from which she springs, by the difficulties
which hover around her, by the wretched habitations in
which she dwells, by the want and sorrow which sometimes journey in her train; but let him ever follow her
as the Angel that guards him, and as the Genius of his
life.   She will bring him out at last into the light of
day, and exhibit him to the world comprehensive in
acquirements, fertile in resources, rich in imagination,
strong in reasoning, prudent and powerful above his
fellows, in all the relations and in all the offices of life.

RELATIONS SUGGESTED BY WIT.

THE first limit to be affixt to that observation of relations, which produces the feeling of wit, is, that they
must be relations which excite *surprise.*   If you tell me
that all men must die, I am very little struck with what
you say, because it is not an assertion very remarkable
for its novelty; but if you were to say that man was like
a time-glass,— that both must run out, and both render
up their dust, I should listen to you with more attention,
because I should feel something like surprise at the
sudden relation you had struck out between two such
apparently dissimilar ideas as a man and a time-glass.

SENSATIONS OF WIT.

THERE is a mode of teaching children geography by
disjointed parts of a wooden map, which they fit together.
I have no doubt that the child, in finding the kingdom

or republic which fits into a great hole in the wooden sea, feels exactly the sensation of wit. Every one must remember that fitting the inviting projection of Crim Tartary into the Black Sea was one of the greatest delights of their childhood; and almost all children are sure to scream with pleasure at the discovery.

THE CAUSE OF WIT, NOT ITS ESSENCE, DEFINABLE.

I AM only defining the *causes* of a certain feeling in the mind called wit;—I can no more define the feeling itself, than I can define the flavour of venison. We all seem to partake of one and the other, with a very great degree of satisfaction; but why each feeling *is* what it is, and nothing else, I am sure I cannot pretend to determine.

ELABORATION OF WIT.

IT is imagined that wit is a sort of inexplicable visitation, that it comes and goes with the rapidity of lightning, and that it is quite as unattainable as beauty or just proportion. I am so much of a contrary way of thinking, that I am convinced a man might sit down as systematically, and as successfully, to the study of wit, as he might to the study of mathematics: and I would answer for it, that, by giving up only six hours a day to being witty he should come on prodigiously before midsummer, so that his friends should hardly know him again.

PUNS.

I HAVE very little to say about puns; they are in very bad repute, and so they *ought* to be. The wit of language is so miserably inferior to the wit of ideas, that it is very deservedly driven out of good company. Sometimes, indeed, a pun makes its appearance which seems for a moment to redeem its species; but we must not be deceived by them: it is a radically bad race of wit.

BANISHMENT OF PUNSTERS.

ONE invaluable blessing produced by the banishment of punning, is an immediate reduction of the number of wits.

CHECK ON WITS.

THE condition of putting together ideas in order to be witty operates much in the same salutary manner as the condition of finding rhymes in poetry;—it reduces the number of performers to those who have vigour enough to overcome incipient difficulties, and makes a sort of provision that that which need not be done at all, should be done *well* whenever it *is* done. For we may observe, that mankind are always more fastidious about that which is pleasing, than they are about that which is useful.

VULGAR DISPLAY.

IF a man have ordinary chairs and tables, no one notices it; but if he stick vulgar gaudy pictures on his walls, which he need not have at all, every one laughs at him for his folly.

TRUE SARCASM.

A TRUE sarcasm is like a sword-stick — it appears, at first sight, to be much more innocent than it really is, till, all of a sudden, there leaps something out of it — sharp, and deadly, and incisive — which makes you tremble and recoil.

RESIST RIDICULE.

I KNOW of no principle which it is of more importance to fix in the minds of young people than that of
the most determined resistance to the encroachments of
ridicule.

BRAVE LAUGHTER.

LEARN from the earliest days to inure your principles
against the perils of ridicule: you can no more exercise
your reason, if you live in the constant dread of laughter,
than you can enjoy your life, if you are in the constant
terror of death.

MISCONSTRUCTIONS.

LET men call you mean, if you know you are just;
hypocritical, if you are honestly religious; pusillanimous,
if you feel that you are firm; resistance soon converts unprincipled wit into sincere respect; and no after-time can
tear from you those feelings which every man carries
within him who has made a noble and successful exertion
in a virtuous cause.

INCONGRUITY THE BASIS OF HUMOUR.

As you increase the incongruity, you increase the
humour; as you diminish it, you diminish the humour.
If a tradesman of a corpulent and respectable appearance,
with habiliments somewhat ostentatious, were to slide
down gently into the mud, and dedecorate a pea-green
coat, I am afraid we should all have the barbarity to
laugh. If his hat and wig, like treacherous servants,
were to desert their falling master, it certainly would not
diminish our propensity to laugh; but if he were to fall

into a violent passion, and abuse everybody about him, nobody could possibly resist the incongruity of a pea-green tradesman, very respectable, sitting in the mud, and threatening all the passers-by with the effects of his wrath. Here, every incident heightens the humour of the scene:—the gaiety of his tunic, the general respectability of his appearance, the rills of muddy water which trickle down his cheeks, and the harmless violence of his rage! But if, instead of this, we were to observe a dustman falling into the mud, it would hardly attract any attention, because the opposition of ideas is so trifling, and the incongruity so slight.

BOUNDARIES OF RIDICULE.

The sense of the humorous is as incompatible with tenderness and respect as with compassion. No man would laugh to see a little child fall; and he would be shocked to see such an accident happen to an old man, or a woman, or to his father! It is an odd case to put, but I should like to know if any man living could have laughed if he had seen Sir Isaac Newton rolling in the mud? I believe that not only Senior Wranglers and Senior Optimi would have run to his assistance, but that dustmen, and carmen, and coal-heavers would have run and picked him up, and set him to rights. It is a beautiful thing to observe the boundaries which nature has affixt to the ridiculous, and to notice how soon it is swallowed up by the more illustrious feelings of our minds. Where is the heart so hard that could bear to see the awkward resources and contrivances of the poor turned into ridicule? Who could laugh at the fractured, ruined body of a soldier? Who is so *wicked* as to amuse himself with the infirmities of extreme old age? or to find subject for humour in the weakness of a perishing dissolving body? Who is there that does not feel himself disposed to overlook the little peculiarities of the truly great and wise, and to throw a veil over that ridicule which they have redeemed by the magnitude of their talents, and the splendour of their virtues? Who ever thinks of turning into ridicule our great and ardent hope of a world to come? Whenever the man of humour meddles with these things, he is astonished to find, that in all the great feelings of their nature the mass of mankind always think and act aright;—that they are ready enough to laugh, — but that they are quite as ready to drive away with indignation and contempt, the light fool who comes with the feather of wit to crumble the bulwarks of truth, and to beat down the Temples of God!

BUFFOONERY.

BUFFOONERY is voluntary incongruity.

BULLS.

A BULL,—which must by no means be past over in this recapitulation of the family of wit and humour,— a bull is exactly the counterpart of a witticism: for as wit discovers real relations that are not apparent, bulls admit apparent relations that are not real.

CHARADES.

I SHALL say nothing of charades, and such sort of unpardonable trumpery : if charades are made at all, they should be made without benefit of clergy, the offender should instantly be hurried off to execution, and be cut off in the middle of his dullness, without being allowed to explain to the executioner why his first is like his second, or what is the resemblance between his fourth and his ninth.

PANGS OF LAUGHTER.

LAUGHTER is, to many men, worse than death. Innumerable duels have been fought to prevent the pangs of ridicule, and to revenge them; and there are very few who would not rather be hated than be laughed at.

DREAD OF RIDICULE.

IN polished society, the dread of being ridiculous models every word and gesture into propriety, and produces an exquisite attention to the feelings and opinions of others; it is the great cure of extravagance, folly, and impertinence; it curbs the sallies of eccentricity, it recalls the attention of mankind to the one uniform standard of reason and common sense.

CIVILISATION.

THERE are several meanings included under the term civilisation: it means, having better cups and saucers than we had a century or two centuries ago; better laws, better manners; and it means, also, having nothing to do,—and those who have nothing to do, must either be amused, or expire with gaping.

CORRUPTING EFFECTS OF WIT AND HUMOUR.

I WISH, after all I have said about wit and humour, I could satisfy myself of their good effects upon the character and disposition; but I am convinced the probable tendency of both is, to corrupt the understanding and the heart.

PROFESSED WITS.

PROFESSED wits, though they are generally courted for the amusement they afford, are seldom respected for the qualities they possess.

WITTY PERFORMERS.

A WITTY man is a dramatic performer: in process of time, he can no more exist without applause, than he can exist without air; if his audience be small, or if they are inattentive, or if a new wit defrauds him of any portion of his admiration, it is all over with him,—he sickens, and is extinguished. The applauses of the theatre on which he performs are so essential to him, that he must obtain them at the expense of decency, friendship, and good feeling. It must always be *probable*, too, that a *mere* wit is a person of light and frivolous understanding. His business is not to discover relations of ideas that are *useful*, and have a real influence upon life, but to discover the more trifling relations which are only amusing; he never looks at things with the naked eye of common sense, but is always gazing at the world through a Claude Lorraine glass,—discovering a thousand appearances which are created only by the instrument of inspection, and covering every object with factitious and unnatural colours. In short, the character of a *mere* wit it is impossible to consider as very amiable, very respectable, or very safe.

DIGNITY OF DULLNESS.

THERE is an association in men's minds between dullness and wisdom, amusement and folly, which has a very powerful influence in decision upon character, and is not overcome without considerable difficulty. The reason is, that the *outward* signs of a dull man and a wise man are the same, and so are the outward signs of a frivolous man and a witty man; and we are not to expect that the majority will be disposed to look to much *more* than the outward sign.

MANIFOLD MEN.

THE meaning of an extraordinary man is, that he is *eight* men, not one man; that he has as much wit as if he had no sense, and as much sense as if he had no wit; that his conduct is as judicious as if he were the dullest of human beings, and his imagination as brilliant as if he were irretrievably ruined.

WIT THE FLAVOUR OF THE MIND.

THERE is no more interesting spectacle than to see the effects of wit upon the different characters of men; than to observe it expanding caution, relaxing dignity, unfreezing coldness,—teaching age, and care, and pain, to smile,—extorting reluctant gleams of pleasure from melancholy, and charming even the pangs of grief. It is pleasant to observe how it penetrates through the coldness and awkwardness of society, gradually bringing men nearer together, and, like the combined force of wine and oil, giving every man a glad heart and a shining countenance. Genuine and innocent wit like this, is surely the flavour of the mind.

ELDERLY PEOPLE.

THE Scythians always ate their grandfathers; they behaved very respectfully to them for a long time, but

as soon as their grandfathers became old and trouble-
some, and began to tell long stories, they immediately
ate them; nothing could be more improper, and even
disrespectful, than dining off such near and venerable
relations; yet we could not with any propriety accuse
them of bad taste in morals.

EMOTIONS OF EATING

I SHOULD like to try a Scotch gentleman, upon his
first arrival in this country, with the taste of ripe fruit,
and leave him to judge after that, whether nature had
confined the senses to such dry and ungracious occupations, as whether mere matter could produce emotion.
Such doctrines may do very well in the chambers of a
northern metaphysician, but they are untenable in the
light of the world; they are refuted, nobly refuted,
twenty times in a year at Fishmongers' Hall.   If you
deny that matter can produce emotion, judge on these
civic occasions, of the power of gusts, and relishes, and
flavours!   Look at men when (as Bishop Taylor says)
they are " gathered round the eels of Syene, and the
oysters of Lucrinus, and when the Lesbian and Chian-
wines descend through the limbec of the tongue and
larynx; when they receive the juice of fishes, and the
marrow of the laborious ox, and the tender lard of
Apulian swine, and the condited stomach of the scarus:"
— is this nothing but mere sensation? is there no emotion, no panting, no wheezing, no deglutition? is this
the calm acquisition of intelligence, and the quiet office
ascribed to the senses?—or is it a proof that nature has
infused into her original creations, the power of gratifying that sense which distinguishes them, and to every
atom of matter has added an atom of joy?

HISS.

THE sound of a trumpet suggests the dreadful idea of a battle, and of the approach of armed men; but to all men brought up at Queen's College, Oxford, it must be associated with eating and drinking, for they are always called to dinner by sound of trumpet: and I have a little daughter at home, who, if she heard the sound of a trumpet, would run to the window expecting to see the puppet-show of Punch, which is carried about the streets. So with a hiss: a hiss is either foolish, or tremendous, or sublime. The hissing of a pancake is absurd; the first faint hiss that arises from the extremity of the pit on the evening of a new play, sinks the soul of the author within him, and makes him curse himself and his Thalia! the hissing of a cobra di capello is sublime, — it is the whisper of death!

MAY MORNINGS.

WALK in the fields in one of the mornings of May, and if you carry with you a mind unpolluted with harm, watch how it is impressed. You are delighted with the beauty of colours; are not those colours beautiful? You breathe vegetable fragrance; is not that fragrance grateful? You see the sun rising from behind a mountain, and the heavens painted with light; is not that renewal of the light of the morning sublime? You reject all obvious reasons, and say that these things are beautiful and sublime, because the accidents of life have made them so; I say they are beautiful and sublime BECAUSE GOD HAS MADE THEM SO! that it is the original, indelible character impressed upon them by Him, who has opened these sources of simple pleasure, to calm, perhaps, the perturbations of sense, and to make us love that joy which is purchased without giving pain to another man's heart, and without entailing reproach upon our own.

STANDARD OF BEAUTY.

WHEREVER the standard of any species of beauty is required, we may safely say it rests in the opinion of candid men, of men who have had experience in that department of beauty, who have feeling for it, and who have competent understandings to judge of the design and reasoning, which are always the highest and most excellent of all beauties. Such men, where they are to be found, form the standard in every department of beauty, and in every ingredient of taste. How such critics are to be found, is another question; that they exist, no man doubts; and their joint influence ultimately prevails, and gives the law to public opinion. But I hear some men asking where they are to be found? and who they are? with a sort of exultation, as if there were any wit, or talent, or importance in the question. They are to be found in Dover Street, Albemarle Street, Berkeley Square, the Temple; anywhere wherever reading, thinking men, who have seen a great deal of the world, are to be found. I myself could mention the names of twenty persons, whose opinions influence the public taste in this town; and then, when opinions are settled here, those opinions go down by the mail-coach, to regulate all matters of taste for the provinces.

FIAT JUSTITIA.

JUSTICE is pleasant, even when she destroys.

INSTRUMENTAL MUSIC.

SEE the effects of a long piece of music at a public concert. The orchestra are breathless with attention, jumping into major and minor keys, executing fugues, and fiddling with the most ecstatic precision. In the midst of all this wonderful science, the audience are gaping, lolling, talking, staring about, and half devoured with ennui. On a sudden there springs up a lively little air, expressive of some natural feeling, though in point of science not worth a halfpenny: the audience all spring up, every head nods, every foot beats time, and every heart also; an universal smile breaks out on every face; the carriage is not ordered; and every one agrees that music is the most delightful rational entertainment that the human mind can possibly enjoy.

PROPORTION NOT THE CAUSE OF BEAUTY.

MR. BURKE contends, and in my humble opinion with great success, that proportion is never of *itself* the original cause of beauty. It is the cause of beauty, as it is an indication of strength and utility in buildings, of swiftness in animals, of any feeling morally beautiful; and it is agreeable, as it is customary in animals, or the proof of the absence of deformity; but no proportion of itself, and without one of these reasons, ever pleases. No man would contend Nature ever intended that 6 to 2, or 9 to 14, are perfection: that the moment a monkey could be discovered and brought to light, the length of whose ear was precisely the cube root of the length of his tail, that he ought to be set up as a model of perfect conformation to the whole simious tribe.

GRACE IS EASE.

GRACE is either the beauty of motion, or the beauty of posture. Graceful motion is motion without difficulty or embarrassment; or that which, from experience, we know to be connected with ingenuous modesty, a desire to increase the happiness of others, or any beautiful moral feeling. A person walks up a long room, observed by a great number of individuals, and pays his respects as a gentleman ought to do;—why is he graceful? Because every movement of his body inspires you with some pleasant feeling; he has the free and unembarrassed use of his limbs; his motions do not indicate forward boldness, or irrational timidity;—the outward signs perpetually indicate agreeable qualities. The same explanation applies to grace of posture and attitude: that is a graceful attitude which indicates an absence of restraint; and facility, which is the sign of agreeable qualities of mind: apart from such indications, one attitude I should conceive to be quite as graceful as another.

BEAUTIFUL PIGS.

Go to the Duke of Bedford's piggery at Woburn, and you will see a breed of pigs with legs so short, that their stomachs trail upon the ground; a breed of animals entombed in their own fat, overwhelmed with prosperity, success, and farina. No animal could possibly be so disgusting if it were not useful; but a breeder, who has accurately attended to the small quantity of food it requires to swell this pig out to such extraordinary dimensions,—the astonishing genius it displays for obesity, — and the laudable propensity of the flesh to desert the cheap regions of the body, and to agglomerate on those parts which are worth ninepence a pound,—such an observer of its utility does not scruple to call these otherwise hideous quadrupeds a beautiful race of pigs.

MONOTONY OF ORDER.

I WENT for the first time in my life, some years ago, to stay at a very grand and beautiful place in the country, where the grounds are said to be laid out with consummate taste. For the first three or four days I was perfectly enchanted; it seemed something so much better than nature, that I really began to wish the earth had been laid out according to the latest principles of improvement, and that the whole face of nature wore a little more the appearance of a park. In three days' time I was tired to death; a thistle, a nettle, a heap of dead bushes, anything that wore the appearance of accident and want of intention, was quite a relief. I used to escape from the made grounds, and walk upon an adjacent goose-common, where the cart-ruts, gravel-pits, bumps, irregularities, coarse ungentleman-like grass, and all the varieties produced by neglect, were a thousand times more gratifying than the monotony of beauties the result of design, and crowded into narrow confines with a luxuriance and abundance utterly unknown to nature.

THE LOVE OF THE BEAUTIFUL.

WHAT are half the crimes in the world committed for? What brings into action the best virtues? The desire of possessing. Of possessing what? — not mere money, but every species of the beautiful which money can purchase. A man lies hid in a little, dirty, smoky room for twenty years of his life, and sums up as many columns of figures as would reach round half the earth, if they were

laid at length; — he gets rich : what does he do with his
riches?   He buys a large well-proportioned house : in
the arrangement of his furniture, he gratifies himself with
all the beauty which splendid colours, regular figures, and
smooth surfaces, can convey; he has the beauties of
variety and association in his grounds; the cup out of
which he drinks his tea is adorned with beautiful figures;
the chair in which he sits is covered with smooth shining
leather ; his table-cloth is of the most beautiful damask;
mirrors reflect the lights from every quarter of the room ;
pictures of the best masters feed his eye with all the
beauties of imitation.   A million of human creatures are
employed in this country in ministering to this feeling
of the beautiful.   It is only a barbarous, ignorant people
that can ever be occupied by the necessaries of life *alone.*
If to eat, and to drink, and to be warm, were the only
passions of our minds, we should all be what the lowest
of us all are at this day.   The love of the beautiful calls
man to fresh exertions, and awakens him to a more
noble life; and the glory of it is, that as painters imitate,
and poets sing, and statuaries carve, and architects rear
up the gorgeous trophies of their skill, — as everything
becomes beautiful, and orderly, and magnificent, — the
activity of the mind rises to still greater, and to better,
objects.

CONTRASTED PLEASURES.

THE joy of a washerwoman who has just got the
20,000*l.* prize in the lottery, and the joy of a sensible,
worthy man, who has just succeeded in rescuing a family
from distress, are both feelings of pleasure ; but while
one is dancing in frantic rapture round her tubs, the
signs by which the other indicates his satisfaction are
characteristic of nothing but tranquillity and peace.

A NOBLE ACTION.

A London merchant, who, I believe, is still alive, while he was staying in the country with a friend, happened to mention that he intended, the next year, to buy a ticket in the lottery; his friend desired he would buy one for him at the same time, which of course was very willingly agreed to. The conversation dropped, the ticket never arrived, and the whole affair was entirely forgotten, when the country gentleman received information that the ticket purchased for him by his friend, had come up a prize of 20,000*l*. Upon his arrival in London, he inquired of his friend where he had put the ticket, and why he had not informed him that it was purchased. "I bought them both the same day, mine and your ticket, and I flung them both into a drawer of my bureau, and I never thought of them afterwards." "But how do you distinguish one ticket from the other? and why am I the holder of the fortunate ticket more than you?" "Why, at the time I put them into the drawer, I put a little mark in ink upon the ticket which I resolved should be yours; and upon re-opening the drawer I found that the one so marked was the fortunate ticket." Now this action appears to me perfectly beautiful; it is *le beau idéal* in morals, and gives that calm, yet deep emotion of pleasure, which every one so easily receives from the beauty of the exterior world.

VALE OF SEVERN.

The sudden variation from the hill country of Gloucestershire to the Vale of Severn, as observed from Birdlip, or Frowcester Hill, is strikingly sublime. You travel for twenty or five-and-twenty miles over one of the most unfortunate, desolate countries under heaven, divided by stone walls, and abandoned to screaming kites and larcenous crows: after travelling really twenty, and to appearance ninety miles over this region of stone and sorrow, life begins to be a burden, and you wish to perish. At the very moment when you are taking this melancholy view of human affairs, and hating the postilion, and blaming the horses, there bursts upon your view, with all its towers, forests, and streams, the deep and shaded Vale of Severn. Sterility and nakedness are thrown in the background: as far as the eye can reach, all is comfort, opulence, product, and beauty: now it is an ancient city, or a fair castle rising out of the forests, and now the beautiful Severn is noticed winding among the cultivated fields, and the cheerful habitations of men. The train of mournful impressions is quite effaced, and you descend rapidly into a vale of plenty, with a heart full of wonder and delight.

AURUNGZEBE.

EVERY body possessed of power is an object either of awe or sublimity, from a justice of peace up to the Emperor Aurungzebe—an object quite as stupendous as the Alps. He had thirty-five millions of revenue, in a country where the products of the earth are, at least, six times as cheap as in England: his empire extended over twenty-five degrees of latitude, and as many of longitude; he had put to death above twenty millions of people. I should like to know the man who could have looked at Aurungzebe without feeling him to the end of his limbs, and in every hair of his head! Such emperors are more sublime than cataracts. I think any man would have shivered more at the sight of Aurungzebe, than at the sight of the two rivers which meet at the Blue Mountains, in America, and, bursting through the whole breadth of the rocks, roll their victorious and united waters to the Eastern Sea.

SUBLIMITY OF ENDURANCE.

I AM going to say rather an odd thing, but I cannot help thinking that the severe and rigid economy of a man in distress, has something in it very sublime, especially if it be endured for any length of time serenely and in silence. I remember a very striking instance of it in a young man, since dead; he was the son of a country curate, who had got him a berth on board a man-of-war, as midshipman. The poor curate made a great effort for his son; fitted him out well with clothes, and gave him fifty pounds in money. The first week, the poor boy lost his chest, clothes, money, and every thing he had in the world. The ship sailed for a foreign station; and his loss was without remedy. He immediately quitted his mess, ceased to associate with the other midshipmen, who were the sons of gentlemen; and for five years, without mentioning it to his parents — who he knew could not assist him, — or without borrowing a farthing from any human being, without a single murmur or complaint, did that poor lad endure the most abject and degrading poverty, at a period of life when the feelings are most alive to ridicule, and the appetites most prone to indulgence. Now, I confess I am a mighty advocate for the sublimity of such long and patient endurance. If you can make the world stare and look on, there, you have vanity, or compassion, to support you; but to bury all your wretchedness in your own mind, — to resolve that you will have no man's pity,

while you have one effort left to procure his respect, —
to harbour no mean thought in the midst of abject
poverty, but, at the very time you are surrounded by
circumstances of humility and depression, to found a
spirit of modest independence upon the consciousness of
having always acted well; — this is a sublime, which,
though it is found in the shade and retirement of life,
ought to be held up to the praises of men, and to be
looked upon as a noble model for imitation.

HOW TO LIVE.

IT is the greatest and first use of history, to show us
the sublime in morals, and to tell us what great men
have done in perilous seasons. Such beings, and such
actions, dignify our nature, and breathe into us a virtuous pride which is the parent of every good. Wherever
you meet with them in the page of history, read them,
mark them, and learn from them, how to live, and how
to die! for the object of *common* men, is only to live.
The object of such men as I have spoken of, was to live
grandly, and in favour with their own *difficult* spirits:
to live, if in war, gloriously; if in peace, usefully, justly,
and *freely ! !*

SUPERIORITY OF MAN.

I CONFESS I feel myself so much at my ease about the
superiority of mankind, — I have such a marked and
decided contempt for the understanding of every baboon
I have yet seen, — I feel so sure that the blue ape without
a tail will never rival us in poetry, painting, and music,
— that I see no reason whatever, why justice may not be
done to the few fragments of soul, and tatters of under-

standing, which they may really possess. I have sometimes, perhaps, felt a little uneasy at Exeter 'Change,
from contrasting the monkeys with the 'prentice-boys
who are teazing them; but a few pages of Locke, or a
few lines of Milton, have always restored me to tranquillity, and convinced me that the superiority of man
had nothing to fear.

INSTINCTS OF ANIMALS.

ALL the wonderful instincts of animals, which, in my
humble opinion, are proved beyond a doubt, and the
belief in which is not decreased with the increase of
science and investigation,—all these instincts are given
them only for the combination or preservation of their
species. If they had not these instincts, they would be
swept off the earth in an instant. This bee, that understands architecture so well, is as stupid as a pebble-stone,
out of his own particular business of making honey;
and, with all his talents, he only exists that boys may
eat his labours, and poets sing about them. *Ut pueris
placeas et declamatio fias.* A peasant girl of ten years
old, puts the whole republic to death with a little smoke;
their palaces are turned into candles, and every clergyman's wife makes mead wine of the honey; and there is
an end of the glory and wisdom of the bees ! Whereas,
man has talents that have no sort of reference to his
existence; and without which, his species might remain
upon earth in the same safety as if they had them not.
The bee works at that particular angle which saves most
time and labour; and the boasted edifice he is construct-
ing is only for his egg: but Somerset House, and Blenheim,
and the Louvre, have nothing to do with breeding.
Epic poems, and Apollo Belvideres, and Venus de .Me-

dicis, have nothing to do with living and eating. We might have discovered pig-nuts without the Royal Society, and gathered acorns without reasoning about curves of the ninth order. The immense superfluity of talent given to man, which has no bearing upon animal life, which has nothing to do with the mere preservation of existence, is one very distinguishing circumstance in this comparison. There is no other animal but man to whom mind appears to be given for any *other* purpose than the preservation of body.

CHANGE OF ANIMAL INSTINCTS.

THE most curious instance of a change of instinct is mentioned by Darwin. The bees carried over to Barbadoes and the Western Isles, ceased to lay up any honey after the first year; as they found it not useful to them. They found the weather so fine, and materials for making honey so plentiful, that they quitted their grave, prudent, and mercantile character, became exceedingly profligate and debauched, eat up their capital, resolved to work no more, and amused themselves by flying about the sugar-houses, and stinging the blacks. The fact is, that by putting animals in different situations, you may change, and even reverse, any of their original propensities. Spallanzani brought up an eagle upon bread and milk, and fed a dove on raw beef. The circumstances by which an animal is surrounded, impel him to do so and so, by the changes they produce in his body and mind.

MEN AND ANIMALS.

IF man were a solitary animal, like a lion or a bear, he would not be so superior to all animals as he is. If he had the hoof of oxen instead of hands, he would not be so superior: neither would he, if he had less perfect organs of speech; nor if his life were confined to a very few years, instead of being extended to seventy. But all these things will not do by any means *alone*, as the degraders of human nature have said; for there are some animals which very nearly possess all these advantages, and yet are perfectly contemptible, when compared even with the lowest of men.

MAN THE OBJECT OF CREATION.

BUT the great source of man's superiority is, the immense and immeasurable disproportion of those faculties, of which nature has given the mere rudiments to brutes; that this disproportion has made man a speculative animal, even where his mere existence is not concerned; that it has made him a progressive animal; that it has made him a religious animal; and that upon that mere superiority, and on the very principle that the chain of mind and spirit terminates here with man, the best and the most irrefragable arguments for the immortality of the soul are founded, which natural religion can afford: that independent of revelation, it would be impossible not to perceive that man is the object of the creation, and that he, and he *alone*, is reserved for another and a better state of existence.

UNIFORMITY OF ACTIONS IN ANIMALS.

THE bees now build exactly as they built in the time of Homer; the bear is as ignorant of good manners as he was two thousand years past; and the baboon is still as unable to read and write, as persons of honour and quality were in the time of Queen Elizabeth. Yet it is not from any lack of inconveniences, nor any extraordinary contentedness with their situation, that any species of animals remains in such a state of sameness. The wolf often kills twenty times as much as he wants; and if he could hit upon any means of preserving his superfluous plunder, he would not perish of hunger as often as he does. To lay traps for the hunters, and to eat them as they were caught, would be far preferable to all those animals who are the cause, and the contents of traps themselves.

MEN OVERCOME, ANIMALS SUBMIT.

ANIMALS, like men, are goaded by wants and sufferings; but, contrary to the nature of men, they do not overcome, but endure them. The flesh of the savage was originally as strong a temptation to the bear, as the flesh of the bear was to the savage. The wants of the one impelled him to invention; the other retained his original stupidity, in spite of his wants.

ABSENCE OF PROGRESS.

THIS sameness of habits in animals does not *demonstrate* that they are not guided by reason, but it renders it in the highest degree improbable that they should be.

But the Chinese are stationary, and so are the Hindoos; —they are now exactly what they were twenty centuries ago. Certainly they are: but, then, they are so from religious prejudice, transmitted from parent to child; and if it can be proved, (which it cannot,) that bees and ants only gain their habits from older bees and ants, I admit the whole question of instinct is very materially changed:

but the fact is the reverse; and if the fact were the reverse also with the Chinese,—if a young Chinese, brought out of his own country very young, were, without ever having seen another Chinese, to begin at the age of five or six to eat rice with two sticks, to clothe himself in blue and nankeen, and adore the great idol Foo, we must call this sameness the sameness of instinct; but as he does these foolish things because he lives with other Chinese, it is the sameness proceeding from imitation, and strengthened, as we happen to know it to be, by religious association.

AN OLD STORY.

EVERY one knows the old story of the tailor and the elephant, which, if it be not true, at least shows the opinion the Orientals, who know the animal well, entertain of his sagacity. An eastern tailor to the court was making a magnificent doublet for a bashaw of nine tails, and covering it, after the manner of eastern doublets, with gold, silver, and every species of metallic magnificence. As he was busying himself on this momentous occasion, there passed by, to the pools of water, one of the royal elephants, about the size of a broad-wheeled waggon, rich in ivory teeth, and shaking, with its ponderous tread, the tailor's shop to its remotest thimble. As he passed near the window, the elephant happened to look in; the tailor lifted up his eyes, perceived the proboscis of the elephant near him, and, being seized with a fit of facetiousness, pricked the animal with his needle: the mass of matter immediately retired, stalked away to the pool, filled his trunk full of muddy water, and, returning to the shop, overwhelmed the artisan and his doublet with the dirty effects of his vengeance.

ANIMAL EXPERIENCE.

ANIMALS profit by experience, as we do,—not so *much*, but in the same manner.

BREVITY OF LIFE.

I THINK it is Helvetius who says, he is quite certain we only owe our superiority over the ourang-outangs to the greater length of life conceded to us; and that, if our life had been as short as theirs, they would have totally defeated us in the competition for nuts and ripe blackberries. I can hardly agree to this extravagant statement: but I think, in a life of twenty years the efforts of the human mind would have been so considerably lowered, that we might probably have thought Helvetius a good philosopher, and admired his sceptical absurdities as some of the greatest efforts of the human understanding. Sir Richard Blackmore would have been our greatest poet; our wit would have been Dutch; our faith, French; the Hottentots would have given us the model for manners, and the Turks for government; and we might probably have been such miserable reasoners respecting the sacred truths of religion, that we should have thought they wanted the support of a puny and childish jealousy of the poor beasts that perish.

COMBATIVE PROPENSITY.

A LION lies under a hole in a rock; and if any other lion happen to pass by, they fight. Now, whoever gets a habit of lying under a hole in a rock, and fighting with every gentleman who passes near him, cannot possibly make any progress.

DOMINION OF MONKEYS.

A THIRD method, in which man gains the dominion over other animals, is by the structure of his body, and the mechanism of his hands.   Suppose, with all our understanding, it had pleased Providence to make us like lobsters, or to imprison us in shells like cray-fish, I very much question if the monkeys would not have converted us into sauce.

THE HUMAN HAND.

THERE can be no doubt, however, but that the destiny of man, and the extent of his faculties, have been very considerably influenced by the mechanism of the hand.

HUMAN STATURE.

IF man had been only two feet high, he could not possibly have subdued the earth, and roasted and boiled animated nature in the way he now does.

PAST AND FUTURE.

MAN is so far from being influenced only by the moment which is passing over his head, that he looks back to centuries past for the guide of his actions, and to centuries to come for their motive.

THE SOUL OF BRUTES.

To talk of God being the soul of brutes, is the worst and most profane degradation of divine power. To suppose that he who regulates the rolling of the planets, and the return of seasons, by general laws, interferes, by a special act of his power, to make a bird fly, and an insect flutter,—to suppose that a gaudy moth cannot expand its wings to the breeze, or a lark unfold its plumage to the sun, without the special mandate of that God who fixes incipient passions in the human heart, and leaves them to produce a Borgia to scourge mankind, or a Newton to instruct them,—is not piety, or science, but a most pernicious substitution of degrading conjectures, from an ignorant apprehension of the consequences of admitting plain facts.

INDISCREET CHAMPIONS OF RELIGION

THE enemies of the soul's immortality I do *not* fear; I know how often they have been vanquished before; and I am quite sure that they will be overthrown again with a mighty overthrow, as often as they *do* appear. But I confess I have some considerable dread of the indiscreet friends of religion. I tremble at that respectable imbecility which shuffles away the plainest truths, and thinks the strongest of all causes wants the weakest of all aids. I shudder at the consequences of fixing the great proofs of religion upon any other basis, than that of the widest investigation, and most honest statement of facts.

A MIND MADE UP.

REPOSE is agreeable to the human mind; and decision is repose. A man 'has made up his opinions; he does not choose to be disturbed; and he is much more thankful to the man who confirms him in his errors, and leaves him alone, than he is to the man who refutes him, or who instructs him at the expense of his tranquillity.

WORDS.

WORDS are an amazing barrier to the reception of truth.

WORD CONTROVERSIES.

DEFINITION of words has been commonly called a mere exercise of grammarians: but when we come to consider the innumerable murders, proscriptions, massacres, and tortures, which men have inflicted on each other from mistaking the meaning of words, the exercise of definition certainly begins to assume rather a more dignified aspect.

TASTE FOR STUDY AN ACQUIRED TASTE.

WITHOUT study, no man can ever do anything with his understanding. But in spite of all that has been said about the sweets of study, it is a sort of luxury, like the taste for olives and coffee — not natural, very hard to be acquired, and very easily lost.

LIVE WITH ABLE MEN.

ONE of the best methods of rendering study agreeable is, to live with able men, and to suffer all those pangs of inferiority, which the want of knowledge always inflicts.

VIGOROUS STUDY.

THERE is nothing so horrible as languid study; when you sit looking at the clock, wishing the time was over,

or that somebody would call on you and put you out of
your misery. The only way to read with any efficacy, is
to read so heartily, that dinner-time comes two hours
before you expected it. To sit with your Livy before
you, and hear the geese cackling that saved the capitol;
and to see with your own eyes the Carthaginian suttlers
gathering up the rings of the Roman knights after the
battle of Cannæ, and heaping them into bushels; and to
be so intimately present at the actions you are reading
of, that when anybody knocks at the door, it will take
you two or three seconds to determine whether you are
in your own study, or in the plains of Lombardy, looking
at Hannibal's weather-beaten face, and admiring the
splendour of his single eye;—this is the only kind of
study which is not tiresome; and almost the only kind
which is not useless: this is the knowledge which gets
into the system, and which a man carries about and uses
like his limbs, without perceiving that it is extraneous,
weighty, or inconvenient.

TOTAL REPOSE.

THERE is one piece of advice, in a life of study, which
I think no one will object to; and that is, every now and
then to be completely idle,—to do nothing at all.

THE RULE OF RIGHT.

SLEEP as much as you please, if your inclination lead
you only to sleep as much as is convenient; if not,
make rules. The system in everything ought to be, —
do as you please — as long as you please to do what is
right.

PROCESS OF THOUGHT.

I HAVE asked several men what passes in their minds when they are thinking; and I could never find any man who could think for two minutes together. Everybody has seemed to admit that it was a perpetual deviation from a particular path, and a perpetual return to it; which, imperfect as the operation is, is the only method in which we can operate with our minds to carry on any process of thought.

THE ART OF LISTENING.

THERE are few good listeners in the world who make all the use that they might make, of the understandings of others, in the conduct of their own.

RESPECT FOR OTHERS.

I MAY be very wrong, and probably am so, but, in the whole course of my life, I do not know that I ever saw a man of considerable understanding respect the understandings of others as much as he might have done for his own improvement, and as it was just that he should do.

A CURE FOR CONTRADICTING.

THE habit of contradicting, into which young men,— and young men of ability in particular,—are apt to fall, is a habit extremely injurious to the powers of the understanding. I would recommend to such young men an intellectual regimen, of which I myself, in an earlier period of life, have felt the advantage: and that is, to assent to the two first propositions that they hear every day; and not only to assent to them, but, if they can, to improve and embellish them; and to make the speaker a little more in love with his own opinion than he was before. When they have a little got over the bitterness of assenting, they may then gradually increase the number of assents, and so go on as their constitution will bear it; and I have little doubt that, in time, this will effect a complete and perfect cure.

PERSEVERE.

THERE is one circumstance, I would preach up, morning, noon, and night, to young persons, for the management of their understanding. Whatever you are from nature, keep to it; never desert your own line of talent. If Providence only intended you to write poses for rings or mottoes for twelfth-cakes, keep to poses and mottoes: a good motto for a twelfth-cake is more respectable than a villanous epic poem in twelve books. Be what nature intended you for, and you will succeed: be anything else, and you will be ten thousand times worse than nothing.

UNITY OF THE MIND.

TALENT is talent, mind is mind, in all its branches. Wit gives to life one of its best flavours; common sense leads to immediate action, and gives society its daily motion; large and comprehensive views, its annual rotation; ridicule chastises folly and impudence, and keeps men in their proper sphere; subtlety seizes hold of the fine threads of truth; analogy darts away to the most sublime discoveries; feeling paints all the exquisite passions of man's soul, and rewards him by a thousand inward visitations for the sorrows that come from without. God made it all! It is all good! We must despise no sort of talent; they all have their separate duties and uses; all, the happiness of man for their object: they all improve, exalt, and gladden life.

CAUTION AN AID TO TALENT.

Caution, though it must be considered as something very different from talent, is no mean aid to every species of talent. As some men are so skilful in economy, that they will do as much with a hundred pounds as another will do with two, so there are a species of men, who have a wonderful management of their understandings, and will make as great a show, and enjoy as much consideration, with a certain quantity of understanding, as others will do with the double of their portion; and this by watching times and persons; by taking strong positions, and never fighting but from the vantage ground, and with great disparity of numbers; in short, by risking nothing, and by a perpetual and systematic attention to the security of reputation. Such rigid economy,— by laying out every shilling at compound interest, — very often accumulates a large stock of fame, where the original capital has been very inconsiderable; and, of course, may command any degree of opulence, where it sets out from great beginnings, and is united with real genius.

DISCOURAGEMENT.

Some men get early disgusted with the task of improvement, and the cultivation of the mind, from some excesses which they have committed, and mistakes into which they have been betrayed, at the beginning of life.

They abuse the whole art of navigation because they have stuck upon a shoal; whereas, the business is, to refit, careen, and set out a second time. The navigation is very difficult; few of us get through it at first, without some rubs and losses,—which the world are always ready enough to forgive, where they are honestly confessed, and diligently repaired.

QUICKNESS.

THERE is something extremely fascinating in quickness; and most men are desirous of appearing quick. The great rule for becoming so, is, *by not attempting to appear quicker than you really are;* by resolving to understand yourself and others, and to know what *you* mean, and what *they* mean, before you speak or answer. Every man must submit to be slow before he is quick; and insignificant, before he is important. The too early struggle against the pain of obscurity, corrupts no small share of understandings.

KNOWLEDGE.

IT is not the mere cry of moralists, and the flourish of rhetoricians: but it is *noble* to seek truth, and it is *beautiful* to find it. It is the ancient feeling of the human heart,—that knowledge is better than riches; and it is deeply and *sacredly true!* To mark the course of human passions as they have flowed on in the ages that are past; to see why nations have risen, and why they have fallen; to speak of heat, and light, and the winds; to know what man has discovered in the heavens above, and in the earth beneath; to hear the chemist unfold the marvellous properties that the Creator has locked up in a speck of earth; to be told that there are worlds so distant from our sun, that the quickness of light travelling from the world's creation, has never yet reached us; to wander in the creations of poetry, and grow warm again, with that eloquence which swayed the democracies of the old world; to go up with great reasoners to the First Cause of all, and to perceive, in the midst of all this dissolution and decay, and cruel separation, that there *is* one thing unchangeable, indestructible, and everlasting;—it is worth while in the days of our youth to strive hard for this great discipline; to pass sleepless nights for it, to give up to it laborious days; to spurn for it present pleasures; to endure for it afflicting poverty; to wade for it through darkness, and sorrow, and contempt, as the great spirits of the world have done in all ages and all times.

DO WHAT YOU CAN.

It is the greatest of all mistakes, to do nothing because you can only do little: but there are men who are always clamouring for immediate and stupendous effects, and think that virtue and knowledge are to be increased as a tower or a temple are to be increased, where the growth of its magnitude can be measured from day to day, and you cannot approach it without perceiving a fresh pillar, or admiring an added pinnacle.

ASSOCIATION OF IDEAS.

When two ideas have, by any accident, been joined together frequently in the understanding, the one idea has, ever after, the strongest tendency to bring back the other: for instance, the celebrated Descartes was very

much in love with a lady who squinted; he had so associated that passion with obliquity of vision, that he
declares, to the latest hour of his life he could never see
a lady with a cast in her eye, without experiencing the
most lively emotions.

LOVE NURTURED BY USE.

WHATEVER we love for its uses, we love for itself.   A
man begins to love his horse because he carries him well
out hunting : he ends with loving the horse without the
slightest reference to his utility; and keeps him when
he is blind and lame, with as much attention as in the
vigour of his youth.

THE LOVE OF A STICK.

I REMEMBER once seeing an advertisement in the
papers, with which I was much struck; and which I will
take the liberty of reading :—"Lost, in the Temple
Coffee House, and supposed to be taken away by mistake,
an oaken stick, which has supported its master not only
over the greatest part of Europe, but has been his companion in his journeys over the inhospitable deserts of
Africa; whoever will restore it to the waiter, will confer
a very serious obligation on the advertiser; or, if that
be any object, shall receive a recompense very much
above the value of the article restored."   Now, here is a
man, who buys a sixpenny stick, because it is useful;
and, totally forgetting the trifling causes which first
made his stick of any consequence, speaks of it with
warmth and affection: calls it his companion; and would
hardly have changed it, perhaps, for the gold stick which
is carried before the king.

FEELING.

WHAT was the first command? Not "let there be colours;" not "let the herb be green, and the heavens be blue:" but, "let there be *light!*" and forthwith there was every variety of colour! So with us; the first mandate was not, "let man be affected with anger and gratitude," but "let man feel;" and then, matter let loose upon him, with all its malignities, and all its pleasures, roused up in him his good and his bad passions, and made him as he is,—the best and the worst of created beings.

GRIEF AND PAIN DISCRIMINATED.

The difference between grief and pain is, that we apply the expression *grief* to those uneasy sensations which have not the body for their immediate cause; *pain*, to those which have. The loss of reputation occasions grief; the loss of a limb pain.

EDUCATED GRIEF.

I AM not speaking of the highest-refined London grief,—the grief of civilisation and softness; but the grief of a savage and a child. The grief of nature in its first stage is a violent, impatient, irritating passion, very much resembling anger. The natural effect of grief and pain is, to cry out as loud as possible, and to kick and sprawl in all possible directions; and I believe, if people would do so much more than they do, they would be all the better for it. The sitting on monuments smiling, and the green and yellow melancholy, is quite a subsequent business, entirely the result of education.

PEEVISHNESS AND ENVY.

PEEVISHNESS is resentment, excited by trifles. Envy is resentment excited by superiority,—not by *all* superiority, but by that to which you think you are fairly entitled; for a ploughman does not envy a king, but he envies another ploughman who has a shilling a week more than he has.

EFFECT OF HABIT ON FEAR.

FEAR is the apprehension of future evil. Habit diminishes fear, when it raises up contrary associations, and increases it, when it confirms the first associations. A soldier, who has often escaped, begins to disunite the two ideas of dying and fighting; he connects also with fighting, a sense of duty, a love of glory. Habit, I should think, would increase the sensation of fear, in a person who had undergone two or three painful operations, and was about to submit to another. A man works in a gunpowder-mill every day of his life, with the utmost *sang froid*, which you would not be very much pleased to enter for half an hour: you have associated with the manufactory, nothing but the accidents you have heard it is exposed to; he has associated with it, the numberless days he has passed there in perfect security. For the same reason, a sailor-boy stands unconcerned upon the mast; a mason upon a ladder; and a miner descends by his single rope. Their associations are altered by experience; therefore, in estimating the degree in which human creatures are under the influence of this passion, we must always remember their previous habits.

CONTAGION OF FEAR.

IN the late attack upon Egypt, our soldiers behaved with the most distinguished courage; but a physician did what, I suppose, no soldier in the whole army would have dared to have done;—he slept for three nights in the sheets of a patient who had died of the plague! If the question had been to encounter noisy, riotous, death he probably could not have done it; but where pus and miasma were concerned, he appears to have been a perfect hero. Fear, is the most contagious of all the passions; and the reason is obvious enough why it becomes so: it is much more likely that the cause of your fear should concern me, more than the cause of any other of your passions. If I see you very angry, it is not probable, unless we happen to be intimately connected, that the cause of your anger would prove to be a cause of mine; but if I see you dreadfully frightened, it immediately occurs to me, that I am implicated in the same cause of fear: — you have discovered that the play-house in which we are both sitting, is on fire; you have seen an enraged bull, running in the streets: I am not easy for an instant, till I have discovered the cause of your terror, and satisfied myself that it does not concern us both.

SHYNESS.

THE most curious offspring of shame, is shyness;—a word always used, I fancy, in a bad sense, to signify misplaced shame; for a person who felt only diffident, exactly in proportion as he ought, would never be called shy.

SHYNESS NO VIRTUE.

A SHY person not only *feels* pain, and *gives* pain; but, what is the worst, he incurs blame, for a want of that rational and manly confidence, which is so useful to those who possess it, and so pleasant to those who witness it.   I am severe against shyness, because it looks like a virtue without *being* a virtue; and because it gives us false notions of what the *real* virtue is.

THE SHAME OF THE SOUL.

THAT dread of shame, which virtue and wisdom teach, is, to act so, from the cradle to the tomb, that no man can cast upon you the shadow of reproach; not to swerve on this side for wealth, or on that side for favour; but to go on speaking truly, and acting justly: no man's oppressor, and no man's sycophant and slave.   This is the shame of the soul; and these are the blushes of the inward man; which are worth all the distortions of the body, and all the crimson of the face.

MORAL EDUCATION.

IN a strong mind, fear grows up into cautious sagacity; grief, into amiable tenderness.   Without the noble toil of moral education, the one is abject cowardice, the other eternal gloom; therefore, there is the good, and there is the evil!   Every man's destiny is in his own hands.

THE MEMORY OF HAPPINESS.

MANKIND are always happier for having been happy; so that if you make them happy now, you make them happy twenty years hence, by the memory of it.

PLEASURE FAVOURABLE TO BENEVOLENCE.

THE pleasures of the body are favourable to all the benevolent virtues,—and its pains unfavourable.   No one is so inclined to good nature, courtesy, and generosity, when cold, wet, and dirty, as after pleasant feeding and during genial warmth.

HAPPINESS AN AID TO VIRTUE.

THAT virtue gives happiness, we all know; but if it be true, that happiness contributes to virtue, the principle furnishes us with some sort of excuse for the errors and excesses of able young men, at the bottom of life, fretting with impatience under their obscurity, and hatching a thousand chimeras of being neglected and overlooked by the world. The natural cure for these errors is, the sunshine of prosperity: as they get happier, they get better; and learn, from the respect which they receive from others, to respect themselves. "Whenever," says Mr. Lancaster, (in his book just published,) "I met with a boy particularly mischievous, I made him a monitor; I never knew this fail." The *cause* for the promotion, and the kind of encouragement it must occasion, I confess appear rather singular; but of the *effect*, I have no sort of doubt.

INFLUENCE OF MUSIC.

IT cost Timotheus, I dare say, a great deal of fine playing, to throw the soul of Alexander into a tumult of feeling; but that once accomplished, the bard harped him into any passion he pleased. However this be true of Timotheus and Alexander, it is certainly true of music in general. If we are stupid or indolent, we resist its powers for some time; but when the twangings, and the beatings, and the breathings once reach the heart, and set it moving with all its streams of life, the mind bounds from grief to joy, from joy to grief, without effort or pang;- but seems rather to derives its keenest pleasure from the quick vicissitude of passion to which it is exposed. It is the same with acting. It is difficult to rouse the mind from an ordinary state, to a dramatic state; but that once done, we glide with ease from any passion, to one the most opposite.

REMOTE IMPRESSIONS.

ANY satisfaction we have recently enjoyed, and of which the memory is fresh and perfect, operates on the will with more violence than another, of which the traces are decayed and obliterated. Contiguity in time and place, has an amazing effect upon the passions. An enormous globe of fire, which fell at Pekin, would not excite half the interest which the most trifling phenomenon could give birth to nearer home. I am persuaded many men might be picked out of the streets, who, for 1000 guineas paid down, would consent to submit to a very cruel death, in fifteen years from the time of receiving the money.

GOOD TEMPER, GOOD HUMOUR, GOOD NATURE.

THERE are three expressions in our language, which, because they refer to the kind and degree of the passions, require some explanation in this place;—Temper, Humour, and Nature. When used with adjectives of blame and praise, temper and humour mean nearly the same thing. A good-humoured person, or a good-tempered person, is one in whom the intentions and actions of others do not easily excite bad passions,—who does not mistake the motives by which the rest of the world are actuated towards him. A good-natured person is a man of active benevolence; who seeks to give pleasure to others in little things. Good-temper measures how a man is acted upon by others; good-nature measures how he acts for others. The presumption is, that the two excellences would be found uniformly conjoined together; that a man who was passively benevolent, would be actively so too: but the reverse is often the case in practice. There are many men of inviolable temper, who never exert themselves to do a good-natured thing, from one end of the year to the other; and ·many in the highest degree irritable, who are perpetually employed in little acts of good-nature.

GOOD FEELING.

To bring a large twelfth-cake to a child, is good nature; to give him education, support and protection, though he have no natural claim upon you, is compassion, and the summit of good feeling.

STRENGTH OF MIND.

WHAT we call strength of mind, implies the prevalence of the calm passions above the violent.

CALM PASSIONS.

WITHOUT some calm passion,—some degree of some species of desire,—the mind could not long endure.

PLEASURE OF MISCHIEF.

SCHOOLBOYS climb walls and trees because it is agreeable to them to be afraid of tumbling;—and this explains the pleasures of mischief.

PLEASURE OF EXCITEMENT.

YOUNG men turn soldiers and sailors from the love of being agitated; and for the same reason, country gentlemen leap over stone walls.

PLEASURE OF GRIEF.

THE love of emotion is the foundation of tragedy; and so pleasant is it to be moved, that we set off for the express purpose of looking excessively dismal for two hours and a half, interspersed with long intervals of positive sobbing.

STRENGTH OF DESIRE.

MEN differ, as their desires are vehement or weak. Some can hardly be said to have any desires at all; others would overturn kingdoms, and mingle heaven with earth, to effect the least of all their desires.

THE PASSIONS OF LIFE.

SUCH are a few of the most striking phenomena of the passions, which move the world, and make up the secret life and inward existence of man; for what we do see and know with certainty of any human creature, is, whether he is lodged in marble or in clay, — whether down or straw is his bed,—whether he is clothed in the purple of the world, or moulders in rags. The inward world, the man within the breast, the dominion of thought, the region of passion, — all this we cannot penetrate: we can never tell how a kind and benevolent heart can cheer a desperate fortune: the comfort which the lowest man may feel in a spotless mind, — the firmness which a man derives from loving justice, — the glory with which he rebukes the bad emotion, and bids his passions be still. Therefore, not to the accidents of life, but to the fountains of thought, and to the springs of pleasure and pain, should the efforts of man be directed to rear up such sentiments as shall guard us from the pangs of envy; to make us rejoice in the happiness of every sentient being; to feel too happy ourselves for hatred and resentment; to forget the body or to enslave it for ever; seeking to purify, to exalt, and to refine our nature. This is the rigid discipline of moral philosophy, which, rigid, as it is, is so beautiful and so good, that without it no condition of life is tolerable; with it, none wretched, sordid, or mean.

THE MOTIVE POWER OF LIFE.

Look at the bustle of Bond Street; drive from thence to the Royal Exchange; observe the infinite variety of occupations, movements, and agitations as you go along: nothing can appear more intricate, — more impossible to be reduced to anything like rule or system; and yet, a very few elements put all this mass of human beings into action. If a messenger from heaven were on a sudden to annihilate the love of power, the love of wealth, and the love of esteem, in the human heart; in half an hour's time the streets would be as empty, and as silent, as they are in the middle of the night.

SYMPATHY.

How ridiculous a play would be, of which a hungry man were the hero ! Why? — because we never suffer from extreme hunger, and have very little sympathy for it; there is hardly any such thing known in civilised society; the author himself would, probably, be the only man in the whole play-house, who had ever seriously felt the want of a dinner. But if a nation of savages were to see such a drama acted, they would see no ridicule in it at all; because starving to death is, among them, no uncommon thing: they are advanced such a little way in civilisation, that to fill their stomachs, is the great and important object of life : and I have no doubt, that to an Indian audience, the loss of a piece of venison might be the basis of a tragedy which would fill every eye with tears; but on the contrary, they might be very likely to laugh, to hear a man complain of his wounded honour, if it turned out that he had ten days' provision beforehand in his cabin.

EXTENSION OF KNOWLEDGE.

NOTHING can be more important to the welfare of a community, than the wide extension of rational curiosity in the desire of knowledge; it not only increases the comforts, enlivens the feelings, and improves the faculties of man, but it forms the firmest barrier against the love of pleasure, and stops the progress of corruption. Every nation has its chances for happiness increased, in proportion as it honours and rewards a spirit which, above all things, honours and rewards it.

SIC VOS NON VOBIS.

A GREAT battle is gained, the plan and depositions of which are admirable; the general who conducted the army is considered as a consummate master of the mili-

tary art, and arrives at the very summit of reputation as
an accomplished officer; but this plan of the battle was
drawn out for him the evening before, by one of his
aides-de-camp, whose original conception it was, and to
whom all the merit is really due. Which is the most
enviable situation? His, who is praised without being
praiseworthy; or his, who is praiseworthy without being
praised? Nobody here could entertain a moment's
doubt about the matter, that the praiseworthiness is
preferable to the praise. But why? Merely *from* the love
of praise; merely because it, in the end, procures more
praise.

PROPRIETY AND CONTRAST.

A GREAT deal of the propriety of common behaviour is
regulated by contrast. No one could endure to see a
judge dance, or a bishop vault into his saddle. A very
regulated and subdued pleasantry and relaxation, is all
that can be allowed to men habitually and officially
dignified. Contrast in trifling objects, which can excite
no high emotion, is the source of humour.

LOVE OF TRAVELLING.

IN the rage for travelling, the object is not so much to
gratify the love of novelty as the love of excellence; not
merely to see new things, but new grand things, new
beautiful things, new excellence, in which the grand and
beautiful will, I should think, upon reflection, be found
to have a much greater effect than the new.

USEFUL NOVELTY.

NOVELTY is the foundation of the love of knowledge:
which is nothing but the desire of *useful* novelty.

EXPERIENCE.

THE first time I make a voyage to the West Indies, I am afraid; the tenth time, I am not;—why? not because my sensibility is blunted; but because my reason is instructed: I perceive there are much greater resources in skill and science than I imagined; that the ship can ride with safety over those monstrous waves which at first bid fair to destroy; that an unctuous and weather-beaten personage, by turning a wheel near him, can guide the prodigious animal, in whose inside I am sailing, with the most unerring precision. It is not that I meet the same danger better, but that I have found out it is a much less danger.

HARDSHIP PRODUCED BY HABIT.

A VERY curious part of habit,—that though we feel *no pleasure* in doing the thing, we feel a great pain from *not* doing it.

NATURE'S PENALTIES.

No reason that I know of, can be given, why the habit of having done a thing, should increase the tendency to do it: all reason stops at this point, — it is not possible to explain it. The pain annexed to the interruption of the habit, is the means by which obedience to the law is secured. Nature is too good a legislator to pass any act without annexing a smart penalty to the violation of it.

HABIT OF VICE.

IF we wish to know who is the most degraded, and the most wretched, of human beings;—if it be any object of curiosity in moral science, to gauge the dimensions of wretchedness, and to see how deep the miseries of man can reach; if this be any object of curiosity, look for the man who has practised a vice so long, that he curses it and clings to it; that he pursues it, because he feels a great law of his nature driving him on towards it; but, reaching it, knows that it will gnaw his heart, and tear his vitals, and make him roll himself in the dust with anguish. Say everything for vice which you can say, — magnify any pleasure as much as you please, but don't believe you can keep it; don't believe you have any secret for sending on quicker the sluggish blood, and for refreshing the faded nerve.

THE ORBIT OF HABIT.

THE period of time in which a habit renews its action, or (if I may be allowed the expression) the orbit of a habit, is of very different dimensions. We may have a habit of shrugging up the shoulders every half-hour; or, of eating three eggs every morning; or, of dining at a club once a month; or, of going down to see a relation once a year: but it is difficult to conceive any habit forming itself for a period greater than a year. I can easily conceive that a person who sets off on every 1st of June, to pay a visit, might have the force of habit added to his other inducements, and go, partly because he loved the persons, partly because he had done it before; but is it easy to believe that there is a habit of doing anything every other year? or, how very ridiculous it would sound for two persons to say, "We agreed a long time ago to dine together every Bissextile, or leap year, and it is now grown into a perfect habit!" This limitation of habits to the period of a year, — which I by no means lay any great stress upon, but which has some degree of truth in it, — depends somewhat upon the revolution of names and appearances. To do anything the first day of a month, or on one particular day every year, is to strengthen a habit by the recurrence of names or seasons; but if an action be performed every third or fourth year, the same name and the same appearances have occurred, without being connected with the same deed, and therefore the habit is impaired.

EFFECTS OF HABIT ON HUMAN NATURE.

THERE is no degree of disguise, or distortion, which human nature may not be made to assume from habit; it grows in every direction in which it is trained, and accommodates itself to every circumstance which caprice or design places in its way. It is a plant with such various aptitudes, and such opposite propensities, that it flourishes in a hot-house, or the open air; is terrestrial, or aquatic; parasitical, or independent; looks well in exposed situations, thrives in protected ones; can bear its own luxuriance, admits of amputation; succeeds in perfect liberty, and can submit to be bent down into any of the forms of art: it is so flexible and ductile, so accommodating and vivacious, that of two methods of managing it — completely opposite, neither the one nor the other need to be considered as mistaken and bad.

HABIT OF SECLUSION.

WHO could imagine that men and women would shut themselves up in monasteries, and nunneries, living the absurd life which they do, in such sort of places? — yet, the greater part of nuns and friars, who came over here, immediately shut out the day-light of common sense, and fell to forming nunneries and monasteries again.

THE FIRE OF LIFE.

THE passions are in morals, what motion is in physics: they create, preserve, and animate; and without them, all would be silence and death. Avarice guides men across the deserts of the ocean; pride covers the earth with trophies, and mausoleums, and pyramids; love turns men from their savage rudeness; ambition shakes the very foundations of kingdoms. By the love of glory, weak nations swell into magnitude and strength. Whatever there is of terrible, whatever there is of beautiful in human events, all that shakes the soul to and fro, and is remembered while thought and flesh cling together,—all these have their origin from the passions. As it is only in storms, and when their coming waters are driven up into the air, that we catch a sight of the depths of the sea, it is only in the season of perturbation that we have a glimpse of the real internal nature of man. It is then only, that the might of these eruptions shaking his frame, dissipate all the feeble coverings of opinion, and rend in pieces that cobweb veil, with which fashion hides the feelings of the heart. It is then only that Nature speaks her genuine feelings; and, as at the last night of Troy, when Venus illuminated the darkness, Æneas saw the gods themselves at work,—so may we, when the blaze of passion is flung upon man's nature, mark in him the signs of a celestial origin, and tremble at the invisible agents of God!

THE POWER OF THE HEART.

THE history of the world shows us that men are not to be counted by their numbers, but by the fire and vigour of their passions; by their deep sense of injury; by their memory of past glory; by their eagerness for fresh fame; by their clear and steady resolution of ceasing to live, or of achieving a particular object, which, when it is *once* formed, strikes off a load of manacles and chains, and gives free space to all heavenly and heroic feelings. All great and extraordinary actions come from the heart.

ENGLISH READING.

IN the time you can give to English reading you should consider what it is most needful to have, what it is most shameful to want,—shirts and stockings, before frills and collars. Such is the history of your own country, to be studied in Hume, then in Rapin's History of England, with Tindal's Continuation. Hume takes you to the end of James the second, Rapin and Tindal will carry you to the end of Anne. Then, Cox's "Life of Sir Robert Walpole," and the "Duke of Marlborough;" and these read with attention to dates and geography. Then the history of the other three or four enlightened nations of Europe. For the English poets, I will let you off at present with Milton, Dryden, Pope, and Shakspeare; and remember, always in books keep the best company.

Don't read a line of Ovid till you have mastered Virgil; nor a line of Thomson till you have exhausted Pope; nor of Massinger, till you are familiar with Shakspeare. — [*Letter to his Son*, 1819.]

UNHAPPINESS AT SCHOOL.

My son writes me word he is unhappy at school. This makes me unhappy; but, 1st. There is much unhappiness in human life: how can school be exempt? 2ndly. Boys are apt to take a particular moment of depression for a general feeling, and they are in fact rarely unhappy; at the moment I write, perhaps he is playing about in the highest spirits. 3rdly. When he comes to state his grievance, it will probably have vanished, or be so trifling, that it will yield to argument or expostulation. 4thly. At all events, if it is a real evil which makes him unhappy, I must find out what it is, and proceed to act upon it; but I must wait till I can, either in person or by letter, find out what it is. — [*Memoir.*]

THE ATMOSPHERE OF RELIGION.

Not only is religion calm and tranquil, but it has an extensive atmosphere round it, whose calmness and tranquillity must be preserved, if you would avoid misrepresentation. — [*Memoir.*]

RESPECT.

Not only study that those with whom you live should habitually respect you, but cultivate such manners as will secure the respect of persons with whom you occasionally converse.   Keep up the habit of being respected, and do not attempt to be more amusing and agreeable than is consistent with the preservation of respect.

MAXIMS AND RULES OF LIFE.

REMEMBER that every person, however low, has *rights* and *feelings*. In all contentions, let peace be rather your object, than triumph: value triumph only as the means of peace.

Remember that your children, your wife, and your servants, have rights and feelings; treat them as you would treat persons who could turn again. Apply these doctrines to the administration of justice as a magistrate. Rank poisons make good medicines; error and misfortune may be turned into wisdom and improvement.

Do not attempt to frighten children and inferiors by passion; it does more harm to your own character than it does good to them; the same thing is better done by firmness and persuasion.

If you desire the common people to treat you as a gentleman, you must conduct yourself as a gentleman should do to them.

When you meet with neglect, let it rouse you to exertion, instead of mortifying your pride. Set about lessening those defects which expose you to neglect, and improve those excellences which command attention and respect.

Against general fears, remember how very precarious life is, take what care you will; how short it is, last as long as it ever does.

Rise early in the morning, not only to avoid self-reproach, but to make the most of the little life that remains; not only to save the hours lost in sleep, but to avoid that languor which is spread over mind and body for the whole of that day in which you have lain late in bed.

Passion gets less and less powerful after every defeat. Husband energy for the real demand which the dangers of life make upon it.

Find fault, when you must find fault, in private, if possible; and some time after the offence, rather than at the time. The blamed are less inclined to resist, when they are blamed without witnesses; both parties are calmer, and the accused party is struck with the forbearance of the accuser, who has seen the fault, and watched for a private and proper time for mentioning it.

Don't be too severe upon yourself and your own failings; keep on, don't faint, be energetic to the last.

If you wish to keep mind clear and body healthy, abstain from all fermented liquors.

Fight against sloth, and do all you can to make friends.

If old age is even a state of suffering, it is a state of superior wisdom, in which man avoids all the rash and foolish things he does in his youth, and which make life dangerous and painful.

Death must be distinguished from dying, with which it is often confounded.

Reverence and stand in awe of yourself.

How Nature delights and amuses us by varying even the character of insects: the ill-nature of the wasp, the sluggishness of the drone, the volatility of the butterfly, the slyness of the bug.

Take short views, hope for the best, and trust in God. — [*Memoir.*]

MANAGEMENT OF THE BODY.

THE longer I live, the more I am convinced that the apothecary is of more importance than Seneca; and that half the unhappiness in the world proceeds from little stoppages, from a duct choked up, from food pressing in the wrong place, from a vext duodenum, or an agitated pylorus.

The deception, as practised upon human creatures, is curious and entertaining. My friend sups late; he eats some strong soup, then a lobster, then some tart, and he dilutes these esculent varieties with wine. The next day I call upon him. He is going to sell his house in London, and to retire into the country. He is alarmed for his eldest daughter's health. His expenses are hourly increasing, and nothing but a timely retreat can save him from ruin. All this is the lobster : and when over-excited nature has had time to manage this testaceous encumbrance, the daughter recovers, the finances are in good order, and every rural idea effectually excluded from the mind.

In the same manner old friendships are destroyed by toasted cheese, and hard salted meat has led to suicide. Unpleasant feelings of the body produce correspondent sensations in the mind, and a great scene of wretchedness is sketched out by a morsel of indigestible and misguided food. Of such infinite consequence to happiness is it to study the body !

I have nothing new to say upon the management which the body requires. The common rules are the best: — exercise without fatigue; generous living without excess; early rising, and moderation in sleeping. These are the apothegms of old women; but if they are not attended to, happiness becomes so extremely difficult that very few persons can attain to it. In this point of view, the care of the body becomes a subject of elevation and importance. A walk in the fields, an hour's less sleep, may remove all those bodily vexations and disquietudes which are such formidable enemies to virtue; and may enable the mind to pursue its own resolves without that constant train of temptations to resist, and obstacles to overcome, which it always experiences from the bad organisation of its companion. Johnson says, every man is a rascal when he is sick; meaning, I suppose, that he has no benevolent dispositions at that period towards his fellow-creatures, but that his notions assume a character of greater affinity to his bodily feelings, and that, *feeling* pain, he becomes malevolent; and if this be true of great diseases, it is true in a less degree of the smaller ailments of the body.

Get up in a morning, walk before breakfast, pass four or five hours of the day in some active employment; then eat and drink over-night, lie in bed till one or two o'clock, saunter away the rest of the day in doing nothing! — can any two human beings be more perfectly dissimilar than the same individual under these two different systems of corporeal management? and is it not of as great importance towards happiness to pay a minute attention to the body, as it is to study the wisdom of Chrysippus and Crantor? — [*Memoir.*]

OF OCCUPATION.

A GOOD stout bodily machine being provided, we must be actively occupied, or there can be little happiness.

If a good useful occupation be *not* provided, it is so ungenial to the human mind to do nothing, that men occupy themselves *perilously,* as with gaming; or *frivolously,* as with walking up and down a street at a watering-place, and looking at the passers-by; or *malevolently,* as by teazing their wives and children. It is impossible to support, for any length of time, a state of perfect *ennui;* and if you were to shut a man up for any length of time within four walls, without occupation, he would go mad. If idleness do not produce vice or malevolence, it commonly produces melancholy.

A stockbroker or a farmer have no leisure for imaginary wretchedness; their minds are usually hurried away by the necessity of noticing external objects, and they are guaranteed from that curse of idleness, the eternal disposition to think of themselves.

If we have no necessary occupation, it becomes extremely difficult to make to ourselves occupations as entirely absorbing as those which necessity imposes.

The profession which a man makes for himself is seldom more than a half profession, and often leaves the mind in a state of vacancy and inoccupation. We must lash ourselves up however, as well as we can, to a notion of its great importance; and as the dispensing power is in our own hands, we must be very jealous of remission and of idleness.

It may seem absurd that a gentleman who does not live by the profits of farming should rise at six o'clock in the morning to look after his farm ; or, if botany be his object, that he should voyage to Iceland in pursuit of it. He is the happier however for his eagerness; his mind is more fully employed, and he is much more effectually guaranteed from all the miseries of *ennui.*

When a very clever man, or a very great man, takes to cultivating turnips and retiring, it is generally an imposture. The moment men cease to talk of their turnips, they are wretched and full of self-reproach. Let every man be *occupied,* and occupied in the highest employment of which his nature is capable, and die with the consciousness that *he has done his best ! — [Memoir.]*

OF FRIENDSHIP.

Life is to be fortified by many friendships. To love, and to be loved, is the greatest happiness of existence. If I lived under the burning sun of the equator, it would be a pleasure to me to think that there were many human beings on the other side of the world who regarded and respected me ; I could and would not live if I were alone upon the earth, and cut off from the remembrance of my fellow-creatures. It is not that a man has occasion often to fall back upon the kindness of his friends ; perhaps he may never experience the necessity of doing so ; but we are governed by our imaginations, and they stand there as a solid and impregnable bulwark against all the evils of life.

Friendships should be formed with persons of all ages and conditions, and with both sexes. I have a friend who is a bookseller, to whom I have been very civil, and who would do anything to serve me; and I have two or three small friendships among persons in much humbler walks of life, who, I verily believe, would do me a considerable kindness according to their means. It is a great happiness to form a sincere friendship with a woman; but a friendship among persons of different sexes rarely or ever takes place in this country. The austerity of our manners hardly admits of such a connection; — compatible with the most perfect innocence, and a source of the highest possible delight to those who are fortunate enough to form it. — [*Memoir.*]

FRANK EXPLANATIONS.

I AM for frank explanations with friends in cases of affronts. They sometimes save a perishing friendship, and even place it on a firmer basis than at first; but secret discontent must always end badly. — [*Memoir.*]

OF CHEERFULNESS.

CHEERFULNESS and good spirits depend in a great degree upon bodily causes, but much may be done for the promotion of this turn of mind. Persons subject to low spirits should make the rooms in which they live as cheerful as possible; taking care that the paper with which the wall is covered should be of a brilliant, lively colour, hanging up pictures or prints, and covering the chimney-piece with beautiful china. A bay-window looking upon pleasant objects, and, above all, a large fire whenever the weather will permit, are favourable to good spirits, and the tables near should be strewed with books and pamphlets. To this must be added as much eating and drinking as is consistent with health; and some manual employment for men, — as gardening, a carpenter's shop, the turning-lathe, &c. Women have always manual employment enough, and it is a great source of cheerfulness. Fresh air, exercise, occupation, society, and travelling, are powerful remedies. — [*Memoir.*]

A COUNTRY DINNER PARTY.

DID you ever dine out in the country? What misery human beings inflict on each other under the name of pleasure! We went to dine last Thursday with Mr. ——, a neighbouring clergyman, a haunch of venison being the stimulus to the invitation. We set out at five o'clock; drove in a broiling sun, on dusty roads, three miles, in our best gowns; found Squire and parsons assembled in a small hot room, the whole house redolent of frying; talked, as is our wont, of roads, weather, and turnips; that done, began to grow hungry, then serious, then impatient. At last a stripling, evidently caught up for the occasion, opened the door and beckoned our host out of the room. After some moments of awful suspense, he returned to us with a face of much distress, saying, "the woman assisting in the kitchen had mistaken the soup for dirty water, and had thrown it away, so we must do without it;" we all agreed it was perhaps as well we should, under the circumstances. At last, to our joy, dinner was announced; but oh, ye gods! as we entered the dining-room what a gale met our nose! the venison was high; the venison was uneatable, and was obliged to follow the soup with all speed.

Dinner proceeded, but our spirits flagged under these accumulated misfortunes. There was an ominous pause between the first and second course; we looked each other in the face—what new disaster awaited us? The pause became fearful. At last the door burst open, and the boy rushed in, calling out aloud, "Please Sir has Betty any right to leather I?" What human gravity

could stand this? We roared with laughter; all took
part against Betty, obtained the second course with some
difficulty, bored each other the usual time, ordered our
carriages, expecting our post-boys to be drunk, and were
grateful to Providence for not permitting them to deposit us in a wet ditch. So much for dinners in the
country. — [*Memoir.*]

IMPROMPTU ON MR. JEFFREY RIDING ON A DONKEY.

> WITTY as Horatius Flaccus,
> As great a Jacobin as Gracchus,
> Short, though not as fat, as Bacchus,
> Riding on a little Jackass.

SYDNEY SMITH IN A YORKSHIRE LIVING.

A DINER-OUT, a wit, and a popular preacher, I was suddenly caught up by the Archbishop of York, and transported to my living in Yorkshire, where there had not
been a resident clergyman for a hundred and fifty years.
Fresh from London, not knowing a turnip from a carrot,
I was compelled to farm three hundred acres, and without capital to build a parsonage-house.

I asked and obtained three years' leave from the Archbishop, in order to effect an exchange, if possible; and
fixed myself meantime at a small village two miles from
York, in which was a fine old house of the time of Queen
Elizabeth, where resided the last of the squires, with his
lady, who looked as if she had walked straight out of the
Ark, or had been the wife of Enoch. He was a perfect
specimen of the Trullibers of old; he smoked, hunted,
drank beer at his door with his grooms and dogs, and
spelt over the county paper on Sundays.

At first, he heard I was a Jacobin and a dangerous fellow, and turned aside as I passed: but at length, when he found the peace of the village undisturbed, harvests much as usual, Juno and Ponto uninjured, he first bowed, then called, and at last reached such a pitch of confidence that he used to bring the papers, that I might explain the difficult words to him; actually discovered that I had made a joke, laughed till I thought he would have died of convulsions, and ended by inviting me to see his dogs.

All my efforts for an exchange having failed, I asked and obtained from my friend the Archbishop another year to build in. And I then set my shoulder to the wheel in good earnest; sent for an architect; he produced plans which would have ruined me. I made him my bow: " You build for glory, Sir; I, for use." I returned him his plans, with five-and-twenty pounds, and sat down in my thinking-chair; and in a few hours Mrs. Sydney and I concocted a plan which has produced what I call the model of parsonage-houses.

I then took to horse to provide bricks and timber; was advised to make my own bricks of my own clay; of course, when the kiln was opened, all bad; mounted my horse again, and in twenty-four hours had bought thousands of bricks and tons of timber. Was advised by neighbouring gentlemen to employ oxen: bought four,— Tug and Lug, Haul and Crawl; but Tug and Lug took to fainting, and required buckets of sal-volatile, and Haul and Crawl to lie down in the mud. So I did as I ought to have done at first,—took the advice of the farmer instead of the gentleman; sold my oxen, bought a team of horses, and at last, in spite of a frost which delayed me six weeks, in spite of walls running down with wet, in spite of the advice and remonstrances of friends who predicted our death, in spite of an infant of six months old who had never been out of the house, I landed my family in my new house nine months after laying the first stone, on the 20th of March; and performed my promise to the letter to the Archbishop, by issuing forth at midnight with a lantern to meet the last cart, with the cook and the cat, which had stuck in the mud, and fairly established them before twelve o'clock at night in the new parsonage-house;—a feat, taking ignorance, inexperience, and poverty into consideration, requiring, I assure you, no small degree of energy.

It made me a very poor man for many years, but I never repented it. I turned schoolmaster, to educate my son, as I could not afford to send him to school. Mrs. Sydney turned schoolmistress, to educate my girls, as I could not afford a governess. I turned farmer, as I could not let my land. A man-servant was too expensive; so I caught up a little garden-girl, made like a mile-stone, christened her Bunch, put a napkin in her hand, and made her my butler. The girls taught her to read, Mrs. Sydney to wait, and I undertook her morals; Bunch became the best butler in the county.

I had little furniture, so I bought a cart-load of deals; took a carpenter (who came to me for parish relief), called Jack Robinson, with a face like a full-moon, into my service; established him in a barn, and said, " Jack, furnish my house." You see the result!

At last it was suggested that a carriage was much wanted in the establishment. After diligent search, I discovered in the back settlements of a York coachmaker an ancient green chariot, supposed to have been the earliest invention of the kind. I brought it home in triumph to my admiring family. Being somewhat dilapidated, the village tailor lined it, the village black-

smith repaired it; nay, but for Mrs Sydney's earnest
entreaties we believe the village painter would have
exercised his genius upon the exterior; it escaped this
danger however, and the result was wonderful. Each
year added to its charms : it grew younger and younger;
a new wheel, a new spring; I christened it the *Immortal.*
It was known all over the neighbourhood; the village
boys cheered it, and the village dogs barked at it; but
" Faber meæ fortunæ " was my motto, and we had no
false shame.

Added to all these domestic cares, I was village parson,
village doctor, village comforter, village magistrate, and
Edinburgh Reviewer; so you see I had not much time
left on my hands to regret London.

My house was considered the ugliest in the county,
but all admitted it was one of the most comfortable; and
we did not die, as our friends had predicted, of the damp
walls of the parsonage. — [*Memoir.*]

·EQUITATION.

I USED to think a fall from a horse dangerous, but
much experience has convinced me to the contrary. I
have had six falls in two years, and just behaved like
the three per cents when they fall,—I got up again, and
am not a bit the worse for it, any more than the stock in
question. I left off riding, however, for the good of my
parish and the peace of my family; for, somehow or
other, my horse and I had a habit of parting company.
On one occasion I found myself suddenly prostrate
in the streets of York, much to the delight of the
Dissenters. Another time, my horse Calamity flung
me over his head into a neighbouring parish, as if I had
been a shuttlecock, and I felt grateful it was not into a

neighbouring planet; but as no harm came of it, I might have persevered perhaps, if, on a certain day, a Quaker tailor from a neighbouring village, to which I had said I was going to ride, had not taken it into his head to call, soon after my departure, and requested to see Mrs. Sydney. She instantly, conceiving I was thrown, if not killed, rushed down to the man, exclaiming, "Where is he? where is your master? is he hurt?" The astonished and quaking snip stood silent from surprise. Still more agitated by his silence, she exclaimed, "Is he hurt? I insist upon knowing the worst." "Why, please, ma'am, it is only thy little bill, a very small account, I wanted thee to settle," replied he, in much surprise. After this, you may suppose, I sold my horse: however, it is some comfort to know that my friend Sir George is one fall ahead of me, and is certainly a worse rider. It is a great proof, too, of the liberality of this county, where everybody can ride as soon as they are born, that they tolerate me at all.—[*Memoir.*]

DEFINITION OF A NICE PERSON.

A NICE person is neither too tall nor too short, looks clean and cheerful, has no prominent feature, makes no difficulties, is never misplaced, sits bodkin, is never foolishly affronted, and is void of affectations.

A nice person helps you well at dinner, understands you, is always gratefully received by young and old, Whig and Tory, grave and gay.

There is something in the very air of a nice person which inspires you with confidence, makes you talk, and talk without fear of malicious misrepresentation; you feel that you are reposing upon a nature which God has made kind, and created for the benefit and happiness of society.   It has the effect upon the mind which soft air and a fine climate have upon the body.

A nice person is clear of little, trumpery passions, acknowledges superiority, delights in talent, shelters humility, pardons adversity, forgives deficiency, respects all men's rights, never stops the bottle, is never long and never wrong, always knows the day of the month and the name of everybody at table, and never gives pain to any human being.

If anybody is wanted for a party, a nice person is the first thought of; when the child is christened, when the daughter is married,—all the joys of life are communicated to nice people; the hand of the dying man is always held out to a nice person.

A nice person never knocks over wine or melted butter, does not tread upon the dog's foot, or molest the family cat, eats soup without noise, laughs in the right place, and has a watchful and attentive eye.

DEFINITION OF HARDNESS OF CHARACTER.

HARDNESS is a want of minute attention to the feelings of others.   It does not proceed from malignity or a carelessness of inflicting pain, but from a want of delicate perception of those little things by which pleasure is conferred or pain excited.

A hard person thinks he has done enough if he does not speak ill of your relations, your children, or your country; and then, with the greatest good-humour and volubility, and with a total inattention to your individual state and position, gallops over a thousand fine feelings, and leaves in every step the mark of his hoofs upon your heart.   Analyse the conversation of a well-bred man who is clear of the besetting sin of hardness; it is a perpetual homage of polite good-nature. He remembers that you are connected with the Church, and he avoids (whatever his opinions may be) the most distant reflections on the Establishment. He knows that you are admired, and he admires you as far as is compatible with good-breeding. He sees that, though young, you are at the head of a great establishment, and he infuses into his manner and conversation that respect which is so pleasing to all who exercise authority. He leaves you in perfect good-humour with yourself, because you perceive how much and how successfully you have been studied.

In the meantime the gentleman on the other side of you (a highly moral and respectable man) has been crushing little sensibilities, and violating little proprieties, and overlooking little discriminations; and without violating anything which can be called a *rule,* or committing what can be denominated a *fault,* has displeased and dispirited you, from wanting that fine vision which sees little things, and that delicate touch which handles them, and that fine sympathy which this superior moral organisation always bestows.

So great an evil in society is *hardness,* and that want of perception of the minute circumstances which occasion pleasure or pain!

ADDRESS TO THE MACHINE BURNERS (1828).

To Mr. Swing.

THE wool your coat is made of is spun by machinery, and this machinery makes your coat two or three shillings cheaper,—perhaps six or seven. Your white hat is made by machinery at half price. The coals you burn are pulled out of the pit by machinery, and are sold to you much cheaper than they could be if they were pulled out by hand.   You do not complain of *these* machines, because they do you good, though they throw many artisans out of work.   But what right have you to object to fanning machines, which make bread cheaper to the artisans, and to avail yourselves of *other* machines which make manufactures cheaper to you ?

If all machinery were abolished, everything would be so dear that you would be ten times worse off than you now are.   Poor people's cloth would get up to a guinea a yard.   Hats could not be sold for less than eighteen shillings.   Coals would be three shillings per hundred. It would be quite impossible for a poor man to obtain any comfort.

If you begin to object to machinery in farming, you may as well object to a plough, because it employs fewer men than a spade.   You may object to a harrow, because it employs fewer men than a rake.   You may object even to a spade, because it employs fewer men than fingers and sticks, with which savages scratch the ground in Otaheite.   If you expect manufacturers to turn against machinery, look at the consequence.   They may succeed, perhaps, in driving machinery out of the town they live in, but they often drive the manufacturer *out* of the town also.   He sets up his trade in some distant part of the country, gets new men, and the disciples of Swing are left to starve in the scene of their violence and folly.   In this way the lace manufacture travelled in the time of Ludd, Swing's grandfather, from Nottingham to Tiverton. Suppose a free importation of corn to be allowed, as it ought to be, and will be.   If you will not allow farmers to grow corn here as cheap as they can, more corn will come from America; for every threshing-machine that is destroyed, more *Americans* will be employed, *not* more Englishmen.

Swing! Swing! you are a stout fellow, but you are a bad adviser. The law is up, and the Judge is coming. Fifty persons in Kent are already transported, and will see their wives and children no more. Sixty persons will be hanged in Hampshire. There are two hundred for trial in Wiltshire—all scholars of Swing! I am no farmer: I have not a machine bigger than a pepper-mill. I am a sincere friend to the poor, and I think every man should live by his labour: but it cuts me to the very heart to see honest husbandmen perishing by that worst of all machines, the gallows,— under the guidance of that most fatal of all leaders—Swing!—[*Memoir.*]

ADVICE TO PARISHIONERS.

It is of importance not only that we should do good, but that we should do it in the best manner. A little judgment and a little reflection added to the gift doubles the value. Now it is lamentable to see how ignorant the poor are. I do not mean of reading and writing, but about the common affairs of life. They are as helpless as children in all difficulties. Nothing would be so useful as some short and cheap book, to instruct them what to do, to whom to go, and to give them a little advice; I mean, mere practical advice. I have begun something of this sort for my parishioners; here it is.

If you begin stealing a little, you will go on from little to much, and soon become a regular thief; and then you will be hanged or sent over seas to Botany Bay. And give me leave to tell you, transportation is no joke. Up at five in the morning, dressed in a jacket half blue half yellow, chained on to another person like two dogs, a man standing over you with a great stick, weak porridge for breakfast, bread and water for dinner, boiled beans for supper, straw to lie upon; and all this for thirty years; and then you are hanged there by order of the governor, without judge or jury. All this is very disagreeable, and you had far better avoid it by making a solemn resolution to take nothing which does not belong to you.

Never sit in wet clothes. Off with them as soon as you can: no constitution can stand it. Look at Jackson, who lives next door to the blacksmith; he was the strongest man in the parish. Twenty different times I warned him of his folly in wearing wet clothes. He pulled of his hat and smiled, and was very civil, but clearly seemed to think it all old woman's nonsense. He is now, as you see, bent double with rheumatism, is living upon parish allowance, and scarcely able to crawl from pillar to post.

Off with your hat when you meet a gentleman. What does it cost? Gentlemen notice these things, are offended if the civility is not paid, and pleased if it is; and what harm does it do you? When first I came to this parish Squire Tempest wanted a postilion. John Barton was a good, civil fellow; and in thinking over the names of the village, the Squire thought of Barton, remembered his constant civility, sent for one of his sons, made him postilion, then coachman, then bailiff, and he now holds a farm under the Squire of 500*l.* per annum. Such things are constantly happening.

I will have no swearing. There is pleasure in a pint of ale, but what pleasure is there in an oath? A swearer is a low, vulgar person. Swearing is fit for a tinker or a razor-grinder, not for an honest labourer in my parish.

I must positively forbid all poaching; it is absolute ruin to yourself and your family. In the end you are sure to be detected, —a hare in one pocket and a pheasant in

the other. How are you to pay ten pounds? You have
not ten pence beforehand in the world. Daniel's
breeches are unpaid for; you have a hole in your hat, and
want a new one; your wife, an excellent woman, is about
to lie in,—and you are, all of a sudden, called upon by
the Justice to pay ten pounds. I shall never forget the
sight of poor Cranford, hurried to Taunton Gaol; a wife
and three daughters on their knees to the Justice, who
was compelled to do his duty, and commit him. The
next day, beds, chairs, and clothes sold, to get the father
out of gaol. Out of gaol he came; but the poor fellow
could not bear the sight of his naked cottage, and to see
his family pinched with hunger. You know how he
ended his days. Was there a dry eye in the churchyard when he was buried? It was a lesson to poachers.
It is indeed a desperate and foolish trade. Observe, I am
not defending the game-laws, but I am advising you, as
long as the game-laws exist, to fear them, and to take
care that you and your family are not crushed by them.
And, then, smart stout young men hate the gamekeeper,
and make it a point of courage and spirit to oppose him.
Why? The gamekeeper is paid to protect the game,
and he would be a very dishonest man if he did not do
his duty. What right have you to bear malice against
him for this? After all, the game in justice belongs to
the land-owners, who feed it; and not to you, who have
no land at all, and can feed nothing.

I don't like that red nose, and those blear eyes, and
that stupid downcast look. You are a drunkard. Another pint, and one pint more; a glass of gin and water,
rum and milk, cider and pepper, a glass of peppermint,
and all the beastly fluids which drunkards pour down
their throats. It is very possible to conquer it, if you
will but be resolute. I remember a man in Staffordshire

who was drunk every day of his life.   Every farthing he
earned went to the ale-house.   One evening he stag-
gered home, and found at a late hour his wife sitting
alone, and drowned in tears.   He was a man not deficient
in natural affections; he appeared to be struck with the
wretchedness of the woman, and with some eagerness
asked her why she was crying.   "I don't like to tell you,
James," she said, "but if I must, I must; and truth is,
my children have not touched a morsel of anything this
blessed day.   As for me, never mind me; I must leave
you to guess how it has fared with me.   But not one
morsel of food could I beg or buy for those children that
lie on that bed before you; and I am sure, James, it is
better for us all we should die, and to my soul I wish we
were dead."   "Dead!" said James, starting up as if a flash
of lightning had darted upon him; "dead, Sally!   You,
and Mary, and the two young ones dead?   Lookye my
lass, you see what I am now,—like a brute.   I have
wasted your substance,—the curse of God is upon me—
I am drawing near to the pit of destruction,— but there's
an end; I feel there's an end.   Give me that glass, wife."
She gave it him with astonishment and fear.   He turned
it topsy-turvy; and, striking the table with great violence,
and flinging himself on his knees, made a most solemn
and affecting vow to God of repentance and sobriety.
From that moment to the day of his death he drank no
fermented liquor, but confined himself entirely to tea and
water.   I never saw so sudden and astonishing a change.
His looks became healthy, his cottage neat, his children
were clad, his wife was happy; and twenty times the
poor man and his wife, with tears in their eyes, have
told me the story, and blessed the evening of the
14th of March, the day of James's restoration, and have
shown me the glass he held in his hand when he made

the vow of sobriety. It is all nonsense about not being able to work without ale, and gin, and cider, and fermented liquors. Do lions and cart-horses drink ale? It is mere habit. If you have good nourishing food, you can do very well without ale. Nobody works harder than the Yorkshire people, and for years together there are many Yorkshire labourers who never taste ale. I have no objection, you will observe, to a moderate use of ale, or any other liquor you can *afford* to purchase. My objection is, that you cannot afford it; that every penny you spend at the ale-house comes out of the stomachs of the poor children, and strips off the clothes of the wife.

My dear little Nanny, don't believe a word he says. He merely means to ruin and deceive you. You have a plain answer to give:—" When I am axed in the church, and the parson has read the service, and all about it is written down in the book, then I will listen to your nonsense, and not before." Am not I a Justice of the Peace, and have not I had a hundred foolish girls brought before me, who have all come with the same story? —" Please, your Worship, he is a false man; he promised me marriage over and over again." I confess I have often wished for the power of hanging these rural lovers. But what use is my wishing? All that can be done with the villain is to make him pay half-a-crown a week, and you are handed over to the poor-house, and to infamy. Will no example teach you? Look to Mary Willet,— three years ago the handsomest and best girl in the village, now a slattern in the poor-house! Look at Harriet Dobson, who trusted in the promises of James Harefield's son, and, after being abandoned by him, went away in despair with a party of soldiers! How can you be such a fool as to surrender your character to the stupid flattery of a ploughboy? If the evening is pleasant, and birds sing, and flowers bloom, is that any reason why you are to forget God's Word, the happiness of your family, and your own character? What is a woman worth without character? A profligate carpenter, or a debauched watchmaker, may gain business from their skill; but how is a profligate woman to gain her bread? Who will receive *her?*

But this is enough of my parish advice. — [*Memoir.*]

PROFESSION OF THE LAW.

The Law is decidedly the best profession for a young man, if he has anything in him. In the Church a man is thrown into life with his hands tied, and bid to swim; he does well if he keeps his head above water. But then in the law he must have a stout heart and an iron digestion, and must be regular as the town clock, or he may as well retire. Attorneys expect in a lawyer the constancy of the turtle-dove.—[*Memoir.*]

CHURCH PREFERMENT.

To give to every clergyman who has gone through the expense of an English University, and who is married and settled in the country, the income which they ought in decency and in justice to receive, would require, not only the confiscation of *all* the cathedral and episcopal property, but some millions of money in addition. A church provided for as ours now is, can obtain a well-educated and respectable clergy only by those hopes which are excited by the unequal division and lottery of preferment. This is the real cause which has brought capital and respectability into the English Church, and peopled it with the well-educated sons of gentlemen,— an object of the greatest importance in a rich country like England. Nothing would so rapidly and certainly ensure the degradation of the Church of England, as the equal division of all its revenues among all its members. —[*Memoir.*]

ADVICE TO A LADY.

KEEP as much as possible in the grand and common road of life ; patent educations or habits seldom succeed. Depend upon it, men set more value on the cultivated minds than on the accomplishments of women, which they are rarely able to appreciate. It is a common error, but it is an error, that literature unfits women for the everyday business of life. It is not so with men : you see those of the most cultivated minds constantly devoting their time and attention to the most homely objects. Literature gives women a real and proper weight in society, but then they must use it with discretion; if the stocking is *blue*, the petticoat must be *long*, as my friend Jeffrey says; the want of this has furnished food for ridicule in all ages.

Never give way to melancholy; resist it steadily, for the habit will encroach. I once gave a lady two-and-twenty recipes against melancholy: one was a bright fire; another, to remember all the pleasant things said to and of her; another, to keep a box of sugar-plums on the chimneypiece, and a kettle simmering on the hob. —[*Memoir.*]

THE SCARS OF LIFE.

EVERY one must go to his grave with his heart scarred like a soldier's body, — sometimes a parent, sometimes a child, a friend, a husband, or a wife. Thus the bands of this life are gradually loosened, and death at last is more welcome than the comfortless solitude of the world. —[*Memoir.*]

FAREWELL.

ALL adieus are melancholy; and principally, I believe, because they put us in mind of the last of all adieus, when the apothecary, and the heir apparent, and the nurse who weeps for pay, surround the bed: when the curate, engaged to dine three miles off, mumbles hasty prayers; when the dim eye closes for ever in the midst of empty pill-boxes, gallipots, phials, and jugs of barley-water.   At that time,—a very distant one, I hope, my dear Madam,—may the memory of good deeds support you!—[*Memoir.*]

JOURNEY OF LIFE.

WE talk of human life as a journey, but how variously is that journey performed!   There are some who come forth girt, and shod, and mantled, to walk on velvet lawns and smooth terraces, where every gale is arrested, and every beam is tempered.   There are others who walk on the Alpine paths of life, against driving misery, and through stormy sorrows, over sharp afflictions; walk with bare feet, and naked breast, jaded, mangled, and chilled. —[*Memoir.*]

MELANCHOLY IN WOMEN.

GOD has made us with strong passions and little wisdom.   To inspire the notion that infallible vengeance will be the consequence of every little deviation from our duty is to encourage melancholy and despair. Women have often ill health and irritable nerves; they want moreover that strong coercion over the fancy which judgment exercises in the minds of men; hence they are apt to cloud their minds with secret fears and super-stitious presentiments.   Check, my dear Madam, as you value their future comfort, every appearance of this in your daughters; dispel that prophetic gloom which dives into futurity, to extract sorrow from days and years to come, and which considers its own unhappy visions as the decrees of Providence. We know nothing of to-morrow; our business is to be good and happy to-day.—[*Memoir.*]

EXPENDITURE OF LIFE.

LIVE always in the best company when you read. No one in youth thinks on the value of time. Do you ever reflect how you pass your life? If you live to seventy-two, which I hope you may, your life is spent in the following manner:—An hour a day is three years; this makes twenty-seven years sleeping,—nine years dressing,—nine years at table,— six years playing with children,—nine years walking, drawing, and visiting,—six years shopping,—and three years quarrelling.—[*Memoir.*]

A ONE-BOOK MAN.

SOME men have only one book in them; others, a library.—[*Memoir.*]

SHAKES OF THE HAND.

THERE is nothing more characteristic than shakes of the hand. I have classified them. There is the *high official,*—the body erect, and a rapid, short shake, near the chin. There is the *mortmain,*—the flat hand introduced into your palm, and hardly conscious of its contiguity. The *digital,*—one finger held out, much used by the high clergy. There is the *shakus rusticus,* where your hand is seized in an iron grasp, betokening

rude health, warm heart, and distance from the Metropolis; but producing a strong sense of relief on your
part when you find your hand released and your fingers
unbroken.   The next to this is the *retentive shake,*—
one which, beginning with vigour, pauses as it were to
take breath, but without relinquishing its prey, and
before you are aware begins again, till you feel anxious
as to the result, and have no shake left in you.   There
are other varieties, but this is enough for one lesson.—
[*Memoir.*]

MISS FOX.

MISS FOX was mentioned, who was at that time at
Bowood: "Oh, she is perfection; she always gives me
the idea of an aged angel."

A UTILITARIAN.

HE is of the Utilitarian school.   That man is so hard
you might drive a broad-wheeled waggon over him, and
it would produce no impression; if you were to bore holes
in him with a gimlet, I am convinced sawdust would
come out of him.   That school treat mankind as if they
were mere machines; the feelings or affections never
enter into their calculations.   If everything is to be
sacrificed to utility, why do you bury your grandmother
at all? why don't you cut her into small pieces at once,
and make portable soup of her?—[*Memoir.*]

CARELESSNESS.

I ALWAYS say to young people, Beware of carelessness,
no fortune will stand it long; you are on the high road
to ruin, the moment you think yourself rich enough to be
careless. — [*Memoir.*]

VALUE OF BEAUTY.

NEVER teach false morality. How exquisitely absurd to tell girls that beauty is of no value, dress of no use! Beauty is of value; her whole prospects and happiness in life may often depend upon a new gown or a becoming bonnet, and if she has five grains of common sense she will find this out. The great thing is to teach her their just value, and that there must be something better under the bonnet than a pretty face for real happiness. But never sacrifice truth. — [*Memoir.*]

VALUE OF GOOD MANNERS.

MANNERS are often too much neglected; they are most important to men, no less than to women. I believe the English are the most disagreeable people under the sun; not so much because Mr. John Bull disdains to talk, as that the respected individual has nothing to say, and because he totally neglects manners. Look at a French carter; he takes off his hat to a neighbour carter, and inquires after "la santé de madame," with a bow that would not have disgraced Sir Charles Grandison; and I have often seen a French soubrette with a far better manner than an English duchess. The true point at which a sensible girl should aim in manners is to be well-behaved without being insipid. It is far better nevertheless to fail in the latter than in the former point; but life is too short to get over a bad manner; besides, manners are the shadows of virtue. — [*Memoir.*]

FALLACIES OF SOCIETY.

IT is astonishing the influence foolish apothegms have upon the mass of mankind, though they are not

unfrequently fallacies.   Here are a few I amused myself with writing, long before Bentham's book on Fallacies.

Fallacy I. — Because I have gone through it, my son shall go through
it also.

A MAN gets well pummelled at a public school; is
subject to every misery and every indignity which seventeen years of age can inflict upon nine and ten; has his
eye nearly knocked out, and his clothes stolen and cut to
pieces; and twenty years afterwards, when he is a chry-
salis, and has forgotten the miseries of his grub state, is
determined to act a manly part in life, and says, "I passed
through all that myself, and I am determined my son shall
pass through it as I have done: " and away goes his bleat-
ing progeny to the tyranny and servitude of· the long
chamber or the large dormitory. It would surely be much
more rational to say, " Because I have passed through it,
I am ·determined my son shall not pass through it;
because I was kicked for nothing, and cuffed for nothing,
and fagged for everything, I will spare all these miseries
to my child." It is not for any good which may be
derived from this rough usage; that has not been weighed
and considered; few persons are capable of weighing its
effects into character; but there is a sort of compensatory
and consolatory notion, that the present generation
(whether useful or not, no matter) are not to come off
scot-free, but are to have their share of ill-usage; as if
the black eye and bloody nose which Master John Jackson received in 1800, are less black and bloody by the
application of similar violence to similar parts of Master
Thomas Jackson, the son, in 1830. This is not only sad
nonsense, but cruel nonsense. The only use to be derived
from the recollection of what we have suffered in youth,

is a fixed determination to screen those we educate from every evil and inconvenience, from subjection to which there are not cogent reasons for submitting. Can anything be more stupid and preposterous than this concealed revenge upon the rising generation, and latent envy lest they should avail themselves of the improvements time has made, and pass a happier youth than their fathers have done?

Fallacy II. — I have said I will do it, and I will do it; I will stick to my word.

THIS fallacy proceeds from confounding resolutions with promises. If you have promised to give a man a guinea for a reward, or to sell him a horse or a field, you must do it; you are dishonest if you do not. But if you have made a resolution to eat no meat for a year, and everybody about you sees that you are doing mischief to your constitution, is it any answer to say, you have said so, and you will stick to your word? With whom have you made the contract but with yourself? and if you and yourself, the two contracting parties, agree to break the contract, where is the evil, or who is injured?

Fallacy III. — " I object to half measures, — it is neither one thing nor the other."

BUT why *should* it be either one thing or the other? why not something between both? Why are half-measures necessarily or probably unwise measures? I am embarrassed in my circumstances;—one of my plans is, to persevere boldly in the same line of expense, and to trust to the chapter of accidents for some increase of fortune;— the other is, to retire entirely from the world, and to hide myself in a cottage;—but I end with doing neither, and take a middle course of diminished expenditure.   I do neither one thing nor the other, but possibly act wiser than if I had done either.   I am highly offended by the conduct of an acquaintance ; I neither overlook it entirely nor do I proceed to call him out; I do neither, but show him, by a serious change of manner, that I consider myself to have been ill-treated.   I effect my object by half-measures.   I cannot agree entirely with the Opposition or the Ministry ; it may very easily happen that my half-measures are wiser than the extremes to which they are opposed.   But it is a sort of metaphor which debauches the understanding of *foolish* people ; and when half-measures are mentioned, they have much the same feeling as if they were cheated—as if they had bargained for a whole bushel and received but half.   To act in extremes is sometimes wisdom ; to *avoid* them is sometimes wisdom ; every measure must be judged of by its own particular circumstances. — [*Memoir.*]

MATRIMONY.

DID you ever hear my definition of marriage ?   It is, that it resembles a pair of shears, so joined that they cannot be separated ; often moving in opposite directions, yet always punishing any one who comes between them. — [*Memoir.*]

THOMAS BABINGTON MACAULAY.

I always prophesied his greatness from the first moment I saw him, then a very young and unknown man, on the Northern Circuit.   There are no limits to his knowledge, on small subjects as well as great; he is like a book in breeches . . .   Yes, I agree, he

is certainly more agreeable since his return from India.
His enemies might perhaps have said before (though I
never did so) that he talked rather too much ; but now
he has occasional flashes of silence, that make his conversation perfectly delightful. But what is far better
and more important than all this is, I believe Macaulay
to be incorruptible. You might lay ribbons, stars,
garters, wealth, titles, before him in vain. He has an
honest, genuine love of his country, and the world could
not bribe him to neglect her interests. — [*Memoir.*]

CLASSES OF MANKIND.

I HAVE divided mankind into classes. There is the
Noodle, — very numerous, but well known. The Afflic-
tion-woman, — a valuable member of society, generally
an ancient spinster, or distant relation of the family, in
small circumstances : the moment she hears of any
accident or distress in the family, she sets off, packs up
her little bag, and is immediately established there, to
comfort, flatter, fetch, and carry. The Up-takers, — a
class of people who only see through their fingers' ends,
and go through a room taking up and touching everything, however visible and however tender. The
Clearers,—who begin at the dish before them, and go on
picking or tasting till it is cleared, however large the
company, small the supply, and rare the contents. The
Sleep-walkers,—those who never deviate from the beaten
track, who think as their fathers have thought since the
Flood, who start from a new idea as they would from
guilt. The Lemon-squeezers of society, — people who
act on you as a wet-blanket, who see a cloud in the sunshine, the nails of the coffin in the ribbons of the bride,
predictors of evil, extinguishers of hope; who, where

there are two sides, see only the worst, — people whose very look curdles the milk, and sets your teeth on edge. The Let-well-aloners, — cousins-german to the Noodle, yet a variety; people who have begun to think and to act, but are timid, and afraid to try their wings, and tremble at the sound of their own footsteps as they advance, and think it safer to stand still. Then the Washerwomen, — very numerous, who exclaim, "Well! as sure as ever I put on my best bonnet, it is certain to rain," &c. There are many more, but I forget them.

Oh yes! there is another class, as you say; people who are always treading on your gouty foot, or talking in your deaf ear, or asking you to give them something with your lame hand, stirring up your weak point, rubbing your sore, &c. — [*Memoir.*]

TASTE FOR MUSIC.

ALL musical people seem to me happy; it is the most engrossing pursuit; almost the only innocent and un-punished passion.

SHADOWS OF GRIEF.

WHY destroy present happiness by a distant misery, which may never come at all, or you may never live to see it? for every substantial grief has twenty shadows, and most of them shadows of your own making.

WIT.

A MAN of small understanding is merry where he can, not where he should. Lightning must, I think, be the wit of heaven.

GREAT PATRIOTS.

No man, I fear, can effect great benefits for his country without some sacrifice of the minor virtues.

FACETIÆ.

THE reigning bore at one time in Edinburgh was ——: his favourite subject, the North Pole. It mattered not how far south you began, you found yourself transported to the north pole before you could take breath; no one escaped him. Sydney Smith declared he should invent a slip-button. Jeffrey fled from him as from the plague, when possible; but one day his arch-tormentor met him in a narrow lane, and began instantly on the north pole. Jeffrey in despair, and out of all patience, darted past him exclaiming "D— the north pole!" Sydney Smith met him shortly after, boiling with indignation at Jeffrey's contempt of the north pole. "Oh, my dear fellow," said he, "never mind; no one minds what Jeffrey says, you know; he is a privileged person; he respects nothing, absolutely nothing. Why, you will scarcely believe it, but it is not more than a week ago that I heard him speak disrespectfully of the equator!"

Some one asked if the Bishop of —— was going to marry. "Perhaps he may," said Sydney Smith; "yet how can a bishop marry? How can he flirt? The most he can say is, 'I will see you in the vestry after service.'"

Oh, don't read those twelve volumes till they are made

into a *consommé* of two. Lord Dudley did still better, he waited till they blew over.

Talking of tithes: "It is an atrocious way of paying the clergy. The custom of tithe in kind will seem incredible to our posterity; no one will believe in the ramiferous priest officiating in the cornfield."

Our friend —— makes all the country smell like Piccadilly.

Sydney Smith observed how many of the most eminent men of the world had been diminutive in person; and after naming several among the ancients, he added, "Why, look there, at Jeffrey; and there is my little friend ——, who has not body enough to cover his mind decently with; his intellect is improperly exposed."

Don't mind the caprices of fashionable women; they are as gross as poodles fed on milk and muffins.

Simplicity is a great object in a great book; it is not wanted in a short one.

The great charm of Sheridan's speaking was his multifariousness of style.

Fox wrote drop by drop.

When I took my Yorkshire servants into Somersetshire, I found that they thought making a drink out of apples was a tempting of Providence, who had intended barley to be the only natural material of intoxication.

We naturally lose illusions as we get older, like teeth, but there is no Cartwright to fit a new set into our understandings. I have, alas, only one illusion left, and that is the Archbishop of Canterbury.

Speaking of the long debates in the House: "Why will not people remember the Flood? If they had lived before it, with the patriarchs, they might have talked any stuff they pleased; but do let them remember how little time they have under this new order of things."

Going one morning to join a breakfast party at the Clarendon, Sydney Smith, on entering the room, unexpectedly found his friend Jeffrey prostrate on his back, and Mr. Henning, the sculptor, in the act of covering his face with plaster of Paris, in order to take his cast. On seeing his friend in this woeful condition, as he stood by him Sydney burst forth in the words of Mark Antony, "Oh, mighty Jeffrey! dost thou lie so low? Are all thy conquests, glories, triumphs, spoils, shrunk to this little measure?" when he was abruptly silenced, in full career, by the voice of old Henning, exclaiming, "Stop, stop, Mr. Smith! for Heaven's sake stop! If Lord Jeffrey laughs, my cast is spoilt."

The charm of London is that you are never glad or sorry for ten minutes together; in the country you are the one and the other for weeks.

There is a New Zealand attorney just arrived in London, with 6*s.* 8*d.* tattooed all over his face.

Yes, he has spent all his life in letting down empty buckets into empty wells; and he is frittering away his age in trying to draw them up again.

If you masthead a sailor for not doing his duty, why should you not weathercock a parishioner for refusing to pay tithes?

" How is —— ? " " He is not very well." " Why, what is the matter ? "   " Oh, don't you know he has produced a couplet? When our friend is delivered of a couplet, with infinite labour and pain, he takes to his bed, has straw laid down, the knocker tied up, expects his friends to call and make inquiries, and the answer at the door invariably is, ' Mr. —— and his little couplet are as well as can be expected.' When he produces an Alexandrine he keeps his bed a day longer."

You will find a Scotchman always says what is undermost. I, on the contrary, say everything that comes uppermost, and have all sorts of bad jokes put upon me in consequence. An American published a book, and declared I had told him there were more mad Quakers in lunatic asylums than any other sect ; — quite an invention on his part. Another time Prince P—— M—— published my conversations ; so when I next met him, I inquired whether this was to be a printed or manuscript one, as I should talk accordingly. He did his best to blush.

Never neglect your fireplaces: I have paid great attention to mine, and could burn you all out in a moment. Much of the cheerfulness of life depends upon it. Who could be miserable with that fire ? What makes a fire so pleasant is, I think, that it is a live thing in a dead room.

Such is the horror the French have of our *cuisine* that at the dinner given in honour of Guizot at the Athenæum, they say his cook was heard to exclaim, " Ah, mon pauvre maître ! je ne le reverrai plus."

I believe the parallelogram between Oxford Street, Piccadilly, Regent Street, and Hyde Park, encloses more intelligence and human ability, to say nothing of wealth and beauty, than the world has ever collected in such a space before.

When I praised the author of the New Poor Law the other day, three gentlemen at the table took it to themselves, and blushed up to the eyes.

Yes! you find people ready enough to do the Samaritan, without the oil and twopence.

It is a great proof of shyness to crumble bread at dinner. "Oh, I see you are afraid of me" (turning to a young lady who sat by him), "you crumble your bread. I do it when I sit by the Bishop of London, and with both hands when I sit by the Archbishop."

Addressing Rogers: "My dear R., if we were both in America, we should be tarred and feathered; and lovely as we are by nature, I should be an ostrich and you an emu."

I once saw a dressed statue of Venus in a serious house —the Venus Millinaria.

You flavour everything; you are the vanille of society.

I fully intended going to America; but my parishioners held a meeting, and came to a resolution that they could not trust me with the canvas-back ducks: and I felt they were right, so gave up the project.

My living in Yorkshire was so far out of the way that it was actually twelve miles from a lemon.

Of course, if ever I do go to a fancy ball at all, I should go as a Dissenter.

I think it was Luttrell who used to say "———'s face always reminded him of boiled mutton and near relations."

Don't you know, as the French say, there are three sexes—men, women, and clergymen?

One of my great objections to the country is, that you get your letters but once a day; here they come every five minutes.

On some one offering him oat-cake, "No, I can't eat oat-cake, it is too rich for me."

Harrowgate is the most heaven-forgotten country under the sun. When I saw it there were only nine mangy fir trees there; and even they all leaned away from it.

Dining at Mr. Grenville's, Sydney Smith as usual arrived before the rest of the party. Some ladies were shortly after announced; as Mr. Grenville, with his graceful dignity and cheerfulness, went forward to receive them, Sydney Smith, looking after him, exclaimed to Mr. Panizzi, "There, that is the man from whom we all ought to learn how to grow old!"

The conversation at table turned on a subject lately treated of in Sir Charles Lyell's book, the phenomena which the earth might present to the geologists of some future period; "Let us imagine," said Sydney Smith, "an excavation on the site of St. Paul's. Fancy a lecture, by the Owen of some future age, on the thigh-bone of a Minor Canon, or the tooth of a Dean,— the form, qualities, the knowledge, tastes, propensities, he would discover from them."

Some one spoke of the state of financial embarrassment of the London University. "Yes, it is so great, that I understand they have already seized on the air-pump, the exhausted receiver, and galvanic batteries; and that bailiffs have been seen chasing the Professor of Modern History round the quadrangle."

Conversing in the evening, with a small circle, round Miss Berry's tea-table, Sydney Smith observed the entrance of a no less remarkable person, both for talents and years, dressed in a beautiful crimson velvet gown. He started up to meet his fine old friend, exclaiming, "exactly the colour of my preaching cushion!" and leading her forward to the light, he pretended to be lost in admiration, saying, "I really can hardly keep my hands off you; I shall be preaching on you, I fear," &c., and played with the subject to the infinite amusement of his old friend and the little circle assembled round her.

Playfair was certainly the most delightful philomath I ever knew.

Have you heard of Niebuhr's discoveries? All Roman history reversed; Tarquin turning out an excellent family man, and Lucretia a very doubtful character, whom Lady Davy would not have visited.

The ladies having left the room, at a dinner at Sir G. Philip's, the conversation turned on the black population of America. Sydney Smith turning to an eminent American jurist, who was here some years ago, said, "Pray, Mr. ———, do tell us why you can't live on better terms with your black population." "Why to tell you the truth, Mr. Smith, they smell so abominably that we can't bear them near us." "Possibly not," said Sydney Smith, "but men must not be led by the *nose* in that way: if you don't like asking them to dinner, it is surely no reason why you should not make *citizens* of them.

> 'Et si non alium latè jactaret odorem,
> *Civis* erat.'" *

Some one complaining of the interminable length of the speeches in Parliament, he said, "Don't talk to me of not being able to cough a speaker down: try the whooping-cough."

Mr. Monckton Milnes was talking to Alderman ———, when the latter turned away: "You were speaking," said Sydney, "to the Lord Mayor elect. I myself felt in his presence like the Roman whom Pyrrhus tried to frighten with an elephant, and remained calm."

When so showy a woman as Mrs. ——— appears at a place, though there is no garrison within twelve miles, the horizon is immediately clouded with majors.

To take Macaulay out of literature and society, and put him in the House of Commons, is like taking the chief physician out of London during a pestilence.

* Virgil, Georgics, ii. 132. *Laurus* in the original.

Praise is the best diet for us, after all.

ONE day Mr. Rogers took Mr. Moore and Sydney Smith home in his carriage, from a breakfast; and insisted on showing them, by the way, Dryden's house, in some obscure street. It was very wet; the house looked very much like other old houses; and having thin shoes on, they both strongly remonstrated; but in vain. Rogers got out himself, and stood expecting them to do likewise; but Sydney Smith, laughing and leaning out of the carriage, exclaimed, " Oh! you see why Rogers don't mind getting out, he has got goloshes on;—but, my dear Rogers, lend us each a golosh, and we will then each stand on one leg, and admire as long as you please."

When Prescott comes to England, a Caspian Sea of soup awaits him.

An American said to Sydney Smith, "You are so funny, Mr. Smith! do you know you remind me of our great joker, Dr. Chamberlaque." " I am much honoured," he replied, " but I was not aware you had such a functionary in the United States."

At Mr. Romilly's there arose a discussion on the Inferno of Dante, and the tortures he had invented. " He may be a great poet," said Sydney Smith, " but as to inventing tortures, I consider him a mere bungler, — no imagination, no knowledge of the human heart. If I had taken it in hand, I would show you what torture really was. For instance (turning to his old friend Mrs. Marcet), you should be doomed to listen, for a thousand years, to conversations between Caroline and Emily, where Caroline should always give wrong explana- tions in chemistry, and Emily in the end be unable to distinguish an acid from an alkali. You, Macaulay, let me consider? — oh, you should be dumb. False dates and facts of the reign of Queen Anne should for ever be shouted in your ears; all liberal and honest opinions should be ridiculed in your presence; and you should not be able to say a single word during that period in their defence." "And what would you condemn me to, Mr. Sydney?" said a young mother. "Why, you should for ever see those three sweet little girls of yours on the point of falling downstairs, and never be able to save them. There, what tortures are there in Dante equal to these?"

Daniel Webster struck me much like a steam-engine in trousers.

When I began to thump the cushion of my pulpit, on first coming to Foston, as is my wont when I preach, the accumulated dust of a hundred and fifty years made such a cloud, that for some minutes I lost sight of my congregation.

Nothing amuses me more than to observe the utter want of perception of a joke in some minds. Mrs. Jackson called the other day, and spoke of the oppressive heat of last week. "Heat, Ma'am!" I said; "it was so dreadful here, that I found there was nothing left for it but to take off my flesh and sit in my bones." "Take off your flesh and sit in your bones, Sir? Oh, Mr. Smith! how could you do that?" she exclaimed with the utmost gravity. "Nothing more easy, Ma'am: come and see next time." But she ordered her carriage, and evidently thought it a very unorthodox proceeding.

Miss ——, too, the other day, walking round the grounds at Combe Florey, exclaimed, "Oh, why do you chain up that fine Newfoundland dog, Mr. Smith?" "Because it has a passion for breakfasting on parish boys." "Parish boys!" she exclaimed, "does he really eat boys, Mr. Smith?" "Yes, he devours them, buttons and all." Her face of horror made me die of laughing.

I like pictures, without knowing anything about them; but I hate coxcombry in the fine arts, as well as in anything else. I got into dreadful disgrace with Sir G. Beaumont once, who standing before a picture at Bowood, exclaimed, turning to me, "Immense breadth of light and shade!" I innocently said, "Yes; about an inch and a half." He gave me a look that ought to have killed me.

At a large dinner party some one else announced the death of Mr. Dugald Stewart; one whose name ever brings with it feelings of respect for his talents and high character. The news was received with so much levity by a lady of rank, who sat by Sydney Smith, that he turned round and said, "Madam, when we are told of the death of so great a man as Mr. Dugald Stewart, it is usual, in civilised society, to look grave for at least the space of five seconds."

They do nothing in Ireland as they would elsewhere. When the Dublin mail was stopped and robbed, a sweet female voice was heard behind the hedge, exclaiming, "Shoot the gintleman, then, Patrick dear!"

We were all assembled to look at a turtle that had been sent to the house of a friend, when a child of the party stooped down and began eagerly stroking the shell of the turtle. "Why are you doing that, B——?" said Sydney Smith. "Oh, to please the turtle." "Why, child, you might as well stroke the dome of St. Paul's, to please the Dean and Chapter."

Some one naming —— as not very orthodox, "Oh," said Sydney Smith, "accuse a man of being a Socinian, and it is all over with him; for the country gentlemen all think it has something to do with poaching."

I hate bare walls; so I cover mine, you see with pictures. I took the advice once of two Royal Academicians, but brought their consultation to an abrupt determination by saying, Gentlemen, I forgot to mention that my highest price is five-and-thirty shillings. The public, it must be owned, treat my collection with great contempt; and even Hibbert, who has been brought up in the midst of fine pictures, and might know better, never will admire them. But look at that sea-piece, now; what would you desire more? It is true, the moon in the corner was rather dingy when I first bought it; so I had a new moon put in for half-a-crown, and now I consider it perfect.

Some one mentioned that a young Scotchman, who had been lately in the neighbourhood, was about to marry an Irish widow, double his age and of considerable dimensions. "Going to marry her!" he exclaimed, bursting out laughing; "going to marry her! impossible! you mean, a part of her; he could not marry her all himself. It would be a case, not of bigamy, but trigamy: the neighbourhood or the magistrates should interfere. There is enough of her to furnish wives for a whole parish. One man marry her!—it is monstrous. You might people a colony with her; or give an assembly with her; or perhaps take your morning walks round her, always provided there were frequent resting-places, and you are in rude health. I once was rash enough to try walking round her before breakfast, but only got half-way and gave it up exhausted. Or you might read the Riot Act and disperse her; in short, you might do anything with her but marry her.

PARSONIC DEER.

OPPOSITE was a beautiful bank with a hanging wood of fine old beech and oak, on the summit of which presented themselves, to our astonished eyes, two donkeys, with deer's antlers fastened on their heads, which ever and anon they shook, much wondering at their horned honours; whilst their attendant donkey-boy, in Sunday garb, stood grinning and blushing at their side. "There, Lady ——! you said the only thing this place wanted to make it perfect was deer; what do you say now? I have, you see, ordered my gamekeeper to drive my deer into the most picturesque point of view. Excuse their long ears, a little peculiarity belonging to parsonic deer. Their voices, too, are singular; but we do our best for you, and you are too true a friend of the Church to mention our defects."

REFLECTION.

WE are told, "Let not the sun go down on your wrath." This of course is best; but, as it generally does, I would add, Never act or write till it has done so. This rule has saved me from many an act of folly. It is wonderful what a different view we take of the same event four-and-twenty hours after it has happened.

STYLE OF SIR JAMES MACKINTOSH.

It struck me last night, as I was lying in bed, that Mackintosh, if he were to write on pepper, would thus describe it—

" Pepper may philosophically be described as a dusty and highly pulverized seed of an oriental fruit; an article rather of condiment than diet, which, dispersed lightly over the surface of food with no other rule than the caprice of the consumer, communicates pleasure, rather than affords nutrition; and, by adding a tropical flavour to the gross and succulent viands of the North, approximates the different regions of the earth, explains the objects of commerce, and justifies the industry of man."

MOCK SPEECH OF SIR JAMES MACKINTOSH.

" Mackintosh's chief foible was indiscriminate praise. I amused myself the other day," said he, laughing, " in writing a termination of a speech for him; would you like to hear it?   I will read it to you:—

" 'It is impossible to conclude these observations without expressing the obligations I am under to a person in a much more humble scene of life,—I mean, Sir, the hackney-coachman by whom I have been driven to this meeting. To pass safely through the streets of a crowded metropolis must require, on the part of the driver, no common assemblage of qualities. He must have caution without timidity, activity without precipitation, and courage without rashness; he must have a clear perception of his object, and a dexterous use of his means. I can safely say of the individual in question, that, for a moderate reward, he has displayed unwearied skill; and to him I shall never forget that I owe unfractured integrity of limb, exemption from pain, and perhaps prolongation of existence.

"'Nor can I pass over the encouraging cheerfulness with which I was received by the waiter, nor the useful blaze of light communicated by the link-boys, as I descended from the carriage. It was with no common pleasure that I remarked in these men, not the mercenary bustle of venal service, but the genuine effusions of untutored benevolence: not the rapacity of subordinate agency, but the alacrity of humble friendship. What may not be said of a country where all the little accidents of life bring forth the hidden qualities of the heart,—. where her vehicles are driven, her streets illumined, and her bells answered, by men teeming with all the refinements of civilised life?

"'I cannot conclude, Sir, without thanking you for the very clear and distinct manner in which you have announced the proposition on which we are to vote. It is but common justice to add, that public assemblies rarely witness articulation so perfect, language so select, and a manner so eminently remarkable for everything that is kind, impartial, and just.'"

The Dean of —— deserves to be preached to death by wild curates.

The advice I sent to the Bishop of New Zealand, when he had to receive the cannibal chiefs there, was to say to them, "I deeply regret, Sirs, to have nothing on my own table suited to your tastes, but you will find plenty of cold curate and roasted clergyman on the sideboard;" and if, in spite of this prudent provision, his visitors should end their repast by eating him likewise, why I could only add, " I sincerely hoped he would disagree with them." In this last sentiment he must cordially have agreed with me; and, upon the whole, he must have considered it a useful hint, and would take it kindly.   Don't you think so?

RECEIPT FOR A SALAD.

To make this condiment, your poet begs
The pounded yellow of two hard-boil'd eggs;
Two boil'd potatoes, pass'd through kitchen sieve,
Smoothness and softness to the salad give.
Let onion atoms lurk within the bowl,
And, half suspected, animate the whole.
Of mordant mustard add a single spoon,
Distrust the condiment that bites so soon;
But deem it not, thou man of herbs, a fault,
To add a double quantity of salt;
Four times the spoon with oil from Lucca brown,
And twice with vinegar procured from town;
And, lastly, o'er the flavour'd compound toss
A magic soupçon of anchovy sauce.
Oh, green and glorious! Oh, herbaceous treat!
'Twould tempt the dying anchorite to eat:
Back to the world he'd turn his fleeting soul,
And plunge his fingers in the salad-bowl!
Serenely full, the epicure would say,
Fate cannot harm me, I have dined to-day.

STATE OF PARTIES IN 1813.

To John Allen, Esq.

January 1st, 1813

My dear Allen,

*   *   *   *   *

As to politics, everything is fast setting in for arbitrary power. The court will grow bolder and bolder; a struggle will commence, and if it ends as I wish, there will be Whigs again, or if not, a Whig will be an animal described in books of natural history, and Lord Grey's bones will be put together and shown, by the side of the monument, at the Liverpool Museum. But when these things come to pass, you will no longer be a Warden, but a brown and impalpable powder in the tombs of Dulwich. In the meantime, enough of liberty will remain to make our old-age tolerably comfortable; and to your last gasp you will remain in the perennial and pleasing delusion that the Whigs are coming in, and will expire mistaking the officiating clergyman for a King's messenger.

RESTORATION OF THE BOURBONS.

March 10th, 1814.

Dear Allen,

I CANNOT at all enter into your feelings about the Bourbons, nor can I attend to so remote an evil as the encouragement to superstitious attachment to kings, when the proposed evil of a military ministry, or of thirty years more of war, is before my eyes. I want to get rid of this great disturber of human happiness, and I scarcely know any price too great to effect it. If you were sailing from Alicant to Aleppo in a storm, and, after the sailors had held up the image of a saint and prayed to it, the storm were to abate, you would be more sorry for the encouragement of superstition than rejoiced at the preservation of your life; and so would every other man born and bred in Edinburgh.

My views of the matter would be much shorter and coarser; I should be so glad to find myself alive, that I should not care a farthing if the storm had generated a thousand new, and revived as many old saints. How can any man stop in the midst of the stupendous joy of getting rid of Buonaparte, and prophesy a thousand little peddling evils that will result from restoring the Bourbons? The most important of all objects is the independence of Europe: it has been twice very nearly destroyed by the French; it is menaced from no other quarter; the people must be identified with their sovereign. There is no help for it; it will teach them in future to hang kings who set up for conquerors. I will not believe that the Bourbons have no party in France. My only knowledge of politics is from the York paper; yet nothing shall convince me that the people are not heartily tired of Buonaparte, and ardently wish for the cessation of the conscription; that is, for the Bourbons.

CHEERFULNESS IN RELIGION.

I ENDEAVOUR in vain to give my parishioners more cheerful ideas of religion; to teach them that God is not a jealous, childish, merciless tyrant; that he is best served by a regular tenour of good actions,—not by bad singing, ill-composed prayers, and eternal apprehensions But the luxury of false religion is, to be unhappy!

DISTANCE IN LONDON.

A FEW yards in London dissolve or cement friendship.

NON-INTERVENTION.

FOR God's sake, do not drag me into another war! I am worn down, and worn out, with crusading and defending Europe, and protecting mankind; I *must* think a little of myself. I am sorry for the Spaniards —I am sorry for the Greeks—I deplore the fate of the Jews; the people of the Sandwich Islands are groaning under the most detestable tyranny; Bagdad is oppressed; I do not like the present state of the Delta; Thibet is not comfortable. Am I to fight for all these people? The world is bursting with sin and sorrow. Am I to be champion of the Decalogue, and to be eternally raising fleets and armies to make all men good and happy? We have just done saving Europe, and I am afraid the consequence will be, that we shall cut each other's throats. No war, dear Lady Grey! — no eloquence; but apathy, selfishness, common sense, arith-- metic! I beseech you, secure Lord Grey's swords and pistols, as the housekeeper did Don Quixote's armour. If there is another war, life will not be worth having.

"May the vengeance of Heaven" overtake all the Legitimates of Verona! but, in the present state of rent and taxes, they must be *left* to the vengeance of Heaven. I allow fighting in such a cause to be a luxury; but the business of a prudent, sensible man, is to guard against luxury.

There is no such thing as a "just war," or, at least, as a *wise* war.

INDEX

INDEX.

THE END.

GENERAL LIST OF WORKS

PUBLISHED BY

MESSRS. LONGMANS, GREEN, AND CO.

PATERNOSTER ROW, LONDON.

Historical Works.

LORD MACAULAY'S WORKS. Complete and Uniform Library Edition. Edited by his Sister, Lady TREVELYAN. 8 vols. 8vo. with Portrait, price £5 5s. cloth, or £8 8s. bound in tree-calf by Rivière.

The **HISTORY of ENGLAND** from the Fall of Wolsey to the Death of Elizabeth. By JAMES ANTHONY FROUDE, M.A. late Fellow of Exeter College, Oxford. VOLS. I. to X. in 8vo. price £7 2s. cloth.

VOLS. I. to IV. the Reign of Henry VIII. Fourth Edition, 54s.

VOLS. V. and VI. the Reigns of Edward VI. and Mary. Third Edition, 28s.

VOLS. VII. and VIII. the Reign of Elizabeth, VOLS. I. and II. Fourth Edition, 28s.

VOLS. IX. and X. the Reign of Elizabeth, VOLS. III. and IV. 32s.

The **HISTORY of ENGLAND** from the Accession of James II. Lord MACAULAY.

LIBRARY EDITION, 5 vols. 8vo. £4.

CABINET EDITION, 8 vols. post 8vo. 48s.

PEOPLE'S EDITION, 4 vols. crown 8vo. 16s.

An **ESSAY on the HISTORY of the ENGLISH GOVERNMENT** and Constitution, from the Reign of Henry VII. to the Present Time. By JOHN EARL RUSSELL. Fourth Edition, revised. Crown 8vo. 6s.

On **PARLIAMENTARY GOVERNMENT in ENGLAND:** Its Origin, Development, and Practical Operation. By ALPHEUS TODD, Librarian of the Legislative Assembly of Canada. In Two Volumes. VOL. I. 8vo. 16s.

HISTORY of the REFORM BILLS of 1866 and 1867. By HOMERSHAM COX, M.A. Barrister-at-Law. 8vo. 7s. 6d.

Antient Parliamentary Elections, a History shewing how Parliaments were Constituted, and Representatives of the People Elected, in Ancient Times. By the same Author. 8vo. 8s. 6d.

Whig and Tory Administrations during the Last Thirteen Years. By the same Author. 8vo. 5s.

A

The **HISTORY** of **ENGLAND** during the Reign of George the Third. By the Right Hon. W. N. MASSEY. Cabinet Edition. 4 vols. post 8vo. 24s.

The **CONSTITUTIONAL HISTORY** of **ENGLAND**, since the Accession of George III. 1760—1860. By Sir THOMAS ERSKINE MAY, C.B. Second Edition. 2 vols. 8vo. 33s.

HISTORICAL STUDIES. By HERMAN MERIVALE, M.A. 8vo. price 12s. 6d.

The **OXFORD REFORMERS** of **1498**; being a History of the Fellow-work of John Colet, Erasmus, and Thomas More. By FREDERIC SEEBOHM. 8vo. 12s.

LECTURES on the **HISTORY** of **ENGLAND**, from the earliest Times to the Death of King Edward II. By WILLIAM LONGMAN. With Maps and Illustrations. 8vo. 15s.

The **HISTORY** of the **LIFE** and **TIMES** of **EDWARD** the **THIRD.** By WILLIAM LONGMAN. With 9 Maps, 8 Plates, and 16 Woodcuts. 2 vols. 8vo. 28s.

HISTORY of **CIVILISATION** in England and France, Spain and Scotland. By HENRY THOMAS BUCKLE. Fifth Edition of the entire Work, with a complete INDEX. 3 vols. crown 8vo. 24s.

WATERLOO LECTURES: a Study of the Campaign of 1815. By Colonel CHARLES C. CHESNEY, R.E. late Professor of Military Art and History in the Staff College. 8vo. with Map, 10s. 6d.

HISTORY of **GRANT'S CAMPAIGN** for the **CAPTURE** of **RICH-MOND**, 1864—1865 : with an Outline of the Previous Course of the American Civil War. By JOHN CANNON. Post 8vo. 12s. 6d.

DEMOCRACY in **AMERICA.** By ALEXIS DE TOCQUEVILLE. Translated by HENRY REEVE. 2 vols. 8vo. 21s.

HISTORY of the **REFORMATION** in **EUROPE** in the Time of Calvin. By J. H. MERLE D'AUBIGNÉ, D.D. VOLS. I. and II. 8vo. 28s. VOL. III. 12s. VOL. IV. 16s. VOL. V. price 16s.

HISTORY of **FRANCE**, from Clovis and Charlemagne to the Accession of Napoléon III. By EYRE EVANS CROWE. 5 vols. 8vo. £4 13s.

The **HISTORY** of **GREECE.** By C. THIRLWALL, D.D. Lord Bishop of St. David's. 8 vols. fcp. 8vo. price 28s.

The **TALE** of the **GREAT PERSIAN WAR**, from the Histories of Herodotus. By GEORGE W. COX, M.A. New Edition. Fcp. 3s. 6d.

GREEK HISTORY from Themistocles to Alexander, in a Series of Lives from Plutarch. Revised and arranged by A. H. CLOUGH. Fcp. with 44 Woodcuts, 6s.

CRITICAL HISTORY of the **LANGUAGE** and **LITERATURE** of Ancient Greece. By WILLIAM MURE, of Caldwell. 5 vols. 8vo. £3 9s.

HISTORY of the **LITERATURE** of **ANCIENT GREECE.** By Professor K. O. MÜLLER. Translated by the Right Hon. Sir GEORGE CORNEWALL LEWIS, Bart. and by J. W. DONALDSON, D.D. 3 vols. 8vo. 21s.

HISTORY of the **CITY** of **ROME** from its Foundation to the Sixteenth Century of the Christian Era. By THOMAS H. DYER, LL.D. 8vo. with 2 Maps, 15s.

HISTORY of the **ROMANS** under the **EMPIRE**. By the Rev. C. MERIVALE, LL.D. 8 vols. post 8vo. 48s.

The **FALL** of the **ROMAN REPUBLIC**: a Short History of the Last Century of the Commonwealth. By the same Author. 12mo. 7s. 6d.

The **HISTORY** of **INDIA**, from the Earliest Period to the close of Lord Dalhousie's Administration. By JOHN CLARK MARSHMAN. 3 vols. crown 8vo. 22s. 6d.

INDIAN POLITY: a View of the System of Administration in India. By Major GEORGE CHESNEY, Fellow of the University of Calcutta. 8vo. with Map, 21s.

HISTORY of the **FRENCH** in **INDIA**, from the Founding of Pondichery in 1674 to its Capture in 1761. By Lieutenant-Colonel G. B. MALLESON, Bengal Staff Corps. 8vo. 16s.

REALITIES of **IRISH LIFE**. By W. STEUART TRENCH, Land Agent in Ireland to the Marquess of Lansdowne, the Marquess of Bath, and Lord Digby. With Illustrations from Drawings by the Author's Son, J. TOWNSEND TRENCH. Third Edition, with 30 Plates. 8vo. 21s.

JOURNALS, CONVERSATIONS, and ESSAYS relating to **IRELAND**. By NASSAU WILLIAM SENIOR. 2 vols. post 8vo. 21s.

MODERN IRELAND; its Vital Questions, Secret Societies, and Government. By an ULSTERMAN. Post 8vo. 6s.

IRELAND in 1868 the **BATTLE-FIELD** for **ENGLISH PARTY STRIFE**: its Grievances, Real and Factitious; Remedies, Abortive or Mischievous. By GERALD FITZGIBBON. Second Edition. 8vo. 8s. 6d.

AN ILLUSTRATED HISTORY of **IRELAND**, from the Earliest Period to the Year of Catholic Emancipation. By MARY F. CUSACK. Second Edition, revised and enlarged. 8vo. 18s. 6d.

CRITICAL and **HISTORICAL ESSAYS** contributed to the *Edinburgh Review*. By the Right Hon. LORD MACAULAY.

    LIBRARY EDITION, 3 vols. 8vo. 36s.

    CABINET EDITION, 4 vols. post 8vo. 24s.

    TRAVELLER'S EDITION, in One Volume, square crown 8vo. 21s.

    PEOPLE'S EDITION, 2 vols. crown 8vo. 8s.

GOD in **HISTORY**; or, the Progress of Man's Faith in the Moral Order of the World. By the late Baron BUNSEN. Translated from the German by SUSANNA WINKWORTH; with a Preface by Dean STANLEY. In Three Volumes. VOLS. I. and II. 8vo. 30s.

HISTORY of **EUROPEAN MORALS**, from Augustus to Charlemagne. By W. E. H. LECKY, M.A. 2 vols. 8vo. price 28s.

HISTORY of the **RISE** and **INFLUENCE** of the **SPIRIT** of **RATIONALISM** in **EUROPE**. By W. E. H. LECKY, M.A. Third Edition, revised. 2 vols. 8vo. 25s.

The **HISTORY** of **PHILOSOPHY**, from Thales to Comte. By GEORGE HENRY LEWES. Third Edition. 2 vols. 8vo. 30s.

EGYPT'S PLACE in **UNIVERSAL HISTORY**; an Historical Investigation. By Baron BUNSEN, D.C.L. Translated by C. H. COTTRELL, M.A. With Additions by S. BIRCH, LL.D. 5 vols. 8vo. price £8 14s. 6d.

MAUNDER'S HISTORICAL TREASURY; comprising a General Introductory Outline of Universal History, and a series of Separate Histories. Latest Edition, revised and brought down to the Present Time by the Rev. G. W. Cox, M.A. late Scholar of Trinity College, Oxford. Fcp. 10s. 6d.

HISTORY of the NORMAN KINGS of ENGLAND. Drawn from a New Collation of the Contemporary Chronicles, by Thomas Cobbe, of the Inner Temple, Barrister-at-Law. 1 vol. 8vo. [*Nearly ready.*

HISTORY of the CHRISTIAN CHURCH, from the Ascension of Christ to the Conversion of Constantine. By E. Burton, D.D. late Prof. of Divinity in the Univ. of Oxford. Eighth Edition. Fcp. 3s. 6d.

SKETCH of the HISTORY of the CHURCH of ENGLAND to the Revolution of 1688. By the Right Rev. T. V. Short, D.D. Lord Bishop of St. Asaph. Seventh Edition. Crown 8vo. 10s. 6d.

HISTORY of the EARLY CHURCH, from the First Preaching of the Gospel to the Council of Nicæa, A.D. 325. By Elizabeth M. Sewell, Author of 'Amy Herbert.' Fcp. 4s. 6d.

The ENGLISH REFORMATION. By 'F. C. Massingberd, M.A. Chancellor of Lincoln and Rector of South Ormsby. Fourth Edition, revised. Fcp. 8vo. 7s. 6d.

Biography and *Memoirs.*

DICTIONARY of GENERAL BIOGRAPHY; containing Concise Memoirs and Notices of the most Eminent Persons of all Countries, from the Earliest Ages to the Present Time. Edited by W. L. R. Cates. 8vo. 21s.

LIVES of the TUDOR PRINCESSES, including Lady Jane Grey and her Sisters. By Agnes Strickland, Author of 'Lives of the Queens of England.' Post 8vo. with Portrait, &c. 12s. 6d.

MEMOIRS of BARON BUNSEN. Drawn chiefly from Family Papers by his Widow, Frances Baroness Bunsen. Second Edition, abridged; with 2 Portraits and 4 Woodcuts. 2 vols. post 8vo. 21s.

LIFE and CORRESPONDENCE of RICHARD WHATELY, D.D. late Archbishop of Dublin. By E. Jane Whately. Popular Edition, with Additions and Omissions. Crown 8vo. with Portrait, 7s. 6d.

LIFE of the DUKE of WELLINGTON. By the Rev. G. R. Gleig, M.A. Popular Edition, carefully revised; with copious Additions. Crown 8vo. with Portrait, 5s.

HISTORY of MY RELIGIOUS OPINIONS. By J. H. Newman, D.D. Being the Substance of Apologia pro Vitâ Suâ. Post 8vo. 6s.

FATHER MATHEW: a Biography. By John Francis Maguire, M.P. for Cork. Popular Edition, with Portrait. Crown 8vo. 3s. 6d.

THE LIFE of FRANZ SCHUBERT. Translated from the German of K. Von Hellborn, by A. D. Coleridge, M.A. late Fellow of King's College, Cambridge. With an Appendix by G. Grove. 2 vols. post 8vo. with Portrait, 21s.

REMINISCENCES of FELIX MENDELSSOHN-BARTHOLDY; a Social and Artistic Biography. By ELISE POLKO. Translated from the German by Lady WALLACE. With additional Letters addressed to English Correspondents. Post 8vo. with Portrait and View, 10s. 6d.

FELIX MENDELSSOHN'S LETTERS from *Italy and Switzerland,* and *Letters from* 1833 *to* 1847, translated by Lady WALLACE. New Edition, with Portrait. 2 vols. crown 8vo. 5s. each.

FARADAY as a DISCOVERER. By JOHN TYNDALL, LL.D. F.R.S. Professor of Natural Philosophy in the Royal Institution of Great Britain. With Two Portraits. Crown 8vo. 6s.

MEMOIRS of SIR HENRY HAVELOCK, K.C.B. By JOHN CLARK MARSHMAN. Cabinet Edition, with Portrait. Crown 8vo. price 5s.

CAPTAIN COOK'S LIFE, VOYAGES, and DISCOVERIES. 18mo. Woodcuts, 2s. 6d.

LIFE of Sir JOHN RICHARDSON, C.B. sometime Inspector of Naval Hospitals and Fleets. By the Rev. JOHN McILRAITH. Fcp. 8vo. with Portrait, 5s.

LIFE of PASTOR FLIEDNER, Founder of the Deaconesses' Institution at Kaiserswerth. Translated from the German by CATHERINE WINKWORTH. Fcp. 8vo. with Portrait, 3s. 6d.

VICISSITUDES of FAMILIES. By Sir J. BERNARD BURKE, C.B. Ulster King of Arms. New Edition, remodelled and enlarged. 2 vols. crown 8vo. 21s.

THE EARLS of GRANARD: a Memoir of the Noble Family of Forbes. Written by Admiral the Hon. JOHN FORBES, and edited by GEORGE ARTHUR HASTINGS, present Earl of Granard, K.P. 8vo. 10s.

GEORGE PETRIE, LL.D. M.R.I.A. &c. formerly President of the Royal Hibernian Academy; his Life and Labours in Art and Archæology. By WILLIAM STOKES, M.D. &c. Physician-in-Ordinary to the Queen in Ireland. 8vo. 12s. 6d.

ESSAYS in ECCLESIASTICAL BIOGRAPHY. By the Right Hon. Sir J. STEPHEN, LL.D. Cabinet Edition (being the Fifth). Crown 8vo. 7s. 6d.

ESSAYS on EDUCATIONAL REFORMERS: the Jesuits, Locke, J. J. Rousseau, Pestalozzi, Jacotot, &c. By the Rev. R. H. QUICK, M.A. Trin. Coll. Cantab. Post 8vo. 7s. 6d.

ESSAYS, BIOGRAPHICAL and CRITICAL. By A. L. MEISSNER, Ph.D. Professor of Modern Languages in Queen's College, Belfast, and in the Queen's University in Ireland.   [*Nearly ready.*

MAUNDER'S BIOGRAPHICAL TREASURY. Thirteenth Edition, reconstructed, thoroughly revised, and in great part rewritten; with about 1,000 additional Memoirs and Notices, by W. L. R. CATES. Fcp. 10s. 6d.

LETTERS and LIFE of FRANCIS BACON, including all his Occasional Works. Collected and edited, with a Commentary, by J. SPEDDING, Trin. Coll. Cantab. VOLS. I. and II. 8vo. 24s. VOLS. III. and IV. price 24s.

Criticism, Philosophy, Polity, &c.

The **INSTITUTES of JUSTINIAN;** with English Introduction, Translation, and Notes.   By T. C. SANDARS, M.A. Barrister, late Fellow of Oriel Coll. Oxon.   Fourth Edition.   8vo. 15*s.*

SOCRATES and the **SOCRATIC SCHOOLS.**   Translated from the German of Dr. E. ZELLER, with the Author's approval, by the Rev. OSWALD J. REICHEL, B.C.L. and M.A.   Crown 8vo. 8*s.* 6*d.*

The **ETHICS of ARISTOTLE,** illustrated with Essays and Notes. By Sir A. GRANT, Bart. M.A. LL.D.   Second Edition, revised and completed. 2 vols. 8vo. price 28*s.*

ELEMENTS of LOGIC.   By R. WHATELY, D.D. late Archbishop of Dublin.   Ninth Edition.   8vo. 10*s.* 6*d.* crown 8vo. 4*s.* 6*d.*

Elements of Rhetoric.   By the same Author.   Seventh Edition. 8vo. 10*s.* 6*d.* crown 8vo. 4*s.* 6*d.*

English Synonymes.   By E. JANE WHATELY.   Edited by Archbishop WHATELY.   5th Edition.   Fcp. 3*s.*

BACON'S ESSAYS with **ANNOTATIONS.**   By R. WHATELY, D.D. late Archbishop of Dublin.   Sixth Edition.   8vo. 10*s.* 6*d.*

LORD BACON'S WORKS, collected and edited by R. L. ELLIS, M.A. J. SPEDDING, M.A. and D. D. HEATH.   Vols. I. to V. *Philosophical Works,* 5 vols. 8vo. £4 6*s.*   VOLS. VI. and VII. *Literary and Professional Works,* 2 vols. £1 16*s.*

On **REPRESENTATIVE GOVERNMENT.**   By JOHN STUART MILL. Third Edition.   8vo. 9*s.*   Crown 8vo. 2*s.*

On **LIBERTY.**   By JOHN STUART MILL.   Fourth Edition.   Post 8vo. 7*s.* 6*d.*   Crown 8vo. 1*s.* 4*d.*

Principles of Political Economy.   By the same Author.   Sixth Edition.   2 vols. 8vo. 30*s.*   Or in 1 vol. crown 8vo. 5*s.*

A System of Logic, Ratiocinative and Inductive.   By the same Author. Seventh Edition. Two vols. 8vo. 25*s.*

ANALYSIS of Mr. MILL'S SYSTEM of LOGIC.   By W. STEBBING, M.A. Fellow of Worcester College, Oxford.   Second Edition.   12mo. 3*s.* 6*d.*

UTILITARIANISM.   By JOHN STUART MILL.   Third Edition.   8vo. 5*s.*

Dissertations and Discussions, Political, Philosophical, and Historical.   By the same Author.   Second Edition, revised.   3 vols. 8vo. 36*s.*

Examination of Sir W. Hamilton's Philosophy, and of the Principal Philosophical Questions discussed in his Writings.   By the same Author. Third Edition.   8vo. 16*s.*

An **OUTLINE of the NECESSARY LAWS of THOUGHT:** a Treatise on Pure and Applied Logic.   By the Most Rev. WILLIAM, Lord Archbishop of York, D.D. F.R.S.   Ninth Thousand.   Crown 8vo. 5*s.* 6*d.*

The **ELEMENTS** of **POLITICAL ECONOMY.** By Henry Dunning Macleod, M.A. Barrister-at-Law. 8vo. 16*s.*

A Dictionary of Political Economy; Biographical, Bibliographical, Historical, and Practical. By the same Author. Vol. I. royal 8vo. 30*s.*

The **ELECTION** of **REPRESENTATIVES,** Parliamentary and Municipal; a Treatise. By Thomas Hare, Barrister-at-Law. Third Edition, with Additions. Crown 8vo. 6*s.*

SPEECHES of the **RIGHT HON. LORD MACAULAY,** corrected by Himself. Library Edition, 8vo. 12*s.* People's Edition, crown 8vo. 3*s.* 6*d.*

LORD MACAULAY'S SPEECHES on **PARLIAMENTARY REFORM** in 1831 and 1832. 16mo. 1*s.*

INAUGURAL ADDRESS delivered to the University of St. Andrews. By John Stuart Mill. 8vo. 5*s.* People's Edition, crown 8vo. 1*s.*

A DICTIONARY of the **ENGLISH LANGUAGE.** By R. G. Latham, M.A. M.D. F.R.S. Founded on the Dictionary of Dr. Samuel Johnson, as edited by the Rev. H. J. Todd, with numerous Emendations and Additions. In Two Volumes. Vol. I. 4to. in Two Parts, price £3 10*s.* In course of publication, also, in 36 Parts, price 3*s.* 6*d.* each.

THESAURUS of **ENGLISH WORDS** and **PHRASES,** classified and arranged so as to facilitate the Expression of Ideas, and assist in Literary Composition. By P. M. Roget, M.D. New Edition. Crown 8vo. 10*s.* 6*d.*

LECTURES on the **SCIENCE** of **LANGUAGE,** delivered at the Royal Institution. By Max Müller, M.A. Fellow of All Souls College, Oxford. 2 vols. 8vo. First Series, Fifth Edition, 12*s.* Second Series, Second Edition, 18*s.*

CHAPTERS on **LANGUAGE.** By Frederic W. Farrar, F.R.S. late Fellow of Trin. Coll. Cambridge. Crown 8vo. 8*s.* 6*d.*

WORD-GOSSIP; a Series of Familiar Essays on Words and their Peculiarities. By the Rev. W. L. Blackley, M.A. Fcp. 8vo. 5*s.*

A BOOK ABOUT WORDS. By G. F. Graham, Author of ' English, or the Art of Composition,' ' English Synonymes,' ' English Grammar Practice,' ' English Style,' &c. Fcp. 8vo. [*Nearly ready.*

The **DEBATER;** a Series of Complete Debates, Outlines of Debates, and Questions for Discussion. By F. Rowton. Fcp. 6*s.*

MANUAL of ENGLISH LITERATURE, Historical and Critical. By Thomas Arnold, M.A. Second Edition. Crown 8vo. price 7*s.* 6*d.*

SOUTHEY'S DOCTOR, complete in One Volume. Edited by the Rev. J. W. Warter, B.D. Square crown 8vo. 12*s.* 6*d.*

HISTORICAL and **CRITICAL COMMENTARY** on the **OLD TESTAMENT;** with a New Translation. By M. M. Kalisch, Ph.D. Vol. I. *Genesis,* 8vo. 18*s.* or adapted for the General Reader, 12*s.* Vol. II. *Exodus,* 15*s.* or adapted for the General Reader, 12*s.* Vol. III. *Leviticus,* Part I. 15*s.* or adapted for the General Reader, 8*s.*

A Hebrew Grammar, with Exercises. By the same Author. Part I. *Outlines with Exercises,* 8vo. 12*s.* 6*d.* Key, 5*s.* Part II. *Exceptional Forms and Constructions,* 12*s.* 6*d.*

A LATIN-ENGLISH DICTIONARY. By J. T. WHITE, D.D. of Corpus Christi College, and J. E. RIDDLE, M.A. of St. Edmund Hall, Oxford. 2 vols. 4to. pp. 2,128, price 42s. cloth.

White's College Latin-English Dictionary (Intermediate Size), abridged for the use of University Students from the Parent Work (as above). Medium 8vo. pp. 1,048, price 18s. cloth.

White's Junior Student's College Latin-English and English-Latin Dictionary. Square 12mo. pp. 1,058, price 12s.

Separately { The ENGLISH-LATIN DICTIONARY, price 5s. 6d.
The LATIN-ENGLISH DICTIONARY, price 7s. 6d.

An ENGLISH-GREEK LEXICON, containing all the Greek Words used by Writers of good authority. By C. D. YONGE, B.A. New Edition. 4to. 21s.

Mr. YONGE'S NEW LEXICON, English and Greek, abridged from his larger work (as above). Revised Edition. Square 12mo. 8s. 6d.

A GREEK-ENGLISH LEXICON. Compiled by H. G. LIDDELL, D.D. Dean of Christ Church, and R. SCOTT, D.D. Master of Balliol. Fifth Edition. Crown 4to. 31s. 6d.

A Lexicon, Greek and English, abridged from LIDDELL and SCOTT'S *Greek-English Lexicon.* Twelfth Edition. Square 12mo. 7s. 6d.

A SANSKRIT-ENGLISH DICTIONARY, the Sanskrit words printed both in the original Devanagari and in Roman Letters. Compiled by T. BENFEY, Prof. in the Univ. of Göttingen. 8vo. 52s. 6d.

WALKER'S PRONOUNCING DICTIONARY of the **ENGLISH LAN-**GUAGE. Thoroughly revised Editions, by B. H. SMART. 8vo. 12s. 16mo. 6s.

A PRACTICAL DICTIONARY of the **FRENCH** and **ENGLISH LAN-**GUAGES. By L. CONTANSEAU. Thirteenth Edition. Post 8vo. 10s. 6d.

Contanseau's Pocket Dictionary, French and English, abridged from the above by the Author. New Edition, revised. Square 18mo. 3s. 6d.

NEW PRACTICAL DICTIONARY of the **GERMAN LANGUAGE;** German–English and English-German. By the Rev. W. L. BLACKLEY, M.A. and Dr. CARL MARTIN FRIEDLÄNDER. Post 8vo. 7s. 6d.

Miscellaneous Works and *Popular Metaphysics.*

The ESSAYS and CONTRIBUTIONS of A. K. H. B., Author of ' The Recreations of a Country Parson.' Uniform Editions :—

Recreations of a Country Parson. FIRST and SECOND SERIES, crown 8vo. 3s. 6d. each.

The Common-place Philosopher in Town and Country. Crown 8vo. 3s. 6d.

Leisure Hours in Town; Essays Consolatory, Æsthetical, Moral, Social, and Domestic. Crown 8vo. 3s. 6d.

The Autumn Holidays of a Country Parson; Essays contributed to *Fraser's Magazine* and to *Good Words*. Crown 8vo. 3*s.* 6*d.*

The Graver Thoughts of a Country Parson. First and Second Series, crown 8vo. 3*s.* 6*d.* each.

Critical Essays of a Country Parson. Selected from Essays contributed to *Fraser's Magazine*. Crown 8vo. 3*s.* 6*d.*

Sunday Afternoons at the Parish Church of a Scottish University City. Crown 8vo. 3*s.* 6*d.*

Lessons of Middle Age, with some Account of various Cities and Men. By A. K. H. B. Author of 'The Recreations of a Country Parson.' Crown 8vo. 3*s.* 6*d.*

Counsel and Comfort spoken from a City Pulpit. Crown 8vo. 3*s.* 6*d.*

Changed Aspects of Unchanged Truths: Memorials of St. Andrews Sundays. Crown 8vo. 3*s.* 6*d.*

SHORT STUDIES on GREAT SUBJECTS. By James Anthony Froude, M.A. late Fellow of Exeter Coll. Oxford. Third Edition. 8vo. 12*s.*

LORD MACAULAY'S MISCELLANEOUS WRITINGS :—
Library Edition. 2 vols. 8vo. Portrait, 21*s.*
People's Edition. 1 vol. crown 8vo. 4*s.* 6*d.*

The REV. SYDNEY SMITH'S MISCELLANEOUS WORKS; including his Contributions to the *Edinburgh Review*. 2 vols. crown 8vo. 8*s.*

The Wit and Wisdom of the Rev. Sydney Smith. a Selection of the most memorable Passages in his Writings and Conversation. 16mo. 5*s.*

EPIGRAMS, Ancient and Modern ; Humorous, Witty, Satirical, Moral, and Panegyrical. Edited by Rev. John Booth, B.A. Cambridge. Second Edition, revised and enlarged. Fcp. 7*s.* 6*d.*

The PEDIGREE of the ENGLISH PEOPLE; an Argument, Historical and Scientific, on the *Ethnology* of the English. By Thomas Nicholas, M.A. Ph.D. 8vo. 16*s.*

The ENGLISH and THEIR ORIGIN: a Prologue to authentic English History. By Luke Owen Pike, M.A. Barrister-at-Law. 8vo. 9*s.*

ESSAYS selected from CONTRIBUTIONS to the *Edinburgh Review*. By Henry Rogers. Second Edition. 3 vols. fcp. 21*s.*

Reason and Faith, their Claims and Conflicts. By the same Author. New Edition, accompanied by several other Essays. Crown 8vo. 6*s.* 6*d.*

The Eclipse of Faith; or, a Visit to a Religious Sceptic. By the same Author. Twelfth Edition. Fcp. 5*s.*

Defence of the Eclipse of Faith, by its Author ; a rejoinder to Dr. Newman's *Reply*. Third Edition. Fcp. 3*s.* 6*d.*

Selections from the Correspondence of R. E. H. Greyson. By the same Author. Third Edition. Crown 8vo. 7*s.* 6*d.*

CHIPS from a GERMAN WORKSHOP; being Essays on the Science of Religion, and on Mythology, Traditions, and Customs. By MAX MÜLLER, M.A. Fellow of All Souls College, Oxford. Second Edition, revised, with an Index. 2 vols. 8vo. 24s.

ANALYSIS of the PHENOMENA of the HUMAN MIND. By JAMES MILL. A New Edition, with Notes, Illustrative and Critical, by ALEXANDER BAIN, ANDREW FINDLATER, and GEORGE GROTE. Edited, with additional Notes, by JOHN STUART MILL. 2 vols. 8vo. price 28s.

An INTRODUCTION to MENTAL PHILOSOPHY, on the Inductive Method. By. J. D. MORELL, M.A. LL.D. 8vo. 12s.

Elements of Psychology, containing the Analysis of the Intellectual Powers. By the same Author. Post 8vo. 7s. 6d.

The SECRET of HEGEL: being the Hegelian System in Origin, Principle, Form, and Matter. By J. H. STIRLING. 2 vols. 8vo. 28s.

The SENSES and the INTELLECT. By ALEXANDER BAIN, M.A. Professor of Logic in the University of Aberdeen. Third Edition. 8vo. 15s.

The EMOTIONS and the WILL. By the same Author. Second Edition. 8vo. 15s.

On the STUDY of CHARACTER, including an Estimate of Phrenology. By the same Author. 8vo. 9s.

MENTAL and MORAL SCIENCE: a Compendium of Psychology and Ethics. By the same Author. Second Edition. Crown 8vo. 10s. 6d.

The PHILOSOPHY of NECESSITY; or, Natural Law as applicable to Mental, Moral, and Social Science. By CHARLES BRAY. Second Edition. 8vo. 9s.

The Education of the Feelings and Affections. By the same Author. Third Edition. 8vo. 3s. 6d.

On Force, its Mental and Moral Correlates. By the same Author. 8vo. 5s.

The FOLK-LORE of the NORTHERN COUNTIES of ENGLAND and the Borders. By WILLIAM HENDERSON. With an Appendix on Household Stories by the Rev. S. BARING-GOULD, M.A. Post 8vo. 9s. 6d.

Astronomy, Meteorology, Popular Geography, &c.

OUTLINES of ASTRONOMY. By Sir J. F. W. HERSCHEL, Bart. M.A. Ninth Edition, revised ; with Plates and Woodcuts. 8vo. 18s.

SATURN and its SYSTEM. By RICHARD A. PROCTOR, B.A. late Scholar of St John's Coll. Camb. 8vo. with 14 Plates, 14s.

Handbook of the Stars. By the same Author. With 3 Maps. Square fcp. 5s.

CELESTIAL OBJECTS for COMMON TELESCOPES. By the Rev. T. W. WEBB, M.A. F.R.A.S. Second Edition, revised, with a large Map of the Moon, and several Woodcuts. 16mo. 7s. 6d.

NAVIGATION and NAUTICAL ASTRONOMY (Practical, Theoretical, Scientific) for the use of Students and Practical Men. By J. MERRIFIELD, F.R.A.S and H. EVERS. 8vo. 14s.

DOVE'S LAW of STORMS, considered in connexion with the Ordinary Movements of the Atmosphere. Translated by R. H. Scott, M.A. T.C.D. 8vo. 10s. 6d.

PHYSICAL GEOGRAPHY for SCHOOLS and GENERAL READERS. By M. F. Maury, LL.D. Fcp. with 2 Charts, 2s. 6d.

A TREATISE on the ACTION of VIS INERTIÆ in the OCEAN; with Remarks on the Abstract Nature of the Forces of Vis Inertiæ and Gravitation, and a New Theory of the Tides. By William Leighton Jordan, F.R.G.S. With 12 Charts and Diagrams. 8vo. 14s.

M'CULLOCH'S DICTIONARY, Geographical, Statistical, and Historical, of the various Countries, Places, and Principal Natural Objects in the World. New Edition, with the Statistical Information brought up to the latest returns by F. Martin. 4 vols. 8vo. with coloured Maps, £4 4s.

A GENERAL DICTIONARY of GEOGRAPHY, Descriptive, Physical, Statistical, and Historical: forming a complete Gazetteer of the World. By A. Keith Johnston, LL.D F.R.G.S. Revised Edition. 8vo. 31s. 6d.

A MANUAL of GEOGRAPHY, Physical, Industrial, and Political. By W. Hughes, F.R.G.S. With 6 Maps. Fcp. 7s. 6d.

The STATES of the RIVER PLATE: their Industries and Commerce. By Wilfrid Latham, Buenos Ayres. Second Edition, revised. 8vo. 12s.

MAUNDER'S TREASURY of GEOGRAPHY, Physical, Historical, Descriptive, and Political. Edited by W. Hughes, F.R.G.S. With 7 Maps and 16 Plates. Fcp. 10s. 6d.

Natural History and Popular Science.

ELEMENTARY TREATISE on PHYSICS, Experimental and Applied. Translated and edited from Ganot's *Eléments de Physique* (with the Author's sanction) by E. Atkinson, Ph. D. F.C.S. New Edition, revised and enlarged; with a Coloured Plate and 620 Woodcuts. Post 8vo. 15s.

The ELEMENTS of PHYSICS or NATURAL PHILOSOPHY. By Neil Arnott, M.D. F.R.S. Physician Extraordinary to the Queen. Sixth Edition, rewritten and completed. Two Parts, 8vo. 21s.

SOUND: a Course of Eight Lectures delivered at the Royal Institution of Great Britain. By John Tyndall, LL.D. F.R.S. Crown 8vo. with Portrait of *M. Chladni* and 169 Woodcuts, price 9s.

HEAT CONSIDERED as a MODE of MOTION. By Professor John Tyndall, LL.D. F.R.S. Third Edition. Crown 8vo. with Woodcuts, 10s. 6d.

LIGHT: Its Influence on Life and Health. By Forbes Winslow, M.D. D.C.L. Oxon. (Hon.). Fcp. 8vo. 6s.

An ESSAY on DEW, and several Appearances connected with it. By W. C. Wells. Edited, with Annotations, by L. P. Casella, F.R.A.S. and an Appendix by R. Strachan, F.M.S. 8vo. 5s.

A TREATISE on ELECTRICITY, in Theory and Practice. By A. De la Rive, Prof. in the Academy of Geneva. Translated by C. V. Walker, F.R.S. 3 vols. 8vo. with Woodcuts, £3 13s.

The **CORRELATION** of **PHYSICAL FORCES.** By W. R. GROVE, Q.C. V.P.R.S. Fifth Edition, revised, and followed by a Discourse on Continuity. 8vo. 10s. 6d. The *Discourse on Continuity*, separately, 2s. 6d.

MANUAL of **GEOLOGY.** By S. HAUGHTON, M.D. F.R.S. Revised Edition, with 66 Woodcuts. Fcp. 7s. 6d.

A **GUIDE** to **GEOLOGY.** By J. PHILLIPS, M.A. Professor of Geology in the University of Oxford. Fifth Edition, with Plates. Fcp. 4s.

The **STUDENT'S MANUAL** of **ZOOLOGY** and **COMPARATIVE** PHYSIOLOGY. By J. BURNEY YEO, M.B. Resident Medical Tutor and Lecturer on Animal Physiology in King's College, London. [*Nearly ready.*

VAN DER HOEVEN'S HANDBOOK of **ZOOLOGY.** Translated from the Second Dutch Edition by the Rev. W. CLARK, M.D. F.R.S. 2 vols. 8vo. with 24 Plates of Figures, 60s.

Professor **OWEN'S LECTURES** on the **COMPARATIVE ANATOMY** and Physiology of the Invertebrate Animals. Second Edition, with 235 Woodcuts. 8vo. 21s.

The **COMPARATIVE ANATOMY** and **PHYSIOLOGY** of the **VERTE-** brate Animals. By RICHARD OWEN, F.R.S. D.C.L. With 1,472 Woodcuts. 3 vols. 8vo. £3 13s. 6d.

The **FIRST MAN** and **HIS PLACE** in **CREATION,** considered on the Principles of Common Sense from a Christian Point of View. By GEORGE MOORE, M.D. Post 8vo. 8s. 6d.

The **PRIMITIVE INHABITANTS** of **SCANDINAVIA**: containing a Description of the Implements, Dwellings, Tombs, and Mode of Living of the Savages in the North of Europe during the Stone Age. By SVEN NILSSON. Translated from the Third Edition; with an Introduction by Sir J. LUBBOCK. With 16 Plates of Figures and 3 Woodcuts. 8vo. 18s.

BIBLE ANIMALS; being an Account of the various Birds, Beasts, Fishes, and other Animals mentioned in the Holy Scriptures. By the Rev. J. G. WOOD, M.A. F.L.S. Copiously illustrated with Original Designs, made under the Author's superintendence and engraved on Wood. In course of publication monthly, to be completed in 20 Parts, price 1s. each, forming One Volume, uniform with 'Homes without Hands.'

HOMES WITHOUT HANDS: a Description of the Habitations of Animals, classed according to their Principle of Construction. By Rev. J. G. WOOD, M.A. F.L.S. With about 140 Vignettes on Wood (20 full size of page). New Edition. 8vo. 21s.

MANUAL of **CORALS** and **SEA JELLIES.** By J. R. GREENE, B.A. Edited by JOSEPH A. GALBRAITH, M.A. and SAMUEL HAUGHTON, M.D. Fcp. with 39 Woodcuts, 5s.

Manual of Sponges and Animalculæ; with a General Introduction on the Principles of Zoology. By the same Author and Editors. Fcp. with 16 Woodcuts, 2s.

Manual of the Metalloids. By J. APJOHN, M.D. F.R.S. and the same Editors. Revised Edition. Fcp. with 38 Woodcuts, 7s. 6d.

A **FAMILIAR HISTORY** of **BIRDS.** By E. STANLEY, D.D. F.R.S. late Lord Bishop of Norwich. Seventh Edition, with Woodcuts. Fcp. 3s. 6d.

The **HARMONIES of NATURE and UNITY of CREATION.** By Dr. GEORGE HARTWIG. 8vo. with numerous Illustrations, 18s.

The **Sea and its Living Wonders.** By the same Author. Third (English) Edition. 8vo. with many Illustrations, 21s.

The **Tropical World.** By the same Author. With 8 Chromoxylographs and 172 Woodcuts. 8vo. 21s.

The **POLAR WORLD**; a Popular Description of Man and Nature in the Arctic and Antarctic Regions of the Globe. By Dr. GEORGE HARTWIG. With 8 Chromoxylographs, 3 Maps, and 85 Woodcuts. 8vo. 21s.

CEYLON. By Sir J. EMERSON TENNENT, K.C.S. LL.D. Fifth Edition; with Maps, &c. and 90 Wood Engravings. 2 vols. 8vo. £2 10s.

KIRBY and SPENCE'S INTRODUCTION to ENTOMOLOGY, or Elements of the Natural History of Insects. 7th Edition. Crown 8vo. 5s.

MAUNDER'S TREASURY of NATURAL HISTORY, or Popular Dictionary of Zoology. Revised and corrected by T. S. COBBOLD, M.D. Fcp. with 900 Woodcuts. 10s. 6d.

The **TREASURY of BOTANY,** or Popular Dictionary of the Vegetable Kingdom; including a Glossary of Botanical Terms. Edited by J. LINDLEY, F.R.S. and T. MOORE, F.L.S. assisted by eminent Contributors. Pp. 1,274, with 274 Woodcuts and 20 Steel Plates. 2 Parts. fcp. 20s.

The **ELEMENTS of BOTANY for FAMILIES and SCHOOLS.** Tenth Edition, revised by THOMAS MOORE, F.L.S. Fcp. with 154 Woodcuts. 2s. 6d.

The **ROSE AMATEUR'S GUIDE.** By THOMAS RIVERS. Twelfth Edition. Fcp. 4s.

The **BRITISH FLORA**; comprising the Phænogamous or Flowering Plants and the Ferns. By Sir W. J. HOOKER, K.H. and G. A. WALKER-ARNOTT, LL.D. 12mo. with 12 Plates, 14s. or coloured, 21s.

LOUDON'S ENCYCLOPÆDIA of PLANTS; comprising the Specific Character, Description, Culture, History, &c. of all the Plants found in Great Britain. With upwards of 12,000 Woodcuts. 8vo. 42s.

MAUNDER'S SCIENTIFIC and LITERARY TREASURY. New Edition, thoroughly revised and in great part re-written, with above 1,000 new Articles, by J. Y. JOHNSON, Corr. M.Z.S. Fcp. 10s. 6d.

A DICTIONARY of SCIENCE, LITERATURE, and ART. Fourth Edition, re-edited by W. T. BRANDE (the Author), and GEORGE W. COX, M.A. assisted by contributors of eminent Scientific and Literary Acquirements. 3 vols. medium 8vo. price 63s. cloth.

The **QUARTERLY JOURNAL of SCIENCE.** Edited by JAMES SAMUELSON and WILLIAM CROOKES, F.R.S. Published quarterly in January, April, July, and October. 8vo. with Illustrations, price 5s. each Number.

Chemistry, Medicine, Surgery, and the Allied Sciences.

A DICTIONARY of CHEMISTRY and the Allied Branches of other Sciences. By HENRY WATTS, F.R.S. assisted by eminent Contributors. Complete in 5 vols. medium 8vo. £7 3s.

ELEMENTS of CHEMISTRY, Theoretical and Practical. By WILLIAM A. MILLER, M.D. LL.D. F.R.S. F.G.S. Prof. of Chemistry, King's Coll. London. 3 vols. 8vo. £3. PART I. CHEMICAL PHYSICS, 15*s.* PART II. INORGANIC CHEMISTRY, 21*s.* PART III. ORGANIC CHEMISTRY, 24*s.*

A MANUAL of CHEMISTRY, Descriptive and Theoretical. By WILLIAM ODLING, M.B. F.R.S. PART I. 8vo. 9*s.* PART II. *just ready.*

A Course of Practical Chemistry, for the use of Medical Students. By the same Author. New Edition, with 70 Woodcuts. Crown 8vo. 7*s.* 6*d.*

Lectures on Animal Chemistry, delivered at the Royal College of Physicians in 1865. By the same Author. Crown 8vo. 4*s.* 6*d.*

HANDBOOK of CHEMICAL ANALYSIS, adapted to the UNITARY *System* of Notation. By F. T. CONINGTON, M.A. F.C.S. Post 8vo. 7*s.* 6*d.* —CONINGTON's *Tables of Qualitative Analysis,* price 2*s.* 6*d.*

The DIAGNOSIS, PATHOLOGY, and TREATMENT of DISEASES of Women; including the Diagnosis of Pregnancy. By GRAILY HEWITT, M.D. Second Edition, enlarged; with 116 Woodcut Illustrations. 8vo. 24*s.*

LECTURES on the DISEASES of INFANCY and CHILDHOOD. By CHARLES WEST, M.D. &c. Fifth Edition, revised and enlarged. 8vo. 16*s.*

A SYSTEM of SURGERY, Theoretical and Practical. In Treatises by Various Authors. Edited by T. HOLMES, M.A. &c. Surgeon and Lecturer on Surgery at St. George's Hospital, and Surgeon-in-Chief to the Metropolitan Police. 4 vols. 8vo. £4 13*s.*

The SURGICAL TREATMENT of CHILDREN'S DISEASES. By T. HOLMES, M.A. &c. late Surgeon to the Hospital for Sick Children. Second Edition, with 9 Plates and 112 Woodcuts. 8vo. 21*s.*

LECTURES on the PRINCIPLES and PRACTICE of PHYSIC. By Sir THOMAS WATSON, Bart. M.D. New Edition in preparation.

LECTURES on SURGICAL PATHOLOGY. By J. PAGET, F.R.S. Edited by W. TURNER, M.B. New Edition in preparation.

On CHRONIC BRONCHITIS, especially as connected with GOUT, EMPHYSEMA, and DISEASES of the HEART. By E. HEADLAM GREENHOW, M.D. F.R.C.P. &c. 8vo. 7*s.* 6*d.*

A TREATISE on the CONTINUED FEVERS of GREAT BRITAIN. By C. MURCHISON, M.D. New Edition in preparation.

CLINICAL LECTURES on DISEASES of the LIVER, JAUNDICE, and ABDOMINAL DROPSY. By CHARLES MURCHISON, M.D. Post 8vo. with 25 Woodcuts. 10*s.* 6*d.*

ANATOMY, DESCRIPTIVE and SURGICAL. By HENRY GRAY, F.R.S. With 410 Wood Engravings from Dissections. New Edition, by T. HOLMES. M.A. Cantab. Royal 8vo. 28*s.*

The THEORY of OCULAR DEFECTS and of SPECTACLES. Translated from the German of Dr. H. SCHEFFLER by R. B. CARTER, F.R.C.S. With Prefatory Notes and a Chapter of Practical Instructions. Post 8vo. 7*s.* 6*d.*

OUTLINES of PHYSIOLOGY, Human and Comparative. By JOHN MARSHALL, F.R.C.S. Surgeon to the University College Hospital. 2 vols. crown 8vo. with 122 Woodcuts, 32*s.*

ESSAYS on PHYSIOLOGICAL SUBJECTS. By GILBERT W. CHILD, M.D. F.L.S. F.C.S. of Exeter College, Oxford. 8vo. 5s.

PHYSIOLOGICAL ANATOMY and PHYSIOLOGY of MAN. By the late R. B. TODD, M.D. F.R.S. and W. BOWMAN, F.R.S. of King's College. With numerous Illustrations. VOL. II. 8vo. 25s.
VOL. I. New Edition by Dr. LIONEL S. BEALE, F.R.S. in course of publication; PART I. with 8 Plates, 7s. 6d.

COPLAND'S DICTIONARY of PRACTICAL MEDICINE, abridged from the larger work and throughout brought down to the present State of Medical Science. 8vo. 36s.

The **WORKS of SIR B. C. BRODIE,** Bart. collected and arranged by CHARLES HAWKINS, F.R.C.S.E. 3 vols. 8vo. with Medallion and Facsimile. 48s.

On **ANILINE and its DERIVATIVES:** a Treatise on the Manufacture of Aniline and Aniline Colours. By M. REIMANN, Ph.D. L.A.M. To which is added the Report on the Colouring Matters derived from Coal Tar shewn at the French Exhibition of 1867. Edited by WILLIAM CROOKES, F.R.S. With 5 Woodcuts. 8vo. 10s. 6d.

A **MANUAL of MATERIA MEDICA and THERAPEUTICS,** abridged from Dr. PEREIRA's *Elements* by F. J. FARRE, M.D. assisted by R. BENTLEY, M.R.C.S. and by R. WARINGTON, F.R.S. 8vo. with 90 Woodcuts, 21s.

THOMSON'S CONSPECTUS of the BRITISH PHARMACOPŒIA. 25th Edition, corrected by E. LLOYD BIRKETT, M.D. 18mo. price 6s.

MANUAL of the DOMESTIC PRACTICE of MEDICINE. By W. B. KESTEVEN, F.R.C.S.E. Third Edition, revised, with Additions. Fcp. 5s.

GYMNASTS and GYMNASTICS. By JOHN H. HOWARD, late Professor of Gymnastics, Comm. Coll. Ripponden. Second Edition, revised and enlarged, with 135 Woodcuts. Crown 8vo. 10s. 6d.

The Fine Arts, and *Illustrated Editions.*

MATERIALS for a HISTORY of OIL PAINTING. By Sir CHARLES LOCKE EASTLAKE, sometime President of the Royal Academy. VOL. II. 8vo. 14s.

HALF-HOUR LECTURES on the HISTORY and PRACTICE of the Fine and Ornamental Arts. By WILLIAM B. SCOTT. New Edition, revised by the Author; with 50 Woodcuts. Crown 8vo. 8s. 6d.

LECTURES on the HISTORY of MODERN MUSIC, delivered at the Royal Institution. By JOHN HULLAH. FIRST COURSE, with Chronological Tables, post 8vo. 6s. 6d. SECOND COURSE, on the Transition Period, with 40 Specimens, 8vo. 16s.

SIX LECTURES on HARMONY, delivered at the Royal Institution of Great Britain in the Year 1867. By G. A. MACFARREN. With numerous engraved Musical Examples and Specimens. 8vo. 10s. 6d.

The **CHORALE BOOK for ENGLAND:** the Hymns translated by Miss C. WINKWORTH; the tunes arranged by Prof. W. S. BENNETT and OTTO GOLDSCHMIDT. Fcp. 4to. 12s. 6d.
Congregational Edition. Fcp. 2s.

SACRED MUSIC for FAMILY USE; a Selection of Pieces for One, Two, or more Voices, from the best Composers, Foreign and English. Edited by JOHN HULLAH. 1 vol. music folio, price 21s.

The NEW TESTAMENT, illustrated with Wood Engravings after the Early Masters, chiefly of the Italian School. Crown 4to. 63s. cloth, gilt top; or £5 5s. elegantly bound in morocco.

LYRA GERMANICA; the Christian Year. Translated by CATHERINE WINKWORTH; with 125 Illustrations on Wood drawn by J. LEIGHTON, F.S.A. 4to. 21s.

LYRA GERMANICA; the Christian Life. Translated by CATHERINE WINKWORTH; with about 200 Woodcut Illustrations by J. LEIGHTON, F.S.A. and other Artists. 4to. 21s.

The LIFE of MAN SYMBOLISED by the MONTHS of the YEAR. Text selected by R. PIGOT; Illustrations on Wood from Original Designs by J. LEIGHTON, F.S.A. 4to. 42s.

CATS' and FARLIE'S MORAL EMBLEMS; with Aphorisms, Adages, and Proverbs of all Nations. 121 Illustrations on Wood by J. LEIGHTON, F.S.A. Text selected by R. PIGOT. Imperial 8vo. 31s. 6d.

SHAKESPEARE'S MIDSUMMER NIGHT'S DREAM, illustrated with 24 Silhouettes or Shadow-Pictures by P. KONEWKA, engraved on Wood by A. VOGEL. Folio, 31s. 6d.

SHAKSPEARE'S SENTIMENTS and SIMILES, printed in Black and Gold, and Illuminated in the Missal Style by HENRY NOEL HUMPHREYS. Square post 8vo. 21s.

SACRED and LEGENDARY ART. By Mrs. JAMESON.

Legends of the Saints and Martyrs. Fifth Edition, with 19 Etchings and 187 Woodcuts. 2 vols. square crown 8vo. 31s. 6d.

Legends of the Monastic Orders. Third Edition, with 11 Etchings and 88 Woodcuts. 1 vol. square crown 8vo. 21s.

Legends of the Madonna. Third Edition, with 27 Etchings and 165 Woodcuts. 1 vol. square crown 8vo. 21s.

The History of Our Lord, with that of his Types and Precursors. Completed by Lady EASTLAKE. Revised Edition, with 31 Etchings and 281 Woodcuts. 2 vols. square crown 8vo. 42s.

Arts, Manufactures, &c.

DRAWING from NATURE. By GEORGE BARNARD, Professor of Drawing at Rugby School. With 18 Lithographic Plates, and 108 Wood Engravings. Imperial 8vo. price 25s. Or in Three Parts, royal 8vo. 7s. 6d. each.

GWILT'S ENCYCLOPÆDIA of ARCHITECTURE, with above 1,100 Engravings on Wood. Fifth Edition, revised and enlarged by WYATT PAPWORTH. Additionally illustrated with nearly 400 Wood Engravings by O. Jewitt, and more than 100 other new Woodcuts. 8vo. 52s. 6d.

ITALIAN SCULPTORS; being a History of Sculpture in Northern, Southern, and Eastern Italy. By C. C. PERKINS. With 30 Etchings and 13 Wood Engravings. Imperial 8vo. 42s.

TUSCAN SCULPTORS, their Lives, Works, and Times. With 45 Etchings and 28 Woodcuts from Original Drawings and Photographs. By the same Author. 2 vols. imperial 8vo. 63s.

ORIGINAL DESIGNS for **WOOD-CARVING**, with **PRACTICAL IN**-structions in the Art. By A. F. B. With 20 Plates of Illustrations engraved on Wood. 4to. 18s.

HINTS on HOUSEHOLD TASTE in FURNITURE, UPHOLSTERY, and other Details. By CHARLES L. EASTLAKE, Architect. With about 90 Illustrations. Square crown 8vo. 18s.

The ENGINEER'S HANDBOOK; explaining the Principles which should guide the Young Engineer in the Construction of Machinery. By C. S. LOWNDES. Post 8vo. 5s.

The ELEMENTS of MECHANISM. By T. M. GOODEVE, M.A. Professor of Mechanics at the R. M. Acad. Woolwich. Second Edition, with 217 Woodcuts. Post 8vo. 6s. 6d.

LATHES and TURNING, Simple, Mechanical, and **ORNAMENTAL.** By W. HENRY NORTHCOTT. With about 240 Illustrations on Steel and Wood. 8vo. 18s.

URE'S DICTIONARY of ARTS, MANUFACTURES, and MINES. Sixth Edition, chiefly rewritten and greatly enlarged by ROBERT HUNT, F.R.S. assisted by numerous Contributors eminent in Science and the Arts, and familiar with Manufactures. With above 2,000 Woodcuts. 3 vols. medium 8vo. price £4 14s. 6d.

HANDBOOK of PRACTICAL TELEGRAPHY, published with the sanction of the Chairman and Directors of the Electric and International Telegraph Company, and adopted by the Department of Telegraphs for India. By R. S. CULLEY. Third Edition. 8vo. 12s. 6d.

ENCYCLOPÆDIA of CIVIL ENGINEERING, Historical, Theoretical, and Practical. By E. CRESY, C.E. With above 3,000 Woodcuts. 8vo. 42s.

TREATISE on MILLS and MILLWORK. By W. FAIRBAIRN, C.E. Second Edition, with 18 Plates and 322 Woodcuts. 2 vols. 8vo. 32s.

Useful Information for Engineers. By the same Author. FIRST, SECOND, and THIRD SERIES, with many Plates and Woodcuts. 3 vols. crown 8vo. 10s. 6d. each.

The Application of Cast and Wrought Iron to Building Purposes. By the same Author. Third Edition, with 6 Plates and 118 Woodcuts. 8vo. 16s.

IRON SHIP BUILDING, its History and Progress, as comprised in a Series of Experimental Researches. By the same Author. With 4 Plates and 130 Woodcuts. 8vo. 18s.

A TREATISE on the STEAM ENGINE, in its various Applications to Mines, Mills, Steam Navigation, Railways and Agriculture. By J. BOURNE, C.E. Eighth Edition ; with Portrait, 37 Plates, and 546 Woodcuts. 4to. 42s.

Catechism of the Steam Engine, in its various Applications to Mines, Mills, Steam Navigation, Railways, and Agriculture. By the same Author. With 89 Woodcuts. Fcp. 6s.

Handbook of the Steam Engine. By the same Author, forming a KEY to the Catechism of the Steam Engine, with 67 Woodcuts. Fcp. 9s.

A TREATISE on the SCREW PROPELLER, SCREW VESSELS, and Screw Engines, as adapted for purposes of Peace and War; with Notices of other Methods of Propulsion, Tables of the Dimensions and Performance of Screw Steamers, and detailed Specifications of Ships and Engines. By J. BOURNE, C.E. Third Edition, with 54 Plates and 287 Woodcuts. 4to. 63s.

EXAMPLES of MODERN STEAM, AIR, and GAS ENGINES of the most Approved Types, as employed for Pumping, for Driving Machinery, for Locomotion, and for Agriculture, minutely and practically described. Illustrated by Working Drawings, and embodying a Critical Account of all Projects of Recent Improvement in Furnaces, Boilers, and Engines. By the same Author. In course of publication monthly, to be completed in 24 Parts, price 2s. 6d. each, forming One volume 4to. with about 50 Plates and 400 Woodcuts.

A HISTORY of the MACHINE-WROUGHT HOSIERY and LACE Manufactures. By WILLIAM FELKIN, F.L.S. F.S.S. Royal 8vo. 21s.

PRACTICAL TREATISE on METALLURGY, adapted from the last German Edition of Professor KERL's *Metallurgy* by W. CROOKES, F.R.S. &c. and E. RÖHRIG, Ph.D. M.E. VOL. I. comprising *Lead, Silver, Zinc, Cadmium, Tin, Mercury, Bismuth, Antimony, Nickel, Arsenic, Gold, Platinum*, and *Sulphur.* 8vo. with 207 Woodcuts, 31s. 6d.

MITCHELL'S MANUAL of PRACTICAL ASSAYING. Third Edition, for the most part re-written, with all the recent Discoveries incorporated, by W. CROOKES, F.R.S. With 188 Woodcuts. 8vo. 28s.

The ART of PERFUMERY; the History and Theory of Odours, and the Methods of Extracting the Aromas of Plants. By Dr. PIESSE, F.C.S. Third Edition, with 53 Woodcuts. Crown 8vo. 10s. 6d.

Chemical, Natural, and Physical Magic, for Juveniles during the Holidays. By the same Author. Third Edition, with 38 Woodcuts. Fcp. 6s.

LOUDON'S ENCYCLOPÆDIA of AGRICULTURE: comprising the Laying-out, Improvement, and Management of Landed Property, and the Cultivation and Economy of the Productions of Agriculture. With 1,100 Woodcuts. 8vo. 31s. 6d.

Loudon's Encylopædia of Gardening: comprising the Theory and Practice of Horticulture, Floriculture, Arboriculture, and Landscape Gardening. With 1,000 Woodcuts. 8vo. 31s. 6d.

BAYLDON'S ART of VALUING RENTS and TILLAGES, and Claims of Tenants upon Quitting Farms, both at Michaelmas and Lady-Day. Eighth Edition, revised by J. C. MORTON. 8vo. 10s. 6d.

Religious and *Moral Works.*

An EXPOSITION of the 39 ARTICLES, Historical and Doctrinal. By E. HAROLD BROWNE, D.D. Lord Bishop of Ely. Seventh Edit. 8vo. 16s.

ARCHBISHOP LEIGHTON'S SERMONS and CHARGES. With Additions and Corrections from MSS. and with Historical and other Illustrative Notes by WILLIAM WEST, Incumbent of S. Columba's, Nairn. 8vo. 15s.

The ACTS of the APOSTLES; with a Commentary, and Practical and Devotional Suggestions for Readers and Students of the English Bible. By the Rev. F. C. COOK, M.A. Canon of Exeter, &c. New Edition. 8vo. 12s. 6d.

The **LIFE and EPISTLES of ST. PAUL.** By W. J. CONYBEARE, M.A. late Fellow of Trin. Coll.Cantab. and the Very Rev. J. S. HOWSON, D.D. Dean of Chester.

LIBRARY EDITION, with all the Original Illustrations, Maps, Landscapes on Steel, Woodcuts, &c. 2 vols. 4to. 48s.

INTERMEDIATE EDITION, with a Selection of Maps, Plates, and Woodcuts. 2 vols. square crown 8vo. 31s. 6d.

PEOPLE'S EDITION, revised and condensed, with 46 Illustrations and Maps. 2 vols. crown 8vo. 12s.

The **VOYAGE and SHIPWRECK of ST. PAUL;** with Dissertations on the Life and Writings of St. Luke and the Ships and Navigation of the Ancients. By JAMES SMITH, F.R.S. Third Edition. Crown 8vo. 10s. 6d.

The **NATIONAL CHURCH; HISTORY and PRINCIPLES of the** CHURCH POLITY of ENGLAND. By D. MOUNTFIELD, M.A. Rector of Newport, Salop. Crown 8vo. 4s.

EVIDENCE of the TRUTH of the CHRISTIAN RELIGION derived from the Literal Fulfilment of Prophecy. By ALEXANDER KEITH, D.D. 37th Edition, with numerous Plates, in square 8vo. 12s. 6d.; also the 39th Edition, in post 8vo. with 5 Plates, 6s.

The **HISTORY and DESTINY of the WORLD and of the CHURCH,** according to Scripture. By the same Author. Square 8vo. with 40 Illustrations, 10s.

A **CRITICAL and GRAMMATICAL COMMENTARY on ST. PAUL'S** Epistles. By C. J. ELLICOTT, D.D. Lord Bishop of Gloucester & Bristol. 8vo.

Galatians, Fourth Edition, 8s. 6d.

Ephesians, Fourth Edition, 8s. 6d.

Pastoral Epistles, Fourth Edition, 10s. 6d.

Philippians, Colossians, and Philemon, Third Edition, 10s. 6d.

Thessalonians, Third Edition, 7s. 6d.

Historical Lectures on the Life of our Lord Jesus Christ: being the Hulsean Lectures for 1859. By the same Author. Fourth Edition. 8vo. price 10s. 6d.

An **INTRODUCTION to the STUDY of the NEW TESTAMENT,** Critical, Exegetical, and Theological. By the Rev. S. DAVIDSON, D.D. LL.D. 2 vols. 8vo. 30s.

Rev. T. H. HORNE'S INTRODUCTION to the CRITICAL STUDY and Knowledge of the Holy Scriptures. Twelfth Edition, as last revised throughout and brought up to the existing state of Biblical Knowledge under careful Editorial revision. With 4 Maps and 22 Woodcuts and Fac-similes. 4 vols. 8vo. 42s.

Rev. T. H. Horne's Compendious Introduction to the Study of the Bible, being an Analysis of the larger work by the same Author. Re-edited by the Rev. JOHN AYRE, M.A. With Maps, &c. Post 8vo. 6s.

EWALD'S HISTORY of ISRAEL to the DEATH of MOSES. Translated from the German. Edited, with a Preface and an Appendix, by RUSSELL MARTINEAU, M.A. Prof. of Hebrew in Manchester New Coll. London. Second Edition, continued to the commencement of the Monarchy. 2 vols. 8vo. 24s. VOL. II. comprising *Joshua* and *Judges*, for Purchasers of the First Edition, 9s.

The **TREASURY of BIBLE KNOWLEDGE**; being a Dictionary of the Books, Persons, Places, Events, and other matters of which mention is made in Holy Scripture. By Rev. J. AYRE, M.A. With Maps, 16 Plates, and numerous Woodcuts. Fcp. 10s. 6d.

The **GREEK TESTAMENT**; with Notes, Grammatical and Exegetical. By the Rev. W. WEBSTER, M.A. and the Rev. W. F. WILKINSON, M.A. 2 vols. 8vo. £2 4s.
>   VOL. I. the Gospels and Acts, 20s.
>   VOL. II. the Epistles and Apocalypse, 24s.

The **CHURCHMAN'S DAILY REMEMBRANCER of DOCTRINE** and DUTY: consisting of Meditations taken from the Writings of Standard Divines from the Early Days of Christianity to the Present Time; with a Preface by W. R. FREMANTLE, M.A. New Edition. Fcp. 8vo. 6s.

EVERY-DAY SCRIPTURE DIFFICULTIES explained and illustrated. By J. E. PRESCOTT, M.A. VOL. I. *Matthew* and *Mark*; VOL. II. *Luke* and *John*. 2 vols. 8vo. 9s. each.

The **PENTATEUCH and BOOK of JOSHUA CRITICALLY EXAMINED**. By the Right Rev. J. W. COLENSO, D.D. Lord Bishop of Natal. People's Edition, in 1 vol. crown 8vo. 6s. or in 5 Parts, 1s. each.

The **CHURCH and the WORLD**: Three Series of Essays on Questions of the Day. By Various Writers. Edited by the Rev. ORBY SHIPLEY, M.A. FIRST SERIES, Third Edition, 15s. SECOND SERIES, Second Edition, 15s. THIRD SERIES, 1868, price 15s. 3 vols. 8vo. 45s.

The **FORMATION of CHRISTENDOM**. By T. W. ALLIES. PARTS I. and II. 8vo. price 12s. each Part.

ENGLAND and CHRISTENDOM. By ARCHBISHOP MANNING, D.D. Post 8vo. price 10s. 6d.

CHRISTENDOM'S DIVISIONS, PART I., a Philosophical Sketch of the Divisions of the Christian Family in East and West. By EDMUND S. FFOULKES. Post 8vo. price 7s. 6d.

Christendom's Divisions, PART II. Greeks and Latins, being a History of their Dissensions and Overtures for Peace down to the Reformation. By the same Author. Post 8vo. 15s.

The **WOMAN BLESSED by ALL GENERATIONS**; or, Mary the Object of Veneration, Confidence, and Imitation to all Christians. By the Rev. R. MELIA, D.D. P.S.M. With 78 Illustrations. 8vo. 15s.

LIFE of the BLESSED VIRGIN; the **FEMALL GLORY**. By ANTHONY STAFFORD. Together with the Apology of the Author, and an Essay on the Cultus of the Blessed Virgin Mary. Fourth Edition, with Facsimiles of the 5 Original Illustrations. Edited by the Rev. ORBY SHIPLEY, M.A. Fcp. 8vo. 10s. 6d.

CELEBRATED SANCTUARIES of the MADONNA. By the Rev. J. SPENCER NORTHCOTE, D.D. Post 8vo. 6s. 6d.

The **HIDDEN WISDOM of CHRIST and the KEY of KNOWLEDGE**; or, History of the Apocrypha. By ERNEST DE BUNSEN. 2 vols. 8vo. 28s.

The **KEYS of ST. PETER**; or, the House of Rechab, connected with the History of Symbolism and Idolatry. By the same Author. 8vo. 14s.

The **TYPES of GENESIS**, briefly considered as Revealing the Development of Human Nature. By Andrew Jukes. Second Edition. Crown 8vo. 7s. 6d.

The **Second Death and the Restitution of All Things**, with some Preliminary Remarks on the Nature and Inspiration of Holy Scripture. By the same Author. Second Edition. Crown 8vo. 3s. 6d.

ESSAYS and REVIEWS. By the Rev. W. Temple, D.D. the Rev. R. Williams, B.D. the Rev. B. Powell, M.A. the Rev. H. B. Wilson, B.D. C. W. Goodwin, M.A. the Rev. M. Pattison, B.D. and the Rev. B. Jowett, M.A. Twelfth Edition. Fcp. 8vo. 5s.

The **POWER of the SOUL over the BODY.** By George Moore, M.D. M.R.C.P.L. &c. Sixth Edition. Crown 8vo. 8s. 6d.

PASSING THOUGHTS on RELIGION. By Elizabeth M. Sewell, Author of 'Amy Herbert.' New Edition. Fcp. 8vo. 5s.

Self-Examination before Confirmation. By the same Author. 32mo. price 1s. 6d.

Readings for a Month Preparatory to Confirmation, from Writers of the Early and English Church. By the same Author. Fcp. 4s.

Readings for Every Day in Lent, compiled from the Writings of Bishop Jeremy Taylor. By the same Author. Fcp. 5s.

Preparation for the Holy Communion; the Devotions chiefly from the works of Jeremy Taylor. By the same. 32mo. 3s.

PRINCIPLES of EDUCATION Drawn from Nature and Revelation, and applied to Female Education in the Upper Classes. By the Author of 'Amy Herbert.' 2 vols. fcp. 12s. 6d.

The **WIFE'S MANUAL;** or, Prayers, Thoughts, and Songs on Several Occasions of a Matron's Life. By the Rev. W. Calvert, M.A. Crown 8vo. price 10s. 6d.

SINGERS and SONGS of the CHURCH: being Biographical Sketches of the Hymn-Writers in all the principal Collections; with Notes on their Psalms and Hymns. By Josiah Miller, M.A. New Edition, enlarged. Crown 8vo. *[Nearly ready.*

'SPIRITUAL SONGS' for the SUNDAYS and HOLIDAYS throughout the Year. By J. S. B. Monsell, LL.D. Vicar of Egham and Rural Dean. Fourth Edition, Sixth Thousand. Fcp. 4s. 6d.

The **Beatitudes:** Abasement before God; Sorrow for Sin; Meekness of Spirit; Desire for Holiness; Gentleness; Purity of Heart; the Peacemakers; Sufferings for Christ. By the same. Third Edition. Fcp. 3s. 6d.

His PRESENCE—not his MEMORY, 1855. By the same Author, in Memory of his Son. Sixth Edition. 16mo. 1s.

LYRA DOMESTICA; Christian Songs for Domestic Edification. Translated from the *Psaltery and Harp* of C. J. P. Spitta, and from other sources, by Richard Massie. First and Second Series, fcp. 4s. 6d. each.

LYRA GERMANICA, translated from the German by Miss C. Winkworth. First Series, Hymns for the Sundays and Chief Festivals. Second Series, the Christian Life. Fcp. 3s. 6d. each Series.

LYRA EUCHARISTICA; Hymns and Verses on the Holy Communion, Ancient and Modern: with other Poems. Edited by the Rev. ORBY SHIPLEY, M.A. Second Edition. Fcp. 7s. 6d.

Lyra Messianica; Hymns and Verses on the Life of Christ, Ancient and Modern; with other Poems. By the same Editor. Second Edition, altered and enlarged. Fcp. 7s. 6d.

Lyra Mystica; Hymns and Verses on Sacred Subjects, Ancient and Modern. By the same Editor. Fcp. 7s. 6d.

ENDEAVOURS after the CHRISTIAN LIFE: Discourses. By JAMES MARTINEAU. Fourth and cheaper Edition, carefully revised; the Two Series complete in One Volume. Post 8vo. 7s. 6d.

WHATELY'S Introductory Lessons on the Christian Evidences. 18mo. 6d.

INTRODUCTORY LESSONS on the HISTORY of RELIGIOUS Worship; being a Sequel to the 'Lessons on Christian Evidences.' By RICHARD WHATELY, D.D. New Edition. 18mo. 2s. 6d.

BISHOP JEREMY TAYLOR'S ENTIRE WORKS. With Life by BISHOP HEBER. Revised and corrected by the Rev. C. P. EDEN, 10 vols. price £5 5s.

Travels, Voyages, &c.

SIX MONTHS in INDIA. By MARY CARPENTER. 2 vols. post 8vo. with Portrait, 18s.

NARRATIVE of the EUPHRATES EXPEDITION carried on by Order of the British Government during the years 1835, 1836. and 1837. By General F. R. CHESNEY, F.R.S. With 2 Maps, 45 Plates, and 16 Woodcuts. 8vo. 24s.

The NORTH-WEST PENINSULA of ICELAND; being the Journal of a Tour in Iceland in the Summer of 1862. By C. W. SHEPHERD, M.A. F.Z.S. With a Map and Two Illustrations. Fcp. 8vo. 7s. 6d.

PICTURES in TYROL and Elsewhere. From a Family Sketch-Book. By the Authoress of 'A Voyage en Zigzag,' &c. Second Edition. Small 4to. with numerous Illustrations, 21s.

HOW WE SPENT the SUMMER; or, a Voyage en Zigzag in Switzerland and Tyrol with some Members of the ALPINE CLUB. From the Sketch-Book of one of the Party. In oblong 4to. with 300 Illustrations, 15s.

BEATEN TRACKS; or, Pen and Pencil Sketches in Italy. By the Authoress of 'A Voyage en Zigzag.' With 42 Plates, containing about 200 Sketches from Drawings made on the Spot. 8vo. 16s.

MAP of the CHAIN of MONT BLANC, from an actual Survey in 1863—1864. By A. ADAMS-REILLY, F.R.G.S. M.A.C. Published under the Authority of the Alpine Club. In Chromolithography on extra stout drawing-paper 28in. × 17in. price 10s. or mounted on canvas in a folding case, 12s. 6d.

HISTORY of DISCOVERY in our AUSTRALASIAN COLONIES, Australia, Tasmania, and New Zealand, from the Earliest Date to the Present Day. By WILLIAM HOWITT. 2 vols. 8vo. with 3 Maps, 20s.

The **CAPITAL** of the **TYCOON**; a Narrative of a Three Years' Residence in Japan. By Sir RUTHERFORD ALCOCK, K.C.B. 2 vols. 8vo. with numerous Illustrations, 42s.

The **DOLOMITE MOUNTAINS**; Excursions through Tyrol, Carinthia, Carniola, and Friuli, 1861-1863. By J. GILBERT and G. C CHURCHILL, F.R.G.S. With numerous Illustrations. Square crown 8vo. 21s.

GUIDE to the **PYRENEES**, for the use of Mountaineers. By CHARLES PACKE. 2d Edition, with Map and Illustrations. Cr. 8vo. 7s. 6d.

The **ALPINE GUIDE**. By JOHN BALL, M.R.I.A. late President of the Alpine Club. 3 vols. post 8vo. with Maps and other Illustrations:—

Guide to the Eastern Alps, price 10s. 6d.

Guide to the Western Alps, including Mont Blanc, Monte Rosa, Zermatt, &c. Price 6s. 6d.

Guide to the Central Alps, including all the Oberland District. 7s. 6d.

Introduction on Alpine Travelling in General, and on the Geology of the Alps, price 1s. Each of the Three Volumes or Parts of the *Alpine Guide* may be had with this INTRODUCTION prefixed, price 1s. extra.

NARRATIVES of **SHIPWRECKS** of the **ROYAL NAVY** between 1793 and 1857, compiled from Official Documents in the Admiralty by W. O. S. GILLY; with a Preface by W. S. GILLY, D.D. Third Edition. Fcp. 5s.

TRAVELS in **ABYSSINIA** and the **GALLA COUNTRY**; with an Account of a Mission to Ras Ali in 1848. From the MSS. of the late WALTER CHICHELE PLOWDEN, Her Britannic Majesty's Consul in Abyssinia. Edited by his Brother TREVOR CHICHELE PLOWDEN. With Two Maps. 8vo. 18s.

MEMORIALS of **LONDON** and **LONDON LIFE** in the 1th, 14th, and 15th Centuries; being a Series of Extracts, Local, Social, and Political, from the Archives of the City of London. A.D. 1276-1419. Selected, translated, and edited by H. T. RILEY, M.A. Royal 8vo. 21s.

COMMENTARIES on the **HISTORY, CONSTITUTION,** and **CHARTERED FRANCHISES** of the CITY of LONDON. By GEORGE NORTON, formerly one of the Common Pleaders of the City of London. Third Edition. 8vo. 14s.

CURIOSITIES of **LONDON**; exhibiting the most Rare and Remarkable Objects of Interest in the Metropolis; with nearly Sixty Years' Personal Recollections. By JOHN TIMBS, F.S.A. New Edition, corrected and enlarged. 8vo. with Portrait, 21s.

The **NORTHERN HEIGHTS** of **LONDON**; or, Historical Associations of Hampstead, Highgate, Muswell Hill, Hornsey, and Islington. By WILLIAM HOWITT. With about 40 Woodcuts. Square crown 8vo. 21s.

VISITS to **REMARKABLE PLACES**: Old Halls, Battle-Fields, and Scenes Illustrative of Striking Passages in English History and Poetry. By WILLIAM HOWITT. 2 vols. square crown 8vo. with Woodcuts, 25s.

The **RURAL LIFE** of **ENGLAND**. By the same Author. With Woodcuts by Bewick and Williams. Medium 8vo. 12s. 6d.

The **IRISH** in **AMERICA**. By JOHN FRANCIS MAGUIRE, M.P. for Cork. Post 8vo. 12s. 6d.

ROMA SOTTERRANEA; or, an Account of the Roman Catacombs, and especially of the Cemetery of St. Callixtus. Compiled from the Works of Commendatore G. B. DE ROSSI. with the consent of the Author, by the Rev. J. S. NORTHCOTE, D.D. and the Rev. W. B. BROWNLOW. With numerous Engravings on Wood, 10 Lithographs, 10 Plates in Chromo-lithography, and an Atlas of Plans, all executed in Rome under the Author's superintendence for this Translation. 1 vol. 8vo.   [*Nearly ready.*

Works of *Fiction.*

The **WARDEN**: a Novel. By ANTHONY TROLLOPE. Crown 8vo. 2*s.* 6*d.*

Barchester Towers : a Sequel to 'The Warden.' Crown 8vo. 3*s.* 6*d.*

STORIES and **TALES** by ELIZABETH M. SEWELL, Author of 'Amy Herbert,' uniform Edition, each Tale *or* Story complete in a single Volume.

AMY HERBERT, 2*s.*6*d.*	IVORS, 3*s.* 6*d.*
GERTRUDE, 2*s.* 6*d.*	KATHARINE ASHTON, 3*s.* 6*d.*
EARL'S DAUGHTER, 2*s.* 6*d.*	MARGARET PERCIVAL, 5*s.*
EXPERIENCE OF LIFE, 2*s.* 6*d.*	LANETON PARSONAGE, 4*s.* 6*d.*
CLEVE HALL, 3*s.* 6*d.*	URSULA, 4*s.* 6*d.*

A Glimpse of the World. By the Author of 'Amy Herbert.' Fcp. 7*s.* 6*d.*

The Journal of a Home Life. By the same Author. Post 8vo. 9*s.* 6*d.*

After Life; a Sequel to 'The Journal of a Home Life.' Price 10*s.* 6*d.*

UNCLE PETER'S FAIRY TALE for the **XIX CENTURY.** Edited by E. M. SEWELL, Author of 'Amy Herbert,' &c. Fcp. 8vo. 7*s.* 6*d.*

BECKER'S GALLUS; or, Roman Scenes of the Time of Augustus : with Notes and Excursuses. New Edition. Post 8vo. 7*s.* 6*d.*

BECKER'S CHARICLES; a Tale illustrative of Private Life among the Ancient Greeks: with Notes and Excursuses. New Edition. Post 8vo. 7*s.* 6*d.*

NOVELS and **TALES** by G. J. WHYTE MELVILLE :—

The GLADIATORS, 5*s.*	HOLMBY HOUSE, 5*s.*
DIGBY GRAND, 5*s.*	GOOD FOR NOTHING, 6*s.*
KATE COVENTRY, 5*s.*	The QUEEN'S MARIES, 6*s.*
GENERAL BOUNCE, 5*s.*	The INTERPRETER, 5*s.*

TALES of ANCIENT GREECE. By GEORGE W. COX, M.A. late Scholar of Trin. Coll. Oxon. Being a Collective Edition of the Author's Classical Stories and Tales, complete in One Volume. Crown 8vo. 6*s.* 6*d.*

A MANUAL of MYTHOLOGY, in the form of Question and Answer. By the same Author. Fcp. 3*s.*

Poetry and *The Drama.*

THOMAS MOORE'S POETICAL WORKS, the only Editions containing the Author's last Copyright Additions :—

SHAMROCK EDITION, crown 8vo. price 3*s.* 6*d.*
RUBY EDITION, crown 8vo. with Portrait, price 6*s.*
PEOPLE'S EDITION, square crown 8vo. with Portrait, &c. 12*s.* 6*d.*
LIBRARY EDITION, medium 8vo. Portrait and Vignette, 14*s.*
CABINET EDITION, 10 vols. fcp. 8vo. price 35*s.*

MOORE'S IRISH MELODIES, Maclise's Edition, with 161 Steel Plates from Original Drawings. Super-royal 8vo. 31*s*. 6*d*.

Miniature Edition of Moore's Irish Melodies with Maclise's Designs (as above) reduced in Lithography. Imp. 16mo. 10*s*. 6*d*.

MOORE'S LALLA ROOKH. Tenniel's Edition, with 68 Wood Engravings from original Drawings and other Illustrations. Fcp. 4to. 21*s*.

SOUTHEY'S POETICAL WORKS, with the Author's last Corrections and copyright Additions. Library Edition, in 1 vol. medium 8vo. with Portrait and Vignette, 14*s*. or in 10 vols. fcp. 3*s*. 6*d*. each.

LAYS of ANCIENT ROME; with *Ivry* and the *Armada*. By the Right Hon. LORD MACAULAY. 16mo. 4*s*. 6*d*.

Lord Macaulay's Lays of Ancient Rome. With 90 Illustrations on Wood, from the Antique, from Drawings by G. SCHARF. Fcp. 4to. 21*s*.

Miniature Edition of Lord Macaulay's Lays of Ancient Rome, with the Illustrations (as above) reduced in Lithography. Imp. 16mo. 10*s*. 6*d*.

GOLDSMITH'S POETICAL WORKS, with Wood Engravings from Designs by Members of the ETCHING CLUB. Imperial 16mo. 7*s*. 6*d*.

MEMORIES of some CONTEMPORARY POETS; with Selections from their Writings. By EMILY TAYLOR. Royal 18mo. 5*s*.

POEMS. By JEAN INGELOW. Thirteenth Edition. Fcp. 8vo. 5*s*.

POEMS by Jean Ingelow. With nearly 100 Illustrations by Eminent Artists, engraved on Wood by the Brothers DALZIEL. Fcp. 4to. 21*s*.

A STORY of DOOM, and other Poems. By JEAN INGELOW. Fcp. 5*s*.

POETICAL WORKS of LETITIA ELIZABETH LANDON (L.E.L.). 2 vols. 16mo. 10*s*.

BOWDLER'S FAMILY SHAKSPEARE, cheaper Genuine Edition, complete in 1 vol. large type, with 36 Woodcut Illustrations, price 14*s*. or with the same ILLUSTRATIONS, in 6 pocket vols. 3*s*. 6*d*. each.

HORATII OPERA, Pocket Edition, with carefully corrected Text, Marginal References, and Introduction. Edited by the Rev. J. E. YONGE, M.A. Square 18mo. 4*s*. 6*d*.

HORATII OPERA. Library Edition, with Marginal References and English Notes. Edited by the Rev. J. E. YONGE. 8vo. 21*s*.

The ÆNEID of VIRGIL Translated into English Verse. By JOHN CONINGTON, M.A. Crown 8vo. 9*s*.

ARUNDINES CAMI, sive Musarum Cantabrigiensium Lusus canori. Collegit atque edidit H. DRURY, M.A. Editio Sexta, curavit H. J. HODGSON, M.A. Crown 8vo. 7*s*. 6*d*.

EIGHT COMEDIES of ARISTOPHANES, viz. the Acharnians, Knights, Clouds, Wasps, Peace, Birds, Frogs, and Plutus. Translated into Rhymed Metres by LEONARD HAMPSON RUDD, M.A. 8vo. 15*s*.

PLAYTIME with the POETS: a Selection of the best English Poetry for the use of Children. By a LADY. Revised Edition. Crown 8vo. 5*s*.

The HOLY CHILD: a Poem in Four Cantos; also an Ode to Silence, and other Poems. By STEPHEN JENNER, M.A. Fcp. 8vo. 5*s*.

The **ILIAD** of **HOMER TRANSLATED** into **BLANK VERSE**. By ICHABOD CHARLES WRIGHT, M.A. 2 vols. crown 8vo. 21*s.*

The **ILIAD** of **HOMER** in **ENGLISH HEXAMETER VERSE**. By J. HENRY DART, M.A. of Exeter Coll. Oxford. Square crown 8vo. 21*s.*

The **ODYSSEY** of **HOMER**. Translated into Blank Verse by G. W. EDGINTON, Licentiate in Medicine. Dedicated by permission to Edward Earl of Derby. VOL. I. 8vo. with Map, 10*s.* 6*d.*

DANTE'S DIVINE COMEDY, translated in English Terza Rima by JOHN DAYMAN, M.A. [With the Italian Text, after *Brunetti*, interpaged.] 8vo. 21*s.*

HUNTING SONGS and **MISCELLANEOUS VERSES**. By R. E. EGERTON WARBURTON. Second Edition. Fcp. 8vo. 5*s.*

An **OLD STORY**, and other Poems. By ELIZABETH D. CROSS. Second Edition. Fcp. 8vo. 3*s.* 6*d.*

The **THREE FOUNTAINS**, a Fäery Epic of Euboea; with other Verses. By the Author of 'The Afterglow.' Fcp. 8vo. 3*s.* 6*d.*

The **Afterglow**; Songs and Sonnets for my Friends. By the Author of 'The Three Fountains.' Second Edition. Fcp. 8vo. 5*s.*

The **SILVER STORE** collected from Mediæval Christian and Jewish Mines. By the Rev. SABINE BARING-GOULD, M.A. Crown 8vo. 6*s.*

Rural Sports, &c.

BLAINE'S ENCYCLOPÆDIA of **RURAL SPORTS**; Hunting, Shooting, Fishing, Racing, &c. With above 600 Woodcuts (20 from Designs by JOHN LEECH). 8vo. 42*s.*

Col. **HAWKER'S INSTRUCTIONS** to **YOUNG SPORTSMEN** in all that relates to Guns and Shooting. Revised by the Author's SON. Square crown 8vo. with Illustrations, 18*s.*

The **DEAD SHOT**, or Sportsman's Complete Guide; a Treatise on the Use of the Gun, Dog-breaking, Pigeon-shooting, &c. By MARKSMAN. Revised Edition. Fcp. 8vo. with Plates, 5*s.*

The **FLY-FISHER'S ENTOMOLOGY**. By ALFRED RONALDS. With coloured Representations of the Natural and Artificial Insect. Sixth Edition; with 20 coloured Plates. 8vo. 14*s.*

A **BOOK** on **ANGLING**; a complete Treatise on the Art of Angling in every branch. By FRANCIS FRANCIS. Second Edition, with Portrait and 15 other Plates, plain and coloured. Post 8vo. 15*s.*

HANDBOOK of **ANGLING**: Teaching Fly-fishing, Trolling, Bottom-fishing, Salmon-fishing; with the Natural History of River Fish, and the best modes of Catching them. By EPHEMERA. Fcp. Woodcuts, 5*s.*

WILCOCKS'S SEA-FISHERMAN; comprising the Chief Methods of Hook and Line Fishing in the British and other Seas, a Glance at Nets, and Remarks on Boats and Boating. Second Edition, enlarged; with 80 Woodcuts. Post 8vo. 12*s.* 6*d.*

The **CRICKET FIELD**; or, the History and the Science of the Game of Cricket. By JAMES PYCROFT, B.A. Fourth Edition. Fcp. 5*s.*

HORSE and **MAN**. By C. S. MARCH PHILLIPPS, Author of 'Jurisprudence,' &c. Fcp. 8vo. 2s. 6d.

The **HORSE'S FOOT**, and **HOW** to **KEEP IT SOUND**. By **W. MILES**, Esq. Ninth Edition, with Illustrations. Imperial 8vo. 12s. 6d.

A Plain Treatise on Horse-Shoeing. By the same Author. Sixth Edition. Post 8vo. with Illustrations, 2s. 6d.

Stables and Stable-Fittings. By the same. Imp. 8vo. with 13 Plates, 15s.

Remarks on Horses' Teeth, addressed to Purchasers. By the same. Post 8vo. 1s. 6d.

ROBBINS'S CAVALRY CATECHISM, or Instructions on Cavalry Exercise and Field Movements, Brigade Movements, Out-post Duty, Cavalry supporting Artillery, Artillery attached to Cavalry. 12mo. 5s.

BLAINE'S VETERINARY ART; a Treatise on the Anatomy, Physiology, and Curative Treatment of the Diseases of the Horse, Neat Cattle and Sheep. Seventh Edition, revised and enlarged by C. STEEL, M.R.C.V.S.L. 8vo. with Plates and Woodcuts, 18s.

The **HORSE**: with a Treatise on Draught. By WILLIAM YOUATT. New Edition, revised and enlarged. 8vo. with numerous Woodcuts, 12s. 6d.

The **Dog**. By the same Author. 8vo. with numerous Woodcuts, 6s.

The **DOG** in **HEALTH** and **DISEASE**. By STONEHENGE. With 70 Wood Engravings. Square crown 8vo. 10s. 6d.

The **GREYHOUND**. By STONEHENGE. Revised Edition, with 24 Portraits of Greyhounds. Square crown 8vo. 10s. 6d.

The **OX**; his Diseases and their Treatment: with an Essay on Parturition in the Cow. By J. R. DOBSON. Crown 8vo. with Illustrations. 7s. 6d.

Commerce, Navigation, and Mercantile Affairs.

BANKING, CURRENCY, and the **EXCHANGES**; a Practical Treatise. By ARTHUR CRUMP. Post 8vo. 6s.

The **ELEMENTS of BANKING**. By HENRY DUNNING MACLEOD, M.A. Barrister-at-Law. Post 8vo.   [Nearly ready.

The **THEORY** and **PRACTICE** of **BANKING**. By the same Author. Second Edition, entirely remodelled. 2 vols. 8vo. 30s.

PRACTICAL GUIDE for **BRITISH SHIPMASTERS** to **UNITED** States Ports. By PIERREPONT EDWARDS. Post 8vo. 8s. 6d.

A DICTIONARY, Practical, Theoretical, and Historical, of Commerce and Commercial Navigation. By J. R. M'CULLOCH, Esq. New and thoroughly revised Edition. 8vo. price 63s. cloth, or 70s. half-bd. in russia.

The **LAW of NATIONS** Considered as Independent Political Communities. By Sir TRAVERS TWISS, D.C.L. 2 vols. 8vo. 30s. or separately, PART I. Peace, 12s. PART II. War, 18s.

Works of Utility and *General Information.*

MODERN COOKERY for PRIVATE FAMILIES, reduced to a System of Easy Practice in a Series of carefully-tested Receipts. By ELIZA ACTON. Newly revised and enlarged Edition; with 8 Plates of Figures and 150 Woodcuts. Fcp. 6s.

On FOOD and its DIGESTION; an Introduction to Dietetics. By W. BRINTON, M.D. With 48 Woodcuts. Post 8vo. 12s.

WINE, the VINE, and the CELLAR. By THOMAS G. SHAW. Second Edition, revised and enlarged, with 32 Illustrations. 8vo. 16s.

A PRACTICAL TREATISE on BREWING; with Formulæ for Public Brewers, and Instructions for Private Families. By W. BLACK. 8vo. 10s. 6d.

SHORT WHIST. By MAJOR A. A thoroughly revised Edition, with an Essay on the Theory of the Modern Scientific Game by PROF. P. Fcp. 3s. 6d.

WHIST, WHAT TO LEAD. By CAM. Fourth Edition. 32mo. 1s.

A HANDBOOK for READERS at the BRITISH MUSEUM. By THOMAS NICHOLS. Post 8vo. 6s.

The CABINET LAWYER; a Popular Digest of the Laws of England, Civil, Criminal, and Constitutional. Twenty-fourth Edition, brought down to the close of the Parliamentary Session of 1868. Fcp. 10s. 6d.

The PHILOSOPHY of HEALTH; or, an Exposition of the Physiological and Sanitary Conditions conducive to Human Longevity and Happiness. By SOUTHWOOD SMITH, M.D. Eleventh Edition, revised and enlarged; with 113 Woodcuts. 8vo. 7s. 6d.

HINTS to MOTHERS on the MANAGEMENT of their HEALTH during the Period of Pregnancy and in the Lying-in Room. By T. BULL, M.D. Fcp. 5s.

The Maternal Management of Children in Health and Disease. By the same Author. Fcp. 5s.

The LAW RELATING to BENEFIT BUILDING SOCIETIES; with Practical Observations on the Act and all the Cases decided thereon; also a Form of Rules and Forms of Mortgages. By W. TIDD PRATT, Barrister. Second Edition. Fcp. 3s. 6d.

NOTES on HOSPITALS. By FLORENCE NIGHTINGALE. Third Edition, enlarged; with 13 Plans. Post 4to. 18s.

COULTHART'S DECIMAL INTEREST TABLES at 24 Different Rates not exceeding 5 per Cent. Calculated for the use of Bankers. To which are added Commission Tables at One-Eighth and One-Fourth per Cent. 8vo. price 15s.

MAUNDER'S TREASURY of KNOWLEDGE and LIBRARY of Reference: comprising an English Dictionary and Grammar, Universal Gazetteer, Classical Dictionary, Chronology, Law Dictionary, a Synopsis of the Peerage, useful Tables, &c. Revised Edition. Fcp. 10s. 6d.

INDEX.

LONDON: PRINTED BY
SPOTTISWOODE AND CO., NEW-STREET SQUARE
AND PARLIAMENT STREET